WILD OPEN HEARTS

A BLUEWATER BILLIONAIRES ROMANTIC COMEDY

KATHRYN NOLAN

That's What She Said Publishing,Inc.

Editing by Faith N. Erline
Cover by Kari March

ISBN: 978-1-945631-54-2 (ebook)
ISBN: 978-1-945631-53-5 (paperback)

092220

For Cait, Erin and Faith—the sisters of my heart. Every positive and affirming example of female friendship I write is based 100% on the three of you.

and

For Lucy, Claire and Pippa—thank you for making this series so damn fun to write (and hilarious).

1

LUNA

*I*t was a beautiful day to be accused of fraud.

I flashed my trademark cheerful smile at Sylvia Lee, the president of my board and my long-time mentor. "Can you repeat that, Sylvia? I'm not sure I heard you correctly."

"Ferris Mark lied to us," she replied, with a face so pinched I winced in sympathy. She tapped a manicured finger on a sheet of paper I really didn't want to examine that closely. "An investigative reporter went undercover at one of their factories and discovered that all of the ingredients they source to cosmetics companies like ours are absolutely, one-hundred-percent tested on animals."

Wild Heart's headquarters were located on Miami Beach's infamous Ocean Drive, which meant my wall-to-wall windows let in a dazzling panorama of white sand and turquoise waves dotted with vibrantly colored beachgoers. I usually felt a decadent love for my tropical hometown. But today, as I watched a lifeguard race by my office window on a skateboard, I was tempted to yank the window open, leap outside, and steal that skateboard for myself.

Because surely, a clumsy escape by skateboard was preferable to the career-ending mess in front of me.

There was a knock at my door. Jasmine Hernandez, the head of Wild Heart public relations, was staring at me with an expression that said *you're so fucked.*

"How bad is it?" I asked Jasmine.

"Nuclear." Her head was down, fingers flying over her cell phone.

I took a sip of my ever-present green smoothie, grimaced, then pushed it away. I opened up a drawer and grabbed an emergency stash of Fritos corn chips—they were one of the only store-brand vegan snacks around, and I'd been mainlining them since college. During moments of stress or anxiety, I could finish a bag in five minutes flat.

I had a feeling this was going to be one of those moments.

Six years ago, Wild Heart inked a massively lucrative deal to sell our eco-friendly and cruelty-free cosmetics throughout the Fischer Home Goods department stores. The deal had solidified my position as one of the youngest self-made billionaires in the world. Wild Heart became the third-largest cosmetics company, right behind Revlon, and was currently valued at $4.5 billion.

Six years ago, to meet our new increased demand from Fischer, I'd made the decision to drop our former supplier and go with Ferris Mark. They were faster. Cheaper. I'd assumed it was a wise business decision—had been proud of it, actually. You *could* be financially successful while maintaining your compassionate values.

I finally scanned the page. *Force feeding, lethal doses, irritation tests.*

Well. Maybe you couldn't.

"Are we sure this is real?" I asked, around a mouth full of corn chips.

My phone started to vibrate. And vibrate. And vibrate. None of this was a positive sign.

I slapped a hand over my phone. Re-pasted my smile on—which was now officially fake. That was new.

"Very real," Sylvia said. "The story is going to break any minute. It's not just Wild Heart that's implicated, but four other major cruelty-free cosmetics lines. Our competitors."

That meant massive amounts of secret, horrible animal testing had been happening for years and none of us knew it. My fingers kept circling *lethal dose testing*, a particularly heinous way of testing the safety of new cosmetics ingredients on animals by getting them to die in a variety of ways. I was all for safety—always—but when I founded Wild Heart at twenty-two, it was on the basis that cosmetics companies had more than enough ingredients at their disposal to produce high-quality makeup. No new ingredients meant no need for safety testing—protecting humans and animals in equal measure.

"We need to pull the products," I said. "Every last one. I don't care how much it costs. And we need a new supplier like yesterday. I'll halt production until then."

An action that would cost us untold amounts of lost revenue. An action that the tiny billionaire-shaped devil on my shoulder was pissed about.

"That's a lot of money," Sylvia said softly, voicing my concerns out loud. "I'm not saying we don't support the same response. I want to make sure you're positive, Luna."

My heart knocked against my chest—*you'll lose it all, you'll lose it all*. I inhaled. Exhaled. Behind Sylvia's head was a framed cover from TIME Magazine: there I was, laughing into the sun in a field of flowers. The headline read: *Luna da Rosa Believes Makeup Can Save the World*.

"We have to do it. It's the right thing to do. And obviously we've been caught in the crossfire," I said firmly, hushing the tiny devil. "We'll make a statement, assure our consumers that we are dedicated to cruelty-free beauty products—"

My phone buzzed so violently it fell to the floor. I picked it up as a flurry of notifications from my social media accounts lit up the screen. I'd always been the face of Wild Heart. From the beginning, I'd positioned myself as America's Vegan Best Friend and Wild Heart had reaped the rewards.

Now I caught the words *Twitter, comments, Luna, fucking fake.*

Could corn chips be delivered to you by the metric ton?

"In the court of public opinion, you're a liar, Luna." Jasmine spoke up from her spot by the door. "We need to get out in front of this before the story breaks. Tell the narrative to the best of our ability."

"Okay," I said, distracted by the vile words spilling across my screen. "The story's already broken though."

I pushed my phone across the desk with one finger. Jasmine strode over, glanced at it. Muttered beneath her breath. I crossed my legs beneath my gauzy hot-pink skirt and pulled my hair over one shoulder, mindlessly braiding it. My bangles clinked up my wrist.

"But Ferris Mark lied to *us*," I said, attempting to process this new information. "Right? I mean, I get feeling upset but we're the victims too. I would never, ever source ingredients that were tested on animals." I jiggled my flip-flops, braided my hair, and tried to ignore the voice in my subconscious screaming at me. *Something's not right.*

"We should have the documentation to prove our innocence," I said, standing up quickly. I swished over to a long row of filing cabinets, scanning for contracts from the year 2015. Yanked open the right cabinet and started flipping through file folders with a righteous passion. "I signed their contract myself so—"

I waved the file in the air. "Here we go," I said, slapping it down on the desk. "This will help. This proves that we were lied to. We'll fix it. I believe that we can fix it."

My internal compass had been stuck on *enthusiastic optimist* since birth.

"Luna, there's another issue." Sylvia's gentle voice had an edge to it I barely recognized. We made eye contact—my mentor seemed pained, and not only at this news.

"One second," I said. "Let me just find this." I dug through the papers, seeking validation that Wild Heart could make this right. I'd founded this company with the sole purpose to do right, to change things for the better throughout our entire industry—how could we be the ones in the *wrong*?

"The reporter has something, Luna," Jasmine piped up. "I doubt you remember this but you—"

"Oh my god, I signed off on it." I was holding the paper, swallowing hard, trying to decipher the ugly truth staring right back at me.

An addendum to our contract. Traditionally, Wild Heart had an extensive due diligence process. It was one of the many ways we ensured the companies we sourced ingredients from not only had a clean animal rights record, but a human rights record as well. That was our promise to consumers, my promise to the world.

That was the promise I made to myself, all those years ago.

The addendum was authorizing Wild Heart to waive our standard policies and to move ahead without an inspection of their production plants.

"You directed the production team to go ahead with Ferris Mark even though they expressed concerns with their ethics.

You made the decision to waive our process because you trusted they were cruelty-free without verifying," Sylvia said.

My signature appeared huge and jubilant on the page—no doubt I'd been excited about the Fischer deal and eager to stay on track.

"The decision to take Ferris Mark at its word was all yours, Luna," Sylvia said.

Our eyes met across the table. Sylvia Lee had smashed through the glass ceiling twenty years ago when she became one of the first female CEOs of a Fortune 500 company. Since then, she'd spent her career taking other female entrepreneurs under her wing, serving on boards and committees and acting as a mentor. For the past ten years, she'd kindly guided me forward and firmly wrangled me in.

The very real disappointment on her face had a fist closing around my throat.

I remembered now, the night I'd signed this. I'd met Emily, Cameron and Daisy for drinks at our favorite tiki bar by the beach, had danced and twirled around and laughed with my favorite women and felt powerful, strong. Because I'd bypassed my board and pulled the trigger on a decision I knew was right—if I didn't think we needed another six months of red tape and bureaucracy, we didn't.

Except—clearly—we had. And now that formerly happy memory was tinged with a distressing, guilt-filled regret.

My phone was lighting up like the Times Square crystal ball on New Year's Eve.

"It's my job to fix this," I said cheerfully, chin up. "Nothing we can't get through. The worst has already happened. It's only up from here."

They stared at me with varying degrees of skepticism.

The large flat-screen TV on my wall caught my attention—

probably because my name was stretched across it. Jasmine snatched up the remote, turning up the volume.

I kept mindlessly braiding my hair—an anxious habit I'd never broken. Well, that and mindlessly devouring junk food.

"An interesting story coming our way from the *Miami Dispatch* this morning," the anchor was saying, "exposing illegal working conditions and animal cruelty at an ingredient plant called Ferris Mark. Sources say well-known Miami-based cosmetics company Wild Heart is a main customer."

They proceeded to cut to my TED Talk from two years ago —where I'm pointing to the audience and declaring, "Cruelty-free cosmetics is the only way forward. Anything less than that is indefensible."

"Goddammit," Jasmine cursed.

"Did Luna da Rosa lie to her customers to make money?" the anchor asked.

"I didn't lie," I said weakly. Which was true. But I'd violated a value I'd always held at the core of my being.

Never let the money change you.

At twenty-two, I'd been a starry-eyed bohemian, intent on changing the world, excited to be part of a new era of female business owners. The night I'd won that first, crucial million dollars, Sylvia had emailed me a few simple thoughts: *Having a lot of money is wonderful, Luna. Money can also make things much more complicated. This will be part of your struggle as a future leader.*

I already knew I liked Sylvia. But I'd deleted the email. Because money had felt like the *key* to changing the world, not the *complication.*

Liar, hypocrite, fake. The words flashed-flashed-flashed across my phone.

"I'm guessing everyone hates me now?" I asked, attempting a lightness I did not even remotely feel.

"Worse," Jasmine said, face serious. "They feel betrayed by you."

I sank back into my chair.

An email popped up on my computer from a name I desperately needed to see.

Daisy Carter-Kincaid.

The subject line read: "Who do we need to stab for you today?"

2

BECK

*J*ack Sparrow was finally going home.

Jack was a nine-year-old, senior Pomeranian with a feisty personality twice the size of his seven pounds. I'd rescued Jack three months ago from a family that had abused him. He'd been terrified of people. All of us— me, Elián, Wes and Jem—took turns sitting outside his kennel, talking softly, getting him used to the sound of human voices that were gentle. Safe. And with training and all the goddamn love we could muster, the real Jack had appeared just in time for Buzz to adopt him.

"You nervous?" I asked, clapping Buzz on the back. He was scowling into the Miami sun, cigarette dangling from his mouth. The old man had been a fisherman his entire life and looked the part—right down to the faded blue anchor tattooed on his arm.

"I've killed a marlin with my bare hands," Buzz grumbled, "don't know why I'd be scared of an old ball of fur that's blind in one eye and almost deaf."

Jem and I shared a look—Buzz hadn't been here when the

bastard had snarled at anyone who got too close to his food bowl.

"Oh, he'll keep you on your toes. Promise," I said, nodding at Jem. Her spiked hair glowed green as she re-appeared with a wiggling Jack Sparrow.

Buzz dropped to one knee. Sized the dog up.

His wife had died two years ago and his adult children had begged him to adopt a dog. They'd chosen Jack Sparrow for their father specifically, although Buzz had given off a disinterested vibe for the entire process.

Except I knew a match when I fucking saw one. Buzz was gruff, intense—but when he'd wandered onto the Lucky Dog campus, I could see a cheerful Jack Sparrow on the bow of his fishing boat, wagging his tail as they cut through the water.

Jack sat, tail wagging, and placed a tiny paw on Buzz's knee.

With a strange look, Buzz clutched Jack to his chest and pressed a palm to his head. "Good boy," he said.

Jack licked his face. I'd seen the dog's records—I wasn't sure once in his life he'd ever been treated nicely by a human being.

"You got whatcha need, Buzz?" I asked, crossing my arms. "Bed, food, toys?"

He stood up, still holding Jack. "I, uh... I don't know, I thought he'd sleep in the bed with me unless you think that's weird."

"Not weird," I said, hiding a smile.

"Well, all right then." Buzz coughed and took the leash Jem presented him. But he didn't let Jack go. "I guess I'll be off."

I stepped forward, passing my hand once more over Jack's tan fur. He'd put Elián and Jem through their paces when it came to training—and there was a moment where I thought he might not be rehabilitated. Jack had been a risk we'd all been nervous taking.

But it was worth it for this moment.

Every adoption day made me think about Willow—the sight of her tail wagging as she walked off with her new family.

"Nice work," I said, nodding at Jem. She was white, twenty-six and had spent a decent amount of her days in juvie as a teenager, just like me. And she'd gone through the same dog-training program, which was how we'd met—at an event where I was mentoring former juvie kids. Her lime-green hair had caught my eye.

That and she had a grit I'd also recognized in myself. *Never again*, it said.

"This was a great one, boss," Jem said, letting out a big sigh. "I'm going to miss that little yappy monster."

I pointed to the parking lot where Buzz was sliding into a large red pickup truck. Jack Sparrow was sitting on Buzz's lap, tongue lolling. The raw, honest smile on the man's face could have been seen from a mile away.

"Yeah," I agreed. "That was a great one."

BECK

*W*es and Jem went back to work—Wes to the shitty trailer we called our office and Jem off to train a bulldog named Princess.

I yanked open the door to the trailer to find Elián flipping through a stack of mail. Elián was Cuban-American with a true understanding of animals and a love for motorcycles that matched my own. He was also Lucky Dog's program director and my best friend.

We started this place together. Though why I ended up in charge, I still wasn't sure. And neither was he, I knew it. That was clear enough given the anxious look on his face right now.

"Jack?" he asked, avoiding whatever bad news was in that pile of mail.

I nodded. "Went great. Buzz will be dressing Jack up in a sailor costume in no time."

Elián grinned. "I can't wait to see it." He hesitated, then handed me a thin envelope, growing serious. "It's from the Miami-Dade Community Foundation."

They were our biggest funder. One of our only funders. At barely four years old, Lucky Dog was as grassroots as you could get, and their two-year grant had kept us open while Elián and I learned the ropes of running a nonprofit.

I tore it open—revealed a short letter telling me that although *Lucky Dog was a very competitive candidate, they would not be funding us at this time.*

"Fuck me," I muttered. Leaned against the wall of the trailer and crossed my arms. "We're out all that cash."

"That was more than half of our income for this fiscal year," he said grimly.

"We'll figure it out," I said, not knowing if I was lying.

"Did you go speak at their annual dinner?" he asked.

"Nope," I replied.

Elián gave me a look.

"That was the night Beatrix came in. It was all hands on deck," I said.

Beatrix was a snarling, 125-pound bull mastiff that had been found near a well-known dog-fighting ring in the city. Deep down, she was a sweetheart—which we were finding out —but that first night, dealing with her had been like trying to lasso a wild horse.

"I'm pretty sure we had her covered," he said simply. "I think you should have gone. I think they would have appreciated, you know, some schmoozing."

I'd rather have been tossed in the ring with Beatrix than have to put on a suit and schmooze. I'd never been good at impressing people—scaring them, sure. With the Mason last name, certain types of people in Miami knew better than to test me. But for a man who'd spent more years in juvie than actual school, those events made me feel foolish.

"Beck," Elián said.

"I know," I growled. "You don't have to say it."

"If I wasn't your best friend, I might try and punch you right now."

"I probably deserve to be punched." I sighed.

I sank into my office chair—financial reports and grant applications littered the space. I knew I needed to pay attention to them. But it was too easy to get distracted by real work. The financial reports made my eyes cross and the grant applications I had to have board members help me write. It all felt like a secret language I was never going to learn.

And the deeper in debt we became—and the less money I raised—the more ashamed I felt.

"We could start producing that shirtless men of Lucky Dog calendar I've always talked about," Elián said. "I'd call it *Puppies and Pecs*."

I scrubbed a hand down my face, smiling in spite of how horrible I felt. "No one wants to see this face on a calendar. Or my pecs. I'd prefer selling off a kidney. And I've got two."

"No need to brag," he said. "And I think organ-selling should be low on our priorities list."

"We've had it worse, you and me," I countered. "Financially, I mean."

"Having it worse doesn't mean this current situation isn't messed up," he said, looking serious again. He tapped his fingers on the desk, sighed. "Listen. We've got bills to pay and not much money left to pay 'em. The board wants us to take out a loan."

"Okay," I said. Sounded like we didn't have a choice. But I didn't like being in *debt*—to anyone or any bank.

"You need to get out there. Raise the alarm. There are people in Miami who love this place and don't want to see its doors close. With the new dumping grounds springing up, we're pretty vital."

"Our doors won't actually close," I said. "Money always comes in." That had been true so far—between board members and the occasional grant I was able to get help with,

Elián and I were patching together our budget. Which actually felt better than the alternative—going out there and begging for money.

"Thirty days," he said. "That's what Christina told me. Thirty days or we close."

Wes walked in—like Jem, he'd been through the same juvie program I mentored in these days. Wes Tran was Vietnamese American and covered in tattoos from his feet up to his neck. He was thin as a rail and never without a baseball cap.

And his heart was so big I actually worried about him. During our first mentoring session, I'd recognized a look I often saw in dogs—an eagerness to please that could be used against you by the wrong type of person. So I hired him. He'd been a non-violent offender—Wes had a penchant for stealing fancy cars but was as gentle as they come.

"Just saw an email come through from the Foundation," Wes said, bobbing his head. "That letter from them too?"

I nodded. Grimaced.

"That blows, dude." He sighed.

"It does blow," I agreed. "A shit-ton."

"What are we gonna do, boss?" Wes asked.

I looked outside, watching Jem place Princess in a sit with a smile on her face.

"Hope for a miracle," I said.

Elián grumbled but I ignored it.

"Coolio," Wes said. "And in the meantime, let me know who you need me to stab."

4
LUNA

I sat with my bare feet in the infinity pool on my back patio, waiting for my best friends to arrive. This was usually my favorite place in my entire mansion—the emerald-colored pool with floating tea-candles, twinkle lights and colorful lanterns strung overhead. Flowering pink hibiscus climbed the walls and palm trees swayed in the ocean-scented breeze.

But there was no peace here for me now.

Tonight I was mindlessly glued to my Instagram feed like those people who rubberneck at car accidents on the highway. Because contrary to my own earlier, naïve opinion, it was not only up from here.

The very last thing I'd posted, before the Ferris Mark news broke, was a video talking about Wild Heart's new body glitter —a fun, shimmery, summer-time product I'd showed off by rubbing it onto my shoulders and letting the sun sparkle off my skin. In the video, I was laughing, light-hearted, silly.

And at the end of the video I flashed a peace sign and said, *"And remember, Wild Heart fans, we are always vegan. Always cruelty-free. That's my promise."*

For whatever reason, I'd really emphasized the words *my promise.*

The comments and direct messages were bad.

Really, really bad.

I peeled open a bag of corn chips from my emergency stash. Shoved a handful into my mouth.

It wasn't that my online life had been free of trolls and bullying—I was a woman of Mexican and Italian heritage, a woman in the spotlight, a vegan, a billionaire—the list went on and on. Online hate wasn't new.

But that was troll-shit—the dregs of humanity spewing their racism or sexism or whatever because I was there and they felt protected by their anonymity.

These comments were from my fans.

"What did we say about looking at your phone?"

I turned around—Emily Stanton, Cameron Whitbury and Daisy Carter-Kincaid stood together like the Charlie's Angels of Friendship, holding vodka and wine.

"I know what you said. But it's just that I'm the actual worst," I said. Then I was actually crying, tears clawing their way up from a deep well of emotion I didn't want to tap into. But these women could accept me for who I was, and in the blink of an eye, I was being wrapped in a tight hug.

Emily, Cameron, Daisy and I were best friends, billionaires and lived in an exclusive community we'd built six years ago called Bluewater. What had started as a way for four best friends to build houses next to each other had become a lush, tropical paradise for the wealthy and the eccentric. The enclave was filled with waterfront mansions, luxury condos, a marina, a private airfield and a tiny village of shops. Bike paths and walking trails wound through the palm trees and along the water. I could most often be found forcing Daisy to practice yoga with me in our state-of-the-art gym. She'd do it

—reluctantly—but only while wearing her unicorn romper. And *only* with her water bottle half-filled with vodka.

From tech executives to funky artists, Bluewater had become its own neighborhood of wacky rich people. I had never lived anyplace so bizarre and beautiful, all at once.

We'd built our four houses on the same street, so it was easier to make time for each other in our jam-packed schedules. The four of us had connected easily over being young, wealthy and constantly in the public eye. Navigating a literal boys club where we'd been frequently dismissed, harassed, discriminated against; lauded constantly for our new hairstyles and never for our business acumen. Without these women, my life would have been painfully lonely.

And they understood intimately the situation I found myself in.

There was no way you could do what we did every single day and not make mistakes.

"What's that digging into my side?" I whispered, sniffling through tears.

"Vodka," Cameron said. "Shhh. It's organic."

"This might be an awkward time to introduce my idea for how you're going to redeem yourself," Daisy said.

"What is it?" I asked, sniffling.

"A sex tape."

I laughed for real.

"Consider this," she continued, tossing her long silver hair. "You accidentally release it. Bam. Your adoring public loves you again."

"Or we take you to Bali," Cameron said, hands on my shoulders.

"I can't believe I'm saying this: I think your sex tape would be perfectly authentic and delightfully trendy, all at the same time," Emily added.

"I'm not making a sex tape," I said, popping open the bottle of wine and sinking back down by the pool. "I am going to eat every last one of these corn chips though."

"How many bags have you had already?" Emily asked, with narrowed eyes.

"I don't know... like thirteen?"

Daisy patted my head and sat next to me. "Good girl."

Daisy was as wildly uninhibited as they came, dragging workaholic Emily, serious Cameron and me to dance head-long into every opportunity for fun that came our way. She was the kind of friend that called you at four in the morning, tossed a beach towel at your face and informed you that she needed a road trip buddy on her way to Tijuana. She was our resident It Girl and her family owned half of Miami, Manhattan and Atlanta. Her massive experience running the Carter-Kincaid real estate holdings was the reason why we were able to transform these 2,500 acres of swampland into Bluewater.

Emily Stanton was our cool, level-headed genius with a brain that had created a revolutionary scar treatment that was going to change lives. Although the past few months, she had been mired in scandal and corporate espionage that required the help of an extremely charming reputation-fixer named Derek—who was now her swoon-worthy boyfriend.

Cameron Whitbury ran a Fortune 500 company that literally built rockets. Her recent need for tighter personal security had brought Jude into her life: her giant—and very handsome—bodyguard. Jude was also now her giant—and very handsome—*fiancé.*

"How are Derek and Jude?" I asked, giving a pointed look to Emily and Cameron. The two shared a secret smile I interpreted to mean: *we're so lucky we're having hot sex every day.*

"Yeah, give your two single besties the gory details," Daisy chimed in, throwing an arm around my shoulders. "And when I say gory, I mean I want to know their dick sizes."

"To the inch," I added. "And if they know the Kama Sutra, tell me all the poses you've done."

"My fiancé's massive dick aside and Kama Sutra expertise aside"—Cameron smirked, waving us off—"why don't you tell us what happened today, Moon?"

"Of course," I said, with forced perkiness. "But first, can I have Roxanne make you guys a green salad or a smoothie? I also brewed a special ginger kombucha mix that's really great for digestion and spiritual—"

"Luna." Daisy laid a stern hand on my shoulder. "You can't distract us with your hippie fairy dust. Give us the damn dirt, girl."

I tucked the edges of my skirt beneath my knees. My stacked gold rings clicked on the cool concrete—they were made to look cheap, yet they'd actually cost me more than a year's worth of rent on my old apartment. The one I'd lived in before I won the Turner VC Award.

"Ferris Mark lied to us," I said, launching into the day's shocking news. I recounted everything—the utter despair at realizing I'd employed and paid a company that force-fed cosmetic ingredients to mice to test fatal reactions, among other things. The news story. The online bullying. The document.

"You signed off on it?" Emily asked.

"I sure did. And gladly too, it would appear," I said.

"Oh, Moon," Daisy said.

"Been there," Cameron said. "It sucks."

"And you know I have too," Emily said. "You'd like to think the opinions of strangers about your morality won't affect you. But you'd have to be superhuman to not be hurt by it."

"That's true, I guess," I said.

I felt almost sick with guilt and embarrassment and a full-body shame that had me achy and uncomfortable. I pressed my forehead to my knees, listened to the sound of crashing waves, a sound I'd lived with since childhood. My gold rings glittered in the pale moonlight. I felt a pinch of... something. More guilt, maybe?

"Thank you for not calling me a big fat fraud like the entire internet," I said.

"The internet can suck it," Cameron said. "It's impossible to avoid this stuff, Moon. I think things will get better after you apologize. That's what Jasmine's going to have you do, right?"

"Yep. That's the first step," I said, feeling a jolt of nerves.

"And what's the rest of the cleanup plan?" Emily asked. "And may I remind you that I happen to know a professional fixer?"

I blew out a breath. "Apologize. Fix all of the errors. Pull the products. Work on a message of transparency. Find a new, reputable supplier. Get everyone to like me again."

"Easy-peasy." Daisy winked.

"You know," Cameron said, tapping her glass, "when we all first met you, the only reason you wanted to make this much money was to give it all away. You were our little bohemian philanthropist."

"That's right," Emily said. "I actually thought you were going to join the Peace Corps."

Once upon a time, I *was* going to join the Peace Corps—but the inspiration for Wild Heart had struck and I'd shifted to majoring in business instead.

"I give money away all the time," I said. "I just don't have time to volunteer like I used to. You know how intense running an enormous business is. My time is all booked up now."

My best friends tilted their heads at me like a trio of judgmental owls.

"What?" I asked. "I have." I traced my history of philanthropy back a few years. I had a handful of favorite nonprofits I used to make large, monthly gifts to. Holding on to that much money when I was newly wealthy had never felt quite right. Surely I'd been giving it away since becoming a *billionaire.*

Right?

"Tomorrow I'll have Jasmine pull some numbers," I finally choked out.

Then I stuffed a handful of chips into my mouth.

"Moon." Daisy nudged my foot with her own. My rings mocked me in the starlight. "Not giving money away doesn't make you a bad person. It is *interesting* though, don't you think? Given what your values are?"

"I've been busy," I said.

Busy becoming the face of Wild Heart, I would have said, had I been feeling more courageous. But until I'd learned the makeup products that my company sold came from an evil company, I had felt like I was helping change the world every day. Words were powerful.

So what if I spent hours online getting the message out there? That's how real change was made.

"Re-dedicating yourself to your values can be a really powerful way to earn trust," Emily said thoughtfully. "I just went through a similar situation with Flawless."

Daisy and Cameron both pinned me with a gaze that indicated their agreement.

I shifted, uneasy. My phone started buzzing away on the concrete—Jasmine calling.

"Take it," Cameron said. "We'll drink until you get back."

"Plus we have to figure out what we're going to do about

the Wealthy Widows at our next HOA meeting," Emily sighed, drumming her fingers on the concrete. In a bout of real madness, after we'd built Bluewater, all four of us also took on the responsibility of running neighborhood meetings every month that tended to drag on until midnight. They were made better with pre-gaming—although Daisy and Cameron had started publicly drinking from flasks as Emily and I tried to keep our neighbors in order.

"What'd they do this time?" The Widows occupied most of our condos and were known for their penchant for mischief and mayhem.

"We'll tell you when you get back," Cameron said. "But it involves rollerblades and Bellinis."

I smiled, grateful for the brief reprieve of normalcy. "I want all of the details." I picked up my phone with trembling fingers. "I love you guys," I said, voice catching through the forced lightness. I kissed each one of them on the top of their heads before padding by and into my house.

"Moon," Daisy said, "just remember. Whatever they say about you, it isn't real, okay? We know who the real Luna da Rosa is."

They were my best friends, the women I trusted the most on this big, beautiful planet. They really did know who I truly was.

But did I?

5

LUNA

*T*he next morning dawned golden and sunny outside my office—tendrils of Miami sun stroked through the windows and bathed Jasmine and Sylvia in a peach-hued light. I had a mug of green tea and was sitting cross-legged on my turquoise couch, pen in one hand and yellow legal pad balanced on my knee.

I'd struggled through my yoga practice that morning—found neither peace in my meditation nor wisdom curled in the flowering vines.

The corn-chip-and-organic-vodka hangover hadn't helped either.

And all of this was worsened by the nonstop hatred spilling across my phone, my laptop, the television. Nasty comments on my social media accounts. An article with my picture in the middle: *When Billionaires Lie.*

Instead of cheerful optimism, I'd moved through my sun salutations and felt twitchy. Weird. Jumpy in the center of my stomach, like I was about to go over the apex of a rollercoaster. But not thrilling jumpy.

It was nerves.

Or maybe something else.

"Let's do this," I said brightly, clapping my hands together. "I'm ready to fix this mistake and move on, stronger than ever."

Jasmine nodded, seemingly energized by a public relations situation she had described as "nuclear."

Sylvia, meanwhile, wore an expression I couldn't even begin to decode.

"I've got a two-pronged idea I think you're going to love," Jasmine said, tapping the TIME Magazine cover in my office. *Luna da Rosa Believes Makeup Can Change the World.* It was soothing, grounding. A shiny talisman that grabbed me by the heart and declared *remember who you are.*

My phone buzzed. Another article.

I stashed my phone away—attempted to focus on Jasmine. She'd been the director of Wild Heart's public relations for the past four years, and I still struggled to get a true read on her.

"Activist. Vegan. Champion for corporate change," Jasmine was saying. "This is your brand."

"It's also who I am," I said.

Jasmine shrugged. "Sure, you can say that. But it's your brand first."

I sipped my tea. Felt twitchy again.

"The first prong is apologizing. I've seen this happen to leaders in your position before—leaders who are both CEO and spokesperson. People buy Wild Heart products because of you, Luna. They trust you. They want to be your friend. They believe if you met in real life you'd actually be their friend."

"I would, actually," I said.

Jasmine repeated: "Sure, you can say that."

"Luna." A knock at the door—Rebecca, my CFO, with a look on her face I recognized from the early days of running this company.

"What happened?" I asked.

"Stock prices for Wild Heart plummeted overnight after the news broke. We need to talk."

"Put a meeting on my calendar." How on earth had I gotten here? *You're going to lose it.* The billionaire devil on my shoulder was the voice of every insecurity—now coming painfully true. I hadn't expected it to develop, hadn't expected a meteoric rise to fame and incredibly lucrative success with Wild Heart to make me experience so much fear. Cameron, Emily and Daisy felt it too—this overwhelming fright that we'd wake one morning and find every penny gone. Every ounce of public goodwill. Every smart idea, innovative vision or strategic thought.

It paralyzed me more than I cared to admit.

"Also, the philanthropic numbers you wanted are right here." Rebecca left a surprisingly thin folder on my desk. I placed a hand over it, seeking the same comfort as the TIME cover.

"Your brand equals trust," Jasmine continued. "You lost that trust yesterday. Regardless of what we know to be true, there's a narrative out there now that you manipulated people into buying Wild Heart's false advertising."

"Which is not true because the supplier we used before Ferris Mark had a perfect animal and human rights record," I shot back. "Why would I suddenly drop my values six years ago if not for the fact that Ferris Mark lied to us?"

"To make more money," Sylvia said simply—the first real words she'd spoken to me this morning. An echo of the email I'd trashed years ago from her: *This will be your struggle as a future leader.*

I was silent.

"People love when celebrities do charity work. It makes them appear real and, most importantly, more trust-worthy.

We need to remind the public of who you really are from a brand perspective."

It was a brilliant idea—drum up public support for Wild Heart. Fix my reputation. Help a nonprofit.

"I like it," I said. "You know, I actually did volunteer with my parents as a kid."

Sylvia nodded at me.

Jasmine charged ahead. "Right. So my idea is to rehabilitate your image through good deeds. Good deeds that we promote online."

I perked up. "That would be really fun and beautiful, actually." Jasmine was handing me a sheet of paper with a list of names. "Are these the organizations you've vetted?"

Sylvia drummed her fingernails on the table.

"They're all fairly well-known with lots of community cache," Jasmine said. "Active social media accounts so you should gain fans too. Sleek, shiny, well-loved. Respected."

I was nodding along, eyes scanning the page. "Can we go see these today?" I asked.

"Of course," she said. "Let me go talk to the team and we'll start calling down the list." She closed the door behind her, leaving Sylvia and me alone for a moment. My stomach roiled. I sensed a conversation coming I didn't want to have.

"What does Wild Heart stand for as a company?" Sylvia asked.

"The intersection of corporate values and social justice," I said automatically. "Proving that you can have a big business that doesn't destroy the environment, violate human rights or test on animals."

She gave me a small smile. "Perfect. With the exception of what's happening right now, do you feel like your company still stands for those things?"

"Yes," I said—and felt strong for the first time in twenty-four hours. "We pay every single one of our employees a livable wage. We prioritize diversity in hiring. Vacation time, flex leave, parental leave—you and I wanted a company that valued our employees and didn't chew them up and spit them out like every other corporation we saw at the time."

"Perfect," Sylvia repeated. "And I agree with your assessment. Now what do you stand for, Luna?"

I shifted in my seat, gripped my mug of tea more tightly. "Animals. Humans. The earth. Peace." As the words left my mouth, that brief surge of strength slipped away.

She noticed. "Now what does your money stand for?"

"Wild Heart's?" I asked. "Competitive salaries. Quality makeup. Attention to—"

"Not your company's," she corrected. "The billion or so dollars you have at your personal disposal. What does it stand for?"

The turquoise couch I was currently sitting on had cost $20,000—a paltry amount for what I currently made. The devil on my shoulder felt smug.

"My money stands for the causes that I care about," I finally said, tapping the file that Rebecca left for me. I flipped it open to the first page, searching for quick corroboration. The top sentence read: *Luna da Rosa, CEO—last personal charitable tax-deduction listed is from six years ago.*

That couldn't possibly be right.

"Luna?" Sylvia prodded.

"Yes?" I asked, shoving the folder aside for a moment.

"What is currently happening to you is all too ordinary, I'm afraid," she said. "However, I happen to think that you aren't even remotely ordinary. Which means you're probably going to struggle more but you'll never doubt who you truly are."

My throat tightened. "I don't doubt that."

She came to sit next to me and handed me a sticky note that read *Lucky Dog.* "What's this?"

"I actually like Jasmine's idea," she said, "so this is my consideration for the nonprofit you choose to dedicate your time to, publicly. I think you'll find your values perfectly in line with theirs."

I typed their name into Google, clicked on their website. Their site indicated that they were four years old, but the design harkened back to 1999. It was poorly made, cheap-looking, and not even remotely mobile-friendly. They had not a single social media account.

Ten years ago, this was the kind of grassroots nonprofit I would have done cartwheels over.

Now?

"I think..." I started, jumpy again, "I think Jasmine's going to want to match me with a place that fits me better."

"Fits your brand better, you mean," she said.

I bit my lip. Started to braid my hair. "That's not bad. That's thinking strategically, Sylvia."

"They work to rehabilitate dogs that are especially tough —candidates for euthanasia, fighting ring dogs, dogs found in hoarding situations or who have been abused."

I scrolled down, interest piqued. There was a display of five photos of five different dogs, all in need of a home. And they were all, well, rough-looking, to say the least.

The day I got the idea for Wild Heart I'd been walking across my college campus, oblivious that my life was about to change. It had bolted through me, igniting a hot-pink glow over my heart, a swell of inspiration I couldn't ignore.

I stared at those dogs.

My heart went *glow*.

Only for a moment. Nothing more.

At one point as a child, I must have been feeding fifteen

different feral cats—and they were mean, ugly things, malnourished and yowling and wild. But my sweet, hippie parents had always ensured I understood that all beings deserved love. A huge tomcat I'd named Billy Joel lived outside our house in Coconut Grove for almost ten years—he was often limping, weepy-eyed, fresh from a fight. But I loved that mean old cat. The dogs this nonprofit worked with were reminiscent of those strays.

Sylvia regarded me closely as I clicked through the site. Jasmine would hate this place. And I was ashamed to admit that, even with that little glow, the strategic side of my brain— the side that seized opportunities and craved innovation— raised a very real warning flag. Because this might be my one real shot to fix my currently spiraling reputation. It'd be naïve to ignore that reality.

"Who's Beck Mason?" I asked, clicking through their list of employees. No pictures or bios, only their email addresses.

"The director," she said.

I shook my head. "No, I mean who *is* he. His name sounds familiar."

Her smile turned mysterious. "Beck's parents are infamous in the city of Miami. Do you know the Miami Devils Motor-cycle Club?"

A tiny lightbulb went off—of course I did. Anyone who had lived in Miami in the last twenty-five years knew that club. They were outlaws who often fought with a rival club—the South Beach Warlocks—over territory. Street fights, gun violence, drug running, wild, parties the police had to break up—they could be seen all over Ocean Drive, riding in packs, wearing leather jackets with a screaming devil's skull on the back.

"His parents run that motorcycle club. Most of the extended family is involved, I believe."

There'd once been a two-month period when I was in high school when parts of Miami were on nightly curfew—too many turf wars between the Devils and the Warlocks.

"Absolutely not," I said, shocked. "He comes from a *violent* crime family?"

"Beck Mason, however, is not even remotely involved," she replied smoothly.

"Working with a nonprofit run by a man with such a storied past is not a smart idea, Sylvia," I said, giving her a pleading look. I kept getting the sense that she was leading me by the hand toward the decision she wanted me to make. "It doesn't matter whether he's involved or not. The media will see a man with a violent, criminal background regardless of whether it's true."

She crossed her arms gracefully. "Does it matter?"

"Does what matter?"

She lifted one shoulder. "What he might have done in his past? If he's on the right path now, will you let something arbitrary prevent you from doing truly amazing work for a nonprofit that needs help?"

Emotionally, I was cresting the top of that rollercoaster now—and what awaited me at the bottom wasn't fun. I shut my eyes for a moment, battling it out in my head. The glow called to me.

Fixing my reputation called to me more.

"I don't believe the kind of reputation this man has is *arbitrary*. And the list Jasmine gave me contains nonprofits that are no less worthy," I countered.

"But is their need as dire?"

I gave her a ghost of a smile. This conversation was making me nostalgic for our early days. As a young leader, I often charged ahead without thinking things through. Sylvia would play this intellectual cat-and-mouse game until I landed on a more pragmatic decision. "I see what you're saying. But I think it's safer and smarter to stick to this list of vetted candidates that aren't run by a man from an infamous crime family. Nothing could be further from my brand *or* my personal values than violence."

I glanced at my watch, saw the time. Grabbed my bag of organic dog food from my lowest desk drawer.

"Back in ten minutes?" Sylvia asked. She knew my schedule.

I placed a hand on her shoulder. Squeezed. I wasn't enjoying any of this—the icky, jumpy, guilty feelings.

Not being in alignment with the woman I'd modeled my entire career off of.

"We'll be okay, right?" I asked her—and I didn't mean only Wild Heart.

"Of course," Sylvia said. "Extraordinary women generally make it through these things okay. But—" Sylvia cut herself off.

"But what?" I prompted.

Sylvia steeled her tone, pinned me with a steady gaze. "Extraordinary women generally make the choice that's right and not always the choice that's safe."

6

LUNA

*B*ehind Wild Heart's headquarters was a thin strip of pavement that faced white sand and a glittering blue-green ocean. I sank down, pushed my shoulder blades to the warm concrete of our building. Inhaled the scent of Miami Beach—a smell I associated with coconuts, sunscreen, salt-water and tequila.

I was ready for my five minutes of daily peace.

But she wasn't here yet.

I flipped open the folder Rebecca had left, analyzing it with a critical eye. Although there wasn't much to analyze—there was a clear trend of my philanthropic giving over the past ten years. And not an upward one.

A drop-off—a spike of giving the first couple years of Wild Heart's existence. At that time, I was serious about developing a foundation arm of my company, a branch that would take Wild Heart profits and reinvest them into Miami's nonprofits and charities. It seemed like the perfect addition to a company that valued social justice above all.

And then... nothing. For the past six years, I'd donated not a single cent. Not from my company. Not personally.

Six years ago I'd signed the contract with Fischer Home Goods and cemented my place as one of the youngest self-made billionaires in the country.

And I'd stopped being charitable.

I rubbed my fingers across my forehead. That gross feeling I'd had since this morning was spreading—from my stomach, up my throat, all the way to my toes. I wanted to jump in the air or curl into a ball. I hadn't been lazy these past years—I'd been working my ass off to permanently change the beauty industry's horrible animal testing policies. I worked twelve-, thirteen-hour days answering what felt like millions of emails, interviewing people, supervising my staff, conducting meetings, evaluating financials, strategizing with the marketing team, approving branding decisions, hiring people, firing people... the list never ended. And none of it had been anticipated when I founded Wild Heart. Being CEO felt like an endless learning curve, but there were aspects of my life that had... shifted.

I swallowed hard around the lump in my throat. Tapped my fingers on the thin folder—evidence of that *shift*.

I opened my Instagram account—home to twelve million followers and an abundance of snide comments and messages. With an iron will, I ignored the red notifications and scrolled through the long panel of images. Yoga, meditation, ocean pics, pretty scenes with my best friends.

Wild Heart products, always.

Sponsored products, often.

I was looking for mentions of service or volunteering, highlighted charities or nonprofits that had captured my attention. A sense of *selflessness* mixed in with my brand.

I scrolled. And scrolled. Even the updates I used to enjoy posting about veganism or animal rights seemed fewer and far between—and only in relation to a product.

The shift, it appeared, had been happening for longer than I'd realized.

And then there were clicks on the pavement, movement, and everything sharp and chaotic in my mind muted to a gentle calm.

Penelope was here. My five minutes of daily peace.

She wasn't the prettiest dog in the world; her tan fur was matted, mangy. She had bites and scratches on her skin. She weighed about thirty pounds—but probably should have weighed forty-five. Penelope was a beach mutt, a dime a dozen on South Beach, and yet she'd chosen Wild Heart as the place where she slept every night.

About six months ago, I started to feed her. I bought her a bowl that said *World's Best Dog* and the most expensive dog food I could find — trying to help her gain weight, trying to earn her trust. These past six months she was now able to sit ten feet away from me.

Which was a drastic improvement.

"Hey there, sweet girl," I crooned. One ragged ear perked up the faintest amount—and I was so happy I could have danced across the sand. She devoured her food, drank water, and stretched out in a patch of shade. Penelope couldn't look me in the eye—too skittish—but if my company made her feel loved, I was more than happy to sit with her.

I loved Penelope. And wasn't that the reason why I started Wild Heart to begin with—that harmony between animals, human beings and the earth?

A splash of yellow caught my eye. Careful not to disturb Penelope, I leaned forward on my knees. Dragged over a ceramic dog bowl that said *you are my sunshine* on the side.

"Are you getting fed twice, pretty girl?" I said, delighted. Maybe she'd put on more weight soon. Maybe she'd even let me pet her—

"Are you ready for our meeting? We've got nonprofits to visit."

Penelope yelped and bolted. I glared at Jasmine, who was watching me coolly. The whole staff knew where to find me during these five minutes—knew and generally didn't interrupt. I could see Penelope down the beach, tail between her legs. Looking fearful as she hunched behind the skinny trunk of a palm tree. The fierce protectiveness I felt for this mutt curled in my heart—and the understanding of that sent images from the Ferris Mark lab rising to the surface of my thoughts.

Lethal dose testing.

Irritation tests.

My gold rings glinted against the thin folder on the ground.

"Luna?" Jasmine said, slightly impatiently. "We've got a long list we need to cull down. You're coming?"

The pictures of those rehabilitated dogs sparked to life.

The right decision?

Or the safe one?

"You know what?" I said, standing and brushing sand from my skirt. "I've changed my mind about that list you've got there. I've chosen the nonprofit I'd like to partner with."

Jasmine arched a manicured brow. "Which one?"

"Lucky Dog," I said. "You'll need to put me in touch with a man named Beck Mason."

7

BECK

"*H*ey, boss?" Wes said, kicking open the door with his combat boot. "I've got bad-ass news. I don't think I have to stab anyone for you."

Elián glanced my way with a grin.

"That so?" I asked, rubbing my eyes. It'd been a sleepless few nights, and not even a long motorcycle ride along Miami Beach had soothed my intense money anxiety. "Tell me about it."

Jem squeezed in behind Wes—and it wasn't hard to miss the blush on his cheeks when he realized she was standing next to him.

"Who are you stabbing?" she asked.

"No one," Elián and I said in unison.

"'Cause I know a guy," she said.

"So do *I*," Wes said. They shared a shy smile.

"We all do. Wes," I said. "What's going on?"

"Oh, yeah. In about twenty minutes a famous billionaire is coming to meet you to discuss getting us money."

I laughed. Elián looked shocked.

But Wes was nodding earnestly. "I'm not lying, swear. I just took a call from a woman named Jasmine Hernandez. She says a lady named Luna da—"

"Luna da Rosa?" Jem asked, jaw dropped.

"Who?" I asked. But Jem was already standing in front of me, pulling open tabs on my computer.

"Luna da Rosa," she said. "She's basically my idol."

Elián looked up from his paperwork. "Did I see a news story about her last night?"

Jem bit her lip. "Yeah. She owns a company here in South Beach called Wild Heart. Cruelty-free makeup. She's totally amazing, you know?"

"I don't know," I said. "I have no idea what the fuck you're talking about."

Jem clapped her hands together. "Here's her page."

I glanced at the number of followers on this site—Instagram. Twelve million.

"Huh," I said. "Who is this?"

"Her company is cruelty-free, super eco-friendly," she said. "It was a huge deal when she started it ten years ago."

Jem was glowing. I was grateful to see it—whoever this Luna person was, I always appreciated seeing Jem and Wes excited.

"Why do you know so much about this woman?" I asked, curious.

Jem shrugged. "When I was in between juvie stints, I got into makeup, different brands. That led me to Luna. Also I, uh, kinda want to go vegan. She's inspiring or whatever."

She ran a hand over her hair, looking embarrassed.

"Me too," Wes added. I narrowed my eyes at him—he'd devoured a double bacon cheeseburger right in front of me yesterday. "I mean, soon. Not right away or anything."

"And this woman cares about abused dogs?" I asked. Because I didn't fucking buy it.

"She's in the middle of some bad press," Elián added. He was scrolling across his computer screen, reading to himself. "That's why I recognized her name. Last night there was a news story. Her company's caught up in a scandal. Turns out for the past few years they've been using ingredients tested on animals. Luna lied."

I glanced back at Jem. "You believe that?"

"No," she said, chin lifted. "Besides, they're already making it right. She's a good person. She messed up, is all."

I didn't think the words *billionaire* and *good person* belonged in the same sentence. And how could it? People with money always made me itchy and people with a lot of money made me furious. Growing up in the Miami Devils Motorcycle Club, money was a tool to manipulate. We either didn't have enough and stole—or worse—to get it. Or we had too much—and stole—or worse—anyway.

"The lady says she wants to come talk to us about a mutually beneficial partnership," Wes continued. "Wanted to know if we happened to have thirty minutes free to talk today. I told her *hell yeah*."

"I don't know why this is happening," Elián said, "but you need to prepare to schmooze the ever-living shit out of her. Who the hell cares what she did? We need her support."

I clenched a fist. Money aside, I was sure she had more fancy degrees than my high-school-dropout situation. And I was a Mason. If she was from Miami, wouldn't she know I wasn't a smart idea for *anyone*?

"I'd rather jump into a pen of stray dogs with my pockets filled with bacon," I said.

"Beck," Elián said, warningly.

The three people I cared about the most in this world were staring at me, waiting.

The three people who depended on me to pay their salaries.

"This her?" I asked, pointing wearily to the screen. A smile broke across Jem's face. She clicked on a tiny photo square and enlarged it. The woman glowed like the sun—flashing white teeth in a beautiful smile. She had dark brown, wavy hair, blond at the ends and expressive, dark eyes, tan skin. Clasped in her hands was a bouquet of pink flowers and she was surrounded by color: blue ocean, blue sky, white sand, yellow shirt, green earrings.

"Huh," I said again.

"We have very few options," Elián said. "It's this or I make you be in that calendar. *Or* say goodbye to both kidneys."

I swallowed thickly. "Okay, I got it. It'll be fine. I want to keep my kidneys."

Jem squeezed my shoulder. "You're going to love her."

8

BECK

$\mathcal{I}$ scowled out the window at the rainbow-colored billionaire walking across the Lucky Dog campus. She had a stern, dark-haired woman by her side with her face in her phone. They'd arrived in a black sedan, tinted windows and there was definitely a driver. A few feet behind them both was a smaller white woman with an earpiece. But other than that, it was only the three of them—Luna had no paparazzi, no fountains of money spraying from behind her.

I wasn't sure what I'd expected.

Luna looked like a tropical flower, dressed in colorful layers and jewelry. The sunlight bounced off of the gold rings stacked on her fingers.

Jem was practically shitting herself, grinning as Luna dropped and held her hand out for Princess to sniff. I snorted. I'd rescued that dog myself and she still cowered whenever I walked into her kennel.

Princess sniffed Luna's hand. Licked it. Wagged her tail.

Elián shot me a look of amusement from where he stood next to her. Jem was laughing shyly at whatever Luna was saying. Wes walked over with a cup of coffee for her and she touched his arm, had him smiling, was gesturing at the space around them.

Elián led Luna and the two other women up the steps and into my trailer. I knew I was glowering like a bastard but suddenly all I could see was Lucky Dog's ugliness—the run-down kennels, the cheap toys, the mud, the bald spots on the grass. I was sitting on a donated desk surrounded by donated furniture. I wasn't sure where Luna lived, but I imagined she had a mansion floating on top of a hill of diamonds.

"Luna, please meet Lucky Dog's executive director, Beck Mason," Elián said.

I stood up. I towered over her—I towered over most people, but she had to tilt her chin to look at me. Luna tossed her hair and extended her hand.

"Pleasure to meet you, Mr. Mason," she said. "Thank you for what you do."

I delayed shaking her hand. I guess I hadn't expected her to offer. I was usually feared when I moved through the streets of Miami. And it wasn't like she really cared about me.

"Hello," I finally said, voice gruff. I closed my fingers around her wrist, my hand engulfing hers. Her hand was warm and soft in mine. "I'm, uh... sure this place isn't what you're used to."

"Looks nice to me," she said. But I caught a wrinkle in her brow as she searched the small, shabby space. A similar wrinkle in her nose, like she'd caught the smell of something bad.

Call me Beck—the words were on the tip of my tongue. I needed to schmooze the hell out of this woman. But her wealthy presence had my hackles up, and the thought of begging anyone for money caused my pride to rear its ugly head. That pride had gotten me out of juvie and on the right track, even as the Mason family had made it clear I was expected to return to a life of crime. But I'd forged ahead, on my own, refusing their help at every turn.

I fucking hated asking for help.

And as Luna flip-flopped over to a chair and sat, I imagined begging *her* for a hand-out. Felt pissed all over again.

"Jasmine Hernandez," the other woman said, shaking my and Elián's hands before going back to her phone.

The woman with the earpiece nodded at me. "Bella," she said. "Personal security."

Elián flashed me a private look. I guessed billionaires usually had security.

Or had my last name scared her?

"Thank you for seeing us on such short notice," Luna said. "I'm sure you're incredibly busy every day. This spontaneous meeting is greatly appreciated."

She looked sincere. But I saw her gaze flick down my body, examine my heavy work boots, old jeans, leather vest. That flick cast around the office again and I caught a look of pity that had my fingers curling into fists.

Jasmine lifted the heel of her expensive-looking shoes, lip curled at what she saw stuck to the bottom.

"Why don't you tell Beck and I why you're here today," Elián said.

Luna's mouth tightened. "I'm not going to beat around the bush. You may or may not have seen the news from yesterday. I own a cruelty-free company called Wild Heart. It was recently discovered that our supplier has been testing on animals this entire time. As you can imagine, since I'm a vegan myself, animal cruelty in any form is abhorrent to me."

Pain crossed her face for a second. I was no vegan—I was wearing a leather vest and ate meat four times a day—but the rainbow billionaire and I could technically agree on the "no cruelty to animals" thing.

"So you're looking for a nonprofit to use to make yourself look better now?" I asked.

"I'm looking to make real change," she replied smoothly.

I gave her my best *I'm-a-repeat-criminal-offender* look. Which Elián always pointed out was never necessary, since my appearance—and my last name—usually scared people. But Luna only cranked up her sunny smile.

"Why are you glaring at me like I have dog shit on my face, Mr. Mason?" Luna asked. The teasing gleam in her eye said *gotcha.*

Elián smirked. Even Jasmine looked up from her phone.

"Because I'm not interested in having Lucky Dog be used, money or not." I shrugged.

"To be clear, we really need money," Elián interrupted. "Badly. Like *a lot* of money."

"Great," Luna said. "Because trust me when I say that my intention is to raise Lucky Dog's profile as well as a significant amount of funding for whatever you need, whatever is most urgent."

"We need funding to rescue more dogs," Elián said, which calmed me a bit.

The dangerous thing about my pride was that it clouded my vision.

"Yes," Luna said. "Let's make that happen. I've basically betrayed the public's trust and my fans' faith in me. They need to reconnect with me, my values, Wild Heart as a brand. I'd like to prove to the world I'm as compassionate as I say I am."

"By filming her experience here," Jasmine said, "working alongside the staff, interviewing them. Interviewing Beck. Real motivational stuff. If you can get your fans to cry, you can get them to buy your products."

I narrowed my eyes—and even Luna looked briefly concerned at Jasmine's words.

"A mutually beneficial partnership," Luna finished quickly. "An immersive fundraising experience that would hopefully grow Lucky Dog's budget for many years to come." She leaned in like she was sharing a secret. "And, obviously, you can expect a large personal gift from me as well."

"Thank you," Elián said. "Very much."

I knew this game.

I held up my palm. "A gift and what?"

Luna tilted her head, quizzical. "What do you mean?"

"What if I don't want you to film here?"

"Why wouldn't you want us to help you?" she asked, lips pursed.

"Because I don't like the idea of being used," I said.

Luna stared at me. I stared back, not even trying to tone down my glower. To her credit, she didn't back down. Instead, she lifted her chin and assessed me cooly.

"I looked at Lucky Dog's website on the way over here," she said. "You have almost no online or social media presence."

"So?"

"Maybe there's a reason why you need help with money."

"I'm not sure you'd fit in here at Lucky Dog. I saw your pictures," I said. "You'll have to get your hands dirty."

She looked actually hurt—and I immediately regretted my full asshole mode.

"I'd love for people to stop using my Instagram feed as a barometer for my work ethic." Luna stood up—shoulders back, spine straight. There was a fire in her eyes I respected, even as my guard was still raised. "I'd love to get my hands dirty here, Mr. Mason. And if you think I've been able, at thirty-two, to become one of the youngest self-made billion-aires in the entire world by posting pictures on Instagram, then you don't know what you're talking about."

She said this sweetly, but I wasn't convinced she was that sweet.

"I don't..." I exhaled through my nose. "I don't want you filming me or interviewing me. I don't want you to blast our private financial situation out to millions of strangers who are going to think I'm doing a shit job. They don't understand what it's like to—"

I clammed up.

Luna assessed me, cocked her head. "I don't understand. I'm offering you the opportunity of a lifetime and you're turning it down because you don't want people to know you need help?"

"Yeah. I am."

"I want to do good," she said. "And I want to do it here."

"You want to use us to improve your reputation," I countered.

"Is that wrong?" she asked. "My reputation is important to me. It's who I am."

We were standing almost toe-to-toe, Jasmine and Elián forgotten in the background.

"I think you should do good just to do it. Not market it." I crossed my arms. Her nostrils flared, but I caught a flash of emotion in those dark eyes. It disappeared as quickly as it appeared. "I don't like strings attached to my money."

"It's not strings. It's media attention," she said.

We were like two boxers in the ring. We could have sold popcorn. And I kept digging and digging, ignoring the look of fury on Elián's face.

"To summarize," Luna said shortly, "I'd like to come work at Lucky Dog a few days a week. Film it. Bring the world to your mission. Raise you an exorbitant amount of money while doing so. And you're saying..."

"No," I said.

Elián looked away from me—which caused a stabbing sensation in my chest. I'd seen my own father have these same stubborn impulses, running the MC with a streak of angry pride.

But I wasn't going to be indebted. Not to anyone. And especially not to someone just trying to use me.

Luna looked almost *sad* for a second. But she tossed her long, wavy hair. Turned away from me to shake Elián's hand. "It's been a pleasure meeting you. Hopefully we'll meet again. Say goodbye to Jem and Wes for me, will you?"

"I will," Elián said. I tried not to notice that Luna had remembered everyone's name. She and her team swept out of the room, taking all of the light with them.

Elián closed the door but didn't turn to me.

"Listen," I started to say, "hear me out—"

"You know that stray from the beach?" he said.

"Uh, yeah," I said, startled by the misdirect.

"She's here and terrified. Jem needs your help. I've got another intake to take care of."

I rubbed my beard. "Okay. I'll go help her. We're cool though, right?"

Elián opened the door, backing out of it with his palms up. "You just sent our last chance out the door."

"You know having my picture online is a complication," I said. "It's been twenty years but I'm pretty damn sure my family is *always* watching. You think the Devils would let their prodigal son partner with a goddamn billionaire and leave him be?"

Elián paused with the door half-open. "You're the one who always says you refuse to let that family dictate who you are," he said. "And now you're letting that fear dictate the future of Lucky Dog. Besides, *you* don't have to be online. But our mission could. The dogs could. All the hope that we

47

create here—no one knows about it. Because you keep it a secret."

"Elián, that's not—" I began. But he was already gone, leaving me to sink down into my donated desk chair, defeated. I focused on the fading Polaroid of Willow I had taped to my computer. It was taken a week before we both graduated from our Positive Results program at Miami-Dade Correctional Facility's juvenile detention program. For more than six months, I worked with Willow, who'd been a giant, terrified, snappy pit-bull mix days away from euthanization when she was placed in my care.

Unconditional love didn't exist in the Mason household. Caring for a living creature was new to me. In the picture, I'm eighteen years old, tall and rangy. We are both transformed. Willow into a dog that is calm, gentle. And me looking confident—knowing that after I got out I didn't have to return to the MC. Could make my own way, free of their stranglehold on me.

Now I felt like shit. What was my goddamn plan, after all? A hundred dogs like Willow were going to come through our doors and if we didn't have enough money, where were they going to go?

I rapped my knuckles on the table.

I knew where they'd go.

Out the window, I saw Jem waving, pointing to Kennel #7. I shut off my computer, closed the file of financial paperwork, and prepared to distract myself.

Luckily, Luna da Rosa had left—because I wasn't sure I could face her anyway.

9

LUNA

*W*hen was the last time I'd been rattled by a man?

Beck Mason had been trying to scare me, and even though I'd never scared easily, I was still upset that I couldn't work here. It was clear they needed help, the whole place screamed *grassroots* in a way that was endearing but also concerning. This place, these dogs, deserved to thrive and I wasn't sure why he'd pushed back so hard—why he'd been put off at the idea of us both benefitting from each other.

It wasn't *using* if both people got what they needed. That was called smart *business*.

There was a shiny Harley Davidson in the parking lot and I assumed it was Beck's. Sylvia had said he was no longer involved with his family, but maybe he still rode his bike. His whole vibe screamed tough-as-nails motorcycle gang member and he was, quite literally, the most colossal person I'd ever seen. He was white, about forty—almost a decade older than me. His shaggy, dirty-blond hair was the same color as his thick beard. And those midnight-blue eyes betrayed only one emotion during our entire stand-off: judgment.

Well, that and a pride I recognized because it mirrored my own. But every time I felt an empathetic urge to reach out, tell him *I've been there*, he'd cross his thick arms over that barrel chest and all I wanted to do was fight back.

Pride versus pride.

I toed my flip-flop through the dirt and the brown grass, eyed the dilapidated equipment. Beck's entire office was the size of the bathrooms at Wild Heart. We didn't use donated pens or computers that were 10 years old. I'd had that twitchy feeling again during my face-off with the shaggy jerk.

More evidence of my *shift*, I guessed.

"I knew Sylvia's idea was a bad one," Jasmine said next to me, fingers flying over her phone. I blew out a breath, stared around me at the kennels filled with dogs getting a second chance at life. They were all shapes and sizes, skittish and confident, healthy and scared, big and small. Even as my heart called out to them, the billionaire devil on my shoulder begged for me to let it go.

"Beck's background is a complication anyway," I said, more to myself than to Jasmine. Bella, the security guard I employed at Bluewater, was scanning the environment as if she expected a roving band of bikers to appear at any second. "And him clearly not liking me wouldn't make for a strategic partnership."

"Exactly," Jasmine said, laying a hand on my arm.

Sylvia's presumed disappointment hung in the air between us.

Right decision or safe decision?

"It's not like I didn't *try*. The executive director said no, so we don't really have an additional recourse," I was saying— still trying to convince myself. We were heading toward the car but my attention kept snagging on a kennel in the far back —a flash of tan fur I vaguely recognized.

"Luna?" Jasmine prodded. I was frozen in my flip-flops, staring at the shabby-looking kennel with #7 painted over the door.

"Wait here," I said slowly, moving toward that #7.

Because it couldn't be, right? I'd left her barely three hours ago on the beach, terrified and shaking behind a palm tree.

But there in one corner, shaking and snapping, was my sweet, beautiful beach mutt. I'd have known that mangy fur anywhere.

Penelope.

And in the corner, crouched like the incredible Hulk, was Beck.

"Hey there, pretty girl," I crooned, fingers hooked into the grate. Like this morning, her ear lifted. She was still shaking, but her eyes went to mine for the first time ever. She stilled.

"What are you doing here?" Beck asked, shock on his face.

"It's Penelope," I said, giant grin blooming. "Can I come in?" All frustration toward him was disappearing with the sudden appearance of my dog.

Beck looked between Penelope and me. Hesitated.

"Okay." He reached over from his spot in the corner and opened the latch. I slid through, careful not to disturb the terrified stray in the corner. Next to her was a cheery yellow bowl that said *you are my sunshine.*

"Is that your food bowl?" I asked. I sat next to him, careful not to touch. It was like sitting next to an actual mountain, except he smelled like fresh soap and bourbon.

"Yeah, it is," he said. Beck had a voice as deep as a canyon.

I pulled up a photo on my phone, scrolling until I found one of Penelope and her food bowl. "See?"

He looked down to the small screen, then back at me.

"I've been feeding her for six months now. I named her because I thought it was really sad that she didn't have a name, on top of not having a family or love or food or a warm place to go at night."

Beck was still staring at me—and I saw a spark of contrition.

"I've been feeding her too," he said gruffly. "Trying to earn her trust so I could bring her here."

"I'm surprised I've never seen you," I said. "I would have remembered seeing a grumpy, leather-wearing biker acting like a jerk outside my office."

Beneath his beard, I thought I saw his lips twitch. "That's your offices? That white industrial building on Ocean Drive?"

"Our headquarters," I said. "We should have protesters there any day now because of the Ferris Mark news. I'm happy you got Penelope out of there. I'd have been devastated if she left because of the people."

"I think she's a candidate for rehabilitation," he said. "I mean, um... she can change."

My heart squeezed painfully. "I think she can change too. How does the rehabilitation process start?"

Beck cleared his throat again. "Hand-feeding. It builds trust quickly."

"Can I try?"

He was surprised. "Let me get you some food."

I watched the white shirt he was wearing stretch across the wide expanse of his shoulders. I could feel dirt staining my skirt, my flip-flops, and repressed the urge to flinch from it. Because I never used to care. But my perfectly-distressed sandals had cost me a grand, and I didn't even know how much I'd paid for this skirt. But it was designer, high-end, and scraping it across mud and dog shit wasn't the best idea.

I think you should do good just to do it.

I'd wanted to flinch at that too—his words had struck a spiky nerve.

I held out my palm, my pricey rings glittering in the sun, and Beck filled my palm with food. Before he could caution me, I let my heart guide me across the kennel, smearing as much dirt across my skirt as possible. And it didn't feel wrong.

Not in the least.

I crooned soft noises at her, hand outstretched.

"Stop there," Beck said gently. "Not too close."

I nodded but didn't turn around. I kept non-threatening eye contact with my girl. She sniffed her way over and took three tentative bites of food. I almost squealed with happiness —but stopped myself.

Penelope scrambled over to her corner, tail between her legs.

"Now come back," Beck instructed.

I beamed at him. "Did you see that?" I said. Without thinking, I gripped the sleeve of his shirt, twisting it. "She ate from my hand, Mr. Mason."

A genuine smile broke across his face. "She likes you. That's... great."

Jasmine was staring at me in horror—probably because I was smeared with mud and clutching a giant stranger.

"You can call me Beck, by the way," he said.

"Grumpy Bearded Jerk is a bit of a mouthful," I admitted.

Another twitch of the lips. "Do you... I mean, do you know who I am?"

"Yes, I do," I said.

"That gonna be a problem?" he asked, glancing toward Bella. Then down to the gold encircling my fingers.

"A problem for what?" I asked.

But he didn't say more. So I stood up, brushing all the dirt I could manage from the skirt. I sensed our conversation was over. Or about to be.

"Luna."

"Yes?" I said, turning around to dust off my ass.

Another long look from Beck. "I don't like being exposed the way you are exposed every day. It makes me uncomfortable. And I'm a stubborn bastard about it."

I bit my lip, leaning against the gate. "I get it. You don't like feeling like you owe anyone."

Understanding flooded his features. "Yeah. That's it."

Jasmine was trying to flag me over but I shook my head at her.

"If we're going to work together, you need to know that I hate pity," he said.

I was momentarily stunned—was Beck considering working with me after all?

"If we're going to... work together?" I ventured, smiling a little.

"The second part of what I said is more important," he replied firmly.

That felt directed at me, which made *me* feel uncomfortable. Had I been obvious back there in his office? My discomfort?

"Okay," I said. "What if I tried my hardest to make it so people don't pity you?"

Beck didn't answer. I thought about what he'd accused me of back in his office—using him to rehabilitate my own image.

"You think I'm going to use you?" I asked.

"Yes," he said.

He was a one-word kind of guy—and that one word hit its intended mark. And I knew what he meant, and I knew how it looked, but I needed him to know I wasn't *actually* like that.

"You know I used to take care of feral cats when I was a kid," I said, toeing the dirt. "In my backyard. I fed them."

Beck's blue eyes softened an iota.

"Every weekend, my parents used to have me pick a

nonprofit in Miami and we'd go volunteer. Homeless shelters, foster youth programs, animal shelters, parks, prisons... you name it, I've done it," I continued. I twisted one of my gold rings, studied Penelope, cowering in the corner. Beck was still silent.

"Listen, I personally signed off on a work order that led to six years' worth of animal cruelty so that I could make money from makeup." My cheeks blazed like the sun above. This felt awful, this churning, anxious, horrible sensation coursing through me. "Let me do a little good now. Here. With you and... and Penelope."

I'd been raised by parents who believed in signs from the universe—and if the appearance of Penelope wasn't a sign that Lucky Dog was the place for me, I wasn't sure what was.

Beck's throat worked as he stared up at me. He let out an irritable sigh. "I'm... sorry. For back there. What I said. I feel like an asshole. People shouldn't judge you like that."

His apology surprised me. He didn't seem the type. "Hazard of the job, I'm afraid," I shrugged. "It happens."

"Well, it shouldn't," he said firmly.

"I agree with you."

There was a long, staring stand-off between us before he said, "I don't want it to look like we're begging."

"My goal would be inspirational," I promised. "Positive. Not embarrassing."

"And I won't be on camera." Beck gave me his hardest stare, his *I'm scaring you* stare, but I only lifted my chin.

"I can agree to that," I said. "I won't film you, I promise. But I will take videos of the dogs and the families on their adoption day. And I get to take five pictures a day."

"Two," he said.

"Four."

"One," he glowered.

"Didn't you promise me you'd never be a grumpy jerk again?"

"Pretty sure I just apologized for being one. Not that it wouldn't repeat."

"Can't teach an old dog new tricks, huh?"

Challenge flared in his eyes. Delight. His mouth was tipping into another smile.

"Three pictures and you can film the adoptions," he conceded.

I held up another finger. "Four."

"Has anyone ever told you you're good at that?" he asked.

"All the time," I replied. "If I work here, can I help with Penelope?"

Beck tilted his head. "Um... sure. Yeah."

"Two people feeding her these past months means she's gotten twice as much love."

Beck and I shared a quick smile. He was peering at me like I was a strange curio in a thrift store.

"To mutually beneficial partnerships," I said, holding out my hand to shake. His fingers were so long they rested on my wrist. We shook, his fingers dragging down my skin, and it must have been the sticky heat and my sudden elation.

Because I felt the tip of each finger.

10

LUNA

*C*ameron was perched on my desk, legs crossed gracefully, auburn hair loose around her shoulders. She was dressed to the nines in a power suit and killer, hot-red stilettos. And she was sweet enough to stop by my office before her next meeting.

"Drink this," she said, placing a large ginger tea in my hand. "It'll make you feel less nervous. And if I see you reach for those Fritos, I'll slap them out of your hand."

I sipped as I was told. Wrinkled my nose at her.

My apology press conference was starting in half an hour.

"Okay," I exhaled, inhaled ginger. "You can read them."

"You're sure?"

I nodded solemnly.

"Listen, they're ridiculous. I can tell that just from scrolling." I hadn't stopped my active social media presence since the news had broken—and after today, a formal and official apology would be broadcast across every site. But I'd figured... what was the harm in continuing to post videos of my yoga poses?

Oh, how wrong I was.

"How do you spell hypocrite?" Cameron quoted. "L-u-n-a."
She rolled her eyes. "That one's really stupid."

I smiled a little. "Yeah, it is."

"Okay, um... how about *I always knew there was a whole lot
of ugly under all of that makeup.*"

I winced. Cameron caught it.

"Sorry," she said, grabbing my shoulder.

"No, no, it's fine," I said, waving it off. "You're making it
better, I promise. I'm a human being. I can't not be compelled
to read these garbage comments. But having a best friend do it
helps immeasurably."

That and I could feel the guilt driving me toward punishment—didn't I deserve this?

"*Sheep fucker.*"

"Excuse me?"

She laughed. "This one says that you're a sheep fucker. You
fuck sheep."

I dropped my head in my hands, a wild-sounding laugh
escaping my lips. "At least half of these comments are from
trolls, I'm guessing?"

"You would be correct." Her voice was kind. "Which is why
you shouldn't read them."

"A lot are from fans," I corrected. "I should read them. One
more, please."

Cameron patted my hand and scrolled. Snorted. "*What a
fucking piece of trash. Although now that I know she eats meat, I'd
fuck her.*"

"Oh my god, I'm not a meat-eater," I sighed, yanking on my
hair. "But I am trash."

Cameron stood, brushing non-existent wrinkles from her
skirt. She dropped a kiss on the crown of my head. "You are
not trash. You *are* my best friend and I love you."

"I feel the same way about you, you gorgeous angel."

"You know I've been through this," she said. "They called me a backstabbing sociopath and accused me of sleeping my way to the top. It's impossible not to get smeared at some point. And it sucks."

"Isn't that the truth?" I sighed. "I assumed it would never be me. But how could I ever uphold a perfect record? I mean, there's only a dozen potential pitfalls presented to me every single day that I have to say *yes*, *no* or *maybe* to with limited information." My gut twisted—a reminder. "Although in the case of Ferris Mark, that's on me. I didn't do the work that needed to get done. And I *still* thought I'd be the Special One. The public figure that escaped scandal for her entire career."

"Don't we all," she said. "But you're owning it now. How do you feel about the statement?"

"Really good, actually," I said. "Apologizing and owning up to my mistakes is the right thing to do as a leader. And I'm ready to move on. Plus, we made a strategic plan for me to work at this nonprofit called Lucky Dog."

I showed Beck's website to her.

"Fits you, Moon," she said.

"That's what I think too," I said.

Her eyes narrowed. "Beck Mason is the director?"

I pulled out my speech for today, waved down Jasmine as she strode towards my office. "You know of him, right?"

"Of course," she said. "Doesn't he run the Miami Devils?" Her face was pinched with concern.

"His parents do," I said, checking my mascara in a hand-mirror. "He has nothing to do with them." Even so, over the last day, I'd battled equal parts excitement and nerves over partnering with Lucky Dog. Sylvia had been pleased with my choice—because she fully believed it was the right thing.

Jasmine was still pissed at me. And igniting the ire of your PR director during a scandal felt ill-advised, to say the least.

But every time those thoughts crept in, I pictured Penelope in that kennel. Beck's quiet patience with her.

"You're not concerned about that?" Cameron asked, brow lifted.

She was my best friend, so I felt fine admitting, "Of course I am."

"I trust your decision though. And you do love animals. Probably too much."

I snorted. "Not possible. And regardless of his background, I don't think Beck Mason would hurt a fly. He's a gentle giant. Although he definitely *looks* like a terrifying motorcycle gang member."

"Ah," Cameron said, a teasing glint in her eye. "A nonprofit hunk, if you will."

Beck Mason was the farthest thing from a hunk I could imagine. "Not so much," I clarified. "He was a presumptive bastard in our meeting and he's going to fight me tooth and nail the whole time. He's the size of a house with this giant beard, arms covered in scars. Leather everything. But... he rescued Penelope. Which is amazing."

"Your Penelope?" she asked, eyes wide.

"The one and only. He rescued my girl."

"Beard and motorcycles, huh?" Cameron said. "Opposite of your type."

"Completely," I assured her. She knew that whenever I had the occasion to date, it was usually surf instructors that juiced regularly and wore hemp. They dressed in board shorts and smelled of salt water. Not that I dated often—too busy, too motivated, too on-the-go to really take it seriously.

But still—I'd never been romantically interested in a man like Beck.

Even though Beck's grin beneath that beard was... intriguing.

"Luna, the camera crews have arrived," Jasmine said, rapping on my door.

"My cue to leave," Cameron said. She wrapped me in a tight hug. "You're going to do great, Moon. This is only temporary, remember that."

I hugged her back. The cheerful, sunny optimist believed her, believed in the natural ebb and flow of our careers. But I'd also seen the dramatic rise—and terrifying free-fall—of people like me; beloved by fans one minute, vilified for life the next.

"I will," I said. "And thank you. For everything. As always."

She squeezed my shoulder, then left.

I shook out my hair and grabbed my apology, prepared to face my attackers with a fierce heart.

"Ready?" Jasmine asked.

"Let's do this," I replied—with a confidence I didn't much feel.

11

BECK

I should have been at the office, working on grants or trying to figure ways to get Lucky Dog fast cash so we could pay our bills.

But this morning I immediately recognized the feeling in my veins.

I needed to ride.

It was a tropical Miami morning as I sped across the Venetian Causeway. Heat shimmered off the road as I tightened my fingers on the throttle.

Speed equaled release. Always had, always would—it was the one thing my family hadn't taken from me, this love for motorcycles. At first, after I'd done my last stint in juvie, I'd been wary of picking up a bike again. Except there was no separating who I was from being on this bike. And on the bike, I was half-man, half-metal.

My route took me past the old Miami Devils MC headquarters. It'd been long shut down now, the members moving from place to place, always one step ahead of law enforcement. Those headquarters had been my home, although a chop shop filled with gang members wasn't a safe place to raise a kid. My parents thought I should be a Miami Devil through and through; I was the child of outlaw royalty and I needed to learn the ropes fast.

It was impossible for me to catch the scent of that place—I was going 90 miles an hour with a helmet on. But I smelled it anyway. Leather, grease, cigarette smoke, and tension. The Devils were half-family, half-enemies. Loyalties shifted like shadows depending on the day. As a kid, and later a teenager, the constant fear sent my walls shooting up—it was like being a junkyard dog, constantly on the defensive. I might have been Beck Mason, the future prince, but that didn't mean I didn't get fucked with constantly.

Rip and Georgie Mason were the kind of parents who'd toss their kid off the pier into shark-infested waters without swimming lessons. Because they believed that a kid's survival instincts would kick in and they'd float, not sink.

And that sharks were a part of life.

Once I'd accidentally knocked over an MC member's beer bottle, spilling the contents everywhere. I'd been eleven, all knees and elbows and height I didn't know what to do with yet. I was clumsy, angering my parents and anyone around me. When I knocked over that beer bottle, I had turned to apologize immediately.

The member had slapped me across the head.

Laughed. They'd all laughed—my parents too. It was meant to be a roughly affectionate gesture. *I'm only messing around with you, kid. Don't take it so personally.*

It had hurt. A lot.

My parents had said nothing.

I knew where I could get money for Lucky Dog—grudges didn't last in the Devils because it was better to have someone in your debt than not at all. The prodigal son could have returned. The MC could have saved our asses ten times over by now with money that was stolen.

And the price of that ask for help would have been higher than I was willing to pay.

I rode down Ocean Drive, slowing as the ocean arced to my left, expensive shops to my right. The sidewalks were filled with pink and purple umbrellas. Latin music was everywhere. A line of palm trees led me right to where we'd captured the stray—Penelope—that Luna and I had both been feeding. I wanted to make sure she didn't have puppies, that we hadn't accidentally left them behind.

And maybe... I'd wanted to bump into Luna.

Not for any reason. Although Jem had casually mentioned that Luna was giving a press conference this morning outside of her offices, which were right next to where we found Penelope on the beach. And we needed to check for puppies. It had made sense to me at the time.

But I also couldn't shake Luna from my brain. It was the way she'd looked after Penelope had eaten from her hand. It was an expression of pure joy.

A throng of people stood outside of Wild Heart's headquarters—an industrial building painted white with *Wild Heart* spray-painted on the side in magenta. Camera crews, news vans, reporters, tourists... Luna had more celebrity than I'd realized. And behind them, with signs, were protesters. She'd mentioned them yesterday and I thought she was exaggerating. They were grouped together, holding signs that said *Animal Killer*.

I narrowed my eyes at them. I saw Luna, walking out with confidence and a piece of paper in her hand. She waved to the cameras, looked at the protesters, and shined that mega-watt smile across the beach.

It hit me square in the chest.

I parked my bike, walked toward the audience. I was a head taller than everyone there—so when Luna looked out she caught my eye. I was torn between embarrassment and interest—didn't want it to seem like I was stalking the rainbow billionaire.

But she waved at me. And against my better judgment... I waved back.

A protester started to make his way past me. I crossed my arms, stared him down.

He fled the other way.

Luna stepped in front of the microphone. Her hair swayed in the breeze and she wore a long pink dress, yellow earrings.

"Thank you, everyone, for coming today," she started. Her voice was steady. "My name is Luna da Rosa and I am the CEO and founder of Wild Heart. I would like to formally apologize for the role that I played in our relationship with the company Ferris Mark. We now know that they lied to us, as well as other companies, and that they engaged in full-scale animal cruelty as they tested on animals. Wild Heart was founded on the promise that we would always be cruelty-free and eco-friendly. A promise that has made us stand out from our competitors in an industry where beauty standards hold more power than animal rights or human rights; where humane working conditions are valued less than cheap lip gloss. When I founded Wild Heart, it was with an ambition to change those standards, to raise the bar. To do better."

Luna paused, looked at her notes. "We broke that promise. I broke that promise when I broke my own procedures and fast-tracked our contract with Ferris Mark. If I'd had us perform our due diligence, I think it's unlikely we would be in this situation right now."

A smattering of chants from the protesters and the flash of cameras couldn't drown out the strength in Luna's voice. It made me feel even shittier for implying yesterday that she wasn't a hard worker—because what she was doing up there was something I would never, ever be able to do. Yet there she stood, clear and honest.

Bella stood nearby, arms crossed in front. A row of security guards and a handful of police officers were shuffling in, which made me feel better about Luna's safety. She had downplayed her celebrity, or maybe I hadn't taken it seriously. She was clearly loved in this city.

Or had been.

"Moving forward, Wild Heart will be even more committed to transparency and we have already started making plans to secure a new supplier. We have also removed any and all products that contained the mislabeled ingredients from both our storefronts and online stores. We will work to regain the trust of our consumers and investors and we thank everyone for their support during this time."

Jasmine leaned in toward the microphone. "We will not be taking questions at this time. Thank you."

Reporters surged forward and the protestors' chants grew louder, angrier. Luna gave a small wave and started to walk around the side of the building. Everything around us suddenly went quiet, which allowed one voice in particular to scream *"Murderer"* right at Luna.

She turned. For one startling moment, she looked... devastated. But then she shook her head, turned back around and left.

I followed her.

12

LUNA

*T*here was no Penelope at the back of our building anymore. She had a new home now, a better one.

But I still needed the peace.

Desperately.

I sank onto the concrete, toes in the sand. Closed my eyes. Tried to block out the outrage in that person's voice. *Murderer.* It was overdramatic and not even remotely true—but I couldn't pretend it didn't hurt. Couldn't find the strength to disregard the opinions of strangers anymore. Police officers and security guards were still milling about behind the building, a precaution Jasmine had suggested. I was grateful for them now.

"Ma'am, this gentleman says he knows you?" I looked up to find Beck scowling down at the ground behind a police officer.

"Mr. Mason," I smiled. I'd been surprisingly bolstered by his sudden appearance in the audience. "You can let him through."

The officer looked at Beck, then back at me, hand on his

police baton. Knowing what I did about Beck's background, I wondered if the officer recognized him.

"I said let him through," I said, more sharply, and the officer complied.

Beck rubbed the back of his head, almost sheepish. He gave me an awkward wave. He was dressed in his uniform of jeans, undershirt and leather vest and he was holding a helmet under one arm.

"Um, hello," he said.

"Hello," I replied. I held out my hand, nodded at it. "Can you pull me up? It hurts my neck to crane up at your giant head."

A funny look from Beck, an *almost* chuckle. But he did as I asked, tugging me gently from the sand. "That's better," I said, lightly touching his shoulder. "I was surprised to see you in the audience. Did you come to see my public shaming?"

My voice was shakier than I realized, adrenaline leaving my body replaced by guilt, sadness.

And another feeling I couldn't quite name.

"Are you okay?" he asked.

"Oh, yeah," I said, throat tight. "Just, you know, it's a lot right now."

Beck nodded, the look on his face as comforting as a hug.

"How'd I do?" I struck a pose, chin tilted.

His eyes crinkled at the sides. "I believed you when you said you're working to change."

"Thank you." I cleared my throat. "I mean that. And I *meant* it."

"Why did that guy yell that at you?" he asked.

"Oh, the protester calling me a murder?" I said. "It's an animal rights protest thing. Technically, in their eyes, I sanctioned the murder of lab animals being used for testing."

"Is it really that bad, what they do to them?" he asked. "I guess I always thought it was no big deal."

"A lot of people think that," I admitted. "When I was twenty-one, I toured a lab as part of a business class in college. This company openly tested on animals, it wasn't a secret. Even though I'd always been a vegan, I didn't really think seeing it would affect me. It did though." I lifted a shoulder, attempting to maintain nonchalance so I didn't break down in front of my new work partner. "If a cosmetics company uses synthetic materials, or materials already safety tested, there's literally no need to test anything on animals. Because when they do, they put them through a lot of pain."

"On purpose?" he asked.

"Yes. On purpose. It's utterly vile. They do this for shampoo, body wash, lipstick, mascara, perfume…" I trailed off. "That's why that man called me a murderer. Which is probably a taste of my own medicine. I was never *that* bad but I've publicly said nasty things about non-vegans in my early twenties I wish I could take back."

Beck's brow furrowed, but he stayed quiet.

"I guess I've learned that the world is a more complicated place than *vegan* versus *non-vegan*. I even used to call out medical research labs for testing on animals."

He looked disappointed. I held my palms out. "I've changed my opinion on that issue, believe me. I would never begrudge medical miracles for humans, even though that means I don't fit the stereotype. But I'd hope we could all agree that shampoo and conditioner aren't life-saving, right?"

"Yes. We can," Beck said.

And maybe this was all part of it. I was uncertain on how to navigate the world when all of my mistakes and shortcomings were now reflected back on me.

"What are you doing here anyway?" I asked.

"I thought Penelope might have had puppies. I wanted to make sure she didn't have a den around here."

"Puppies?" I asked. I bit my lip. "I don't think so. I've been with her for the past six months and she's never looked pregnant."

"Good," he said. "Takes care of that. I'll see you around, I guess?"

"On Tuesday," I said, giving him a movie-worthy wink. "I'm your new employee, remember?"

"Right." He was looking behind me, glowering. I turned—three bikers with vests that had screaming devils stitched into the front were casting a curious gaze our way. Beck's jaw was tight, nostrils flaring.

"You know those guys?" I asked.

"Not anymore," he said. One of the guys—massive, tough-looking—gave Beck a sardonic little wave. Every part of Beck's body tightened.

"Devils, right?" I asked.

He shook his head but didn't respond. An unspoken communication was happening between the mountain man next to me and the trio of bikers behind me. I couldn't even begin to parse it.

"It's been twenty years, but some people are still angry about my choice," Beck finally said, clearing his throat. His stubbornness yesterday was making more sense—those walls, that lack of trust. I didn't feel unsafe with the bikers behind me, but the edgy energy in the air was certainly distressing. I couldn't imagine growing up with this kind of hidden violence.

"People in Miami don't think nice things about me," he continued, drawing me back to the conversation. *Believe me, I know*, I almost said. Jasmine had left a few articles for me on my desk about the Miami Devils. Even recently, they'd had plenty of bad press.

I dug into my purse, scooped out a handful of Sour Patch Kids.

"Well, people in Miami think I'm a hypocritical fake so you're in the right company," I said brightly, feeling a strange urge to comfort this man. "One troll on Instagram called me a *sheep fucker.*"

Beck looked furious before he caught my light expression. A smile tugged at the corner of his mouth. "What does fucking sheep have to do with anything?"

"Who knows?" I laughed. Touched his shoulder again. "Want one of these?"

His brow wrinkled. "What is this?"

"Sour candy." I popped one between my teeth, tilted my head. "Go on. Take it."

"Thank you," he finally said, taking an orange one.

I let out a sigh. "I have to go to my board meeting unfortunately. I'll see you on Tuesday?"

"Okay," he said.

"Thanks for coming back to say hi," I said. "I needed a friendly face."

"Most people don't consider this face *friendly*," he said. "Usually strikes fear in the hearts of children and the elderly."

"Ah," I said with a grin, "good thing I'm not children or the elderly, Mr. Mason."

13

BECK

"*H*appy one-year anniversary of getting out," I said to Wes, clapping him on the shoulder. He was sitting at the computer, sorting what little mail we received. His fingers tapped along to a Black Flag song he was playing from his phone.

"Aw, thanks, boss," he said. "I thought I wouldn't really remember the date. But I did."

"It's hard to forget," I said. "I still remember mine."

Wes eyed Jem, who was marching towards us with a plate in her hands.

"How do you feel?" I asked. It'd been only ten months since he'd started working here. I'd seen a startling change in him.

"Happy," he said, bashful. "I love the dogs. I love my job. I need to stay busy, Beck."

He gave me an honest look.

"I get it," I said. "I'll keep you busy."

"Thank you." He rapped his knuckles again. "Am I doing okay here?"

"You're doing great. Everyone loves you."

"Yeah?" Wes asked. "I like having, you know... a family."

Jem burst through the door and Wes's entire attention landed on her. I hid a smile, glad to see the two of them developing a friendship or a relationship or whatever was happening. Routine and community were the things that had kept me away from the MC after I got out.

Lucky Dog *was* my family now. Which was even more clear to me after seeing those three Devils members on the beach outside Luna's office. In twenty years, I'd only seen them three times—always briefly. I didn't recognize the guy who'd *waved* at me. They weren't stupid—we were surrounded by security on that beach. But I'd felt an unspoken message: *we're watching you.*

I'd shaken it off. Or tried to. This was always the game with them. My parents were expert emotional manipulators, as a court social worker had said once. But last night I'd woken from a nightmare with fractured images. Bars. Tight spaces. Not enough room to breathe.

"What's that?" I asked Jem, dismissing the memory.

"Vegan cookies," she said. She handed one to Wes. "Happy one-year anniversary of getting out."

Wes actually blushed. "Aw, man. Thanks, Jem."

"Any time." She bit into a cookie. Grinned. "I technically made these for Luna and I'm nervous as fuck. Just like you are, Beck."

"I'm not nervous," I scowled. It was Tuesday, Luna's first volunteer day.

Luna suddenly shoved the trailer door open and I jumped so hard everyone around me startled with my spontaneous motion—I accidentally knocked over two empty coffee mugs as Wes threw a stack of mail in the air.

"Good afternoon, new coworkers," Luna said, twirling around as she strode toward the front desk.

"Um... hello," I grumbled, kicking the mugs out of the way and scooping up the envelopes. Why was my heart beating this fast?

Luna was wearing a tank top and colorful yoga pants, hair in a high bun. Normal, I guess. But her running shoes looked more expensive than my motorcycle.

"Are these cookies?" she asked Jem.

"I baked them for you," Jem said. She slapped a hand over her face. "Goddammit, that sounded stalker-ish."

"No way, girl," Luna said, waving a hand. "We're coworkers now. You don't have to feel weird. Also I love cookies. How did you know?"

Jem shrugged, bit her lip. Luna stuffed two cookies into her mouth and gave Jem a double thumbs-up.

"If these cookies were a woman, I'd *marry* them," Wes said. Luna laughed and Jem looked absurdly pleased with herself.

I made a mental note that Wes needed a few dating tips from Elián and me.

Not that I had much advice to share.

Luna finally spun on her heels and saw me.

"Hey there," she said.

"How many camera crews do you have with you today?" I asked.

"Only my usual ten," she said. "On a scale of one to grumpy, what are you today?"

"At least a five," Jem interjected.

"Don't you have kennels to clean?" I said. But I took one of her cookies and bit into it. "These are delicious."

"Thanks, boss." Jem swept out the door, taking Wes with her.

"So a five, huh, boss?" Luna asked, dark eyes twinkling.

"Don't call me boss," I said.

"*H*ow have things been?" I asked, walking Luna into our large training field. That morning I'd read an article about her in *The Miami Herald*. It was an opinion article, written by another local businessman. It had not been nice.

"Not great," she said. "Which I didn't really expect. I thought a fast and open apology would take the worst of it. But Wild Heart stock crashed again today. Remember those comments I told you I'd made back in my twenties?"

"The ones about non-vegans?"

"The very same," she continued. "They're being dredged up and used against me. I had really hoped everything would be, I don't know, *dissolved* after a day. But that was probably extremely naïve of me."

I looked over at her, saw her shaking her head. "I'm sorry, Luna."

"It's not your fault," she said. "Besides, I feel better already, being here."

"Here?" I asked.

"It feels really happy at Lucky Dog. Don't you think?"

I looked around—saw all of our fucked-up shit. It was hard to see it any other way. This place was being held together with duct tape.

"You think showing people what you're doing here will get us more money?"

"And improve my reputation," she said, crossing her fingers. "I mean, I hope."

Luna was staring out at our giant space. I thought about the fury of the protesters, the nasty comments about her online. If I was in her situation, how far would I go to get my perfect reputation back?

"Luna," I said.

"Yes?" she asked cheerfully.

"Don't..." I stubbed at the ground with my boot. "Don't market us for pity. I'm serious. I know we talked about this when you were first here but..."

Luna took a step back at my change in tone. "What?"

"I want the money to come from a place of... I don't know. Hope. Not fear or just because people feel bad for us."

"I get it. And I promise," she said. "But, Beck, you're the one who's afraid to get on camera. Don't you think people would respond to the passion of the founder?"

"I'm not changing my mind on that," I said, arms crossed. "I'm not your prop."

Her nostrils flared. "That's still what you think? That I'm going to use you?"

"Of course."

She mirrored my pose. "Do I really give off the impression that I'm so shallow now?"

"I think people in desperate situations do things they wouldn't normally do," I said.

"You really are a *five* today, aren't you?"

I *almost* smiled. Switched to glowering at the last minute. But she smiled too.

"Okay, okay," she conceded. "You still don't fully trust me. Let's keep going with the tour."

She started to walk away.

"You're not... I mean, you're not mad?"

"Mad?" she said. "No. I don't really get mad. A little frustrated, maybe. I'm the CEO of a company valued at over one billion dollars that I built from the ground up. You think I don't spar with people all damn day? We're merely at an *impasse*."

"Oh," I said, taken aback. *Huh.*

"Let's try this," she said. "If you had all the money in the world at your disposal, what would you do for Lucky Dog?"

"Expand it and double the number of dogs we could treat, from fifteen to thirty. Then triple it. Then open a second location."

Luna thought about that for a second. "I like it. Sounds reasonable. Forward motion without expanding so quickly you can't sustain it. You've got smart vision, Mr. Mason."

"I do?" I didn't. At least, I didn't think I did.

She tapped her lip. "Can I take a picture of this little cutie over here?" It was Beatrix, looking extra snarly and vicious in her cage.

"I doubt she'll be a nice model."

But she was already strolling over, cooing to Beatrix in low tones. The dog didn't come over to her—still too scared for that—but she did open up her mouth for a fully canine grin.

Click went Luna's phone and her thumbs flew over the screen.

"What about this? Do you approve?"

I took the phone, my fingers brushing hers. It was a picture on her Instagram feed with the twelve million followers or whatever. In her profile picture, she wore a crown of white daisies, dark hair flowing, lips red. Next to it: *Vegan. CEO/Founder of Wild Heart. Animal lover and nature nerd. All links to Wild Heart's products in bio.*

"All of these people want to look at your pictures?"

"They sure do." She tapped the one in question. It was the picture of Beatrix but she didn't look like she was in a cage—she looked like a regular dog.

Most importantly, she looked like an adoptable dog.

Beneath it, Luna had captioned: *For the next month I'll be volunteering with local Miami charity Lucky Dog which rescues and rehabilitates dogs like this good girl Beatrix! The great news is that I'm bringing my followers along with me! And if you want to help dogs like Beatrix, click the link in my bio to donate. More money = help more dogs.*

"I had our accountant link a donation page from my site to Lucky Dog," she explained.

I stared at her.

"What?" she asked. "You thought I wasn't serious about any of this?"

"Maybe... kinda?"

She looked hurt. "Well, contrary to current opinion, I really do care, Beck."

"Okay," I said. Because we'd sparred enough today and I was starting to feel bad about it. "I believe you. If your posts are like that, I... think that's fine."

"Some would even say I'm kind of... .an expert on... branding... and... marketing..." Luna tapped her chin, pretending to look around her.

"Okay, fuck, I get it. You're a genius. Now can I give you this fucking tour?"

Luna touched my arm. "I'd love that."

15

LUNA

*B*eck Mason still believed I was going to churn him up and spit him out, all in the name of improving my reputation.

Since the news broke, I'd basically become target practice for any stranger online who could figure out how to leave a comment on Instagram. Besides the usual trolls, I was quickly becoming a living example of the ways in which corporations lie to consumers; the ways in which vegans *suck*; the ways in which leaders manipulate their followers and on and on and on.

So Beck pushing back on my stipulations didn't actually bother me—that was merely business details to hash out. That was my daily life—I was used to that.

But the judgment on his face? That hurt more than everything else this week combined.

"You're going to dial it back, right?" I asked—lightly, but with enough steel in my voice that he actually looked sorry. "Because *five* is a bit much right now after the day I had. Maybe a three?"

Beck nodded. "Do you want to go see Penelope?"

"Please," I grinned. "Pretty please."

"And I'll aim for, uh... zero, actually, if that's okay with you?"

"I mean, if you're a *zero* on the grumpiness scale, where's the fun?"

Beck actually chuckled. "Come on," he said.

I followed him through the training field, back toward kennel #7. "Also, I'm sure you're busy, right? Could Elián give me this tour?"

"Oh, it's no... I mean, I wanted to. It's no problem," he said.

"Well then, sock it to me, boss," I said.

"This field is where the dogs we're working with go through obedience and trust training—getting them used to humans and other dogs. This ring of kennels is where they live. And as they graduate to different levels of training, they eventually work toward this." Beck slapped a shoddy-looking building. "It's a replica of a real house. The dogs we work with, they're afraid of anything new—stairs, couches, being inside —and they're not house trained. Abused dogs, stray dogs, it's important that they feel safe before being adopted out. Gives them the best chance for recovery."

I peeked inside, smiling at the realistic-looking living room they'd created. There was even a fireplace with a cozy rug in front of it. "I love it. What are Jem and Elián trained in?"

"They're animal behavioral specialists. That's how I met Elián. I got a job as a janitor at Miami's SPCA. He was working there."

"He's your friend?" I asked.

"Best friend," he said. "And co-founder, but he doesn't like me calling him that."

"He gave you the glory," I said.

Beck looked embarrassed. "I'm not sure why. I'm a high school dropout who can barely string two words together."

"Maybe it's because you're the right person to lead," I said.

"Maybe." His eyes widened before he looked away from me. *Interesting.*

Beck *was* the right leader for Lucky Dog. Sincere, clearly educated on what these dogs needed, and able to set them up for success. But he didn't see himself that way.

"Let's agree to disagree on that. Because I see a leader sitting in front of me," I said. Beck, however, didn't respond.

"So... how long do they stay here?" I asked, redirecting.

"Give or take thirteen weeks. We spend that time exposing them to humans they can trust. Love, maybe."

"And they can stay even if it takes longer?"

"Until they find their home, yes."

Tears sprang to my eyes.

"That makes me very happy," I said. Beck gave me a tentative smile.

We'd reached Penelope's kennel. She was curled in the corner but not asleep. Scared, on high alert.

"Oh, Beck," I said softly. He reached out, as if to touch me, but then pulled his hand back.

"She'll be okay," he promised. "We're going to work with her today." He led us inside and we both sat gingerly, without making a sound. He scattered food all around us in a circle.

"The more she associates *humans* with *food*, the better. Food equals safety; safety equals trust."

I wrapped my arms around my knees, again aware of the mud staining these brand-new, stupidly expensive yoga pants. It was a brand I followed obsessively—their founder was young and hip and almost unbearably trendy. When they'd reached out for sponsorship, I'd said *yes* enthusiastically, was willing to shill for their brand if they did the same for Wild Heart, obviously.

But as I sat in the hot sun with Beck, it was interesting to note how easily yoga-gear-branding opportunities dominated my attention more than my former passions about animals or the environment.

"How long do you usually sit here with each dog?" I asked.

"As long as it takes," Beck said. "This is the tough part. It's one step forward, two steps back for what feels like forever." He was cradling a brush in his lap. I tapped it with my finger.

"We're going to brush her hair?"

"Maybe," he said. "It's a way for dogs to bond with their humans. Sometimes. A lot of abused dogs are also smacked with brushes so I'm not sure how she'll respond."

That old, familiar fire surfaced in my heart—the same one that had directed me to found Wild Heart. "Do you believe Penelope was abused?"

He grimaced. "I'm not sure. It's a possibility. She could be a stray because she ran from an abusive owner."

I exhaled sharply through my nose.

Beck heard it. Gave me a look of concern. "Lucky you and I were there to rescue her, huh?"

I held his gaze for a moment, throat tight. "Very lucky indeed." I stretched my feet out, leaning back. Dug into my purse for my ever-present glass bottle of kombucha. I'd managed to limit my intake of corn chips and sour gummy candy to a mere handful of each this week. "Want some while we're sitting here?"

"What is it?"

"Kombucha. I brought an extra cup for you."

"You brought this for... me?" he asked.

"It's meant to be shared with friends"

"We're friends?" He looked skeptical.

"Of course. We've had two fights, you've seen me publicly shamed and now we're helping rehabilitate a dog together. Doesn't that make us friends?"

Beck gave me a quizzical look as I poured the carbonated drink into a cup and handed it to him. "What's in it?" he asked.

"A symbiotic colony of bacteria and yeast."

He pressed it back into my hand. "Nope."

"Your loss." But he wouldn't stop eyeing it.

Penelope stirred in the corner, then pulled herself low about a foot across the ground.

I grabbed the sleeve of his shirt and whispered, *"Did you see that?"*

He smiled. "I did."

We sat in silence for a minute, both of us watching for signs of progress from the dog in the corner. He cleared his throat, shifted next to me. "So, uh... when did you start drinking bacteria?"

That startled a laugh from me. Even Beck looked a little amused. "My parents raised me in Coconut Grove. It's a neighborhood here in Miami that still believes it's the Summer of Love. Hippies abound. Bongos everywhere. And kombucha basically ran from our taps."

Beck nodded like he suddenly understood something. "That's why you're the way you are."

"Just about," I agreed. "Even before becoming vegan or starting Wild Heart, my parents had always really emphasized the connections that exist between humans, animals and our planet. That we all have a role to play in making the world a better place."

It was why I felt such a strong connection to the natural beauty of Miami. The ocean was part of my soul, the beach a form of poetry that I craved. I always felt so *sure* that my true path in life was to do my best to be part of protecting that beauty.

Until recently, that is.

"I like that," he said simply.

I turned more fully toward him. "Did you always want to start your own nonprofit?"

He blew out a breath. "Elián and I opened Lucky Dog four years ago. Before that, I did all kinds of jobs at animal hospitals, shelters, other rescues. I learned the field, getting my certification in behavioral training."

"And why did you want to focus on dogs?"

Penelope was inching closer to the food.

"I, uh... well, I was in and out of juvenile detention when I was a teenager." He stopped talking, almost as if he was startled. I didn't push—merely folded my legs under me and waited.

"Anyway," he finally said, "my last time there, I did this program. It paired offenders about to be released with dogs about to be euthanized for behavioral problems. We spent six months with our dogs. They lived with us and we trained them day and night. If all went well, the day of our graduation was the day they got adopted." He coughed a little, cleared his throat. "My dog was named Willow."

He was a calm mountain right now—utterly still—but I sensed a riot of emotions brewing beneath the surface. Sensed and let him be. For now. But I thought about his family, what they'd done.

"What was graduation day like?" I asked.

"Willow was adopted by a family with a giant backyard and four active kids. I wrote them letters, tried to see how she was doing. They never wrote back but, uh..." Another cough. "I think she had the life she deserved."

"You gave that to her," I said.

But Beck merely shrugged.

"Were your... parents... there?" I asked, each word dropped carefully, so as not to disturb.

Beck turned to me. "No. But that's okay. I go to all the graduations now, if I can make it, and that's how I met Jem and Wes."

I let my head drop back against the grate—tried to imagine Beck and his dog. Beck watching the dog leave. Beck looking out into an audience with no friendly faces looking back.

"Well," I finally said, when I'd reined in my emotions, "if I was there, I would have cheered for you."

He didn't respond. But I caught a tentative smile.

I beamed back at him—holding up the cup of kombucha. "Come on. One sip for me."

He sipped it. "It's disgusting."

"Well, at least you tried it."

Jem's lime-green hair caught my attention. She was struggling to haul a bag of gravel into a kennel. Part of me wanted to keep chatting with this enigmatic giant. But I had a job to do—a responsibility—and I didn't want to start my time here by slacking off.

"Hey, I'm here to work, right?" I said.

"Yeah, why?"

I pointed to Jem. "How about I go help her? I love being with Penelope but if you guys need work done..."

"Oh, yeah," he said, slowly standing up. "I lost track of time a bit. She'd love the help and I probably have, you know, emails or something."

"Right," I said, tilting my head. "I've gotten like five hundred emails while sitting here. I'm sure it's the same for you."

"Probably."

I slipped out of the kennel. Waved to Beck. "Come find me later. And thank you for the tour."

And then I all but skipped over to Jem, who smiled shyly when I reached her. And when I turned back to Penelope, Beck was still in her cage. Sitting absolutely still.

Patiently earning her trust.

16

LUNA

"*H*ey, girl," I said, waving my fingers at Jem as I approached. "You need a little help?"

She pointed at her chest. "Me, you mean?"

"Yeah, you, the goddess with the green hair."

Jem bit her lip like she was unsure. "Kinda, to be honest. I'm cleaning out Jack Sparrow's kennel and it's definitely a two-woman job."

I gave her a salute. "On it." I grabbed a bucket and a mop and started attacking the tiled area in the far-left corner. I was just getting into a good rhythm. And then my phone vibrated with a text from Cameron. It was a screen-shot of a headline in an entertainment magazine: *Instagram Model Luna da Rosa Caught in Makeup Fraud.*

"Uggghhhh," I said, trying not to throw my phone at the wall.

"What is it? Did you get dog shit in your hair?" Jem asked.

"Not exactly. This is a very special kind of shit."

I showed her the screen. Her forehead creased. "You're not a model."

"Don't I know it," I said, bumping my shoulder against hers.

There was no shame in the Instagram model game. But Cameron, Daisy, Emily and I were constantly battling the media's need to highlight our sexuality, our outfits, who we were dating *more* than whatever innovative work we were doing. Emily was literally changing lives through a scientific discovery she spearheaded, but her recent haircut was still the main focus of the media.

Another text from Cameron: *Just a reminder that we know you're a talented businesswoman and the baddest bitch around.*

I snorted.

"Is that from your friend?" Jem asked.

"My best friend Cameron."

Jem ran a hand over her hair. "You have good friends."

"That I do."

"I'm kind of obsessed with you," she said quickly. "Okay, sorry, that was a weirdo thing to say."

"It's not weird," I promised. "I'm obsessed with your whole bad-ass vibe. So we're even."

Yanking up all of the old dog bedding, I rolled it in a ball and tossed it into the laundry container in the corner. I started to tackle the overgrown weeds that surrounded the raised dog bed. How expensive would turf be to put in? Would it be helpful? I made a note on my phone to ask Beck later—could definitely be something to ask for donations for.

"I'm vegetarian but really want to go vegan. And I basically own a lifetime supply of Wild Heart's black eyeliner," Jem continued.

"Expertly applied, by the way," I said, giving her an exaggerated wink to show it off. "Hey, do you want some of my kombucha? Grumpy McGrumpy Pants in there wouldn't take it."

Jem propped a shovel in the dirt. "Yeah, actually. That'd be rad."

I poured her a glass of kombucha and we did a little *cheers*.

"Thanks for being nice to me today, Jem," I said, leaning against the grate. "You're probably pretty pissed at me for the Ferris Mark stuff, huh?"

She studied me for a second. "I was pissed a little when I found out, for sure. I mean, I buy your products for a reason."

My stomach hollowed out—it was harder seeing the disappointment of a fan like Jem, who truly wanted her makeup to reflect her values.

"I'm really sorry," I said. "I fucked up. Big time. *Really* big time."

"People make mistakes though, even CEOs or whatever." She shrugged. "Plus, I tossed all of my Wild Heart products already. It'll be okay in the end."

"Will you text me what products?" I said. "I'll get you new ones once everything's fixed."

"Oh... please, you don't have to do that." Her pale cheeks were turning pink.

"Let me," I said. "Consider it payment for rescuing Penelope and all the work you do here every day. I'll stock you with eyeliner for life."

Her entire face lit up. "If you insist..."

"I do," I said. "And I'm working on fixing those mistakes. Because it was a mistake driven by..." I hesitated, searching for the right words. "A mistake driven by impulses I'm not proud of."

Jem shook her head, looking out across the field. I caught a glimpse of Beck scowling at me from his window and I gave him my best *Miss America* wave.

"Wes, Beck and I all met through the same rehabilitation program. We're familiar with mistakes," she said so quietly I almost didn't catch it. I helped her tear open the bag of gravel and deposit it evenly over the ground. I was sweating, dirty, heart racing—my job hadn't been this physical in, well, ever.

"The one with the dogs?" I asked.

"That's the one," she said. "I was really lucky to get a nice judge. She didn't think my future was gonna be that pretty without an intervention, you know? That was six years ago."

I sat back on my heels, brushing a strand of sweaty hair from my forehead. "Did your dog get adopted?"

"Walter," she said. "That was his name. And yeah." She scrolled through her phone and showed me a picture of a family with two little kids and a terrier that looked practically chaotic with happiness.

"Oh, *Jem*," I said, tears springing to the corners of my eyes.

"Oh my god, don't *cry*," she said. "It's not sad. It's happy."

"I cry when I'm happy," I said, laughing a little through the tears. "You're such a fucking *bad-ass*." I clapped a hand over my mouth. "Sorry, are we allowed to curse here?"

"Fuck yeah," she said. "If you don't think the f-word comes out of Beck's mouth a hundred times a day, you've got another thing coming."

"I knew there was a reason why I liked Beck," I said, shaking out a sheet and placing it across the new bed. I folded it with care, tucking it into each corner, fluffing the pillows.

"Not to lean too hard into the canine metaphors, but his bark is way worse than his bite," she said.

I bet I'd like his bite.

I dropped the shovel I was holding and it *clanked* against the concrete.

"Are you okay?"

"Oh, yeah, just super hot," I said, fanning my face. Where the hell had that thought come from? I looked back toward the trailer and Beck was now outside, drinking a cup of coffee that looked doll-sized in his hands. Without his vest on, his chest appeared even more expansive. His chest hair pushed through the v in the shirt.

Maybe... maybe I hadn't wanted to admit to myself that Beck Mason gave off a very real *filthy sex* vibe. He looked like the kind of man who'd leave you marked and breathless and blissed out for weeks.

"He's a good boss though?" I asked, attempting a distraction. He and I were working together, nothing more.

"Beck makes this place what it is," Jem said. "Which is why it's frustrating that he won't let himself be, you know... like the *you* of this place."

"He doesn't like attention," I said.

Jem shook her head back and forth. "Nope nope nope."

I wiped down everything with bleach and water, humming softly as we worked together. I wasn't sure which dog was going into this kennel but it was my goal for it to be the *best*. I brushed every last scrap of dust from the bed and folded the sheets. Arranged the toys with military precision—and noticed how worn and old they were. I placed a Milk-Bone right in the center of the pillow, like a hotel mint.

I snapped a photo. "I only get four designated photos a day per Beck's privacy measures," I said, "but I think this one is worth it. What do you think?"

Jem appeared over my shoulder. "It's beautiful. You really think this will help?"

"I do," I said—the first thing I'd felt certain about in days.

She gave me such a precious, toothy smile I pulled her in for a picture.

"For your page?" she looked horrified.

"Of course," I said, but then thought about Beck's reticence. "Unless you don't want to. Absolutely no pressure if you're not comfortable."

"I look okay?"

"A *literal goddess*," I promised. "Now get in here."

We looked happy in the picture—flushed, tired, real. I hadn't seen a picture of myself like that in a while, actually.

My smart watch beeped. I was about to be late for a production call with the West Coast.

"I have to go," I said. "Thanks for hanging out with me today. I'll send you some recipes later okay?"

Jem was still flushed. "Hey, Luna?"

I turned.

"My mentor in that program used to say that we all deserve second chances, you know? They're only extra scary because when we get them, we're worried we'll ruin them."

"That makes a lot of sense," I said sadly. "I guess... I guess I can relate to that."

"You won't ruin it though." She said this quickly, like she needed courage to do so. And then she bounded off across the training field.

My chest felt tight, a cinched emotion that threatened to cut off air.

I closed my eyes, inhaled. Exhaled. Did it again until the sensation ebbed. Her words were an unexpected kindness, poking at the tender edges of my soul.

Until I turned around and walked into the wall of muscle known as *Beck*.

17

BECK

"Sorry," I said, looking away. "Didn't mean to scare you."

"Never," Luna said. Strands of hair hung loose from her high bun. "I was heading out, actually."

I peered around her shoulder to look inside the kennel. She'd folded all the blankets to make a thick pillow. Placed a stuffed toy nearby. And a Milk-Bone in the middle.

That damn Milk-Bone got me. "You did this?"

She lifted one shoulder, the strap sliding down her skin. "It's silly. I thought if I was scared and alone I'd want to feel safe and welcome and get treats."

I looked over at her. "Thank you."

"You're welcome." She exhaled, wiped those strands of hair back into her bun. "The Ferris Mark thing is messing with my production schedules. I've got to go soothe a few hurt feelings on the West Coast."

"You cleaned dog shit for two hours and now you're going to...?" I wasn't sure where I was going with this *or* my expectations of the rainbow billionaire.

"Be a CEO?" she teased. "Yeah, that's my day. Started at 4:00 am"—she yawned—"but this was the highlight."

Luna peered up at me in the bright Miami sunshine. Her skin looked like it was glowing.

Or maybe that was her in general.

"Thank you for sitting with Penelope," I said.

"It was my absolute pleasure," Luna replied.

A sleek black car pulled into our parking lot next to my busted-looking motorcycle. Luna grabbed her expensive purse, went to leave—and then turned back.

"You know, technically, I've got one officially sanctioned photo left to take. I've only taken three."

"You didn't hit your Instagram quota of fifty posts an hour?"

"What am I, an amateur?" she asked. "I do sixty, easy."

A smile tugged at my lips.

"I could take one of *you*."

"Nope," I said.

"A lot of my fans would be into that shaggy beard."

"This face is terrifying, remember?" I said, pointing at it.

"Well"—she pursed her lips—"you're definitely a *type*."

"What type is that?"

"You know." Her cheeks flushed. "Hot, bearded mountain man."

Her compliment—intended or not—sent a frisson of heat up my spine. When was the last time anyone had said *anything* about my face that was nice?

"I'm still going for grumpy biker," I said.

"Nah." Luna poked her tongue out. "Word on the street is you're a big softie, Mr. Mason."

"Beck," I said automatically.

"I know." Her smile was bewitching. Luna da Rosa was *teasing* me.

"So *hot,* bearded men are your type?" I asked. Two could play at this game.

"*A* type. Certainly not mine."

"I'm going to guess your type would be..." I tapped my chin. "A hippie spin instructor whose name is Carrot?"

"*How'd you know about Carrot?*" she deadpanned.

I let out a laugh—a little surprised.

"I think you'd be surprised at the wave of perverted messages I'd receive about you." Luna placed her phone in my palm, fingertips glancing off my skin. "Since you won't take a picture, take one of me, please."

I stood frozen as Luna undid her hair, running her fingers through it—the breeze tossed the brown and blond waves. She posed and I took it. In the picture, she looked like she was comfortable in her skin, comfortable here, happy with her life. But I knew things were not going great for her right now.

Was this the real Luna? Or a fake?

"Text me updates about Penelope, okay?" she said. "I'll worry about her until I can get back here later this week."

My eyes searched her beautiful dark ones. The sincerity and compassion there seemed real.

"Sure," I said.

"Try not to terrify too many elderly people while I'm gone, Mr. Mason."

I watched Luna get in that car and be driven away.

Jem came up behind me, waving at the car with a look of total love.

"Can we keep her?" she asked.

"Maybe," I grumbled.

18

BECK

*T*hree days later, Elián yanked open the trailer door with a big grin on his face.

"Have you checked Luna's donation page yet?" he asked. "The one for Lucky Dog?"

Before I could answer, he pulled up a website on my computer. $15,652 scrolled across the screen.

"That's how much she's raised for us so far and it's only been up four days."

"Holy shit," I said, leaning forward. "And she's only worked here one day."

"She's convincing," he said. "She'd make a real good executive director, to tell you the truth."

He hadn't meant it as a slight toward me. But I still felt it. Luna had done in one day what I struggled to pull off these past four years.

"We could get a lot of money from this," I admitted. Elián clapped my shoulder.

"That's what I've been saying this whole time. And the timing couldn't be more urgent, with the deadline and all."

I nodded, chastised. We had less than twenty days to fill

the funding gap left by losing that multi-year foundation grant. Christina, the board president, had called me yesterday. She was pleased with all of the new cash.

But it needs to keep coming in, Beck, she'd warned me. *This can't be a one-time thing.*

Meaning I needed to start doing my damn job.

A text came through on my phone. It was Luna.

Can you come by my office today? I have a surprise for you.

"Great news, I'm assuming?"

I shrugged. Typed back, *Okay*.

Luna sent me a string of animated hearts and fireworks. I showed it to Elián. "She's... very excitable."

"I can see that." He gave me an unreadable look before checking his watch. "Also, shit, Jimmy is here for his adoption interview. Wes's friend?"

"I'll do it," I said. Elián stared at the stack of grant applications on my desk. "I'll do those after," I said. "Bring him here. We'll do it together, like old times."

He sighed but left to get Jimmy. In the early days, when we didn't even have enough money to pay ourselves, Elián and I did everything at Lucky Dog together—intake, training, interviews, administration, fundraising. It'd been stressful and overwhelming, but we were best friends and we loved the dogs. We kept each other motivated. And that was enough.

Elián got to stay in that role. And now that I was in charge, I missed those days.

I met Elián and Jimmy outside. We liked to interview candidates while visiting the dogs. It gave us a chance to see how people interacted with the animals—if a connection existed. People went into the adoption process with an idea of what kind of dog was right for them.

They were usually wrong.

"Jimmy?" I asked. He was a white man almost as tall as I

was, which was saying a lot. Tattoos covered his neck and bald head. He wore all leather and smelled like bike grease.

And when I shook his hand, I saw a tattoo—the skull of a screaming devil.

"Yeah, nice to meet you man," Jimmy said smoothly. He looked closer to Wes's age, no more than twenty-five. There was nothing aggressive about his posture or body language.

But I was wary.

"I'm Beck. Beck Mason," I said, and watched the recognition bloom on his face.

He was a Devil. Had to be.

"Thought that was you," Jimmy said. "Wes told me his boss used to ride with the Devils a long time ago, right?

"Twenty years ago," I clarified. "You?" If he was an active member of the club, there was no way I was letting a dog leave with him.

Jimmy looked around briefly, then stepped closer. My hands curled into fists at my side.

"I left two years ago," he said. "Same reason as you did. Or at least what I heard."

"Yeah?" I asked.

"Yeah. It's bad. Rip and Georgie aren't doing too well."

"Spending four decades as criminals can run you down," I said. I felt no sympathy for them.

Jimmy pointed at his tattoo. "I'm getting it removed. I don't want you to think I'm... you know, still involved.

"Okay," I said. "We do background checks for everyone, obviously, but as long as nothing comes back, I trust you."

"I can handle that," he said.

"How do you know Wes again?"

"Juvie," he said. "Way back. You?"

"Same."

Jimmy looked at Elián. "I'm actually the only law-abiding citizen that works at Lucky Dog," Elián chuckled.

Jimmy grinned. "The straight man. I like it. So can we see the dogs or what?"

Elián and I walked Jimmy around the kennels, let him ask questions about our program and dog ownership in general. He'd grown up with dogs, loved them, and felt strongly that it was time for him to have one.

We stopped outside Beatrix's cage—the giant, snarly bull mastiff. He liked her.

"She's a big girl," Jimmy said.

"She'd require a steady hand," I said. "Firm training. But I think she's a sweetheart beneath all that armor."

"What excites you the most about owning a dog?" Elián asked him.

Jimmy tapped his fist on the gate. "I don't know, man. I'm trying to find my way right now. Legally. I think it'd be real nice to work a nine-to-five and come home to a dog who didn't think you were a piece of shit, you know?"

"Yeah, I know," I said. Beatrix was wary in her corner but Jimmy didn't seem bothered. They looked to be a match, at first glance, but I wasn't so sure. We kept walking, Jimmy talking with me about bikes.

We finally reached Betty and Veronica, two bonded Yorkies who'd been rescued from a dog hoarding situation. These lap dogs were going to have to be adopted together as a pair.

"Who are these ladies?" Jimmy asked. Betty and Veronica danced over to the cage, panting excitedly as he pet them.

"They come as a set," I said. Elián was hiding a smile behind his hand—we'd done this job enough to know a *true* match. And as much as we wanted to see Beatrix in a loving home, Jimmy might not be the one.

"Can I go in?" he asked.

I nodded, opened the kennel door. "They didn't need much in terms of rehabilitation, just love. Their owner had kept them with forty-seven other dogs on a farm near the Redlands. Barely any food, barely enough water, lots of fights every day. I think these two protected each other."

Wes had wandered over from the office, smiling at the sight in front of him.

"Jimmy, you found yourself two, huh?" Wes said, hands in his pockets.

"These two?" Jimmy asked. Betty was licking his face and he was laughing. "Nah. I'm going for that giant dog over there."

"Sure," Wes said. "I mean, whatever makes you happy, bro."

If Luna was here, would she be capturing this on video? Could we share this story and be real about it? Because this was the center of my work: the love and companionship that existed between humans and animals. Its power to change them both.

And even more than that—it was also the friendship between Wes and Jimmy. The trust there. The trust between them and the dogs. It was the beating heart of Lucky Dog and I guessed, if I had money, I'd give it... here.

Ideas like this would pop up from time to time, and I'd feel the urge to tell someone. Like a room full of donors or a foundation. But fear never let me go. Never let me shake off being a Mason and the nasty reputation that came with that.

Jimmy was holding Veronica by one hand and staring into her eyes. She was panting, wagging her tail.

I knew a match when I saw one.

My phone vibrated—Luna again.

In an hour I'll have a random fifteen-minute pocket of free time. Come then?

Okay, I typed back.

I expected another round of videos or maybe for an actual glitter rocket to explode from my phone. But instead, Luna sent me a picture of herself holding an envelope with my name on it. It looked suspiciously like a check.

And Luna looked beautiful in the picture: wild dark hair with tiny white flowers braided through the strands.

Hint hint, she texted back.

"I've gotta go," I said. "Luna needs me."

Wes and Elián shot me dual bemused looks.

"I mean, she *has* something for me," I corrected, backing away. "I'll be back soon. Probably. I've got grants or whatever."

"Cool, boss," Wes said. "We'll be here with the Yorkies, holding down the fort."

I strode toward the parking lot, swung a leg over my bike and pulled my helmet on.

I was going to see the Wild Heart office.

19

LUNA

*T*he comment read: *Who knew an Instagram model was smart enough to pull off such a successful fraud? I mean she had us all fooled.*

My stomach lurched like I'd been punched there. I clicked on the profile of the person who'd left the comment. A local Miami businessman: a cheesy, smarmy-looking asshole. I knew his company—knew he paid terribly, treated his employees like shit, and didn't care about the horrible working conditions of the factories he used to produce his office supplies.

The most infuriating part of this entire Ferris Mark debacle was that my own personal mistakes were affecting the change I thought Wild Heart was bringing to the business community. Fair wages. Diverse hiring. Valuing the impact our production had on the earth.

Instead, I worried I was only making things worse. My TED Talk was now filled with vile comments. Half from avid animal-rights activists who hated me. Half from "leaders" in our industry who had been waiting for me to fail.

Outside the wall-to-wall windows, the beach sparkled in

the afternoon sunshine and a pulsing energy emanated from the beachgoers streaming past us towards the water. I could hear the low, rhythmic pulse of Latin music, watched the light glancing off yellow beach umbrellas. It was a perfectly gorgeous, humidly sticky Miami day.

And I was too pissed off to enjoy it.

I sipped my green smoothie and yanked my diffuser closer to my face, inhaling a mango-citrus-ginger blend that I used to create a tranquil, calming atmosphere in my offices. It wasn't working.

Until recently, I'd very rarely felt this kind of fury. But I was furious: at myself, at Ferris Mark, at the people formerly known as my fans. It was a strange, needling sensation that made me want to cry and throw my diffuser all at the same time.

My watch beeped, reminding me about an emergency board meeting in two minutes. I yanked open my lower file cabinet drawer, searching for my contracts folder. My fingers roamed over the pages quickly, aware of the time, when a splash of red caught my eye.

There, shoved at the very bottom of the drawer, was an old photo I'd once had framed on my desk. I was twelve years old, squished on either side by my grinning parents—supportive, even then, of all of my dreams. For the first time ever, I was actually happy my parents were currently back-packing, traveling out of the country with limited cell service. I yearned for their presence as a comfort—but was relieved they didn't have to see their only daughter smeared through the press.

I passed my thumb over the worn picture, the faded smiling faces. In it, we were at a stand I'd set up to raise money for endangered animals by selling friendship bracelets I'd made. My face was dark brown and beach-sandy, my hair a snarled mess, a toothy grin on my face. It wasn't Instagram-worthy; I wasn't looking for the best light or coolest pose.

I'd raised $817 that day—no small feat for a twelve-year-old.

Money can also make things much more complicated. This will be part of your struggle as a future leader.

I bit my lip, caressed the photo.

And stuck it next to my monitor.

Sylvia and the board members barged into my office not a second later. I stood, forgetting about the photo—the memory —immediately. We were going to finalize plans to go back to our old supplier and examine the media reaction to my apology. Derek was letting us borrow his crisis-management team as we worked to fix my reputation. I wasn't looking forward to the meeting.

But at least we were moving forward.

Plus, in an hour I got to see Beck.

To give him a check.

That was the only reason I wanted to see him, of course.

So hot, bearded men are your type?

They hadn't been. The problem was that I was starting to see past Beck's grumpy walls—his handsome face and charming half-grin were slowly revealing themselves beneath all that facial hair. And I still had that sneaking suspicion that Beck was a wild man, sexually-speaking—he was no longer an outlaw, but I bet he fucked like one.

And rode a motorcycle like one too.

I'd never told *anyone* this—never acted on it, too ambitious —but I was the shiny, happy good girl with an illicit interest in Bad Biker Boys. Beck was pressing on those secret buttons.

"Luna?" Sylvia prodded.

I sipped my smoothie, tried to calm down. "I'm ready whenever you are."

Sylvia exchanged a glance with my CTO. "We've got bad news, I'm afraid."

"I figured," I said, steeling myself. "Sock it to me. Can't be worse than last week, right?"

She tapped a stack of papers in front of her. "We've just heard from Fischer Home Goods. They're considering terminating our store contract, which would cost us more than half of our revenue for the fiscal year."

The information slammed into me like a sudden storm front. I looked out the window, immediately seeking refuge in the cloudless teal sky. Except the sky was actually falling now. And it wasn't dramatics.

No.

Everything I had worked so hard to build was tumbling down around me.

20

BECK

*L*una's offices looked like a jungle. Ocean views, green plants. Everyone working there seemed trendy and young and smarter than I'd ever be. I looked down at my black tee-shirt and dirt-covered jeans, touched my beard. Did my entire look scream *outsider*? Or *criminal*?

Once, when I was sixteen, a counselor gave me a pamphlet from the local community college. I'd left it around the clubhouse. Hoped my parents might see it.

My mother did. *The last thing you need is more school*, she'd said, stubbing her cigarette out on the bar top. *Besides, you really think they'd let you in?*

Wild Heart felt like what I'd imagined that school would be like—the colors, the sense of purpose, the chatty conversations. It made me want to turn to the first person who passed me and ask *Are you sure you want to let me in?*

One long wall had glass containers of that drink Luna had given me the other day—*kombucha*. Sections of the office were covered with floor pillows and yoga mats.

"Smoothie? Latte? Green tea?" The receptionist asked me as she took me to the very back.

"Uh, no," I said. I made a mental note to ask Wes if we needed to start serving beverages to our visitors. Wasn't that the kind of thing real executive directors did?

We passed a poster of Luna wearing a crown of roses, applying lipstick with a cheeky grin. *Beauty on the inside. Beauty on the outside,* read the tagline. *At Wild Heart, we're committed to one thing: our values. That means our dedication to makeup that's smart for the planet and never cruel to animals.*

And even though I was pretty damn sure I wasn't their target audience, there was something I liked about it all. I finally understood the public's anger. Wild Heart—from its marketing to this very office—touted all about honesty.

Luna's office door was open. I looked in. She stood at the foot of a long glass table, slightly bent over as she marked pieces of paper with a red pencil.

"This one with the orange. Teal for this one. No lavender. Does that work?" She was backlit by the ocean view, hands propped on her hips. When she looked up at me, her expression brightened even further.

"You're here," she said.

"Take your time," I said. "I'll wait."

Luna bit her bottom lip, made a few more notes for her staff. I studied body language—an old habit, constantly needing to read the room at the MC, the tension in the group, the threat-level in a jail cell. Luna's body was open and accepting. Her staff as well. No wonder the suggestion that her life was a series of Instagram posts was hurtful.

She was a leader.

"Come on in," she finally said. Staff members slid by me and I was aware again of their age, of mine, that I smelled like leather and asphalt while this entire building smelled like the ocean. I couldn't have been more than eight or nine years older than Luna, but I felt our age difference in that moment.

"Welcome to the Wild Heart headquarters. I know you're familiar with the outside, but this is where all the magic happens," she said.

I sat in a green chair I worried would break beneath my weight. "I like it."

"You do?" Luna came around the desk and sat on the edge, right in front of me. When she crossed her legs, the cotton of her long white dress brushed my jean-clad knees. "I designed it myself with one of my best friends, Daisy. She's in real estate, has all the best design connections. For the first five years, we operated out of a one-room office. This was a major upgrade."

"Looks expensive," I added, nodding toward the view.

"It's... very expensive," she agreed. She looked distracted for a moment, then refocused. "I'm really happy you're here, Beck. Also, I've been nervous for you to see everything."

"Why?" I asked.

"I wanted you to like it." Her fingers tugged a tiny braid into existence.

A smile crept up and I didn't hide it. "Well, I do. It fits you. Is that you?" I asked, pointing to a photo of a very young-looking Luna holding a check. "Your first million or whatever?"

"Something like that."

I squinted, could just make out the words on the check. "So it was an award you got?"

"It was," she said. "It's called the Turner Venture Capitalist Award and I was the first woman who'd ever won. That's the night of the pitch competition. You basically go through these huge rounds of cuts for two months until the final ten are chosen. I presented my three-minute plan for Wild Heart in front of two hundred and fifty venture capitalists in Silicon Valley."

I picked up the framed photo—her smile was electric. She was standing with two people I assumed were her parents—she looked just like them.

"That must have been an incredible amount of work," I said.

"Hard work and a massive amount of luck," she said. "That and the right connections, which took a while for Wild Heart to develop. That's initially why I went all out on my role as spokeswoman, putting my entire life all over social media. Connections happen person-to-person, and after a few years, the right people started following me."

"That's how you got the money?"

"The start-up capital, yes," she said. "The first five years sucked. It was basically fundraising twenty-four/seven on a shoestring budget. As you're well aware."

I shifted in my chair. "I'm terrible at it. Believe me."

Luna tilted her head, long hair sliding off her shoulders. "That's not what I see."

I handed the picture back to her, unsure of what to do with the compliment.

"I was a very arrogant twenty-two-year-old," she said. "I told everyone around me who would listen that I had *everything figured out*. Luckily I had a board and a bunch of mentors in the business community that steered me in the right direction. No major issues. Well, I mean... until recently."

Her cheeks flushed a little as she put the photo back. But then she spun around with exaggerated movements and held out that envelope I'd seen in the picture she'd texted.

"Ta-*da*."

"Um, thanks," I said, taking it from her and sliding it open. There it was. A check for ten thousand dollars.

I was glad to be sitting down.

"For me?"

"For Lucky Dog," she said. "Plus we're closing in on fifteen grand in online donations already."

"But it's only been a *week*," I said, almost angry. The world of easy money Luna seemed to wade in and out of boggled my mind. *Ta-da—ten thousand dollars.*

But who was I kidding? The chair I was sitting in probably cost more than my rent.

"Come look," she said, waving me over. "I want to make sure the posts fit the vibe you were going for." I stood over her shoulder, trying not to crowd her space. But still I caught the scent of citrus and sunscreen. Literal fucking *sunshine* is what Luna da Rosa smelled like. She pulled her hair to one side, exposing the side of her throat to me.

"See?" she said. "People are responding to them pretty well." Her photos of Lucky Dog were happy—motivational, not shameful. Like I'd said I wanted. The picture of her and Jem had a smile spreading across my face. "Not too manipulative, right?"

"No," I said, surprised.

She tapped her temple. "Told you I'm good at this."

She pressed the check more firmly into my hand and a surge of ugly pride rose in me.

"Beck," she said, guiding my attention back. "It's not wrong to receive this. No one's using you and no one pities you. It's because you're doing great work and people don't want to see Lucky Dog close."

I took a step back. "Sorry."

"You don't have to apologize," she said.

"How'd you know?"

"Game recognizes game." Luna grinned. "Although I think you're more stubborn than me, but we both like to carve our own path, even if that means clumsily hacking our way through life."

"I don't like owing people," I said.

"You don't owe me a thing," she said firmly. "The bigger picture here is rescuing more dogs."

And your reputation, I almost said. Although that element of distrust was slowly fading away the more time I spent with her.

I looked back at the photos she was showing me. She placed the phone in my palm so I could scroll, read the comments. The panel of images showed Luna's private moments on a public stage. There she was with friends, dancing, drinking, diving into the ocean or bending into a complicated yoga pose. She was making salads and chatting in videos and conducting board meetings.

Luna was *out there* in a way that made me terrified just thinking about it.

The comments on the picture she tapped on were positive in the beginning—seems like there were people who had always supported Lucky Dog. I'd had no idea. When you were a young nonprofit, it was easy to feel invisible.

Ugly bitch—that was comment #476. I pointed to it.

"Ignore it," she said.

"I want to know where this man lives," I said.

Her eyes met mine. "Oh. That's super nice of you but it's really fine. He's a troll. He's trash. I don't know where he lives because their anonymity makes them feel brave when they're not," she said.

Grumbling beneath my breath, I kept scrolling. Beneath that, a sentence that jarred me: *How do we know the money goes to dogs and not Beck Mason's shady motorcycle club?*

She snatched the phone from me. "And ignore that too."

"Are you getting comments about the Miami Devils?" I asked, anger rising. "Because you know I have absolutely nothing to do with them anymore. They can't touch Lucky Dog. I'd never let them."

Luna fiddled with that tiny braid again. "I've gotten... a few comments about the MC. Nothing major. It's people trying to stir things up because they like drama."

Was my past going to continue to stomp all over my present and destroy my future? Because I was pretty damn sure the Devils would love to set fire to any bit of happiness I might try to hold on to.

And if anything got in their way—say, a beautiful woman and her successful company—I knew they wouldn't hesitate to watch that burn too.

"Luna?" We both turned—one of her staff had a giant glass filled with green juice. "I made this for you."

"Thank you," she said. "Can you bring an extra straw? I think Mr. Mason would love some." She glanced at the giant watch on her wrist. "And we officially have four minutes until my next meeting. You should have a little green juice. You look stressed."

I sat back down—putting me eye-level with Luna, who was still propped against her desk. I turned behind me, made sure that Jasmine woman wasn't lurking around us.

"Luna," I started. Hesitated.

"What is it?"

"You've already done so much for us," I started. "But if you really *are* focused on fixing all this shit..." I hesitated for a moment, "... maybe you shouldn't work with a person whose family is notorious for violence and drugs in South Beach."

She turned her head, staring at an old picture near her computer. "No thanks. I'm sticking with you. Now try this."

I gave her my scariest look.

She returned it with her sweetest smile. "I don't care about your past."

I knew she was trying to get off easy with that bewitching grin. "You do though. Or at least you did. There's no way a billionaire with a fucked-up reputation meets me and doesn't consider running away."

Luna lifted her chin, tapping her sandal beneath her skirt. A long few seconds ticked by before she finally said, "I didn't want to work with Lucky Dog at first because of who you were. The complication. You're right, that is true. And *technically* my PR director is having several aneurysms a day over comments like the one you just saw." She worried at her bottom lip. "Sometimes I have given into those same thoughts."

I was silent. It looked like a battle was going on behind her eyes.

But still.

"You think I'm trash." I didn't phrase it as a question.

Luna looked immediately offended. "*Never*," she said firmly. "I have never, *ever* thought that. Your family though? I think they're utterly vile."

"They are vile," I said. "We can agree on that."

She released her braid, clutching the edge of her desk. She glanced back at that photo one more time. "I'm trying out this new thing where I match my internal and external values. Doing what I say I'm going to do because it's right and not necessarily safe or easy. For better or worse, you're stuck with me basically until the end of time, Beck Mason. When we're both ninety, I'll still be begging you to take a selfie with me."

I felt a smile tugging at the corner of my mouth. Maybe the beard would hide it.

"And for what it's worth, you're doing incredible work at Lucky Dog. You deserve that money."

A better man would have walked out the door and ended our partnership before Rip and Georgie Mason stole away this situation.

A smarter man would have been wary of a wealthy woman who'd never known the inside of a jail cell or the pinch of *not enough*.

But I wasn't a better man.

And I sure as shit wasn't a smarter man.

I took the glass from Luna. It was *grass*-green.

"Are we at... what did you call it, another *impasse*?" I asked, lightening my tone.

"I think so." Her lips quirked up.

"What the hell is in this?" I asked.

Luna let out a relieved exhale, sensing my shift in conversation. "Wheatgrass. Lemon. Cucumbers."

I pre-wrinkled my nose. Sipped it. Enjoyed her playful smirk a little too much.

"Tastes like what comes out the back of a lawnmower."

"And Heineken tastes like warm piss."

"That's blasphemy and you know it." Then I took another sip.

"You *like it*," she teased.

"Two sips don't mean a thing," I shot back. But I was suddenly drinking it—whether it was because it tasted all right, or because it kept her smiling, I didn't want to know. "When did you get into all this hippie stuff?"

I handed the glass back to Luna, who placed her pink lips right where mine had been. She sipped, thought for a moment. "Veganism? My parents were always vegetarian, very eco-conscious and into animal rights. When I was eleven, a neighbor told me how eggs and dairy-products were derived from animals and I plopped down on our kitchen floor and cried *very* dramatically."

Her eyes slid toward mine like she was expecting me to make fun of her. But I didn't want to. I could relate. "There's nothing wrong with caring about things like that."

Luna tilted her head, sending her silver earrings shimmering. "That's true. It's always how I've been."

"When you were a kid, did you ever get made fun of for being vegan?"

She shrugged. "People make fun of you whenever you take a stand against anything. It wasn't always easy but *not* being vegan never felt like an option. This, what's happening right now, is exponentially worse. Being caught in a mistake that corrupts your most deeply-held values." She turned her computer screen around. The article looked like it was about her... and it looked mean. "A mistake and a pattern of thinking," she added.

My nostrils flared. I felt protective of the rainbow billionaire again.

Although, if I hadn't known her... wouldn't Elián and I be at the office talking shit about lying rich people right now?

"There isn't a silver lining here," I finally said. "Fucking sucks."

She grasped my arm, squeezed. Heat and sensation shot up my arm. "Thank you for not telling me this is all part of life's beautiful journey."

"Not really the type of guy who talks about journeys, Luna."

"I think I like that about you, Mr. Mason," she replied.

"Do you think I'm disgusting because I eat meat?

"I doubt anyone finds you disgusting, Beck."

"Well, you're not *children* or the *elderly*."

She smiled, running a hand through her hair. "Back in the day... yes. I would have said intense things about you. I care about this; I really think it's better for the world—for people and for animals—if we could find other ways to live."

"And now?"

She bit her lip. "I do wish you were a vegan."

I shifted in my chair, uncomfortable—I'd expected her to say *no way* in that sunshine-y, *sweet* way of hers.

"I believe our planet lives in greater harmony when we don't consume meat, even though I know how unrealistic that is, as many, many people like to point out to me. Meat impacts human rights, the environment, our health, and destroys our ecosystem. I don't want to be a part of that. I want to live in a world where all beings, human and animal, have more than enough to eat, shelter, love, work, safety and freedom from pain."

"I won't ever be a vegan, Luna," I said—clearly. "But I agree with you on the *freedom from pain* bit for animals. And for people. The only way I can get out of bed every morning is knowing that the abused animals I work with are getting better. No longer in pain. If not..."

"It's too dark," she added.

I flexed my fingers. "Yes."

She reached forward, her eyes kind. Touched my leather vest and said, "This causes pain, too."

I opened my mouth. Closed it. "You're right," I finally admitted. She was right, really.

I took in Luna's office—for all of its colorful bohemianness, there was wealth in every item.

"How do you feel about a person who has a lot of money that's spent on things and not charity?" I might have asked it to be shitty, if this was our first meeting. But now I was just curious. Waiting for her response, not trying to piss her off.

But I'd touched a nerve.

She tensed, angry. "I'm assuming you're talking about me?"

"You're the only person I know who has a lot of money, Luna."

Her look almost had me squirming. I imagined she used it

on problem employees or annoying board members. It was fierce as hell.

I leaned back in my chair and crossed my arms. If this was Beatrix—snarling and trying to dominate me—I'd do something similar. Loose, open body language with an edge to it.

To her credit, Luna didn't blink. And neither did I.

"You know," she said, "when I first started Wild Heart, one of the main goals was to use it to start my own foundation."

That struck me as very Luna-like.

"And now?"

A tap of her fingernails. She opened her mouth but suddenly Jasmine was at the door. "Luna, we've got the emergency meeting with Fischer."

"I know," Luna said, eyes still locked with mine.

But then she was smiling at Jasmine and sweeping around the desk, trailing her citrus scent with her. "I was just finishing up with Beck."

I stood—caught Jasmine in the act of changing her expression from irritated to neutral.

"Hello, Beck," she said. "Later this week, I'd like to talk damage control for your family members. I'm concerned your background is going to be a—"

"It's not a problem, Jasmine," Luna said, scooping up files, a pen and her phone. I could see her morphing back into a CEO—she started reading a document and emailing someone at the same time. She was an efficient bundle of good vibes.

"All due respect, Luna, but you pay me to manage situations like Beck."

Luna stopped what she was doing and gave Jasmine an honest-to-god glower that rivaled my own. "Beck is a human, not a situation."

Jasmine looked away, pissed.

Luna, however, gave me a beautiful, but secretive, smile. "You have your check?"

"Uh, yeah. Is everything okay?"

"It's probably the worst day of my professional career," she said. "Which makes twice in two weeks. The work is never done." She patted me on the shoulder—I felt bad, pushing her on the stuff when clearly she was having a shit day. Why hadn't she said anything?

"Can I... help?"

"You can help by letting me work with you tomorrow. Say three-ish?"

But she and Jasmine were already moving out the door, gone before I could technically answer. Leaving me alone in her office, holding a green smoothie. I'd never admit it, but it actually tasted delicious.

21

BECK

I leaned against Betty and Veronica's kennel, my fingers in the grating.

"All the pros," Wes said to Jimmy. "One. You can take them everywhere in a backpack. Two. That means you have two adventure buddies whenever you want to go on a road trip. Three. They can sleep in bed with you and not take up any space."

Jimmy held both wiggling balls of fur up to his face. "You think these pups would come on my bike with me?"

Wes turned to me for confirmation.

"You ever think about getting a sidecar for your bike?" I suggested.

Jimmy laughed—a big, booming one. But he considered it. "I guess I would if it makes them happy?"

And that's how I knew he was the one for them.

A group of well-dressed people was walking toward us from the parking lot. "And, uh, let us know how you feel. But if you want them to go with you, they're all yours."

"These balls of fur are going to love you forever, bro," Wes said.

Jimmy nodded, clapped Wes on the shoulder. "Yeah. I, uh... I don't get a lot of that in my life right now, you know?" Jimmy said.

"Same here," Wes said softly. "I get it from this place though."

If Luna was here, maybe I'd even *want* her to capture this somehow. Because she could do it right. She'd know how.

Maybe I could even be the one speaking in the video.

You could do this.

"Excuse me, Mr. Mason?"

I turned around to that group of sharply dressed people. "Hey," I said, a little too gruffly. I cleared my throat. "Can I help you? Are you lost?"

The man in front—white with dark hair, a little older than me—gave me an odd look. "No, not at all. We're with the Carlisle Foundation and we found out about your nonprofit from Ms. da Rosa. You're her favorite place right now."

"Oh," I said. "Um... sure. She sent you here?"

"No. We decided to pop in. We were in the area. We always find it nice to see nonprofits on a typical day, see how things are really done."

That sounded like rich person code for *catch you off guard*.

"Sure," I said, wiping my fingers on the back of my jeans. I thought about shaking their hands, but the body language in front of me was as cool as ice. "What do you want to know?"

Their suits and their facial expressions didn't technically mean jack shit. But my brain shouted *they're smarter than you*, drowning out my ability to think clearly.

"Perhaps a tour?" an older Black woman with white hair asked.

"Yeah, uh, this way." I'd done a bit of this, but not for a while. I'd always had time to prep—to practice my speech and make sure Lucky Dog appeared to be in working order. But our field was a wreck and all the dogs were barking, and Jem was leading Beatrix through a training session that wasn't going well. The group stared at Wes, Jimmy and Jem—who were all tattooed and spiked.

"Wes and Jem are two of my staff members—trained behavioral specialists—and Jimmy is a potential adopter." Wes and Jem were cheery as they shook hands, while Jimmy stood off to the side. The Carlisle people asked questions about the dogs, about Beatrix—Wes and Jem both did great answering them. But they really were *specialists,* like I'd said. I was just some guy.

"And, Beck, tell us more about your strategic vision for Lucky Dog," the first man asked. "What's your long-term plan for this place?"

"Build more kennels and rescue more dogs," I said. "Miami has become a dumping ground for dogs people don't want and strays are out of control. But they don't have to be euthanized. Rehabilitation is the answer. Also—" I stopped, thought about what I'd witnessed. "What we do is also match. Dog to human. Dog to family. The love that grows between the two is powerful, I think."

Behind them, Wes was giving me two thumbs up.

"But how?" the man asked. "We like to see nonprofits have a longstanding vision. It takes a lot to stay afloat in this financially risky environment. I'm sure you understand, Mr. Mason."

There was a condescending edge when he said the word *Mason*.

"Yeah, I get what you're saying," I said. "The *how* is build more kennels. Save more dogs. Partner up with some inmate programs potentially." I crossed my arms over my chest. "That's about it."

The woman was writing something on a legal pad, which

pissed me off. Because I hadn't even known they were coming, so it felt fucked up that I was now being graded.

"How is Lucky Dog invested?" the man asked. "Mutual funds? Bonds? CDs?"

I didn't have a clue. Our board was small—only three members, and Elián and I were working to grow it. But we didn't *have* investments. Yet.

A flash of color caught my eye—Luna, here for her three o'clock shift.

"I, uh, I don't know."

"The executive director doesn't know what his company's investment portfolio looks like?" the man asked.

"I'm not sure we have one," I said. I didn't know what a mutual fund was and I wasn't going to let this asshole in on that juicy tidbit. "I guess, in my mind, the most important focus is right now. Like what we're going to do for these dogs in the moment. It's a crisis and we're trying to help as many dogs as we can." Half of the group was staring off, looking down, like they were embarrassed for me. And now I *was* embarrassed. I cleared my throat. "But I guess I could get that information for you from my board."

"It's more impressive when the executive director knows it offhand," the man said.

"And it's nice when foundations let nonprofits know when they're coming," said a voice that I recognized.

I whirled around. Luna, in colorful yoga pants. She propped her hands on her hips. "Albert, when you spoke to my staff earlier today, you mentioned coming to Lucky Dog next week. Not on a surprise visit." She seemed as cheerful as ever, but her back was straight and her tone was icier than normal.

Albert flared his nostrils at her. "We thought a surprise would be more fun."

"Or disrespectful of Mr. Mason's time," Luna shot back. I couldn't stop the surprised look that came over my face. But Luna wasn't looking at me. She was staring at Albert. "If you have questions he can't answer, it's probably because he was busy saving a dog's life twenty minutes before you got here."

I'd actually been trying to figure out a financial report that contained far too little money for my liking. Luna's donations couldn't come fast enough—rent was due. And payroll. And health insurance.

"Since you are sponsoring this nonprofit, do you have anything to say about their stock portfolio?"

For a second, Luna looked like she had an idea about where Albert could stick that stock portfolio. But instead she said, "When I founded Wild Heart, all of our cash went into immediate needs. We had no savings and I'm not ashamed to say that. We certainly didn't have anything left over to invest. Beck's in the same position, which is why I'm trying to *raise him money* so that they can stabilize. Do you know a lot of four-year-old nonprofits with robust stock portfolios?"

I wasn't sure what was happening to me—my pride was shrinking the more time I spent around Luna. A few weeks ago, I would have hated being saved like this. I'd never liked that—in the MC, needing help was a sign of weakness. And the members were all too willing to beat weakness out of you. But it wasn't pride that rushed through my nerve endings.

It was lust. I'd written off my attraction to the rainbow billionaire as a curiosity. Luna was like a tropical flower in a bed of weeds. I was just... interested in her.

Except the way you handled flowers was delicately.

What I wanted to do to Luna right now wasn't delicate.

Not that I'd had much in the way of sex the past couple years. I was usually a one-night-stand-after-the-bar kind of guy. And Lucky Dog had consumed my energy, drained me of any desire other than to *work*. I hadn't had the privilege of a writhing woman beneath my body in a long, long time.

Right now, the only woman I could imagine beneath me was Luna. Pinned down by my hips, legs wrapped high on my waist, all that gorgeous dark hair tangled in my fingers as I buried my cock deep inside of her. Watching her defend Lucky Dog—and me—with a cute smile and her *don't-fuck-with-me* tone, I wondered if I could drag her behind my trailer and put my hands on her. And my fingers.

And my mouth.

"I have known some with robust stock portfolios, yes," Albert said coolly.

"Well, good for you," Luna said. "That's not happening for Lucky Dog right now, which is a situation we are rapidly working to fix. And a *great* way for that to happen would be seed funding from your foundation." She flashed a bright, beautiful smile at the rest of the group. "What do you say Jem and Elián introduce you to some of the dogs?"

Elián walked over and greeted everyone. I said goodbye to the suited-up group. Within a minute, Elián and Jem were running the show, and I watched them become looser, more interested.

Before I could say *thank you* to Luna, she was grabbing Wes by the hands. "Tell me you saw the *Bachelor in Miami* last night."

Wes mimed an explosion off the side of his head. "What a mind-fuck, right? Who wouldn't pick Marissa? I *love* Marissa."

"Yeah, and their one-on-one date was *e-lec-tric*."

"What the hell are you two talking about?" I interjected.

"*Bachelor in Miami*," they replied in unison.

"Wait, you don't watch it, boss?" Wes asked.

I shook my head. "No."

"Oh my god, you have no taste," Luna cried, hand on her

forehead. "I'll make you binge-watch it with me, don't worry. We can't be friends if you don't watch it."

Luna was always friendly and I guessed she wasn't serious, but would I really do that? Watch TV with her?

Would that be like... a date?

"What's it about?" I grumbled.

"True fucking love," Wes said.

"I wouldn't know much about that," I said.

Luna tilted her head, snagged her lip. But didn't say anything.

"So, uh, thanks for saving me from those guys," I muttered. "I appreciate it."

"It's no problem," she said, laying her hand on my arm. "I know Albert from way back. He used to run a local bank and at the time I thought he was basically the world's biggest asshole. Since taking over the Foundation, he only does charitable work now, but I've always gotten the impression he enjoys riding in on a white horse and 'rescuing' nonprofits. You're not sitting around, twiddling your thumbs and waiting for him to rescue you, are you?"

"No," I said, chuckling a little. "I'm busy as shit."

"Exactly." She peered over at them, where they were watching Penelope through her kennel. "If they don't end up giving to you, don't stress about it. It's a dry run. By the time I'm done with you, this place will be crawling with donors."

My jaw tensed. I was still riled up from watching Luna go to bat for me. "Okay."

"Hey, boss." Wes gave me the stack of mail he'd been flipping through. "Mail from today. Thought you and Luna would be extra interested." I grabbed it—the envelopes were all slit open. And inside each one: a check.

"Can you count these and send the total to Christina?" I

said to Wes. "Add it to what Luna's brought in from the website."

It was hard to believe but we were getting closer and closer to filling the gap every day. A miracle if I'd ever seen one.

"Look at all these *donations*," she exclaimed. "I knew you could do it."

"*You* did it," I shot back.

"Nope," she said. "I merely took the pictures. What's in the pictures is all you, Mr. Mason."

I needed my cock to stop twitching every time she breathily referred to me as *Mr. Mason*.

"We make a good team," I said, looking at the ground.

"I think so too," she agreed, nudging my shoulder. "Now let's go get you even more, okay?"

22

LUNA

"Okay, but take a picture of me before we start," I instructed Beck. I'd been prepared to haul bags of dog food or hose down kennels, but he'd asked me to help him with Penelope instead. She was less timid now, sitting up straight and panting a little as we settled into our usual corner. This time, Beck and I touched—shoulder to shoulder.

He took my phone. "Okay, but what's interesting about this?"

I held out a long, skinny spoon and a jar of peanut butter. "Shows the process to potential donors," I said. "Let's your adoring public see that you know how to get dogs to trust you. Before this whole mess, my followers used to love to see those behind-the-scenes moments. Meetings, scientists working in labs, testing different products on consumers."

His look was skeptical but he took my phone anyway. "How's my face?" I teased, pursing my lips and tilting my head.

"Beautiful," he said roughly. *Click* went the camera.

Did he just call me *beautiful*?

"Thanks," I said. *Interesting.*

"You only have three left," he said, holding up the requisite fingers. I mimed snapping a photo of him and he actually grinned.

"Okay, Grumpy Pants. Tell me what we're actually doing with this jar of peanut butter."

He touched the handle of the brush that lay between us. "I think she'd let us, specifically *you*, brush her today."

"Me?"

"Yeah," he said. "She trusts you already."

That gave me a shimmery feeling all over my body. I could feel my phone vibrating, imitating my emotional response. But I chose to ignore it—I knew it was only hundreds of voicemails and emails flitting by, things that demanded my urgent attention or rapid-fire response. Ignoring them felt delicious, almost illicit. Since becoming a CEO, I never took vacations, even though self-care and adventure were very *on-brand* for me. But after a yoga class or a long hike, I was strapped back to my laptop.

These moments at Lucky Dog—these moments with Beck —felt stolen, pick-pocketed slivers of joy just for me.

"Do you really think so?" I asked, turning around to face him. He was almost too close. I could see the flecks of green in his dark blue eyes.

"You have a calming energy for her," he said.

"Did Beck Mason say the word *energy*?" I teased. "You'll start sounding like my parents soon."

He chuckled, handed the brush to me. And held out the spoon. Over the course of ten long minutes, he and I sat in serene silence while Penelope ever-so-slowly crawled over to us.

It was a lesson in patience. It was only my body, connected to the concrete. The air on my skin, the sun warming my back. My shoulder, brushing against Beck's burly one.

"There she goes," he whispered, mouth at my ear. Penelope was eagerly eating peanut butter, body relaxed. "Food equals happiness for animals. Happiness equals trust. You brushing her while she's eating should help her connect people to those feelings. Go ahead."

I made a crooning sound. Penelope watched me, but with much less wariness than before. I pressed the brush to her fur and gently tugged through.

Penelope sat down.

"Is that okay?" I whispered, excited.

"Keep going," he said.

I brushed her again and her tail wagged. I was aware that this interaction was probably brief—it wasn't like Lucky Dog worked miracles. But I still kept my movements light, safe, gentle. She shivered a little. Made eye contact with me.

"She likes it," I said, still whispering.

"She likes you," he whispered back. "You're doing a great job."

My throat was as tight as could be. This connection with something more tremendous than myself, more tremendous than my situation, was what my parents had taught me to search for. It's why we'd spent our weekends at foster care homes and local parks. It had been—was supposed to be—my driving motivation in founding Wild Heart, connecting compassion, justice and business.

And in this vital moment, it was all too clear to me how deeply I'd veered off course.

"I haven't felt this way in a long time," I said. I didn't elaborate and Beck didn't push. But he did reach out and very, very lightly touch my hand, the one holding the brush.

Then he pulled away.

Eventually Penelope retreated but Beck and I stayed still, not moving. I put the brush down, wrapping my arms around my knees. I laid my cheek there and looked openly at the man next to me.

"That picture you took," he said, "how many people do you think will look at it?"

I thought for a moment. "I don't know. Maybe four, five million people?"

"That doesn't make you terrified?" he asked.

"Not anymore," I said. "Don't assume I was this way immediately. Being friendly is my jam. But it took time to feel comfortable about exposing myself like that. Even before Ferris Mark, the trolls came after me. That took time to get used to. Time where I had to accept that I wasn't going to please every stranger who hated me on the internet."

Beck looked past me, where the foundation folks were slowly making their way back to the parking lot. He'd stumbled a little bit, in their presence. But no more or less than most people would have. Jem and Elián were naturally enthusiastic and I couldn't stand watching Beck look embarrassed.

It had made me want to clock Albert in the face with my Fendi purse—and generally speaking, I abhorred violence.

"Do you believe you're the right person to lead Wild Heart?" he asked.

I hesitated. Thought about my obnoxiously happy signature on Ferris Mark's contract addendum. *You're fixing it though*, I reminded myself.

"Yes," I managed.

He nodded. "I'm not sure I'm the best person to lead Lucky Dog."

"Why?" I asked. "Because Elián and Jem are more natural on a tour?"

"Yeah."

I lifted one shoulder. "Leadership is about delegating based on your employees' strengths. Elián and Jem are charming with donors, yes. And that's okay. You still impressed the foundation members."

"I didn't," he argued. "You did."

"I've had more practice," I said. "Your comparison doesn't work here, boss."

"Lucky Dog needs a leader like you. Someone who's... charming."

"You were very earnest and honest," I said, trying to ignore my body's response to him calling me *charming*. "Those are the two most important qualities. Everything else can be learned."

Beck was quiet, squinting into the sun.

"There's an article floating around the internet right now you should know about," I said, trying to keep my tone casual. Beck seemed a little more open, a little more vulnerable, and so even though it pained me to mention it, I wanted him to hear this from me. "It's about the time you served in juvenile detention. Some asshole entertainment reporter dug up your mugshots."

Movement rippled through the giant man next to me. Tension, anger maybe. "Can I see?"

I took out my phone, showing him the article in question. It was a garbage piece, reporting on the Ferris Mark scandal and dragging Beck's background and family into it. I'd been relieved to see that donations to Lucky Dog didn't seem to be affected.

But still, the middle of the article featured that picture of me on TIME Magazine, laughing and happy. Next to it, they'd placed one of Beck's mugshots from twenty years ago. He was thinner, angrier, practically snarling into the camera. I placed my phone into his hand.

"This blowback..." I started to say. "It... I mean, I'm really sorry, Beck. It's an absolute disgrace. Now I feel like *I* should..."

"What?" He was staring at the screen, forehead creased.

"Tell you to partner with someone else. Maybe you should *associate* yourself with someone who isn't going to cause such unwanted negative attention on your very deserving nonprofit." I pulled at a fraying string on the bottom of my shirt. "I wouldn't be offended if you wanted me to leave. And I'd still keep giving you donations, make a large gift. That wouldn't go away."

He placed the phone back in my hand, screen down. "I haven't seen that picture in a very long time." I was still, awaiting his judgment. "But it looks like we're stuck with each other," he said, repeating my words from the other day.

The surge of happiness that swelled up in my chest caught me completely off guard. "It might get worse," I said, feeling the urge to protect this man.

"I've been through worse," he said softly.

We shared a smile for a sweet second.

"Can I ask you a nosy question?"

"How nosy?"

"I'm guessing the Miami Devils... your parents... weren't happy that you decided to defect from them?" I'd seen the word *defect* last night while doing research on the culture of outlaw motorcycle clubs. Like formally fleeing your own country, running across borders toward freedom. I'd found the word to be startling in its intensity.

"It's rarely done. And never done if you're blood. I was on high alert for a long time, making sure they didn't come after me." I remembered how he'd reacted that day at the beach, when Devils club members had been strolling past us. The way that one man had *waved* at Beck. Except it hadn't been a wave but a crueler, more threatening act than that. He'd looked prepared for a fight in broad daylight.

"I think it's interesting, courageous, actually," I said, "that even with your family out there, even with people knowing about them, even knowing you'd have to be the public face of this nonprofit, that you still started it. That you and Elián still gave it a go. Everything I've experienced recently, the way people have *turned* on me, it's absolutely the worst thing that's ever happened. I'm not sure, if all of this fraud nonsense had happened *first,* I would have gone through and done something so public. But you did."

"I'm not that public though," Beck conceded, nimbly dodging my compliment as usual. "Elián is frustrated with me."

"I think Elián sees what I see," I said.

"What's that?"

"A dedicated leader."

His expression looked... grateful.

"Hey, Beck?"

We turned—it was Elián with a concerned look on his face.

"What is it?" Beck said.

"Animal control just called. A stray pit bull on the beach at Lummus Park. If we can't get it, it has to go to the kill shelter over on High Street. You want in?"

"What's open?"

Elián turned behind him. "I guess Jack's kennel? You and Jem cleaned it the other day, right?"

"We did," I said, happy to have provided even the tiniest amount of help.

"Let's get her," Beck said.

"I'm coming too," I declared, standing and brushing dirt from my pants.

"It's pretty physically demanding," Beck said.

"And this body can do anything," I tossed back.

And for a delirious second, his eyes traveled the length of the body in question—mine—in such a filthy way my core flooded with heat. I liked it. A lot.

"Let's go then," he said. "Want to take my bike? Jem can follow in the truck if we catch her."

"*When* we catch her," I said, needing to distract myself from sexual thoughts of Beck and his bike. "And you're sure I'll, uh, fit on the back?"

He stood up, barely six inches from me. I had to crane my neck to maintain eye contact. "We'll make it work."

I was the girl who always fantasized about sex on a motor-cycle—but had never actually been on one.

Riding with Beck was going to be absolutely, one-hundred-percent fine though.

Right?

23

LUNA

*I*t was not fine.

It was hot as hell.

I'm about to ride a motorcycle NBD I texted to Cameron, Daisy and Emily. A flurry of those three dots—I imagined they were trying to text the fastest snark.

Who are you riding? Daisy texted. A beat, then: *With. I meant who are you riding with, obviously.*

Beck, I said. The nonprofit hunk's one-word answers were rubbing off on me.

And I needed to stop thinking about words like *riding* and *rubbing off.* Immediately.

"I've got an extra helmet for you," Beck said as we stood by his Harley Davidson that gleamed in the sunlight. His arm behind his head caused his unnaturally large biceps to bulge, making me think of granite boulders.

"Okay, cool," I said. "Should I take my hair down so it can fit?"

"Sure," he rasped.

I tugged apart my high bun and my hair went tumbling to my shoulders. It might have been my imagination but his entire body went taut, the curve of his lips like a tease. "How do I look?"

"Like Cousin It," he said.

"Just the look I was going for," I said. That curved lip became a truly crooked grin and only the buzzing of my phone stopped me from leaning into the gentle giant standing in front of me.

Motorcycle? HOT. I knew you were going to ride Beck, Cameron had texted back.

She and I shared an affinity for motorcycles.

His BIKE. Riding his BIKE. I replied.

Statistically speaking you're going to die on that thing, Emily said, ever the scientist.

Going out in style. That's very Luna, Daisy replied. I was so distracted I didn't realize Beck was standing an inch from me.

"Can I put this on you?"

"Please," I smiled. He tugged the helmet over my hair, and I couldn't help but keep smiling up at him.

"You look like a real badass."

"This is a real fantasy of mine," I said. "I mean *dream. Dream* is what I meant."

"You fantasize about motorcycles?"

Yes.

"Nope. They're death machines that destroy the environment."

He lifted his chin, a flirtatious glint in his eye. "But it's always been your dream to ride one?"

"Absolutely. I know it doesn't make sense," I said airily.

"Well," he said, "death machine or not, we're heading over to Lummus Park. You'll be behind me. Hold on tight. Really tight. You've got to lean into the curves. Follow my lead, okay?"

"Is it scary?" I asked, transfixed by how aroused I was at watching Beck swing a jean-clad leg over the seat, hands already flexing on the grip. He settled into the seat, turned to face me.

"It can be. It's also fun as hell. But I've been riding since I was sixteen years old. You can trust me, Luna."

"I like fun." Also trusting Beck felt incredibly easy in this moment. His posture exuded *competency* and I liked it.

"I thought you would."

"Listen. We both know Miami has the worst drivers. You're not... one of them, right?"

He twisted the throttle—roaring the bike to life. I couldn't entirely hear, but he mouthed the word *never*. And there went that sexy grin again—a grin that had me moving toward him like a sleepwalker. Swinging my own leg over and settling on the seat. His back was like one giant, muscled wall in front of me. My hands landed gently at his side.

Holy shit, there were *vibrations*. It was like sitting on top of the world's most powerful battery-operated vibrator. I tilted my pelvis an inch forward, pressing my sex more firmly to that seat.

"Holy shit," I whispered. Beck was turned away, thankfully, but he adjusted his front mirror so I could see him. Which was good and bad—his handsome face was too alluring as my clit was treated to such dirty treatment.

"Luna," he said, half-shouting. "You need to get closer. Wrap your arms around me."

Ooh, baby.

"Sure thing, boss," I said. I slid forward a couple inches—swallowed a moan—and let myself wrap him in a bear hug, tucking my cheek to the middle of his back. The force of his body was awe-inspiring. I felt overcome in the sexiest way, immediately submissive, immediately wanton.

And between my legs—a persistent *buzz*.

He squeezed my hand clasped around his chest. We were off.

Fun wasn't the word for what happened next. We were a sleek, streamlined body in space, hurtling down a highway toward Biscayne Bay. I was half-convinced we were going to crash, half-convinced we were going to take flight. If I'd grown wings and shot straight into the sky I wouldn't have been more ecstatic. I kept laughing against Beck, my hands gripping him hard. His muscular ass was cupped between my legs and every few minutes I shuddered and sighed as those vibrations pushed me closer and closer toward orgasm. But I *couldn't orgasm* on the back of a motorcycle with *Beck Mason*. So I kept shifting, moving, attempting to distribute the buzzing feeling to other, less sensitive parts of my body. Which ended up being the backs of my thighs and the curve of my ass.

And of course, as I squirmed and wiggled and beat back a rush of arousal, I was doing my best not to slide my palm down that magnificent chest and cup his cock through those jeans. Would Beck be hard for me? Was he as turned on as I was, wrapped together like this as we broke the sound barrier and whipped past cars like they were standing still? Every shoddy, out-of-the-way gas station we passed suddenly seemed rife with erotic adventure. Bike parked out front while I shoved Beck back to the wall and dropped to my knees. Tugged until that zipper exposed what I knew would be magnificence.

Or maybe I'd take him like this—straddling his body on the bike while he let me fuck him raw.

Beck tapped my hand twice—a sign I took to mean *You okay?*

I nodded against his back, flushed, aroused as the wind whipped over my skin and a continual loop of X-rated images played in my mind. By the time we made it to Lummus Park, I was a hot mess of hormones. One false move and I was liable to pop off. As soon as he slowed the bike down to a parking spot, I clambered off, took off my helmet and shook out my hair. The pulse between my legs was incessant and demanding. And my body knew who it wanted: the gentle giant standing in front of me, scanning the beach for a stray dog he was planning on saving.

As he slipped on a pair of sunglasses that made him look *extra* dashing, the only sensation my body conveyed was *need*.

24

BECK

*L*ummus Park was hot, the sun's rays blinding off the white sand. Bathing-suit-clad tourists played beach volleyball or lounged on towels as music drifted past us on the breeze. This was the Miami Beach of movies and tourism videos—a neon-colored paradise.

I'd lived in Miami Beach my entire life. But everyone here existed in a world where I wasn't welcome. I'd had a front-row seat to the mayhem the Miami Devils caused along Ocean Drive. My playground growing up had been the cold concrete floor in the clubhouse.

"Okay, what do we do?" Luna asked, clapping her hands together.

I searched the sand for a dark-brown dog, ignoring the beach balls people were tossing back and forth, and the roar of a pair of jet-skis off the shore. "According to the report, she's a brindle pit mix, not more than thirty pounds. Skittish. Skinny. No collar."

I showed her the supplies I'd brought: slip-collar, gloves and a leash. And the bacon I had in my pocket.

"I feel like a Marvel superhero but for dogs," she said.

"Which one am I?"

"The Incredible Hulk, duh," she said.

I was about to ask her which superhero that made her —but then I saw the dog.

"She's over there," I said, extending my hand. "Follow my arm."

Luna lifted her aviators, squinting. "I don't see her." She rose up on her tiptoes and grabbed my bicep. Our ride out here had my head spinning with lust—the feel of her hand on my chest, face to my back, strong thighs pressed against mine. We'd been joined together as we rocketed down the road and I'd thought about fucking her any number of filthy ways.

But I needed to focus on the stray, not her fingers on my skin.

"How about now?" I asked.

She shook her head. Against my better judgment, I placed my fingers in her soft hair and gently moved her face toward the dog far across the beach.

"Oh, there she is!" she said.

I gave her the heavy-duty gardening gloves. "We'll try and get close to her—with the help of this bacon. Wear the gloves and watch her mouth at all times. Scared dogs snap."

"What if she runs away?"

We began to make our way through hundreds of towels on the sand. I could smell hot dogs and sunscreen.

"Well, it's kind of hard. We don't want to scare her but we might need to run after her. Either way, the most important thing is to get her in the truck, okay?"

"Sure thing, boss."

Her smile was cute.

"You really don't have to call me boss."

"Aye aye, captain."

"Luna," I said.

"On it, *sir*."

She was laughing and loose. Meanwhile my fingers were curling into fists.

Sir made me think of her sinking to her knees in the sand.

But as I watched her wind-tossed hair, my secret desires turned tender.

I wanted to touch her hair.

Dive into it, tangle it, grip it, yank it. *Breathe it in*. Beneath every fantasy I had—of bending her over my bike and tearing those yoga pants in two—lived an urge to smell her hair like a weirdo.

"Beck?" Luna prodded.

I dragged a hand down my face. "Sorry. Uh, I was thinking about the dog. Let's head towards that row of palm trees."

As the two of us neared, I could see the dog lying in the shade. Her ribs were visible and her skin had mange. As soon as we came into view, she hid behind the trunk.

I crouched. Luna did the same. Our body language was *gentle*. Non-threatening.

I held a finger to my lips and Luna nodded. When I pulled out the bacon and placed it on the spot in front of us, the stray was immediately interested. The dog took one... two... three steps closer. Her legs were trembling, eyes wide with mistrust.

The dog looked at Luna. Looked at me. Looked at the food. And bolted.

"*Fuck*," I swore, standing up and holding out my hand to Luna. I pulled her up easily. "You ready for a chase?"

"Aye aye, *sir*," she replied.

25

BECK

The stray made a break for a crowded part of the beach and Luna and I followed it.

"The goal is to follow her quickly without making her feel like she's being chased."

"So... like super-fast walking while pretending to stare at something else?" she suggested.

"Exactly," I replied. "Let's go." The dog was loping around a long row of food trucks, clearly searching for food. I gave a whistle and she turned to me, ears lifted. Walking swiftly now, I held out the bacon.

She bolted again.

"Oh, *shit*," Luna swore, this time grabbing my hand. "Come on, we got her."

We moved through vendors selling pork dumplings and bánh mì, cubanos and street tacos. A frisbee sailed past us and I snatched it out of the air before it hit Luna in the head.

"Whoa, thanks," she said. "Hazards of the job, huh? I guess my biggest hazard is like thumb sprain from Instagramming too hard."

I grinned at her joke and almost walked right into the restroom wall. She stopped me just in time.

"We make a good team," she sighed. "If a clumsy one. Should we split up?"

I gave her a strip of bacon. "Whoever sees her first, okay?"

She snagged her bottom lip. "Feels like we should give her a name. Since we'll probably be chasing her across the entire city."

"Uh... okay. What do you think?"

"Beach Ball," she said.

"How about no," I countered.

"You don't think *Here, Beach Ball* has a nice ring to it?"

My lips twitched. "No, I do not."

Luna must have been wearing glitter on her skin. She was sparkling in the sun.

"What about... Sunshine?" I said.

Luna threw her hands in the air. "That's perfect. We'll get her. I've got bacon, gloves and a *can-do* attitude, as usual. See ya on the other side, boss." And then she slinked off toward the front of the building.

There were plenty of corners and crevices for a dog to hide in as I crept against the back wall. I was concerned—if we couldn't catch her, I didn't want to think about what her future would be.

But I was also having *fun* with Luna.

When was the last time that had happened?

A flash of tan caught my eye. I stilled, listening. I peeked my head around the corner—saw Sunshine's tail. She was hiding beneath a bush. Caught sight of me—and ran away.

I let out a frustrated sigh. Turned the corner. And Luna crashed into me.

"Shit," I said, taking a step back at the impact.

"Oh, sorry," she squealed, face squashed into my chest. I

grabbed her upper arms. Steadied her. She was out of breath —staring at me with determination in her dark eyes. I was tempted to brush the strand of hair from her forehead. "Part of my *can-do* attitude is running into things."

Sunshine streaked past us toward the ocean.

"*Oh, shit,*" we both cried out, breaking into a sprint. Luna and I skated through a volleyball game and leapt over sunbathers arranged like dominoes.

"I see her," Luna called over her shoulder, running faster. Her foot caught in the leash she was carrying and she flew face-first toward the sand.

My arm banded around her waist before she could hit it. I tugged a panting Luna back against me, and her full citrus scent almost knocked me over.

"Nice catch," she gasped. "I'm usually more graceful."

I gently let her go. "Don't, uh, worry about it."

Sunshine was racing like a greyhound toward the waves.

"Are these rescues usually filled with this many wacky hijinks?" Luna asked.

"Not really," I replied. Sunshine looked seconds away from freaking out in the frothy waves. I didn't know if she could swim and I felt fucking awful that we'd put her in this scared, survival-mode position. "Call Jem," I said. "Have her meet us in the parking lot with the med kit and a crate."

I reached behind my head to take off my shirt, but to my utter surprise, Luna was racing into the waves like a lifeguard. Sunshine tried to swim away awkwardly but Luna reached forward, wrapping her arms around her neck.

"Her mouth," I called, completely fucking alarmed. "Luna, watch her—"

But Sunshine went willingly—or was at least extremely excited by the prospect of wet bacon in Luna's hand. Her shaggy head rested on Luna's shoulder as she stood in the waves and walked toward me, soaking wet and grinning.

"I got her!"

I exhaled raggedly. *She was too impulsive.* That had to be the reason why a woman with a net worth of a billion dollars had dived into the waves like this was a two o'clock board meeting. Sunshine was squirming now so I ran to Luna and took hold of the dog. I gave Sunshine another piece of bacon as I slipped the collar over her head.

We both collapsed onto the sand, sweating and exhausted.

"Thank god I'm wearing Wild Heart's classic waterproof mascara in *ebony*," Luna said in a fake commercial voice.

I chuckled, dropped my head to my knee. "That was incredibly fucking dangerous."

She shook her head. "I would have backed off if it seemed like she was going to bite me. But I couldn't stop myself."

"I know what you mean," I finally admitted. Seconds earlier, I'd been prepared to do the same.

The dog was yanking the leash taut, clearly wary of us and terrified of the rope around her neck. I gave her another piece of bacon. "Let's get you some food and safety and a family that loves you."

Luna's head whipped around at that. "I'm really glad we got her, Beck. Really, *really* glad."

"Me too," I said.

Her hand flew to her mouth. She looked shocked.

"What is it?" I asked, scanning her for hidden, ocean-related injuries.

"*My phone.* My phone is in my bag, back on the beach."

"Thank god. It would have been toast in the water," I said.

"But it means I didn't film *a thing.*"

26

LUNA

*a*s I walked back down the beach with Beck, I felt wildly out of control, breath shallow, pulse thready. And it wasn't our sprint and my sudden dash into the ocean.

I was anxious. Anxious because I'd had a golden opportunity to film myself performing an act of bravery and I hadn't. There'd be no Instagram video, no Facebook pic. I could see Jasmine salivating at the idea of Luna da Rosa, current internet villain, redeeming herself by rescuing a stray dog from drowning.

Next to me, Sunshine was a shivering, scared thing—every time she inhaled, I could see the hard edges of her rib cage. Presented with the option, I would have chosen diving in after her every single time. There'd been no *choice,* merely *action,* and I hoped, sincerely, that most other people would have done the same thing.

But I was stumbling into an awkward crossroad. Rebuilding my reputation through Beck's nonprofit hadn't felt weird or ethically complicated before. Even though Beck had been worried we were using him, I knew in my heart we weren't.

Yet now I was torn between this urge to *show* the public that I wasn't the kind of person who would partner with a company like Ferris Mark. And an urge to keep what had happened on the beach private. Not to be manipulative or self-serving.

It was a bizarre flight-or-fight response. My role as Wild Heart spokeswoman had always been fun and silly, a way to merge my personal and professional selves into one brand.

But wasn't I more than a brand?

I grabbed my bag on the beach and found my phone with anxious fingers. "Do you want me to take your picture with Sunshine?" Beck asked gruffly. His eyes were trained on the sand—which made me hyper-aware that my shirt was practically see-through and my nipples were hard.

"Sure." I hesitated. "I won't get too close, but donors should see what a dog looks like when you first meet them."

Which was mournful, terrified, scared. The poor thing was trembling out of control, and as I sank to the sand and wrapped my arms around my knees, I didn't feel right about this at all.

"Luna, you're not smiling," he said.

I plastered on a fake grin that faltered as soon as he gave me my phone back. I stared at the picture, which made me uneasy. Uploaded it to Instagram with the caption: *Dogs like Sunshine need our help. We found this sweet baby on the beach, scared out of her mind. But at Lucky Dog, there's a safe, healing place for her to rehabilitate and find her forever home. Hit the link in my bio to donate.*

"What do you think of this?" I asked. He leaned over my shoulder, his body heat radiating like a furnace.

"Maybe people should see the whole process, like you said," he replied.

I didn't answer, merely stared at a picture that technically was soliciting donations but *actually* was positioning me as a hero to all dogs. *Look at what I did* is what it said.

Good for my reputation. Rebuilding. Earning their trust back. These words had been pounded into my head by Jasmine these past weeks until every single thing I did became an analysis in public approval.

Sunshine was truly cowering now.

"There's Jem," Beck said. "Let's go meet her by the parking lot."

"Is she..." I stopped, suddenly worried I was going to cry. "Beck, is Sunshine going to be okay?"

He studied me for a moment. "Yeah. I think she is. I know it's hard, seeing them like this. It keeps me awake at night sometimes, Luna."

"I can see why," I said, voice tight.

He reached out and squeezed my shoulder—a truly comforting gesture I felt all the way to my toes. "We have to hope though. What else is there?"

"Is that our girl?"

Beck and I whirled around and I was never so happy to see Jem in my life. Her lime-green ponytail scraped the top of the Lucky Dog truck as she climbed out, smiling when she saw Sunshine.

"Luna grabbed her from the ocean," Beck said.

"Right on," Jem said, giving me a shy smile. "I knew you'd be a natural."

"What happens now?" I asked. Beck was rummaging around in the back of the truck, and when he emerged, he held a giant white shirt toward me.

"I'll crate her with lots of food and get her to our vet immediately to do a full medical work-up," Jem said. "It'll be scary for her for a while, but once she's settled back at the campus, the rehabilitation will begin. And we'll start her on a high-calorie diet."

I watched as Beck, speaking in low tones, lifted Sunshine into the crate. She whipped around, snapped at him, but he dodged her teeth and deposited her gently. I crouched down, looked at her face, tried to think about *hope*.

"She's a fighter," Jem said. "Don't worry."

I knew then, standing on this beach with this terrified dog, that I'd do literally anything to help Lucky Dog: money, advocacy, time, contacts, resources. That tiny voice my parents had always taught me to trust was all but yodeling at me, directing my attention toward the animal I'd just held in my arms. This was why I was a vegan, why Wild Heart could change the world if I could manage to get it back on track.

"You can wear my shirt if you want," Beck said, pulling me from my thoughts. "I didn't want you to get cold or anything."

"Oh, thanks," I said, laughing a little. "This thing is basically the size of a tent."

"I'm... big," he said.

"I noticed."

It might have been the high heat of the day, but his cheeks colored.

"Hey, Luna," Jem said, "I tried that white bean and kale salad the other day. It was great."

"*Yay*," I cheered. "I'll have my chef make an extra batch and bring it to you next week."

"Feels like you work at Lucky Dog now," she said.

I pursed my lips. "Things are pretty hard at Wild Heart. Part of me wishes I did work with you."

Jem was trying to get Sunshine to sniff her hand, so she missed the pensive look Beck flashed my way.

"I'll hit the road and text you updates." Jem checked her watch. "You calling it quits, boss?"

"I should probably head back later tonight," Beck said. "But you head home after dropping her off."

Jem turned to me. "Luna, you want a ride? Or will your driver pick you up?"

I glanced at Beck, who was staring out at the ocean.

What I wanted?

Well.

I wanted to keep spending time with Beck.

"I'll figure it out," I said, waving her off. "Beck can always give me a ride home on his bike, right?"

Jem looked between Beck and me. Looked *hard* at me. Widened her eyes in a move I recognized as girl code for *what's going on between you two?*

I gave her the old headshake. *Nothing*, I mouthed.

She widened her eyes *again*. Made a sound in the back of her throat.

Stop, I mouthed, starting to giggle.

"What is happening between you two?" Beck said gruffly.

She shook her head, grinning. "Aw, nothing boss. You two have fun."

And then she drove off, leaving us alone. And maybe it was our sexy ride over here, and rescuing the dog, and the earnest way he'd told me to *hope*...

But looking at Beck Mason was giving me butterflies.

Huge, gigantic ones.

"Thanks again for the shirt," I said, tearing off my tank top and bending over to wring out my sopping wet hair. I shook it out, and when I flipped back up, Beck looked away so fast I worried he'd break his neck.

"I grew up in a hippie neighborhood where my neighbors were pretty *open* about the human body," I told him. "There's nothing to be embarrassed by."

"Not embarrassed," he corrected. "Respectful."

Except the look I'd caught in his eye—the raw, naked lust —had been anything but.

"Suit yourself." I tossed the wet tank top onto his bike and dropped the tent-sized shirt over my head, knotting the ends around my waist. "If only I'd brought my back-up supply of flower crowns. How do I look, boss?"

"Beautiful," he said hoarsely.

I bit my lip, smiling, desperate for this lightness after my dark hopelessness earlier. "Doing what we did today is good for the soul. I can feel it."

"It shows," Beck said. "You, um... you have the kind of face that's easy to read."

"Very true," I agreed. "I'm an open book."

He kicked at a stone in the sand, looking seconds away from calling it a night.

"Can I buy you a drink?" I asked.

"Me?" he said, startled.

"No, the other terrifying-looking biker," I deadpanned.

His mouth tipped up on one side.

"I have a million hours of emails to tackle tonight and I think a drink would help. Just one. We can watch the sunset, my second favorite time of day."

"What's your first?"

"Sunrise. When the world paints herself pink and gold for us."

He stared at me.

"Come on," I said, "I'm not going to force-feed you kombucha."

"You're sure?"

"I'm going to force-feed you kale."

Beck chuckled—but it was a surprised sound. A delighted sound. *I* was delighted.

"There's a dive bar I used to go to right over there, actually," he said. "It's like the last shitty thing still standing on this fancy block."

I peered over, saw a low, dark building that looked moments away from being formally condemned. "Love it."

"You sure about that?"

I lifted my chin, winked. Beck didn't have to know that I now frequented clubs you had to be wait-listed to get into. Not that I waited anymore. I was a bottle-service-VIP girl now.

"Your old MC friends go there?" I asked, purely out of curiosity.

But Beck's jaw tightened, jumping into protection mode. "I used to go there *after* I left. The Devils can't be down at Lummus Park anymore without the cops getting involved. They go inland for their bars. At least, last I heard."

"Well as long as I'm not going to be the reason why a bar fight breaks out... why not? First round's on me, Mr. Mason."

27

BECK

*T*his was a bad idea.

I didn't need to be going to a place that sold alcohol with the rainbow billionaire. Didn't need to be in a place that forced you to speak close together. I was still distracted from watching Luna strip her shirt off—her full breasts swelling against that hot-pink sports bra, the delicious nip of her waist, those lean muscles. When she'd tossed her hair back, she looked like a mermaid. I wanted to press my tongue to her tan skin.

Yet she had been the one to suggest the drinks.

She'd clearly been upset by the state Sunshine was in. But beyond that, her mood had been classic Luna: teasing, funny, happy.

Teasing *me*. Flirting with *me*.

"Here we are," I said, walking up to the piece-of-shit bar frequented by people who had a looser understanding of the word *legal*. I used to drink here back in the day, when I was processing my life *before* and my life *after*. Elián and I had spent plenty a night after a tough day at Lucky Dog here.

Their busted sign read *Dean's* but half the letters were scrubbed off.

Luna's eyes widened. But then she straightened her spine and yanked open the door. The patrons glared, but it didn't affect her. Her feet did stick to the floor and she winced, examining whatever had ended up on the bottom of her expensive-looking shoes.

"It's decades of old gum and spilled beer," I admitted. My hand rested on her lower back as I guided her to the bar, the light touch sending heat rolling through me. Every person in there stared at Luna—she wasn't a regular and she sure as shit didn't look like she belonged in a dive bar. Even wrapped in her hippie clothes, she screamed *first class* all the way.

She held up two fingers for the bartender—a surly man named Stu.

"I can get this," I said, reaching for my wallet.

"Don't you dare," she protested. "Heineken, right? With a kombucha chaser?"

Stu walked over—furious, as usual, that someone was brave enough to ask him for a drink.

"What?" he barked at Luna. My hackles went up until I saw her shine that mega-watt smile his way.

"Hey there, I'm Luna." She extended her hand, glittering with gold rings.

Stu looked at me.

Then he shook her hand. He didn't smile but he wasn't frowning.

"What's your name, sir?"

"Stu. Stuart."

"Very chill vibe in here," she said. "Like 90s-era grunge but more intentional. I love it. It's like watching a Nirvana music video."

I thought Stu might turn his back on her and leave. But he leaned in. "Back in the day, I got into grunge myself. You?"

"Former grunge girl all the way. I love a flannel shirt, you know?"

He flipped the towel from his shoulder and mopped at a spot on his greasy bar. "Good eye. What do you do, Luna?"

He said *Luna* like he'd never heard such a strange word.

"I own one of the largest makeup companies in the world."

He narrowed one eye like a pirate. "Huh."

"Would you take a picture with me?" she asked.

"Yeah, okay," Stu said. I glanced behind me to make sure no other signs of the apocalypse were coming our way. Luna flipped her phone, pursed her lips and flashed the peace sign like a pro. Stu's smile was more grimace but it was definitely a smile. Maybe the first I'd seen on his face in my two decades of drinking here.

"I love it," she cheered. "Now can I grab two shots of your finest whiskey and two bottles of your most expensive Heineken?"

"I've got a bottle of Macallan I haven't opened," Stu said, coughing around his shock.

"Put in on my tab, kind sir."

When she turned back around, braid swinging, I had to hold my jaw closed.

Stu slid the whiskey our way—I'd never had Macallan in all my years of whiskey drinking. Luna clinked our glasses together. "To Sunshine," she said regally.

Then I watched Luna da Rosa sip a shot of $350 whiskey like she was born doing it.

While wearing my shirt.

All the blood in my body rushed south.

"Drink, Beck," she said, laughing.

I did as I was told.

It was the finest liquor I'd ever tasted.

"Fuck me," I said.

"Delicious, right?"

Luna leaned all the way across the bar, giving me a full view of the gorgeous curves of her ass. I was starting to develop a fetish for floral yoga pants.

"Stu, I'm stealing these," she said, grabbing two pink drink umbrellas. He slid us Heinekens, which she scooped up.

"Join me on the beach?" she asked.

"Sure."

Then she twirled around, waved to Stu, and waltzed back outside toward the ocean.

"That lady famous or somethin'?" Stu asked.

"She is," I said.

"I like her." He tossed the rag back over his shoulder and proceeded to yell at a man in the back. I reached forward, grabbed another drink umbrella to give to her.

Tried to quiet the voice in my head that echoed Stu's words.

I liked her too.

Another bad idea.

28

LUNA

"This is the only way I like to truly enjoy a beer courtesy of Heineken," I told Beck. I'd dragged the man over to a picnic bench facing the Atlantic Ocean, waves a frothy peach as the sun began its long descent behind us. Then I told him to wait a few minutes while I procured some extra-special provisions from the food truck across the street.

Now I was sitting barefoot and cross-legged with a plate on my lap and the beer to my right.

"What is this?" Beck asked.

"Alchemy." I nudged his shoulder with mine. "My favorite food stand right over there sells mango on a stick. It's dusted with chili powder and sea salt." I picked up the stick, tugged the sweet fruit free. Licked the salt and chili powder from my fingers while keeping my eyes on his blue ones.

"Lick the salt. Eat the mango. Drink the beer."

He reached forward, mimicked my motions. I watched his lips, closing around the sticky fruit. And it was probably that same *lightness* I'd been feeling, combined with the adrenaline, the handsome man next to me, the scent of his shirt, the sunset—but I held my salt-and-chili-powder fingers out to him.

"Lick," I said.

His gaze informed me I was now playing with fire.

Which was fine by me. I was a child of the earth, a worshiper of the natural elements.

Fire didn't scare me.

Fire intrigued me.

Beck Mason wrapped his thick fingers around my wrist and brought my fingers to his mouth. He sucked the tip of my index finger between lips that were soft, powerful. I felt his tongue—warm—curl around the digit.

"Delicious," he rasped.

"Now drink your beer, boss," I replied. I was going to have to remember every detail of this night so I could relay it at Mordecai's Bistro to Emily, Cameron and Daisy. They would be so *proud.*

We both took pulls of frosty liquid—my mouth exploding with cold bubbles, tart hops, sweet mango, spicy chili and salt.

"What's the word you said?" Beck asked.

"*Alchemy,*" I replied.

"What does it mean?"

"When a process seems magical. Like a transformation. An elixir."

Beck licked the remaining salt from his lips. "I like that."

I smiled, watched the crashing waves for a minute. The humid breeze caressed my skin, wrapping around us both. "Is this what it feels like during your day? This... effervescence?"

His brow furrowed. "What does that word mean?"

"Light. Bubbly," I explained.

"Yeah. Although it's only one dog." Beck said that almost robotically.

"That's not how I see it," I explained. "When we do good in

this world, it doesn't matter how small we believe it to be. Kindness ripples, has an impact long after our connection is finished. To me, you're a hero."

"You'll make me blush," Beck said. He shifted on the table, knee resting on mine.

He didn't move it.

"Does anything really make you blush?" I teased, leaning back on my palms.

"Gorgeous women drinking expensive whiskey."

My heart tripped, spun, fell over itself.

Beck Mason liked me.

The knowledge spread through me like a languid pleasure.

Because I liked him too.

Those butterflies magnified.

"Noted," I said. "For the future."

"You don't feel this way at Wild Heart? *Effervescent*?"

"Sometimes. Or... no. Also yes?"

He chuckled.

"I guess I founded Wild Heart based on that feeling. But my responsibilities are vast and what we do is more at a systems-level, working to change the way corporate values and social justice values intersect. It's thrilling. Innovative. Terrifying." I pulled at the label on my beer, tugging it clean off. "The *effervescence* has rubbed off a little bit, I think. Which isn't bad. Just a change."

A shift, my subconscious reminded me.

"Learning about the animal testing was actually a brutal reminder of how close I am to it. I guess it is more personal than I realized." I sucked a piece of mango into my mouth, experienced that same crash of taste. "I do miss this feeling of personal connection. Rescuing Sunshine... there's no other feeling like it, is there?"

"I don't think so, no," he said. "I struggle with that, being on the front-line, working with dogs rather than with donors. Elián doesn't want me doing things like this. Neither does my board. They want me talking to people. Asking for money."

I tipped my bottle against his. "Well, for tonight, I say fuck 'em."

"Never thought I'd hear Luna da Rosa say *fuck 'em*."

I snorted. "What do you think I'd say?"

"Let them follow their own spiritual path."

I shook my head, laughing into my beer. "I've got many layers, Beck Mason."

"I'm beginning to realize that," he said—and his eyes on mine felt magical.

Alchemy. Maybe there was more *elixir* than alcohol in this Heineken.

"Do you have a dog, Beck?" I asked.

"Me? No. Why?" he said.

"Because you're a dog hero," I said. "I guess this whole time I assumed you had like seventy dogs living with you."

He stared off into the peach-tinted sea. The palm trees around us were transforming into dark, tropical silhouettes. "I already have fifteen dogs at Lucky Dog."

I nudged his knee. "But you don't want *your own* dog?"

"I don't think so," he said. "Ever since Willow..." He stopped.

"Willow... the dog you worked with in that program?" I asked, the memory sliding back. Beck, all alone on his graduation day, watching this dog he'd cared for be taken away by another family.

"It was twenty years ago. I don't admit that to a lot of people because I think they'll think it's stupid."

I winced at that word. "Stupid?"

"It was one dog. Two decades ago. I can't move past that?"

"Beck." I lightly touched his back, then splayed my fingers out. "You loved her very much."

"She saved my life." His voice was thick. "If I hadn't been placed there, if she hadn't been my dog, I'd be running the Miami Devils right now, in and out of prison, stuck in a cycle of violence."

My stomach twisted, imagining Beck transplanted into this dark alternative future.

"I know that she was never really *my* dog. But there's a connection that happens. When a terrified animal looks at you and trusts you. Only you. You feel responsible for them. You... love them."

I was silent, utterly transfixed by this mountain of a man next to me.

"Dogs like Willow are disposable in our society. That always made me angry. Because she wasn't nice looking or perfect or had all the right pedigrees or came from the right breeder."

"Our society thinks that people like that are disposable too," I said. Beck looked at me with the most brazen sincerity I'd ever seen on his face. It stole my breath away.

"I think..." I paused, wanting to get the words right, "I think in this world we get to love whatever we want as passionately as we want. Even if it doesn't *fit*. Our time on this earth is too precious not to live with our hearts wide open."

"Even if that hurts?" he asked.

I wanted to ask more about his background—because I wasn't sure if he had received any true open-hearted love as a kid.

"Maybe we look for other people who can love us like that," I said. "Or animals."

I yanked off my hair tie, letting the braided strands be

tugged free by the ocean breeze. A batch of wind swept them up and I giggled, attempting to free my face from my curls.

"You have something. Stuck in your hair." Beck's deep voice was rougher than normal.

"Can you get it?"

He reached forward, the tips of his fingers alighting in my hair. They swept through the strands, searching. "It's a flower."

A tiny white flower was crushed between his fingers. "A gift," I said. "From the universe."

His throat worked. I could see him contemplating—and if the thought was *making a move* on me, I wanted him to know I was wide, wide, wide open.

"That felt good," I said. "Your fingers. Can you keep going?"

I tilted my neck.

"I can," Beck said. He slid those fingers through my hair, immediately scratching at the base of my scalp. I let out a moan that was practically pornographic.

We both went absolutely still.

"I love head massages," I said, voice breathy. "Keep going."

I was leaning against him now, eyes fluttering. I knew he would; his whole persona screamed *I will protect you*. And I liked that about him, liked that I felt comfortable asking for what I wanted without shame, that he'd give it to me, effortlessly.

Beck's expression was dreamy, fingers sifting, stroking, scratching. His palm landed on my neck and he squeezed, massaging the tension there. I purred. He growled—I heard it, right below the sound of the waves.

"You take a lot of girls to Dean's?" I managed to ask. "It's quite the romantic destination. Peanuts. Stu's scowl. High-class beverages."

"No," he said. "I haven't taken any women anywhere for a long time, Luna."

His thumb swept around my throat, landed on my pulse point. Caressed it.

"How about you?" he asked. "You must take a lot of your yoga boyfriends to your spin classes or whatever."

"Excuse me," I laughed. "I take them to my hot pilates classes and then to a quick bongo session."

"Carrot, right?"

"They're all named Carrot, yes." I was still grinning, body relaxed and unbearably aroused by Beck's handiwork. I tilted my head forward shamelessly, and he put a second hand into my hair. Worked those fingers through. Beneath the veil of my hair, I bit my lip, swallowed a sigh. Tried not to focus on the outline of the *incredibly huge* erection in his jeans.

He gathered all of my hair off to one side—no easy feat. Gave it the *gentlest* tug—but it sent a spike of lust between my legs. I complied, fully lifting my head. His face was inches from my own.

"Do gorgeous women drinking whiskey really make you blush?" I whispered, staring at his mouth.

"More than blush," he said. "Nervous."

This man.

"Good nervous?" I asked.

One big hand left my hair, cupped my face. His thumb swiped across my lower lip and I tasted heat and salt, sugary mango.

"The best kind of nervous," he said.

Beck was going to kiss me. I could feel it, wanted it *so very badly*. His thumb on my lip was the sweetest pressure. We were both frozen, suspended. Balancing on the edge of what felt very much like my destiny.

His thumb left my lip. Both hands left my hair. Beck sat all the way up, knee separating from mine. With a grimace, he finished his beer and placed it back on the picnic table.

"I should, uh... probably get you home," he said. "Don't you think?"

I struggled to arrange my features to look neutral and not hurt.

Beck had pulled away from me.

"That works," I managed, clearing my throat. "I live in Bluewater. Do you know where that is?"

He nodded like I was proving a point. "Of course. I can take you there."

I finished my beer, throat parched, thoughts racing toward figuring out what I had done wrong. Sure, kissing the man whose nonprofit I was supposed to be helping probably wasn't the *best* idea—it was a complication—but I was too tempted by this man to care.

Didn't Beck feel the same way?

29

BECK

*I*t was those damn gold rings that did it. Right before I was about to press my lips to Luna's, one of the diamonds had caught the light, flashing right into my eye. I didn't believe in messages from the universe—that was a Luna thing—but if I *did,* that felt like an important one. Even with the fun and flirtation of this day, it didn't erase the vast differences between us. Not a bit.

Kissing an ex-con on the beach would be fun for a woman like her.

A woman like Luna *dating* someone like me felt entirely out of the question.

And if I was honest, I still didn't entirely trust her motivations toward both me and my organization. It was all so complicated. I believed Luna truly cared, but she also had obligations to a life I'd never have access to.

We were quiet, conversation strained, as we put on our helmets. I had no idea what her thoughts were, but mine were focused on the fact that she lived in Bluewater—the most exclusive neighborhood in the entire city. And as we rolled up to two giant golden gates with *BB* in the middle and an actual security guard, I had to accept a fact about her that I'd known this whole time but never had thrown in my face.

Luna da Rosa was a *billionaire.*

I knew this. Fuck, it was the reason I'd stopped myself from kissing her. But seeing the reality of her wealth was a different thing entirely. We coasted along a street with more mansions than I'd ever seen in my entire life. Pools, fountains, a marina, what looked like an airfield—and a constant row of never-ending palm trees. We leaned around a curved road where four mansions were distinctly placed. She tugged on my chest, pointed at one and I came to a stop, shutting off the engine.

"This is my house," she said, pointing to a Mediterranean-style ranch home with an open courtyard covered in purple jacaranda and pink hibiscus bushes. It was the largest fucking house I'd ever seen in my entire life.

"Oh," I said, feeling mute at the sight of the mansion in front of me. "Okay."

Luna pulled the helmet off, shaking out her hair, releasing the scent of oranges. My fingers curled into fists at my side, remembering the feel of those curls.

"Thank you for the ride," she said. "Thanks for letting me help with Sunshine. And the drink. And for helping me feel... happy."

I nodded. Looked away. Luna leaned down, trying to catch my eye. "Did I do something wrong, Beck?"

My eyes slid back to her mansion. "No."

"Well, it felt like one second we were laughing about Carrot and now we're standing in front of my house like... like the way we were when we first met."

"An impasse," I said, remembering her word.

"Seriously, please talk to me." I heard the plea in her voice.

There was no denying that she and I had been growing closer over the past week. More honest with each other.

"I'm not this," I said. "After I leave this neighborhood, I'm driving home to a one-bedroom apartment on the shitty side of Miami. This... this *extravagance* will never come for me. Not in this lifetime and not in any others."

Luna tilted her chin, face a mixture of anger and regret. "I've worked really hard to earn this extravagance, Beck. Earning a billion dollars by the time I was twenty-six didn't happen because I was lazing around on a beach. I've worked my ass off for this. I won't feel bad about it."

"I'm not asking you to," I hedged. Although I was. "We can keep laughing and joking that we're *stuck with each other* all we want. But we're different. Our lives are different. Our bank accounts aren't even in spitting distance of each other. This," I said, waving to the wealth standing behind me, "isn't something I can brush off."

And please don't use me.

I almost said the words—one more truth to hand over to her. But facing the expensive-reality of Luna's life was reminding me of all the reasons why I hadn't trusted her to begin with. *Rich CEO Saves Broke Ex-Convict's Nonprofit.* That story made me feel like shit, a charity case to drum up sympathy and paint her in a positive light.

"I'd never ask you to deny it," she finally said. "I thought... I thought you'd want to see where I lived. I thought"—her teeth snagged her lip—"I thought you'd be interested." She had a strange inflection on *interested*. If it wasn't so dark out, I'd worry she'd see my cheeks redden.

"It's not that I'm not interested," I managed. One side of her mouth lifted, hopeful. "But you can't pretend you don't notice where our friendship doesn't make sense."

"Sure, I've noticed it," she said, chin lifted again. "Is that what you wanted to hear?"

"I don't know," I admitted, suddenly exhausted. Why did I care about this shit anyway? Friend or not, Luna da Rosa was really only a CEO that was volunteering at my nonprofit. That was all.

Luna was worrying at her bottom lip, all the flirtatious lightness of earlier drained away. "Impasse is right, Mr. Mason."

"Maybe I'm..." I shrugged. "Like an eight or whatever on the grumpiness scale."

Luna actually smiled. "I actually think you've been a *zero* for a week straight now."

"Happy to hear, I guess," I said. I knew I sounded gruff. Awkward. I wanted to slip back into the dream of that beach; the mangoes, the sunset, her hair beneath my fingers.

"I should go get back to work, I guess," she said, walking slowly down her incredibly long driveway. "I'll see you in a few days at Lucky Dog."

"Thanks for the drink," I mumbled.

Her expression was a mystery. "Good night." She waved, then turned to walk down the path, shining in the moonlight.

I got on my bike and roared off to my shitty apartment on the other side of town.

30

LUNA

*W*hat the hell had just *happened*?

One second, Beck was tenderly stroking through my hair in a way that left me breathless.

The next? We were awkwardly at an *impasse* again in front of my house—Beck's walls all the way back up. And me, unsure of what I'd done, or not done, or how to fix it. *The shift* was alive and well tonight, as I walked through my driveway beneath a dark canopy of stars, salt on the breeze. Because I'd been proud, excited, to show off Bluewater and the amazing things that we'd done. But wouldn't I feel the same way that Beck did if I was dating a man so much wealthier than I was— like *so much more*?

Wouldn't a neighborhood of super rich people, no matter how funky or loving or beautiful, make me feel guarded?

"Pssst. Moon." I turned, jumping, to find Emily slipping out from the small path that encircled my courtyard.

"Is having that much sex with Derek every day making you *quieter*?" I teased, laughing breathlessly. "You could have killed me. I could have died and come back reincarnated as like a cheeseburger."

"The horror," Emily mused. "Can I come in?"

"Please," I said, wrapping her into a side-hug. I flicked on the colorful lights and lamps that adorned my living room. Put the kettle on and lit a tray of candles. I made Emily a cup of chamomile tea, grateful for the distraction. Beck's words had left me unsettled. It didn't feel like an argument, necessarily. It just felt... complicated.

"What's up, beautiful?" I asked, handing her a small, teal coffee mug. "Where are Cameron and Daisy? And Derek?"

Her lips quirked. "Daisy is on a spontaneous trip to Bali with, I believe, a European prince."

I snorted into my own mug.

"Cameron's with Jude. Derek has a late meeting. I thought I'd come over because, you know, the picture that's floating around. With Beck."

"Wait, what?" I reached for my phone, stowed safely in my bag. When I pulled it out, my screen was filled with notifications and missed calls from Jasmine. "Oh my god, my phone's been *on silent this whole time*."

I tapped open the screen, frantically searching. Emily placed a steadying hand on my arm.

"Moon," she said. "Where were you that you had your phone on silent for the first time in a decade?"

I looked at my friend. "I was having a beer with Beck at Lummus Park after we rescued a stray dog together."

Understanding flooded her features. A tiny smile. "The picture makes more sense now. And I'll preface this by saying it's only floating around gossip blogs and lifestyle websites. I don't think it's a setback. I'm sure Jasmine does though."

A text from Jasmine. Three, actually. The last one: *This photo is going to be an issue with our Fischer Home Goods meeting tomorrow.*

"Oh, *shit*," I muttered.

I finally found it—I'd been tagged on Instagram. It looked like a classic paparazzi shot, the picture focused on my face.

"Oh my god, I see what you mean," I said, fingers flying to my mouth.

Emily laid her head against my shoulder. "I actually think it's very cute," she admitted.

In it, I looked like I'm about to make passionate love to *Beck's face*. It must have been snapped just before we almost kissed—we'd been so wrapped up in the moment, it would have taken a lot for us to be distracted.

Heat flared across my body as I was wrenched back to that moment in time. Because I'd been on the other end of Beck's expression—had born witness to the carnal hunger in his eyes. Although his fingers in my hair had been utterly tender.

It was the kindness in the way he'd stroked my hair that felt especially persistent in the face of the awkward interaction we'd had. There was a glow in my heart that was starting to feel like Beck. And if my parents had taught me anything, it was to trust that glow, that nudge from the universe insisting that you'd found something beautiful.

This extravagance will never come for me—not in this lifetime, not in any others.

I had never used to care about things like mansions and infinity pools and personal security. But becoming a billionaire had literally expanded all of the areas in my life. It was only natural to grow into them. And I'd resented his insinuation I should be ashamed—men had been allowed to flaunt their excessive wealth since the dawn of time. I felt proud to take up that space, to exert the power of my hard work and success.

I still felt *off* though.

"Did you see the caption?" Emily asked. "I can always talk to Derek, see if he can get it removed."

I shook my head, preoccupied. It read: *Disgraced CEO Luna da Rosa seen here canoodling with the Executive Director of Lucky Dog, the nonprofit she has been publicly supporting since news broke of the animal cruelty scandal. Beck Mason's parents are Georgie and Rip Mason, notorious for their violent club fights, extortion, and racketeering activities out of the Miami Devils MC.*

"This is a... complication," I said, echoing my fears from the beginning. Emily's head was near my own, fingers landing on the complication in question.

"I have to say, as your best friend, this looks like a very fun complication, Moon," she said. I touched my lips, remembered the pressure of Beck's thumb there. The joy of reaching forward, wrapping my arms around Sunshine. Knowing she was going to get that second chance, would find love and happiness.

"I've been doing a lot of soul-searching since the Ferris Mark news," I admitted to her. "I'm not even sure I actually *see* this as a complication anymore, even though I know it is from a business standpoint."

The devil on my shoulder stirred and I shushed it.

"What's going to happen with the Fischer meeting?" she asked, tucking her legs underneath her.

"They're skittish because of the cost of pulling all of those damaged products. And the cost of Wild Heart's damaged reputation. There's another cosmetics line that's cruelty-free and scandal-free and it's looking like they're going to drop us in favor of them."

"Assholes," she said. "Although you know its only business. It's awful being on the end of it, but all of us know what that's like. I hate Fischer for doing this to you, Moon, but I fully believe it's not personal for them. And that you'll find an even better storefront partner. I mean, you're Luna da Rosa. You always find a way."

"It feels personal though," I said quietly. "Maybe that's the ultimate downfall of making myself the *face* of Wild Heart. All of that personal branding. I made a massive professional mistake that I'm working to fix but the public is taking it out on me *personally*."

Emily squeezed my hand. "You know I went through something similar. At the end of the day, you have to go with what feels right, which is terrifying. Because you can lose everything."

"No kidding," I said.

She tapped the photo. "This seems pretty right, don't you think?"

I thought about that little girl in the photo now taped to my computer. What would she do?

"It really does," I said.

And I owe Beck an apology, I realized.

A brightly-colored parrot flew through the room, taking advantage of the back patio doors I'd left wide open. He flapped his rainbow wings once before settling on the top of the couch.

I cooed, running my finger down his feathers. "A visit from Frank? If this isn't a sign from the universe, I don't know what is." Frank was a free-range parrot who'd taken up residence in Bluewater a few years ago. He was sweet as sugar—but his previous owner had taught him to curse like a sailor.

"Evening, shitheads," Frank squawked.

"Frank is very wise," Emily said. "And I think he'd agree that you like Beck and should ask him on a date and smoosh his face and have all of his babies."

I dropped my head back on her shoulder. "Oh god, is it that obvious?"

"That you *like-like* Beck?" She laughed. "Yes. Yes, it is. And from the look of this picture, I'd say he likes you too."

I didn't disagree—Beck and I had a connection. An intimacy, an honesty—that was why I'd pushed him to spill tonight. We'd already sparred enough to breach those walls, to hand each other parcels of vulnerability like rare jewels. I owed him that much in return after how I'd made him feel tonight, intentional or not.

"Fuckfaces," Frank added.

"So wise," Emily grinned.

Two hours later, after conquering the majority of my inbox and doing a wind-down meditation by the pool, I pulled up the picture again. The one of me and Beck. I didn't stare at the two of us, our body language, the sweet way his fingers were curled in my hair.

I read the comments.

Every single one.

People seemed to hate the Mason family as much as they hated—or pretended to hate—me. Beck's family had certainly been behind their fair share of fraud and money laundering, so of course the implications about the two of us were strange and far-fetched: Beck was seducing me for my money, which he was funneling to his parents. I was using Beck to get to his parents who I was paying to "take out" my enemies. The money I raised for Beck was going to his nonprofit, which was nothing more than a front. Beck was a criminal, therefore I was a criminal. My bohemian, love-and-light persona was a sham because would someone like me willingly associate with a family filled with violence?

My fingers pressed to my brow. That wasn't necessarily a totally off-the-wall question.

Because I didn't know.

The Luna who was more obsessed with her money than her values liked fitness instructors who also believed in what I believed in.

This new Luna—trying to navigate life after being exposed so painfully to the public—liked men like Beck, who were not vegan and had no money... but who had hope.

Did that make *any sense*?

I clicked over to my Instagram profile—the picture of me and Sunshine was still there, and it felt like it'd been taken a year ago instead of this afternoon. I pulled it up and experienced that same *pinch* in my gut. But I read the comments, every single one. And for the most part?

They were positive.

Even Jasmine had mentioned it in one of her many increasingly frantic text messages. *That picture of you and the stray is solid gold!! People love dogs, Luna. Keep playing that angle. Are there any other dogs you can rescue and can you film it next time?*

The issue being that Beck wasn't an angle.

What I'd done wasn't an angle.

Using it to improve *my* reputation, however, was.

I deleted the picture.

31

BECK

*T*he next morning I got to Lucky Dog early. My nerves were heightened. It reminded me of how I used to be as a kid. Jumpy. After leaving Luna, I was restless all night—I felt guilty *and* kind of pissed.

It wasn't comfortable.

Nor was the call I'd gotten from Elián, telling me about the picture of Luna and I that was online. *Beck Mason's parents are the infamous Georgie and Rip Mason, notorious for their violent club fights, extortion and racketeering out of the Miami Devils MC.*

Yeah, no shit.

And the thing Rip and Georgie hated more than the cops was media attention.

I'd inspected the campus as the sun rose, relieved to find the dogs fine, happy, unaffected. But at half-past six, I wasn't surprised when I heard the familiar roar of motorcycles, racing down the road right outside Lucky Dog. My ear picked out four, maybe five bikes. I'd stood outside my trailer, clutching a cup of coffee and scowled at the noise. There were plenty of riders who enjoyed the cool morning air. It didn't *mean* it was the Devils.

And when they'd ridden past, tires squealing, I *thought* I saw leather jackets on all five of them. Skulls on the back of each.

But I couldn't be sure.

I didn't fucking like it. Them coming here, to me, I could handle.

What if they came for Luna?

Which was why when I saw—and then heard—Luna's car crunching over the gravel in our driveway, I thought I was dreaming.

She was real though. It was barely seven in the morning and Luna was striding toward me with a cup of coffee in her hand and a bag that smelled delicious. She was makeup-less and smiling at me in the sunshine.

A dream, indeed.

"An apology coffee," she said, pressing it into my hands. "And apology donuts."

"What are you apologizing for?" I asked.

"Can I come in?" she asked, biting her lip.

I opened the door to my office, tilted my head to invite her inside. She slid past me, keeping our bodies apart, and settled on the old couch along the back wall.

"From Carbs 'n Coffee," she said. "I figured you for a classic old-fashioned donut and black coffee."

Impressed, I opened the bag. Held out a piece for her. "I ate two vegan ones on the way over."

I settled on the edge of my desk. "Thank you," I said.

She tucked a strand of hair behind her ear. "I felt really weird when you left last night. And as you know, I'm trying to correct my mistakes, analyze my actions more. And I..." She paused, took a deep breath. "I think taking you to the enclave without talking to you about it first was an unnecessary power dynamic shift. To be clear,

I'm *not* apologizing for my success. I earned that mansion."

"I kind of... wanted you to."

"I know you did," she said, smiling more broadly than I expected. "Operating in this world as a billionaire is one thing. Doing it as a woman is another. I take that responsibility seriously and I never want to feel ashamed for achieving something that men get to do all the time."

I sipped the coffee, turning this over. "I agree. I'm sorry."

"It's okay, really," she said. "Because beyond that, on a *personal* level, I get why it made you pissed off or uncomfortable or whatever. Like I was throwing it in your face. I'd never, ever do that to you on purpose, Beck. But I was probably doing it unconsciously."

"I think I was kind of being a dick though," I admitted.

"And I think *I* was kind of being insensitive though," she said, eyebrow lifted.

I took another sip, my eyes on her luminous ones. "Would you call this the nice kind of impasse?"

"I think so." She bit her lip. "I'm really sorry, Beck."

"I'm sorry, Luna," I said.

"Friends again?" She held her hand out, indicating for me to shake. I shook it like we had that first day. And like that first day, my fingers wrapped around her small wrist, her palm touching mine like a shock. The interesting kind. I let my thumb stroke across her inner wrist. Her breathing hitched.

"Friends," I said roughly. Tried not to indulge the fantasy that called to me with Luna looking so pretty in my office. Of sinking to my knees and spreading her bare legs. Showing her with my mouth how much I appreciated her honesty.

"Tell me about Bluewater," I said instead. "I want to know about where you live."

"You sure you're interested?" she asked.

I nodded. Sipped.

"My three best friends are also billionaires," she said. "We wanted a place that was for us. We wanted to be neighbors so we could see each other all the time. Daisy, who's a real estate mogul, created a design that was pretty epic. So now we live with a bunch of weird and kooky rich people." She smiled. "At the end of the day, the four of us at least have each other, to listen when we're victims of misogyny or harassment or manipulation from our male peers. Friends help. Feeling safe helps." Luna leaned in like she was sharing a secret. "Also we accidentally designed the bay that our four houses face to look like a uterus."

I coughed around my coffee. "You're serious?"

"Totally," she said. "And our street? It's one of the ovaries."

I laughed for real, releasing a day's worth of odd tension. She giggled, sitting back against the couch. "I'm not joking. I live on a street shaped like an ovary with my three best friends. As you know, celebrating the beauty of the female form is a priority of mine."

If someone had told me a month ago that I'd be sitting with an extremely rich woman, joking about ovaries and drinking a coffee she'd brought me... I would have called that person a damned liar.

"To have friends like that, family like that," I said, "well, you're lucky. They don't seem to use money like a weapon."

Luna tilted her head. "I'm extremely lucky, yes. Did your parents use money like a weapon?"

I cleared my throat. "If we didn't have enough, and we almost never did, it was easy to get a fourteen-year-old to go out and get some for you."

Her face darkened. "Was that where your arrests came from?"

"Not always," I admitted. "I guess sometimes I wanted my parents to... notice me."

That sentence landed like a *thud* between us. But Luna didn't make a cheesy *oh, poor you* sound or spew some Hallmark bullshit. "Then I'm happy you have a new family now. Lucky Dog. Wes and Jem and Elián. The dogs. All of their adoptive humans. And if you ever need *more* family, we've got extra room at Bluewater."

Her smile lit up every dark shadow in my heart.

"I'll keep that offer in mind," I said, voice thick.

"Like you said, money can be used for evil. It can also be used for good. I've let my money control me. I want to change that, starting with Lucky Dog. Thank you for letting me have that experience here. For helping me learn."

"Of course," I replied.

Luna looked at the watch on her wrist, sighed. "As much as I'd love to stay here all day, I've got a crucial meeting in two hours I need to prepare for."

Luna stood gingerly, making her way toward me like she wasn't entirely sure about it. The tips of her toes touched the tips of my shoes. I was still leaning against the desk, which put me closer to eye-level with the rainbow billionaire, who was suddenly stepping into my space, fingers resting lightly on my ribcage. I felt the soft brush of her lips on my cheek, those same lips hovering at my ear. My fingers gripped the desk as her closeness set my entire body on fucking fire.

"On a personal note," she whispered, "if you were inclined as to ask me on a date, I'd say yes." Luna stepped back, looking pretty and girlish and filled with hope. "So you should ask me."

32

LUNA

I sat at the head of the table at the Wild Heart conference room, staring at a group of people who no longer seemed to respect me very much.

I'd pushed to have this meeting with Fischer Home Goods at the Wild Heart offices because I wanted them to fully understand that what happened with Ferris Mark was absolutely horrible, but that we weren't—and never would be—a fraudulent company. Around the room hung framed magazine and newspaper articles about Wild Heart—our high pay standards, our diverse board and leadership, our eco-friendly packaging, all of it was displayed openly and celebrated. I'd removed large photos or articles with my face in them, trying to distance the amazingness of Wild Heart from whatever complicated feelings the public had about my role as spokeswoman.

This morning, after leaving Beck's office, I'd watched my TED Talk, re-igniting the fire in my belly that had led me to pull *zero* punches in that speech. I hadn't hesitated to call out big cosmetics brands and label them hypocrites. Didn't hesitate to splash the human and animal rights violations prevalent in our industry across that screen and call for change. Now. None of my speech had been for image or branding or Instagram or Jasmine. It had all been *my vision*.

If Fischer Home Goods was going to terminate their contract, they were going to have to wrench it from my sunshine-y, vegan hands.

Sylvia sat next to me. One minute before the meeting began, she passed a sticky note my way.

Remember what you stand for.

So different from the aggravated frustration from Jasmine and her team this morning—they were pissed about the picture, pissed about the caption.

Pissed that I'd deleted the photo of me and Sunshine.

This little note of uncomplicated support meant so much more than Jasmine's media concerns.

I beamed at Sylvia, nodded at her.

"Thank you, everyone, for coming," I said, aiming as much light as I could at their head of in-store products, Kristin Langley. "I know it's been a tense couple of weeks since the Ferris Mark news broke, but I really appreciate your kindness and understanding during this time."

Kristin's expression let me know she felt neither kindness *nor* understanding but I forged ahead.

"Today we'll be discussing negotiations of our storefront contract with Fischer Home Goods. There have been discussions"—*threats*—"of terminating the contract, so I want to do everything in my power as the founder and CEO of Wild Heart to guarantee your trust in us. Such a drastic action need not occur. Kombucha?"

They weren't really a kombucha crowd, but I still poured some for a few of the willing visitors and then settled back into my chair. "Tell me your concerns. I'm here to listen," I said, accessing a deep, zen-like space to keep from freaking out or tearing up all the papers on the table and running away. Daisy could hide me out on her yacht and Cameron and Emily would helicopter in corn chips, I was sure of it.

"Let me be clear," Kristin said. "We're here to formally end our partnership with Wild Heart. Just so there's no confusion."

I kept my smile broad and hid any strain. "I see. I want to remind you that until Ferris Mark lied to us, and four other major cosmetics companies, our relationship was nothing but incredibly beneficial. Financially and from a marketing perspective. Young people in America care about the causes that Wild Heart stands for. Not only cruelty-free products, but a company that pays its employees a living wage, a company that values gender, racial and ethnic diversity in its hiring practices. A corporation that puts social justice at the center of its decision making."

"Until you didn't," Kristin said. "And that's the issue. I know you're working with a new supplier now, but the public fallout has been too severe. It's easier for us to cut contact with you altogether." She smiled like a snake. "You understand. The public doesn't want to buy products at Fischer Home Goods from a company they believe has lied to them."

"I *don't* understand, actually," I said. "Since my work with Lucky Dog, the tide has been turning and my PR team is working on rebranding and re-messaging with a focus on honesty and transparency. We fully intend to correct the mistakes that were made. In fact, many of them have been corrected already."

"How does your connection with the Miami Devils play into this?" she asked, crossing her arms.

The question threw me for such a loop that three awkward seconds ticked with no pithy response from me.

"What are you referring to, Kristin?" Sylvia asked sharply. "Wild Heart has never had a connection with a motorcycle gang. That's preposterous and, I might add, not relevant to a business negotiation."

"It is if your CEO is dating a member, openly. Fischer is a national company but based in Miami, like Wild Heart. We're all very familiar with their reputation." Kristin leaned in across the table. "Careful. It's tarnishing your perfect one, Ms. Da Rosa."

Her quick, icy tone felt like an actual slap across the face. Two years ago, Kristin and I had been colleagues, working together to make a partnership we hoped would be lucrative *and* revolutionary.

This happened to me quite a bit. Between my active social media accounts and my generally bouncy personality, people usually assumed I was a vapid, glittering fairy without any bite.

"Careful," I repeated to Kristin. "My personal life and the personal life of Beck Mason is of absolutely zero concern to you, Fischer Home Goods *or* the consumers. This company is valued at over a billion dollars and has been credited with changing the production standards of the beauty industry. You either want to continue partnering with an innovator or you don't."

"We don't," Kristin said. "I'll have the termination papers sent over within the hour."

The Fischer team stood as one and exited the Wild Heart headquarters. Kristin didn't even have the decency to look disappointed, or bittersweet, or *something*.

She just left.

Absent their scrutiny, and in the relative comfort of Sylvia's presence, I let my head drop into my hands. For a moment, no more. I wanted to be back in Beck's office, stepping into his body heat and scent. If Beck were here, he'd wrap me into a bear hug—no question.

"It really is easier for them, Luna," Sylvia said, interrupting my thoughts. "It's business. If they smell danger, they'll drop you and pick up another company. Money works fast, you know that. And even though you believe Wild Heart is vital and innovative, they only see you as a maker of mascaras. And there are many mascara makers in this industry for them to choose from."

"We're not special," I repeated bitterly.

"You are," Sylvia said. "*You* are special. They're not."

I stalked over to the conference room door. Locked it. Leaned against it and crossed my arms over my chest.

"Can I ask your honest opinion, Sylvia?"

"Of course," she said. I trusted her opinion—more than Jasmine's, I was realizing.

"What's the board thinking right now?" I asked. I was the majority shareholder in the company and every single member was a trusted colleague I'd personally brought on. But that didn't make me entirely safe.

"The board is committed to Wild Heart and you. You've done an excellent job, Luna. They trust you."

I blew out a relieved breath. I might have been feeling confused about aspects of my job lately, but at least I wasn't at risk of losing it. Not like what happened with Emily.

"We just lost our main source of revenue," I said, pointing out the door. "I thought the Ferris Mark thing would drop but it's sticky. It's all over me."

"Yes, it is," she said. "Some stories aren't let go of that easily. You are a threat, Luna. To the way things are done. If they see a chance to drag you through the mud, they'll take it over and over."

I swallowed around a lump in my throat. "At least I know now," I said, voice wavering. "But am *I* making a mistake? Working with Lucky Dog and adding extra fuel for the fire?"

"Is your question really about Lucky Dog or are you asking me about Beck Mason?"

I opened my mouth to answer. Stopped. Felt my cheeks get hot. "Nothing is *formally* happening with Beck and me. But it might happen and I want to know if I'm going to take this company down with me. People's jobs are on the line. Our mission is on the line. Are my personal choices sacrificing what's best for Wild Heart?"

"You're a woman, a CEO, a public persona," Sylvia said. "Your choices will continue to be picked apart and analyzed forever. You won't ever escape it."

I looked out the window, found no comfort in Miami's shimmering waves.

"That wasn't the answer I wanted," I said.

"I know it's not."

"I thought light attracted light. I'm always nice, I care deeply about things, I'm all about good causes—"

"That doesn't matter," she said. "Your detractors will be many. Always. You think I didn't feel the same pressure? Because I did. But you cannot live your life dictated by the opinions of strangers."

A knock on the window. Jasmine, pointing at one of the giant screens on the wall. *Turn it on*, she mouthed. She looked furious. Sylvia turned it on—to the business news network we always had on.

"In the wake of the Ferris Mark scandal, things aren't looking up for Miami's own Wild Heart. First, the animal cruelty. Then the news that Luna da Rosa had openly defied her own policies to work with them. And now, the latest word that Fischer Home Goods, the second-largest chain of stores in the country, will no longer be selling their products. This was the partnership that garnered Ms. da Rosa's billionaire status and put Wild Heart officially on the map with the other reputable cosmetics brands."

My gold rings caught the light from the sun, twinkling with all of their expensive goodness. The Fischer contract had only been possible because of my rash decision to go with Ferris Mark—because I'd run the numbers and had predicted, if all went as planned, my net worth would break the billion-dollar mark. It had been an exciting gamble, a tease, a fun game, to roll the dice and let the universe reward me for my hard work.

The devil on my shoulder had won that day. There'd been no regard for social justice, only money.

"Luna, are you okay?" Sylvia asked.

"Of course," I said brightly, with my last remaining ounce of strength. "One second, I need to get some air."

"Luna."

I stopped, turned. It was Jasmine, barreling through the door and brandishing her phone like a sword. "It's nuclear again. They're ganging up on you now."

"I know," I sighed. Sylvia caught my eye across the table.

"We need to strategize, immediately," Jasmine said. "Does Beck have any dogs coming that are particularly tragic or trau-matized? You could do a video. Maybe shot in black and white. We could even stage it."

"No," I said clearly. But Jasmine was scrolling through her phone as always. "Also, if the media is going to continue to bring up Beck's family, we could flip it. Use it. What if you surprised Beck at his office by bringing his parents there? Show both of you confronting them, put you in a hero's light, working together."

"No," I said again.

From behind her, Sylvia gave me an approving nod.

"You're making it hard to do my job," Jasmine said.

"I know," I said. "We'll figure it out. But I want to move forward intentionally. And I don't want to manipulate or use Beck or the dogs in any way."

"You told Beck in your first meeting it's not manipulation if it's mutually beneficial." Her smile was wry. "So what's the problem?"

My hand was on the door and I was already moving. I needed a break from this conversation. "I've changed my mind."

I stepped outside to Jasmine's protests, kicked off my shoes, and sank my bare toes into the sand. Inhaled. Exhaled. Tried to feel every grain of sand along the soles of my feet—a meditation technique my mother used to have me do when I was a little kid. *Grain, grain, grain* went my focus. It was a pointless endeavor—you couldn't actually feel every grain— but it had the benefit of calming your mind after a few minutes.

The clarity materialized—about the meeting and Jasmine's emergency ideas. Deep down, even when I felt like the sky was truly falling, I believed *good* was still coming my way. Fischer had been very clear about their intentions and yet I hadn't let myself believe it. Because I had apologized, was working with Lucky Dog, doing something trustworthy with my time.

It still wasn't working. But now Jasmine's ideas felt... icky to me.

I could try my hardest—and my life might never go back to the way it was.

Maybe it was time I started to accept that.

My phone pinged.

Beck.

My cheeks were still hot and I realized I was smiling even in the midst of this mini personal crisis I was having with my toes in the sand. There was a video plus a text that said: *I had to ask Jem to help me send this. She says hi and that she misses you. Thought you would want to see this.*

The video was Beck, looking bearded and handsome and giant standing in the middle of the Lucky Dog training field. In his right hand, he held a minuscule treat between his fingers. Face open but stern, he said, "Penelope. Sit."

Before him was my girl—my straggly, mangy, skinny stray dog looking cleaner, more filled out and *sitting on command.*

I pressed the phone to my chest. *Glow* went my heart.

Before I could think too hard I fired off a text back: *I can't tell you how much I needed to see this video right at this moment. Thank you, Beck. You're doing such a great job with our girl."*

Behind me, people were streaming into my office— Jasmine's staff. The fall-out was continuing and now we had a potential financial crisis on our hands. I curled my toes, squished sand, yearned to tear off my clothing and dive naked into that sea-green water.

I don't think I'll be around this week. Bad news for Wild Heart and I have to be here to fix it. Send your prayers to the universe that all goes well. I'll keep posting photos to raise you more money, okay? And I'll send a case of kombucha to Lucky Dog for you.

Okay, Beck texted back.

I smirked. The man was a one-word machine.

Thank you again for talking with me this morning, I wrote. *And if you want to ask me on a date later, you know where to find me.*

He didn't text anything back.

33

BECK

*L*una hadn't been at Lucky Dog for an entire week.

According to my staff, I was in a bad mood.

Which wasn't true—I just wanted to slam doors and prowl around and scowl at every question because I liked it that way. But I guess we'd all gotten used to a weekly infusion of Luna's cheery light and without it I felt stuck in grumpy darkness.

Her influence wasn't entirely absent though. Right now, Elián and I were sitting on the stairs outside the office, sharing a six-pack of beer, and watching Luna's website update with more and more donations for Lucky Dog. We were approaching $100,000 in total donations over two weeks, which was one-third of our budget gap, the one we needed to close by the end of this month.

It also meant that my staff could be paid next week. I didn't think that was going to happen before Luna decided I was *stuck* with her.

"Can you show me what she's been posting?" I asked Elián. Luna had texted that she'd been secretly taking more than four photos every time she visited. She had plenty to upload and share from the comfort of her office. Elián showed me her Instagram page. It was filled with attractive pictures of our campus. I scanned the same horizon—saw our dusty field, the shabby equipment, everything looking old and cheap.

Luna's pictures were colorful and hopeful. We looked like a happy place for happy dogs that needed a little bit of extra help. There were portraits of every single dog we had with funny captions. Silly photos of Wes and Jem, training sessions with Elián.

"She's good, man," Elián said.

"Is that a lie?" I asked. "What she posted?"

"I don't think it is," he said. "I think she really loves it here. You can tell how she talks about it. Donors want to give to her because she's authentic. She's not trying to guilt them into giving. I think she's trying to inspire them."

I ran a hand through my hair, pondering that. "She is good," I admitted. "I feel bad that my family is fucking things up for her this week."

"Media that bad, huh?" he asked, squinting at the setting sun.

I shouldn't have brought it up—I had to clamp down on my anger to keep it from boiling over. After that paparazzi shot, the Devils were back in the public eye, though mostly it was re-posting the same mug shots or sharing bizarre theories. About ten years ago, I'd kicked around the idea of sealing or expunging my juvenile record—a real clean slate. But I hadn't gone through with it, mostly because I wanted to avoid even talking about it at all costs.

Now I wished I had.

"Bad. It's all fake. They're trying to drag her down. Dragging up old stories about me that I'd forgotten about. Or aren't real."

"Have your parents reached out to you?" Elián asked.

I huffed into my beer. "No," I said. "I'm only useful to Rip and Georgie if I come back begging. They'll stay away until that happens. But the MC's letting me know they're around. Couple times. I think they rode past here the other morning. A couple guys on the beach giving me the eye, that kind of thing."

"Jesus, man," he said. "If they give you problems, tell me, okay?"

I nodded. The first five years after I'd left the MC, I was looking over my shoulder all the time, worried they'd drag me back kicking and screaming. But twenty years was a long time and before Luna I'd felt—finally—*safe*.

Luna da Rosa was a disruption to my life in more ways than one.

One of them was that I hadn't been able to stop thinking about her for seven days straight and the thoughts were so filthy I had to fuck my own hand every single night.

"We need to talk about what's next," Elián said. "The money is amazing. We're *probably* out of the crisis. Now we gotta do something about it."

"What do you mean?" I opened two more beers, passed one to him.

"Those foundation people were assholes. But they kinda had a point, Beck. I know you don't want to do it because it seems risky, but we have to invest now. We have to develop a strategic plan and formalize our goals. All of these donors"— Elián pointed at the screen with the tip of his beer—"will want accountability for this massive public interest in us. We have to court them. Make sure they'll give again."

"More kennels, more dogs," I shrugged, wanting to clam up.

But he wouldn't let me. He threw an arm around my shoulders, patted my back. "Not having a high school diploma doesn't mean jack shit and you know that. Everything I just said we can get help with. Board members. Volunteers. Shit, *Luna* can do this stuff for us. If you asked her she'd rally together the best brains in the business."

Elián handed me a stack of square envelopes. "Like these. What are all these?"

"Invitations to community events and other fundraisers."

They were all addressed to Mr. Beck Mason, Executive Director. "Don't they know I'm a violent criminal or whatever?"

"Not everyone cares about trashy gossip," Elián said, grinning as he took a swig. "You're starting to be in high demand. Well, maybe not *high*. But like a low-to-medium demand."

I flipped through the stack. Foundations, Rotary club meetings, church groups.

"Some of them want you to speak," he said, tapping an envelope.

I grimaced. "That's too bad."

Elián sat forward, elbows on his knees. "Do you remember when I met you at the Miami SPCA? I'd never seen someone so angry and unsure. You were like Beatrix over there, snarling at anyone who got too close."

I lifted a shoulder. "Hazard of juvie. Hazard of the club. If you don't come out swinging, the other person will."

"And I didn't," he said. "And you hated me in the beginning because of it."

Elián was only five years older than I was, but I remembered thinking of him as being wise when I'd finally let him be my friend.

"Yeah," I said, smiling a little.

"You barely said a word," he continued.

"Still don't."

"No," he countered. "You're more talkative than you realize now, especially around Luna."

I shifted at that. Was that true?

"You're never going to be a chatty guy, Beck," he said, "but my point is that you can grow. I've watched you grow. And you've never abandoned this cause or these dogs or your staff. You're growing. Lucky Dog is now growing. That means you have to be a leader now."

I watched Luna's website light up with money. And she'd done it by telling the truth without shame. Telling people straight out: We need your help. You can give it.

I sent a text her way: *Elián and I are watching your website. Lots of money. Thank you.* It took me a minute—if writing on a computer was hard, that shiny text screen was even harder. The texts I received from Luna were cheery and funny. It caused ugly self-esteem things to rise in me.

And I was ignoring all the times she'd asked me on a date this week and I'd said nothing.

"Maybe Luna can help me with some of this stuff," I said, feeling butterflies or moths or giant fucking pandas stomping through my insides and stirring shit up.

"Maybe you can finally take Luna on that date," Elián said.

"Jem's got a big mouth," I sighed, although I was a little pleased.

"You like Luna."

"... yeah." I allowed.

Another nudge from Elián. "I know the excuses you're going to throw out there. I'm going to stay one step ahead and tell you those excuses ain't worth shit."

"You mean the fact that she's a famous billionaire and I'm motorcycle trash?"

The look he gave me spoke volumes. And he didn't even

know about Luna bringing me coffee and apologies last week, trying to find common ground for our very different lives.

I had no excuse, really.

It had been a long time since I'd ever felt this passionately about a woman and I worried that if I got Luna on a date, I'd scare her away with my feelings. My feelings and my lust, which wasn't nice. But it was demanding.

"I'm going to go on a long ride," I said, "grab a burger. And when I get home, I'll give Luna a call and ask her out the old-fashioned way."

"Classy guy."

"I have a feeling a week from now we'll be having this same conversation about Jem and Wes."

"Wes's got a crush on Jem, doesn't he?"

"A big one," I replied.

$105,000, $105,500, $105,700... the numbers went tick, tick, tick as I finished my beer with Elián. Wes had a crush. I was going to put myself out there. Lucky Dog was raking in the dough.

Things were looking up.

34

LUNA

I was here to eat a cheeseburger. With bacon.

Or at least *try* to. I had my driver drop me off at a burger stand off the side of the highway that looked inconspicuous and moments away from being shut down for health-code violations. And if I contracted a strange, tropical disease from my first-time eating meat since I was eleven years old—so be it.

It was the punishment I deserved.

I'd spent the past week working long, exhausting days with my staff and my board, attempting to secure a store that could replace, even partially, our lost revenue from Fischer Home Goods. Jasmine had me doing fluff pieces for any magazine or online forum that wasn't trying to smear my reputation further. I was posting about Lucky Dog constantly, attempting to reroute my personal *and* professional brand, all while watching our stock prices take a deep, terrifying dive.

There was a slew of hate messages in various inboxes across all of my social media platforms. I tried to stay upbeat all week—tried to hold tight to my values, my new path, Sylvia's words resonating constantly in my mind.

KATHRYN NOLAN

The right thing or the safe thing?

I didn't want to be an ordinary leader.

I wanted to be *extraordinary*.

Except today Claudia Bardot had decided to add her hat into the ring of online bullies. Claudia was a famous actress— a famous *vegan* actress—and when I was twenty-four and just starting out, she'd discovered Wild Heart products and become obsessed. We became fast friends... and Claudia became one of my earliest admirers. Her fans became my fans and I owed a lot of my early success to the buzz she built about my makeup and my company and the way we were doing things differently.

Today Claudia Bardot had disowned me. Publicly.

I understood her hurt at my perceived betrayal, understood the pain of realizing a brand you've loved is cruel to animals. But I thought... I hoped... she'd talk to me to learn the real story.

I hoped she was the kind of friend who could see me for who I really was.

Instead, she'd issued a comment today severing any ties to Wild Heart and to me. Her words had been short, but brutal: *It's heart-wrenching when you discover that a woman you idolize has been lying to you for years, building her brand of social justice based on hypocrisy. At this point, I'm not even sure Luna da Rosa is an actual vegan. She is, however, an expert actress.*

"What do you fucking want?" the woman behind the counter barked at me.

"Bacon cheeseburger and fries, please," I said in a small voice. I'd contemplated a disguise but then—who cared? If the world believed I was fake, I might as well embrace it.

Except as I sat on the rickety table beneath an equally-rickety umbrella, I felt only an unsettled nausea and tears as I stared at the greasy burger.

I'd hit multiple lows over the past three weeks—Ferris Mark. Learning I was at fault. The online hate. The protesters calling me a murderer. Losing the contract. Losing Claudia.

This cheeseburger, however?

Was the *lowest*.

None of this felt okay though. None of this felt *right*. Which I found odd, since at this point, I was ready to throw in the towel and admit defeat. *Your detractors will be many*, Sylvia had said.

I wasn't sure I had the strength left to push back against them.

Which was why I was going to give in to them.

As soon as I stopped dry heaving.

"Luna?"

A giant nonprofit hunk was stalking my way with a look of utter disbelief on his handsome, bearded face.

"What the *fuck*" I hissed to myself, hiding under the table since that was the only idea I had at the time. Until Beck's shaggy head dropped down to pin a gaze on me that said *gotcha*.

"Evening," he said. He dropped to his knees. I squinted up at him like I hadn't been sure it was him.

"Beck?" I asked, like we were bumping into each other at the farmer's market. "Oh my god. *Hey*."

He passed a hand over his mouth, hiding a smirk. "What are you doing beneath the table at a burger joint?"

"Market research," I said weakly.

"On the ground?"

"Being a CEO is about vision, Beck," I said. "Opportunity exists in every grain of sand and straw wrapper."

"I wouldn't know," he mused. "I'm just here to enjoy a juicy burger like the rest of us meat-eating evildoers."

At the mention of the words *juicy burger,* my stomach

twisted violently. I slapped a hand over my mouth. His smirk grew into a look of concern, narrowed eyes searching mine.

"Me too," I said weakly.

A beat passed. Beck was too kind, too perceptive to bear witness to my personal nadir.

"Do you mind if I join you?"

"Under the table?"

"If I fit," he said, shrugging his gigantic shoulders.

"You're definitely too big," I said. And immediately my brain flashed a memory of Beck's cock outlined through his jeans while his fingers worked a heavenly magic on my scalp.

"Is that so?" His lips quirked.

"I mean, some would say."

"Luna," he said, chuckling now.

"I'm very busy under here," I said airily. "This could even be an interesting corporate retreat if you think about it. A cozy way to incubate new and invigorating ideas."

"I'm going to get a burger," he said. "And I'm buying us more beer. I'm fine talking to you like this but it might be easier if you sat in a chair."

"We keep ending up at these impasses, Mr. Mason," I said, laughing a little. Then smacking my damn forehead on the table.

"Ouch—shit," I said. I untangled myself from the ground gingerly, Beck's strong hand lifting me. He swiped his thumb across my forehead with more tenderness than I could handle.

"Lying about eating a burger and saying the word *shit*," he mused. "Sounds like you could use a friend."

Beck turned around before I could answer, so I was left with his magnificent ass in those jeans, his helmet beneath his arm, and the sly grin he flashed me when he caught me staring. If Beck Mason was in a *grinnin' mood* I wasn't going to make it through this night with my clothes on. Grumpy Beck had his own appeal.

Beck with a crooked grin could cause spontaneous orgasms.

I distracted myself by methodically picking up the burger. Trying to bring it to my mouth.

Putting it back down. I did this fifteen times over before he returned, hitching a leg over a chair so small I feared for its engineering.

"For you," he said, placing a second Heineken next to me. "*Warm horse piss,* as you call it, no mangoes this time."

"Not as much alchemy," I noted. His blue eyes blazed with kindness and good humor. "Well, maybe a little bit."

"I asked Barb what she had for vegans and she gave me this plate of lettuce and tomatoes. Thought it might suit you better."

Rabbit food—I'd heard it called that before. But suddenly the thought of crisp lettuce and fresh tomatoes was so compelling I could have wept. I dropped the burger and stuffed the lettuce into my mouth.

"Thank you," I said, placing a hand on his wrist. "Truly. And please don't make fun of me for being here."

Beck shook his head. "Never."

We ate in companionable silence for a moment. Beck seemed curious, not judgmental. And finally he said, "Rough day?"

I laughed—startling the silence. It was a cathartic sound. "Rough week," I said. "We lost that Fischer contract and the media hasn't been too kind. We're in trouble, financially." I took out my phone and showed him the comment from Claudia, gave him a summary of our relationship.

"You're not these things this woman is saying about you," he said. "You know that, right?"

"Aren't I?" I reached for the burger, determined.

He touched the top of my hand, stilling me. "What does this prove?"

The palm trees swayed over our heads as cars from the nearby highway sped by.

"That they're right."

He narrowed his eyes.

"And they *are*," I said.

He slowly slid the paper plate of greasy meat away from me.

"Sounds like a crock of shit to me," he said. "I've watched you try and eat this for twenty minutes now. It's not happening. It's not *you*. What the fuck does this Claudia person know anyway?"

"It's just..." I swallowed hard against a throat that felt locked. "It's easier to stop fighting. I mean, I'm willing to keep going professionally for the sake of Wild Heart. But personally? I thought I might as well eat the damn cheeseburger."

"Have you checked the Lucky Dog donation page yet?" he asked.

I shook my head.

"A hundred and twenty-five thousand before I left tonight. And that's not including what's come in the mail. We're getting close to closing our funding gap. All of the dogs in our care right now are going to end up with loving homes because of *you*."

I pointed at Beck's chest. "That's because of *you*."

"Yeah, but the money helps, don't you think?" And there was that grin—that burst of sexy, charming lightness across his usually scowling face.

"It does," I said, slowly loosening.

"That's who you are, Luna," he said. "And *I'm* eating this burger."

A smile flew across my face so fast I worried I'd pulled a cheek muscle. Beck caught it, returned it—and for a sweet minute, we smiled at each other beneath the swaying palm trees. We hadn't *really* talked about Our Moment On The Beach—a moment I was fully prepared to escalate to a hot, gasping make-out on a public bench before he pulled back. We'd talked about what happened afterward, at Bluewater, but not those charged, heavy seconds.

And now here he was.

I could see his motorcycle in the parking lot. "My, uh, driver... .I sent him home for the night. Didn't want any witnesses to my rock bottom meat excursion."

Beck's gaze stayed locked on mine. "That's a good excuse for me to give you a ride home."

Do it do it do it do it—chanted the voices in my head that sounded an awful lot like my best friends.

"So this is a *date,* Beck Mason." I pointed between our paper plates. "You bought me a beer and some lettuce. And you're escorting me home on your motorcycle."

I expected him to tease me back. But instead he said, "It *is* a date. Our first one."

I tugged at the collar of my worn sweatshirt. All week I'd been asking Beck out on a date via text message and he hadn't replied. Meanwhile, Emily had been kind enough to troll through my closet and pick out 77 different potential first date outfits, none of which included this old University of Miami sweatshirt and basketball shorts. Had I even re-applied deodorant before coming over here?

"Well, okay, then," I finally said. "Although I've *heard* that boys with motorcycles have less-than-noble intentions."

"Not a boy," he corrected. "And you heard right."

"Come here often?" I finally asked, when I was able to function again after having Beck confirm his *less-than-noble intentions* toward me. My body felt hot, nerves fizzing.

"I come here at least once a week, sometimes with Elián," he replied. "Usually by myself. It's my favorite spot in town."

"Are you fairly solitary, Mr. Mason?" I asked.

Beck took a bite of his burger and I watched his jaw work. "I like people. But I might like dogs more."

"A lot of people connect more easily with animals," I said. "Do you like parties? Festivals? Concerts?"

He shook his head. "I like, well, this. One on one conversation. I like Elián, my best friend. And Wes and Jem." His cheeks went the slightest shade of pink beneath his beard. "I like you."

Beneath our tiny table, he slid his knee between my legs. I placed my hand on his knee, squeezed.

"Rooms with a lot of people make me nervous," he said. "I spent most of my childhood at the MC's old clubhouse. We had a house about a mile away, but the clubhouse was where everything happened. They didn't see any issue with their son playing with blocks in the corner while guns were being waved around."

I paused in the act of bringing a slice of tomato toward my mouth. Watched Beck.

"What was that like?" I asked, trying to keep my tone casual.

"Like spending every day with a live bomb in the middle of the room. And the fuse isn't lit but half the people in it have matches. Does that make sense?"

"It does," I said. Horrified. "Always waiting for the *potential* of explosion."

Beck took a long drink of beer. "Juvie was like that, although most of the guys I was with weren't actually violent. Just... backed into a corner. It was always loud."

"Is that why you don't like being the center of attention?"

"Where I come from, having eyes on you isn't safe," he said after a beat. "Less attention, less trouble."

Beneath the table, I squeezed his knee harder. His left hand found mine and intertwined our fingers together, swiping his thumb in circles on the inside of my wrist.

"Speaking of," he said. "Elián informed me this evening that I have to actually start doing my job."

"For real?" I asked.

"Yeah, yeah." He grinned. "No more chasing down stray dogs. Lucky Dog needs to invest. Speak to the public. Go to events. Start thinking long-term."

"It's a hard shift, but you'll do it," I said. "I experienced the same thing once Wild Heart was really taking off. It's hard to leave the front line but you have the makings of a true leader, Beck Mason."

"Don't lie," he said, edge to his voice.

"I'm not lying," I replied. "And are you asking for my help?"

He nodded.

"I've got some connections," I said. "What if I helped you find board members who have expertise in those areas?"

"Yes," he said. "Like that."

I brought my other hand to join his beneath the table. "What if we went to an event together? I could be your date."

"I wouldn't embarrass you?"

"Of course not," I said. Louder than I intended because Kristen's comments about my "association" with Beck suddenly reappeared in my anxieties. I'd thought I'd shaken off her insinuation that his supposed reputation was impacting Wild Heart. I allowed myself the briefest of fantasies—I *liked* picturing the two of us at an event together. I would be nothing but proud to have him on my arm.

But would it ultimately affect the success of Wild Heart?

Your detractors will be many.

"Luna?" he prodded.

I shook my head, re-focused on the gentle giant in front of me. Who looked so *dashing* all of a sudden I feared swooning off this rickety chair. Because Beck was watching me with such a happiness it caused my heart to kick around my chest like a soccer ball. What was *happening*? We were easily sliding head-first into this date and I hadn't felt this silly or relaxed or comfortable with a man in a long time.

Did those anxieties matter? Would the old Luna have cared even one bit?

"Nothing. Just picturing how devastatingly handsome you would look in a suit," I said.

He popped a French fry into his mouth. Winked at me.

Yep. I was definitely going to swoon off this damn chair.

"So, uh... what first date questions do you want to ask me?" I asked. "Zodiac sign... favorite color...?"

"Why did you choose a job in makeup?" he asked. "I've been wondering."

"Oh," I said, surprised. "Well, I *love* makeup and I always have. The beauty industry is a source for a lot of harm in this country and in many others. And I thought, if I could have an impact on *one* bad thing it could do a lot of good. Cosmetics is a $170 billion industry. It gets a lot of attention, it's on every television screen and magazine. If I could create a cosmetics company that was dedicated to values of justice then maybe other industries would follow."

I tapped my beer against Beck's. "It's why it's more than *one* dog that you rescue. Just like Wild Heart is more than *one* sale of lipstick. It multiplies, radiates, *expands* every day."

Beck looked at me. Looked down at the remaining half of my cheeseburger.

"Luna."

"Beck."

"I have an idea."

"What is it?" I leaned back on my palms, content with the sun warming my legs and this man's palms gripping my knees.

"I want to take your picture for Instagram. With the burger."

36

BECK

"*B*ut you caught me at a low point," Luna said, pointing at the grease dripping from my cheeseburger. "This isn't for public consumption. I still can't believe you saw me doing that on our *first date*."

"Could it be for your fans?" I asked. "And I'm honestly asking, not judging."

Luna bit her lip, putting down the burger. She moved to braid her hair but I caught her fingers. Brought her hand to my mouth and kissed her palm instead.

And then I kept holding her hand.

Holding Luna da Rosa's hand. When was the last time I'd experienced handholding?

It was romantic—just our fingers, sliding back and forth. Her bare thigh beneath my palm under the table. When I'd seen her sitting at this table, about to stuff a burger into her mouth, I'd sworn it was a waking dream.

But no.

Luna was sitting on a shitty lawn chair, holding a burger while wearing a ratty old sweatshirt.

I'd never seen anything more lovely in my life.

It was all of my hopes *and* all of my fears—letting her see the passion I had for her. Recognizing those same feelings in her eyes, the openness of her body. I could read her body language pretty well now and Luna was giving me all the green lights.

But she's still a fucking billionaire, an ugly voice chimed in. Easy to forget when she was dressed in a ragged sweatshirt that looked like it was from my closet. At the end of the night though, when I drove her home, it would be to her mansion.

"You mean tell my millions of Instagram followers that I almost became an actual hypocrite and ate all of this meat?" she asked me.

"Yes," I said.

Luna's lips started to curve, head tilting. I could practically see the gears turning in her head.

"It's almost *too* honest. Which means Jasmine would hate it," she said. "Which makes me want to do it more."

"Trouble in PR paradise?" I asked.

"Concerns," she said. "I'm having concerns. But that's not up for discussion tonight. Not on our first date." She chewed on her lettuce, thoughtful. "What would I say though?"

I lifted a shoulder, let her mull it over.

"I guess..." Her fingers tapped on the table. "I guess it's a reminder, right? I can take ownership of the ways that I've turned my back on my values. Let money take priority. And I can still be that girl at eleven who became a vegan and meant it. The people who hate me now, who think I'm a fraud, they can't...they can't..."

"They can't change you," I finished.

Her lips transformed into a full Luna-grin.

"I like it. The universe is telling me *yes*," she said.

"You can't say no to that," I said somberly. I grabbed her phone.

She looked down at herself. "Tell me the truth. Does this old sweatshirt and basketball shorts make me look trendy? Because I'm trying really hard not to try hard and by not trying hard I'm cooler than everyone else?"

"Sure," I shrugged.

"*Beck*." She laughed.

I reached forward and tucked a strand of wayward hair behind her ear. Swiped my thumb across her cheekbone. "When I saw you tonight you looked so lovely, I thought you were a dream."

She swallowed hard. "So I *do* look okay then."

I chuckled. "Hold up the burger. You'll walk me through how you look like, you know, you do?"

"Like an *Instagram influencer*," she teased. "If we were doing that it'd take hours. But I think your point is that I should be myself. No poses."

I pointed to the burger again. She dutifully held it. "I forgot to tell you. Penelope should be ready for adoption applications in a month."

Luna's face changed: happiness, joy, compassion. I hit *click*.

That was the real Luna da Rosa.

"Beck," she said, hands flying to her throat. "Oh, I'm so *thrilled* to hear that."

"I know," I grinned. "I can tell. And here's your picture."

"Nope," she laughed. "That's one of two hundred. Keep that finger limber, boss."

"I think we got it on the first try," I said softly. "Take a look."

She took the phone, examined her portrait. Gave me a strange look. "I... love it. Thank you."

"You don't actually have to post it," I said. "It could also be only for you and me. To commemorate our date."

She flushed prettily and put down the burger. "If that was the case, then you would have to be in the picture too."

"Is that so?"

"Yes. Although, now I'm upset with myself. If I'd known we were going on a date, I would have packed more flower crowns."

My lips tugged at the ends. "I'm... sorry I didn't answer you. Earlier. Words aren't my strong suit."

"That's right," she said, smirking. "I forgot I'm supposed to be kind of mad at you. Your text messaging flirt game needs some work. Because *no response* doesn't really make a girl swoon."

"Noted for the future," I said, repeating her words from the other night.

"You have to sweep her off her feet, show her how you feel, Mr. Mason. *Fireworks*." She wiggled her fingers in the air.

"Showing I can do. Actions I can do." Then I slid the table between us to the right. Reached forward and dragged Luna into my lap. She gasped as my arms wrapped around her waist.

"How's this?" My lips hovered an inch from hers.

"G—good," she whispered.

"Should we take that picture now?"

She nodded, eyes mischievous and locked on my mouth. "Yes, please."

"Do it then." I nudged my nose across her jaw.

With a playful smile, she held her phone out and snuggled against me. Flipped the camera around until I could see tiny versions of ourselves. As she prepared to take the picture, I leaned in and gave her a sloppy kiss on the cheek. *Click* went her phone as she exploded in laughter. I dragged my mouth across her cheek and buried my nose in her hair. I'd been dreaming of it since the night on the beach.

"Will you take me home now, Beck?" she asked, voice shaking.

"Of course," I said. She showed me her phone—I usually hated pictures of myself, hadn't taken one in years. I'd certainly spent more of my life frightening people than being admired. I knew some people found me sexually attractive, but I'd never once felt like I was a person with a face to be admired. Only feared. Despised, even. The recent news stories featuring my mug shots—which I'd thought I'd never see again—had made it clear how people felt about my face.

This picture, however, told a different story. Luna was laughing, filled with light, with my arms holding her tight. I looked happy as I kissed her, and she looked comfortable, and we could have been newlyweds for the obvious amount of trust between us.

My natural instinct to read body language sent back one message: *this is real, Beck.*

It had to be, right?

37

LUNA

*B*eck and I roared down the highway on his motorcycle, a crystal-blue ocean to our right that grew darker and darker as the sun set and the stars burst forth. Palm trees danced overhead as the engine's delicious vibration echoed between my thighs. I was breathless, free, leaning with Beck into every turn, aroused by the sight of his hands on this dangerous machine. The sexy competence of it all was enough to send my head spinning. On sharp turns, I just let myself feel—big man, loud bike, ocean breeze, salt air. The endless fear and turmoil that had plagued me since we'd first gotten the news about Ferris Mark was evaporating the faster Beck took us, the more curves we hugged as we raced toward home.

I didn't know what was going to happen next on this date. Didn't know if it was right or wrong, courageous or foolish, if it would make Jasmine happy or Sylvia cheer.

All I knew was that whatever *step* the universe had been pushing me toward this entire time I was ready for now.

So, *so ready*.

Bluewater was beautiful drenched in moonlight as we

pulled in, the still water sparkling, my eccentric neighbors taking evening strolls. As Beck slowed to a gentle speed, I caught the eyes of Mr. and Mr. Jones, who were retired business executives, at least in theory, although Daisy, Cameron, Emily and I had spent a lot of nights over a lot of cocktails debating whether or not they were international spies. We swung past the lagoon where I could make out Steve's tail—our resident alligator who'd lost his leg to a boat prop. Of everyone in the community, I was the most comfortable taking rotisserie chicken to feed our scaly friend, who seemed to have a soft spot for me. We circled the airfield, where I glimpsed Emily and Derek, dressed to the nines and boarding a helicopter. He was probably sweeping my best friend up and away to a fancy, romantic dinner.

Which meant, as we curved around our ovary-shaped block toward my house, that left only Cameron and Daisy as potential *spies*. While their houses were innocuously dark, they'd both invested in infrared glasses for gossip-mongering purposes.

I pressed my cheek harder to the space between Beck's shoulder blades, desperate to breathe in his scent one last time. He idled us across my long driveway, beneath the palm trees, then behind ten-foot-tall hedges lit with tiny white fairy lights. My garage held no cars but was instead a converted open studio for yoga and meditation, lit with dangling teal and magenta lamps. The whole scene cast us in a muted, colorful glow as he pulled to a stop—moon overhead, waves nearby, the constant splash of the fountain.

"This is me, as you know," I said. I was wrapped around Beck like a spider monkey but I couldn't move. I was too busy jumping mental hula-hoops, trying to figure out if I should invite Beck Mason into my home. I wanted to, even if we didn't *do* anything but drink cups of ginger tea and stare at each other by the pool. Even if he held my hand as I—

"I haven't been on a date in a long time," he said, voice husky, "but I think at some point one person has to let go."

"Are you sure? I've heard one person carries the other person on their back for the rest of the night. So joke's on you, Beck."

He chuckled quietly. Wrapped his hands around mine and held on tight. I hadn't realized how much I was craving this strangely intimate backward hug, but now that I was getting it I soaked it in.

"You don't have to go anywhere, Luna," he said.

"I do though," I said, already envisioning an inbox that would basically *scream* at me until I tackled the mountains of messages. "As much as I'd love to keep doing whatever this is."

I slid from the back. Removed my helmet and placed it on the ground. Shook out my hair way more dramatically than I needed to—but Beck seemed to like my hair and I liked teasing Beck.

"When was the last time you were on a first date?" I asked, shaking the wayward strands from my face.

"A very long time," he said. "Not a lot of bar hook-ups end in first dates."

"Ah," I said. "I see."

"When was the last time you saw Carrot?"

I tapped my lip, pretending to think. "I squeeze him in between Kale and Basil." He was smiling, but I wanted to give him a serious answer too. "I go on dates, lots of dates. I hook up with guys but it doesn't mean much to me. I love *love* in this world, cultivating it, giving it space to grow between people, between people and the environment. But..." I tilted my head in the moonlight. "It's never been my personal priority. Wild Heart is number one."

"Ah," he repeated my own words. "I see."

"Actually, let me clarify," I said. "I've had many dates. But none like this one."

"Okay," he replied

"We should do it again sometime, is what I mean."

Beck was straddling his bike and devouring me with a look so sexually hungry, I took a step back, dazed. His body vibrated with a restrained passion that I was desperate to see unleashed. But his whole vibe *also* screamed *I'm a gentleman* and so I doubted I'd get to see that side of him tonight.

"Okay," he repeated.

"What did I tell you about *fireworks*, Beck?" I said. "You've got to show a girl that you—"

A thick arm banded around my waist and pulled me to his chest.

On the bike, he was closer to my height and my brain over-loaded being face-to-face with a man this devilishly hand-some. This sincere, this compassionate. This *kind*.

His fingers were in my hair, confident, tilting my head back.

And then I was being kissed. Kissed. *Kissed by Beck Mason.* His lips were strong beneath that beard, movements deliber-ate, a rough kiss of feeling but also sensual, sweet. His hands held me still as his mouth moved with mine, drank me in, ravaging my lips with expert precision.

With a deep growl, he grabbed my ass and yanked me so I was straddling him on his bike. My arms wrapped around his neck and I pressed every single inch of my body against his massive one. One heartbeat, one ragged breath. Between my legs, his cock was as hard as the metal bars behind me—but his fingers caressed up my spine, my jaw, the nape of my neck. He kept kissing me, stealing my breath, searing our lips together while knuckles trailed along my neck. Those strong lips left my mouth, nipped at my jaw. One kiss along my throat... another... then another. His teeth scraped my skin as I fisted my hands in his white shirt and shuddered. A kiss, a bite, the tip of his tongue licking into my mouth, parting my lips. Our rejoining was filthier now, hungrier—evidenced by the out of control moans coming from the back of my throat. I wasn't sure who was gasping, who was clutching. Part, breathe, kiss—his lips were sure, the kiss absent of any awkwardness. The kiss was Beck showing me his desire with his mouth and tongue.

It was the most exquisite seduction of my life.

With a barely restrained snarl, Beck yanked me, positioning my sex right over his rigid, jean-clad erection. We finally, *finally,* parted, both of us dragging in deep breaths, staring at each other. I was wrapped around him on his motorcycle behind my privacy bushes and so turned on I felt faint.

"Luna," Beck said, scraping those teeth against my neck.

"Yes, Beck?" I let out a long sigh, shivering.

"Since this is our first date, I'm not going to fuck you." He closed his teeth around my throat. Bit hard. A mark of possession.

I loved it.

"Oh... okay," I said, voice shaking. I was reaching the point where coherent speech was no longer possible.

"I'm a gentleman."

"Bullshit."

His chest rumbled with laughter—but he rolled his hips expertly and my head fell back at the intense sensation.

"Oh, *god,* okay, I take it back."

"I'm a gentleman, which means I won't fuck you, sweetheart. But I am going to make you come right now." Another roll. "If that's what you want?" He paused, drew my chin down so we could lock eyes. "Is that what you want?"

"Yes," I said.

"Perfect," he said, nipping my lip. "Because I'll make you come just like this."

"Yes, *yes*," I sobbed. He was rolling his hips, thrusting up, a rhythm maddeningly slow, gloriously perfect. Our bodies writhed together like we'd been born doing this, dry-fucking each other on the back of a motorcycle. It would have been filthy—it *was* filthy—but it was also such a graceful expression of human lust I couldn't stand it. I gripped his thick hair and crashed my mouth onto his, grinding hard right where I needed it. Beck squeezed my flesh, spread my ass cheeks, kept me in place as our tongues danced.

I grasped the ends of my sweatshirt and tossed it over my head. His gaze competed for the night air in heat-levels, and both felt sultry, velvety. Off went my sports bra, because suddenly I needed to be bare-breasted in front of this hungry man.

"*Luna*," Beck bit out. He pressed our foreheads together, admiring my half-naked form. "Can I touch you there?"

"Please," I said softly, kissing his hair. I could feel his breath on my nipples, his rough palms skating up my ribcage. When they landed on my breasts it was almost too much sensation—I was still grinding myself shamelessly on his cock, and now his thumbs were stroking my skin, pebbling my nipples as he peered at me with a look of abject wonder.

"I want you to keep grinding on me," Beck said firmly, "and I want you to listen to every fantasy I've had about you since the day we fucking met."

"I thought..." I sighed, "I thought you weren't good with words, Mr. Mason."

Another bite—sharper this time. "Call it inspiration."

I smiled a little, leaned back on the handlebars to give him a shameless show of my hips working over his body. "Tell me."

He leaned forward, sucked my breast into his mouth with a greedy groan. "Every night, I fuck my fist and take you in a million different ways, sweetheart." His fingers tangled in the ends of my long hair, giving me a slow, gentle pull until my breasts arched fully into his face. He licked his tongue along my cleavage, lapping at the drop of sweat there. "I fuck you filthy and fast. Slow and long. Hard." Beck gave me a particularly intense thrust and I had to muffle a cry. "I've bent you over this bike, eaten your pussy on my kitchen table. Taken you in my shower again and again and again."

"The... the shower?" I gasped. That was a special fantasy of mine. "More. Tell me more."

Beck's hot mouth moved to my other breast, tasting me like a dessert he'd waited a lifetime to savor. His tongue flattened, stroked, while his cock kept *pressing* at my clit. "All that hot water, Luna. All that steam. Your naked body against glass while I fuck you from behind in the spray."

There was a tightening at the base of my spine, my body expanding and contracting with every dirty word out of his mouth. "Can you picture me there, Luna? Your face pressed to the wall while I slide inside you?"

Oh, I could. Beck would stretch me, and there'd be a bite of pain followed by the sweetest friction in the entire world.

"You would feel like paradise," he said, grinding me roughly now.

Getting me there, close, close, *close*. I was so out of my mind I had to bury my face in his neck and sob.

"I think about fucking you in your office."

"I want... I want that, Beck," I mumbled, reaching a precipice, racing towards it. I was grinding on Beck Mason on his motorcycle, mindless with it, while he muttered sex fantasies into my ear.

"Can you picture me there, under your desk?"

I sobbed a *yes*.

"Don't you think a woman like you deserves to have a man on his knees with his mouth between her legs?"

"So close..." I chanted. "Oh, *god*. It's too good."

"Nothing's too good for you, Luna," he praised. "Fuck me, sweetheart. Take what you deserve."

He gripped my cheeks and slammed our mouths together. It was the kind of kiss that obliterated your senses. It sent stars spinning and waves crashing as I climaxed. Aftershocks burst like pops of color while I sucked in heaving gulps of humid night air.

And then Beck, pulling me hard to his massive chest and *holding me*. Stroking my naked, slick skin. Kissing my temple. When our eyes finally met, my heart leapt with pure, unfiltered joy.

While my brain said *uh-oh*.

Beck Mason had given me The First Kiss to End All Kisses, after a surprise first date that both delighted and comforted me, after weeks of watching his shy grins, his kind actions, his true heart—all the many ways he moved through this world with real compassion. He performed beautiful deeds for this world every day, on purpose and without an audience.

Uh-oh.

My body was shifting, releasing the lust, the heady arousal. Welcoming even more *feelings* for him. I was falling, I was sure of it. What else could explain this weightlessness?

Beck's thumb traced my bottom lip. "For the record, Luna —that's how I show a woman how I feel."

Fireworks.

38

LUNA

J woke up a changed woman.
　　　　Literally.

The sun streamed in through my white, gauzy curtains—
and my first sense was birdsong, ocean waves. It was another
balmy morning in Miami.

The memory of last night came roaring back, momentarily
stealing my breath. The Kiss. That orgasm. My body writhing
against Beck's massive one, on his bike, in the middle of my
courtyard. The sensations had been otherworldly, not like
anything I'd ever experienced before with any other lover. I
wanted him here now, naked, in my bed—wanted the ability
to explore every plane of his body with my mouth, wanted
Beck gasping, unable to take any more pleasure.

Except he would, right? His passion for me felt like an
endless thing in the most beautiful way. Never before had I
actually experienced the feeling of being devoured.
Worshipped. The knowledge of that infused my mind with
thoughts I hadn't let myself examine for a long time.

Thoughts about compassion. Image. Money.

My gold rings were stacked next to a picture of my parents

and me in my early twenties, grinning cheesily on a random hiking trail, packs strapped to our backs. My parents were both teachers, as big-hearted as you could get, and yet their actions weren't monetized. My entire life they had quietly toiled, volunteering with me when they could, helping their neighbors, teaching their students with kindness. Spending time with me in nature, always gently encouraging my attention to the connections that existed between all of us. Every leaf and grain of sand as integral to our planet as the tusk of an elephant, a white whale, stray cats and honeybees. It was one, harmonious web—which was why every action we took as human beings had a reaction, no matter how small. For them, it was no act. And really, my compassion wasn't an act either—it felt as essential to my body as water, as air.

"Namaste, bitch." Daisy was standing on my patio, waving excitedly at me through the glass of the patio door. Behind her, of course, were Cameron and Emily.

I jumped, clutching the sheets to my chest.

"What do you want?" I mock-yelled, waving them away half-heartedly. "I'm naked and thinking about Beck."

"Girl, I *bet* you are," Cameron cheered. "Get dressed. It's not Sunday but we brought you surprise Drag Queen Brunch."

I cheered, shaking my wild hair loose. A glance at my phone let me know I was in meetings for eight straight hours until I could *finally* sneak away to Lucky Dog before dinner. Eight *long* hours where I knew I'd be distracted by thoughts of Beck all day.

But I had forty-five minutes before I had to get ready for work—it was barely 6:30 in the morning, but when your best friends were adept at running the world, they carved out time to bring you brunch at dawn. Mordecai's Bistro hosted an extremely popular Drag Queen Brunch on Sundays that all four of us attended once a month. It was our special, sacred time to overindulge and gossip and laugh our way through whatever rough things had come up during the week. It also had the added benefit of being a meeting space for four local romance authors that we all read and followed *obsessively*.

I tossed on a sundress and slipped barefoot out onto the patio, where Roxanne was already setting up coffee and bright yellow bowls of ripe mangoes and sliced oranges. I placed a hand on her shoulder, thanked her, and joined my best friends at the infinity pool. They'd laid out the best vegan breakfast that Mordecai's offered—complete with mimosas.

"A kiss for you, you, and *you*," I said, kissing each one on the top of the head. Emily and Cameron were both dressed in stylish running clothes while Daisy wore a hot-purple tracksuit. "This is literally the nicest thing ever."

Emily held out a donut, teasingly—and when I reached for it, she yanked it away. "You can only have this if you tell us about what happened with Beck last night."

I snatched it, bit into it with a fake growl. "I'll spill all the deets. But I need your help with blowing up my reputation on Instagram."

"Go on," Daisy said, lifting her sunglasses.

"Last night I almost ate a bacon cheeseburger from a burger stand off the highway called Mel's."

There was a long pause. And then Cameron said, "*Thank god.*"

I snorted. "I only contemplated doing it because I felt wretched."

"Cameron means thank *god* you're a human being," Emily said, patting my hand. "I mean, we know you're a human being. An extremely good human being. But being tempted doesn't make you weak. It makes you real."

I shook my head. Watched a trio of birds land in the palm tree closest to me. "Is that how I come off though? Not real?"

My best friends exchanged a look. "You're a billionaire, Luna. A smart one. A savvy one. The media might play at making you out to be a glittery Instagram influencer, but we all know that beneath that flower-crown is the mind of a savage businesswoman," Emily said. "You couldn't have gotten here without it, that ability to see an opportunity and use it to your advantage."

I trailed my toes through the warm water. "But?"

"You're almost too aware of your brand," Cameron said. "Which isn't a criticism, really. Because we all are. But I think if there's anything that's coming from this Ferris Mark shit, it's that the public's opinion is mercurial, impossible to predict, and impossible to truly cultivate. You, Luna da Rosa, have to exist within the middle of that feeling proud of who you are and your decisions. They'll love you *and* hate you regardless of what you do."

I tilted my head, picked up a slice of orange. "Sylvia said something similar to me last week."

"What does all of this have to do with burgers and Beck?" Daisy prodded.

"Look at the picture he took of me last night." I crawled closer, showed them my phone. In the picture I look like, well... myself. "Beck thought I could tell people about *not* eating this burger. Not giving in to the lies they're telling about me."

"You need to post that," Emily said. "Take it from someone who's now very seriously dating a fixer. The public loves it when you're truly real. Not that you should do it for that. But that you should do it as, I don't know, a hard reset? How you're truly going to be open and accountable moving forward?"

"Your actions in public and your actions in private being

one and the same," I said, bringing the tips of my fingers together. I'd been mulling this over since meeting Beck. You could say a lot about his surly attitude, but he didn't change his behavior for anyone. Public *or* private. Even with the sudden reappearance of his past, and his family, in the media all over again.

"I'm going to do it," I said, biting my lip on a smile. "Whatever shit people want to keep throwing at me *and* Beck is stickier than I would have imagined. I've done everything I can. Apologized publicly. Fixed the problem. Implemented better policies so the same mistake can't repeat itself. Rededicated myself to my values." I felt buoyed by the warm, kind smiles of my friends. "I have to keep living now."

Daisy handed me another donut. "And you can start by eating this second donut."

"That works. I'm *starving*." I devoured it in seconds.

"Speaking of starving," she continued, "tell us you sexed with Beck last night and are going to marry him and have a bunch of bearded babies."

I wrinkled my nose. "Not exactly. But our first kiss was so amazing I literally came."

Cameron started to slow clap and I threw a piece of donut at her.

"And...?" Emily said.

I bit my lip, taking my phone back to swipe to the very last one. If Beck's life was the ability to prioritize *actions* over *words* then this picture said it all. I placed the phone on the concrete between the three of them. Sat back and watched their reactions.

Emily was the first to react—her entire face lit up, like a switch being thrown. And then she reached over and grabbed my hand, squeezing tightly.

"Oh, Moon," she said. "You're falling in *love*."

39

BECK

ourteen hours, fifty-five minutes and... shit, how many seconds had it been?

I scrubbed a hand down my face, fought the urge to pace our administrative offices. Next to me, Jem had set up a table with ingredients in our makeshift kitchen, where we brewed pot after pot of coffee and ate slices of pizza on Fridays. It had a stove, an old refrigerator and a microwave. That morning, I'd asked Jem if she'd ever seen Luna mention anything *vegan* that she liked. She had screamed the words *peanut butter chocolate bars*. Right in my fucking ear. So now Jem was lining a piece of wax paper while I stirred maple syrup and peanut butter with clumsy motions.

"She'll love them," Jem said, nudging me with her shoulder. "I promise. Is there an occasion?"

"Um." I stirred and stirred. "To say thank you."

"For what?"

For giving me the greatest kiss I'd ever experienced and for climaxing on my cock like a dark-haired angel.

"Everything she's done. You know, the money or whatever."

"Sure." Jem smirked, placing a bowl of chocolate into the microwave. "That doesn't sound like a lie at all."

Wes kicked the front door open and yelled, "Guess who's getting adopted *today*." He had Betty and Veronica in his arms. Jem had given them tiny pink bows for their collars and they tilted their heads as Wes spun around.

I grinned. "Jimmy coming by today?"

"He is, boss. And he's mad excited. He told me he's happy he has a two-bedroom apartment since he's planning on Betty and Veronica here having their own space to really stretch out."

"The right match," I said. Jem nodded in agreement.

"When's Luna coming by today?" Wes asked. "I need to talk to her about *Bachelor in Miami* last night."

"Any minute now," I said, attempting to inject as much casualness in my voice as I could muster.

And it's been fourteen hours, fifty-eight minutes and fuck it, it'd been too much time since I'd said good night to Luna after our date. I'd carefully tugged her shirt back on, given her another kiss, made sure she'd gotten in the front door safely, and then rode home with the dopiest grin on my face. A grin that was still on my face.

Wes and Jem had been giving me shit about it all day.

Elián, however, had clapped me on the back and said, "I'm happy for you."

Nothing had happened. It was one date. One kiss. One orgasm.

And yet it felt, to me, as if everything had happened.

This morning Luna had also posted the picture of her and the cheeseburger. She had that hopeful-happy-compassionate look on her face. The caption read: *Hey there Wild Heart fans: You might have noticed the internet has had some choice words to say about me and my values over the past few weeks—especially about one of my deepest-held values: the rights of animals. I cannot begin to tell you the extent of my regret for our involvement with Ferris Mark and I remain dedicated to ensuring a mistake like that never, ever happens again. But on a personal note, I've been a dedicated vegan since I was eleven years old. Yesterday, disparaged and hopeless, I took a stab at eating this burger and abandoning my beliefs: giving in to the absolute worst of what people have said about me.*

I couldn't do it. Regardless of my mistakes, that value cannot be taken from me—not by trolls or mean commenters or trashy media or hurtful gossip. This is what lives in my heart and it is mine and mine alone. Please don't give up on me—and please don't ever give up on your values. Treasure them.

A friendly reminder to go donate to Lucky Dog when you have a chance. It is a truly special place. And if anyone on this page says another WORD about Beck Mason that isn't positive, I will block you. Love and light—Luna

It was the growth I'd seen Luna going through these past two weeks. But she'd also defended me. It didn't feel like a post that was using me or my nonprofit—but embracing my past, for better or worse.

It was dangerous—this hope that what she and I had could be real.

As I stirred chocolate, I kept glancing out the window—which meant I saw Luna first, floating through the campus. She stopped at Penelope's kennel for more than fifteen minutes. I could see her lips moving, watched her stick one finger through the bars and gently stroke Penelope's nose. Saw the way that beach mutt stared at Luna like she understood she was her rescuer. Luna was dressed in a long skirt with blue flowers and a white tank top. White flowers were braided into her hair. And when she burst into the admin trailer, my team admired her like she was royalty.

"My people," she exclaimed, throwing her hands into the air. Jem giggled and let Luna pull her in for a hug. She kissed Betty, then Veronica, and then gave Wes a kiss on the cheek that had him blushing.

"Wes, what if I told you I booked us a tour of the *Bachelor in Miami* house?"

"Shut up," he said. "You didn't. Jimmy is gonna *flip.* Can I bring him?"

"Of course," she said. "Or anyone else here or at Lucky Dog or in your life that you'd like." Jem was carefully mixing the final pieces of the peanut butter bars, so she missed Luna nodding her head and winking at my green-haired staff member.

"Oh," Wes said. "Um... yeah. Lemme think about who I'd bring and I can let you know?"

"Sure thing," she exclaimed. "And please tell me these pups are going home today."

"My buddy Jimmy is coming by in a bit to adopt them."

"Beautiful," she said, finally allowing her dark-eyed gaze to slide my way. "Hello, Beck."

"Hello, Luna," I said.

She ran a hand through her hair, and the heat in her expression sent blood rushing to my cock. "What are you making, boss?"

"Jem helped me cook this dessert for you," I said.

She glanced down into the pan. "Beck Mason, did you bake me chocolate peanut butter bars?"

"Yes," I said simply.

Her arms slid around my waist. It startled me, this public affection. But hadn't she hugged and kissed everyone else in the room?

I wrapped my arms around her and let my lips fall on top of her head.

I didn't miss the bug-eyed look that passed between Wes and Jem.

"Thank you," she said. "They're my favorite."

I winked at Jem over Luna's head. "I might have had an inside source."

Luna pulled back, but not very far. She leaned against the counter and dipped her finger in the chocolate. "Beck Mason. Vegan chef."

I lifted a shoulder. "I'm a man of many talents."

She smirked. "I had an idea this morning that I think Jem can help me with. I'm still totally down to keep using my platform to raise money for Lucky Dog. But I think the *right* thing to do is help Lucky Dog create its own platform. Just to keep things, you know, on the up and up."

Luna caught my eye. "Things are changing and I want to ensure Lucky Dog is ready for success, regardless of what people might say. The real benefit of me being here is raising awareness and having a digital footprint that captures that."

"You're sure about that?" I asked, one eyebrow raised. One last burst of stubborn privacy appeared. But then I thought about stories like Jimmy's. True stories, stories I could tell.

"It's time to toss those rotary phones and enter the 21st century, Mr. Mason," Luna said.

"Okay," I said.

Wes and Jem's heads whipped my way.

"What? It's so strange I'm saying *okay* to this?"

"When will the plague of locusts get here?" Jem asked, tapping her chin.

"And I think Jem should run it," Luna finished.

"Me?" Jem asked.

"Yeah, you," Luna said, nudging her hip.

"What if we interviewed Jimmy about why he's adopting Betty and Veronica?" I suggested.

Luna's eyes widened. "That's a great idea."

"And I'll be in it," I said, pausing to spread chocolate across the pan of bars.

"It's locusts before the four horsemen, right?" Jem said behind me.

"Smart-ass," I said, chuckling. "Whether we wanted it or not, Luna coming here has both exploded Lucky Dog and brought back all of the shit about my parents and the MC. I don't have any excuses left, do I? I have to be who I am and fuck anyone else."

Luna crossed her arms across her chest and gave me a lazy, pleasing perusal. "Funny. I was having this same conversation with my best friends this morning."

We shared a smile.

"Listen," I said. "You should know that Jimmy used to be a member of the Devils but not anymore. It's a strange coincidence. That okay?"

"Absolutely. You feel nervous about being on camera?"

"Absolutely," I repeated. My gut was already churning. "I want Jem to set all of this up but I want this video to be on your page too. All of those followers should see this, right? If we want to have the best impact?"

Luna's face looked kind. She touched my arm lightly. "Spoken like a true executive director. And you're exactly right. It *will* have the best impact."

I ducked my head—but not before catching her secret smile at me.

"When will Jimmy be here?" she asked.

"Fifteen minutes. Hey, can I see you in my office for a minute? There's a financial report I thought you could help me with."

"Always," she said. "After you, boss."

I placed my hand low on Luna's back and led her from the

wandering eyes of my employees, who, I was sure, already knew that we were... dating? Was that what we were now? She waved to Elián, who was working with Beatrix. Blew a kiss at Penelope. Swung her hips as she walked into my office.

I had her up against the door as soon as I'd shut it. A second later I was lifting her up. I pinned her to the wall with my hips as my hands landed on either side of her face. The layers of her skirt fell away. Her bare legs wrapped around my body.

"Beck," she purred, "did you really bake me dessert?"

"To say thank you," I said. "For our date."

"You should kiss me now," she demanded.

Her full lips opened for me immediately. Our kiss last night had shown me that Luna and I were made for this.

We fit.

There was no hesitation, only a deep connection. This kiss was everything I'd dreamed of since I'd left her last night. Our mouths ravaged each other. My hips rocked, cock grinding against her pussy. Our breathing became ragged. Pants. Moans. Whimpers. It was zero to sixty with this woman and if I wasn't careful I was going to be fucking her through this door with the eleven minutes we had left before my interview.

"Luna, I can't stop thinking about you," I growled, mouth in her hair, her throat, teeth on her ear, hands, fingers, everywhere roaming, stroking. My hips thrust urgently between her legs and she was already trembling. "That's probably not professional or makes things complicated or fucks up your reputation or—" I was babbling, and I'd never actually done that in my entire forty years on this planet.

Luna gripped my face, lips swollen. "Today at work, I was thinking about you so much that I dropped our industrial-sized blender and it spilled frozen bananas all over the floor.

Then I spilled tea down my shirt and sent the same email four times to the same person."

I let a slow, easy smile slide up my face. "I guess we're on the same page."

She returned it. "I guess we are, *sir*."

I bit her lip and gave her a particularly vicious roll of my hips. "Luna, what did you mean in there about things changing?"

She threaded her fingers through my beard, tugged it hard. Just like I liked. "I've been learning a lot from you. I want to do what you said—doing good things but not for good media, or likes or subtle manipulation that gets fans to buy my products. I can still be... I think..." I kissed her forehead, "I want to be who I am *today* without losing the woman I was when I started Wild Heart."

"Everything you've done is the reason Lucky Dog can stay open," I told her.

"But I'm focused on being authentic," Luna said. "And if we're dating, I don't want all of that tangled up for people online, affecting *your* nonprofit. Besides, the glory really should go to Lucky Dog. I'm an innocent bystander."

"I saw your post," I said, kissing her temple. Her ear. "You stood up for me."

"Of course, Beck. You would do the same."

"Are we really dating?"

How many dates was *dating*? We were entering territory I hadn't walked through in years.

"Fucking me against the door in your office constitutes a second date," she whispered.

I slipped my palm beneath her skirt, out of my *mind* for this woman. What time was it? When did I need to do an interview in front of twelve million people? The only thing I could register was her slick flesh, the hungry cries that fell from her lips as I stroked her gorgeous cunt.

"I can be fast," Luna was saying, fingers flying to my belt. "Fast and quiet, which would surprise a lot of people—"

"Yo, boss?"

Luna and I went as still as statues, my palm landing over her mouth. Her eyes were laughing as I kept her pinned to the door Wes was banging on.

"Uh, yeah, Wes?"

Luna's shoulders were shaking. I smirked at her, removed my palm but placed a finger over her lips. She bit it.

"Jimmy is here and everyone wants to know when you're gonna be famous or whatever?"

"Right this second," Luna called, giggling. "He's coming."

"Cool beans, boss. See you in a sec."

"Cool beans," Luna repeated to me. But I silenced her silly expression with a tender kiss, sliding my fingers into her hair to hold her in place. When we parted, she was out of breath.

"Are you around later? I need to fuck you with my mouth."

"Jesus, Beck," she said, voice shaking. "Yeah... uh, yes. I'm around."

"Come here. After everyone leaves, okay?" I set her down gently, kissing her cheek. Arranged the layers of her skirt and straightened the straps of her shirt.

"Do I look suitably ravaged?" she asked.

"Not anymore," I said. I reached forward, took her hand. "Will you help me? With the video?"

"Of course. Anything you need."

She brushed lint from my shirt. "Let's go make it possible for you to rescue even more dogs, boss."

40

LUNA

*I*n twenty minutes, I'd worked my magic in the Lucky Dog administrative offices. I arranged two black chairs in the corner that looked the least drab and dreary. Then I set up Jem as the videographer and Wes as the treats-procurer, for whenever Betty and Veronica got antsy.

Jimmy ambled into the office and I was immediately struck by his size and his all-black outfit, not to mention the tattoos that scrolled across his neck.

"Are you Betty and Veronica's dog dad?" I asked.

His answering smile told me all I needed to know.

"Luna, your phone keeps ringing," Jem called to me. Her green hair looked practically neon—although maybe that was the light flush to her cheeks. That seemed to happen whenever Wes was around now.

"It's Jasmine. Ignore it," I said.

Because I certainly had been. In the past two weeks, I'd lost Wild Heart its most lucrative contract, had a trashy paparazzi picture taken of me that confirmed my burgeoning relationship with a man whose family ran Miami's most notorious crime family, *and then* I'd posted an inflammatory picture of myself talking about how I'd *almost* eaten a cheeseburger.

Jasmine was furious with me.

And I hadn't missed the many, tiny ways in which she was trying to manipulate my image.

She'd called me seven times in the last hour, even though I'd informed my staff that I would be here all night. I was even contemplating playing hooky tomorrow. Which I'd never done. Ever. Not even from the varied waitressing jobs I'd held throughout high school and college.

Except Beck Mason was standing right next to me, holding a Yorkie so tiny it fit in the palm of his giant hand. Stroking its fur with a gentleness that never ceased to astonish me. And the thought of whisking that man away for a day of unbridled freedom was too tempting to ignore.

"What?" he asked, when he caught me staring.

"Nothing," I said, smiling. "You look handsome for the camera."

He looked down at his usual uniform of white undershirt and jeans. "I guess."

"Go sit over there." I pointed toward the chairs and Jimmy and Beck deposited themselves into them—even though their combined bulk made the chairs look comically small. "We'll be filming this live. If you mess up, just go with it. No one will know. We want people to see what an adoption day looks like at Lucky Dog, so be yourselves. Casual."

They both nodded—stoic.

"The chemistry between you two is electric," I said with a smile. "What's that on your lap by the way?"

"My questions," Beck said. "I don't want to forget them."

I gave him the thumbs-up and Jem the go-ahead. "Ready in thirty seconds?"

"Wait." The edge in Beck's voice caught my attention. He

crooked his finger at me. I walked over, crouched next to him. Jimmy seemed distracted by his two adorable dogs. "You're not going to be in this with me?" Beck whispered.

I bit my lip. "I want this to be for you, Beck. Not for me. This is bigger than rebuilding my reputation. This is making sure that moments like this"—I looked over at Jimmy—"continue to happen. It has to come from you."

That blinding vision I'd experienced this morning hadn't abated. And the first step was making sure I was truly propping up Lucky Dog—and not only my ego or reputation.

Beck looked away, cleared his throat. "Okay."

I placed a hand on his knee, squeezing until he looked back at me. "I'll be right here, beaming at you."

A flicker of a smile. "I'll need it."

"You're a leader, Beck Mason. No one can take that away from you." I swished back over to Jem and said, "Let's start."

For a second, Beck and Jimmy were frozen in place, probably entranced with that red, blinking light I knew could cause a rush of stage fright. I did as promised—giving Beck as much of a brilliant smile as I could, until I felt him exhale in response.

I winked—and he barely concealed a grin.

"Thank you, everyone, for watching," Beck said. "My name is Beck Mason and I'm the executive director of Lucky Dog."

Behind me, Elián was standing, leaning against the wall of the trailer. Jem sat next to me, Wes off to the side. We were all staring at Beck.

"For the past three weeks, Luna da Rosa has been working and volunteering here. She has done a lot for us here and we can't thank her enough." Beck looked toward me and I could feel a deep flush in my cheeks. I was trying to push the spotlight off myself, but there was no way I could deny what those words meant to me. "We have been struggling to raise money and when Luna met us, we were at risk of closing our doors in thirty days if the funds didn't come. Luna has made that happen. And that is why we're here today. To show what donations make happen at Lucky Dog." Beck looked at Jimmy, who waved into the camera. In his lap, the Yorkies sat patiently, looking like dogs in a dog food commercial.

I caught Jem's eye. *Perfect*, I mouthed.

"Jimmy is adopting two dogs today, a bonded pair named Betty and Veronica. We rescued them from a hoarding situation, where they were being kept with forty-seven other dogs on a large property outside of Miami. They were starving when we found them."

Jimmy's jaw clenched.

Beck looked at his piece of paper. "What does this mean to you, Jimmy?"

The other man blew out a breath. "I mean, I'll be honest, if that's okay?"

Beck nodded.

Jimmy touched a tattoo on his arm. "Things are changing for me. I need to live a life that's more..." he thought for a second "... legal."

"That's good," Beck said, with a shadow of a smile. "We're very supportive of *legal*."

"Where I was before, the people I was with before—" Jimmy looked pointedly at Beck. "It wasn't really a situation where you were accepted for being who you are. The pressure to do things you didn't want to do was huge and I... well, I hated it. It felt like a vise was around my chest all the time. Like I couldn't breathe."

I watched Beck, who seemed to be struggling a little bit to keep a neutral expression. Jimmy was talking about his time with the Miami Devils. I was sure of it.

"When I finally left that situation, I wanted to experience

love. Caring for something that wasn't only me and my needs. Working towards kindness, giving and receiving." Jimmy peered at the dogs in his lap with pure adoration. I blinked— and tears were already rolling down my cheeks.

Jem's hand landed between my shoulder blades.

"Dogs will do that," Beck said simply.

"Fuck yeah, they will," Jimmy said. Then he looked right at me and said, "Sorry for cursing."

"Cursing is allowed," I said in a stage whisper.

Beck looked back at his paper. "Why rescue though? Why Lucky Dog?"

"I don't know, man," Jimmy said, smiling. "People make a lot of assumptions about me. Probably do to you, huh?"

"About what?" Beck asked.

"Your value."

Now it was my turn to look at Jem and Wes. Wes was swallowing hard, over and over. Jem's eyes were shining. I reached down to take her hand.

"My lack of value, you mean," Beck said.

Jimmy laughed sardonically. "Exactly. I ain't rich. I'm not smart. I've got nothing to show for my life except a busted-up bike and, uh... well, my dogs." The reality of that—that he was beholden to these animals—draped over him like a blanket. But it wasn't negative—it was pride, and not the bad kind.

The beautiful kind.

This. This moment right here, between these two people, was so real and raw I felt it *grip me.* Like a fist was closing around my body and yanking me forward. I was compelled, crying and squeezing Jem's hand.

"I guess I've always wanted to feel a love like that, you know?" Jimmy said. "And it pisses me off that we devalue people all the time. Pisses me off that we do it to dogs too. I

239

know they weren't like the nicest looking dogs when you got them. But that doesn't mean they don't deserve a home."

Beck swallowed thickly. "Yeah. I agree."

Beck looked at his paper again. It felt like the room was holding its collective breath. Because I could *see* what was happening on Beck's face. The turmoil there. But I didn't know what he wanted to say.

Beck Mason looked right at me, as if needing the comfort. I smiled—as full a smile as I could—and placed a hand over my heart. *You can do it*, I mouthed. Whatever it was he was going to do.

"So, uh," he started, clearing his throat, "it's not a secret anymore about who I am. It was actually never a secret. I'm a Mason. My parents run the Miami Devils MC and when I was a teenager, I served five different sentences in a juvenile detention facility. A lot of people have seen my mugshots now." He put his notes down. "It's hard to have your past dragged up by strangers. Made fun of. To have assumptions made about you. To be picked apart. But I don't want to feel shame about that. So I won't." Beck kept staring at me. "Because what does that say about people like you or me, who have done time but are back on the right path? Or have been involved in a criminal organization and gotten out? There's no shame."

"I think it's more like courage, don't you?" Jimmy said.

I was weightless again—heart wild and open and reaching toward Beck.

"A couple of weeks ago I wouldn't have said that. But I think you're right," Beck replied. "Courage."

Tears were streaming down Jem's face. I took the camera from her, held it steady—and held her in a one-armed hug with my free arm.

"I say all that because a dog did that for me. I never used to say that because I always worried I sounded foolish. But I did this program my last time in juvie where I worked with this dog. Willow." Beck's voice wavered at the end. "She was a real good girl. She's the reason I'm here. Without her..."

"Yeah," Jimmy said. "I get it. You need things in this life that are bigger than you."

My body was vibrating. That electric, hot-pink *glow* I'd gotten the day the idea for Wild Heart had struck into my brain like lightning was repeating itself. The universe was shaking wisdom loose for me and I knew what it was. Money. Good. Evil. The way it flows through our lives and touches everything, the impact it leaves.

What if Wild Heart started giving away money, like I'd always planned?

"That's why I started this place," Beck said. "It's about dogs. But it's also about people. The way they impact each other. And yeah. I don't want to live in a society that tosses anyone away—animals or people. We're not some huge fancy place and we never will be. But I guess I want to help as much as I can."

"You're doing a great job," Jimmy said. He turned to the camera. "Everyone should donate here."

They both laughed, the room lightening a little bit. Jem sniffed next to me.

"Everyone should donate here," Beck said. "And one last thing. Well, two, I guess. The more money we raise, the more dogs we can rescue. The more people we can help find something real, like Jimmy did. Please don't give up on us. We promise to keep expanding for as long as we can."

I looked at the camera, preparing to turn it off.

"The other thing was about Luna."

I shook my head. *No,* I mouthed. *About you.* I pointed at him.

"Luna da Rosa made a mistake and she's making it better,"

Beck said. "And I can personally say that she has more compassion and integrity in her little finger than most people do in their whole body. I trust her. And I believe in her." He coughed a little. "And thank you."

I clicked *off*. Glanced down at my phone to see the response to the live video. Checked it against the donation page.

"Well," I said, "the video was about ten minutes long and you raised another $100,000 in that time."

Elián *hooted* behind me and Jem screamed.

"Great job, boss," I said to Beck. If I didn't touch this man soon, I was going to lose my mind.

"Sure," he said. "We all did a great job."

Then I watched Beck hug Wes. Hug Jem. Whisper something in their ears that had them nodding.

When he walked over to me, he surprised me—placing a palm to my cheek.

"You didn't have to say those things about me," I said softly.

"Yes, I did," he replied.

Fireworks.

41

BECK

*T*hose ten minutes had been a rush.

And fucking terrifying.

A strange peace came over me at the end. Like a truth had been knocked free so I could show it to the world. According to Luna, millions of people were watching it.

In reality?

The only person in that room was Luna.

Even as Jimmy's words made me remember my own past, even as I watched Jem and Wes respond to a feeling we all could identify with—being *worthless* to the world.

But really, Luna da Rosa held my attention. She was the only one I was speaking to.

Two of the longest hours of my life went by—we sent Betty and Veronica home with Jimmy and busied ourselves with the usual. Luna and Jem trained Penelope. Elián helped me put everything I'd said into that video into a speech I could use. Wes counted checks and answered volunteer requests. It was a good goddamn day, sliding into a good goddamn night. And when seven o'clock hit, I sent everyone home.

Everyone except Luna.

The knock came at 7:02. For the past two hours, I'd been filled with lust and emotion. It wouldn't take much for me to become an animal. Luna stepped in, slid the door shut. There was a dirty paw-print in the middle of her white tank top. Her skirt was dusty at the ends. Her makeup was smudged. Luna was coming to me as authentic as she'd ever been.

"Lock the door," I said. I had to force the words through my tight throat.

She did. I nodded at the open blinds and she closed them with trembling fingers.

"Come here." I patted the spot on my desk directly in front of me.

She sat prettily in front of me, looking like a gift. I rolled my chair forward. Pulled the tie from her hair. Pressed my nose to the loose tendrils. Inhaled as she sighed. My arms came around her body and my hands knocked every fucking thing from my desk—highlighters, pens, cups, leashes, dog food, sticky notes. All of it clattered to the floor.

I sat back, placed my palms on her knees. Spread her legs slowly. All that hair fell in a curtain around her face.

"Thank you again. For what you said about me," she whispered. My fingers wrapped around her bare ankles, slid up her calves, shifting the fabric of her skirt, revealing delicious inches of skin. "I haven't been feeling very confident about myself recently."

"Luna." I meant to say more but her inner thighs were exposed now. I dragged my beard across them, nuzzling the skin. "*Luna.*"

"Yes?" Her voice shook.

I opened my mouth, breathing her in, tasting her. "I said those things because I like you. Because you've shown me the kind of person you really are." My fingers kept shifting, shifting. She tilted her hips so I could shove the material past her waist, exposing pale-pink underwear. "And I know you understand how thankful I am for your help."

"I do. Of course, I do."

"Good." I hooked my fingers into the lace and dragged them down her legs with an obsession—each tug, every part of her leg, the beautiful sight of her pussy right in front of my face. There for me to enjoy and explore.

I spread her legs further.

"Because now I'm going to fuck you with my mouth," I rasped, pulling her toward me by the hips. "Because I really like you, Luna. A lot. It's hard for me to express myself. But you should know this. And if you don't come on my face right now, I might fucking die."

I leaned into her wet folds and finally inhaled the *true* scent of her—earth, salt, sugar, woman—and I couldn't stop my tongue from swiping up her sex.

"*Beck*." A plea. My palms spanned the round curves of her ass. I squeezed, dragged her closer, and swept my tongue up and down. "I need... I need..."

"Anything you need, say it," I growled, eyes looking up at her from between her legs.

"I really like you too," she gasped, wrapping her fingers in my hair. She rocked her hips, brushing her clit against my mouth. I smirked and held her still. "My friends, they..." She was already panting. "They said I was *falling* for you."

"Is that true, sweetheart?" Endearments weren't my thing, but I'd called her *sweetheart* three times now. If any woman was my sweet *heart*, it was Luna da Rosa. I kissed the inside of her thighs, taking my time, biting her flesh. I smelled her arousal, could feel her legs already trembling and I'd barely licked her. This beauty was going to come from anticipation alone.

I'd never felt so alive, so in control, so *fucking vulnerable*.

"I've never felt this way about anyone. Ever," she whispered.

I stood so fast the chair fell over. Then I was bending Luna back, taking her mouth in a furious kiss. She moaned loudly, gripping my hair, spreading her legs even wider as my fingers caressed her pussy. I slid my index finger inside and was gripped by wet heat that had me fisting her hair. Pulling it. My palm grazed her clit and she cried out, head falling back, exposing her throat to my lips. She bent back farther and my mouth landed on her breasts, pulling her nipples through the fabric. I'd done this in my dreams and in my fantasies. The reality was even more beautiful.

I wasn't sure what to do with all this extra emotion. So I put it into my actions, pushing her back onto the desk and dropping to my knees. I shoved the rest of her skirt over her hips, dragged her ass to the edge of the desk, and dropped my tongue directly onto her clit.

"*Holy shit*," she cried out, almost laughing—but this wasn't going to be funny.

"Tell me when you first thought about this," I said. "About us."

Us.

I gave her clit a few long strokes that had breath coming fast through her nose.

"The day on the beach. I kept thinking... *god, that's amazing*... I kept thinking about your beard and what it would... what it would feel like." She gave in to a long groan. I pulled an even sexier sound from her lips when I fluttered my tongue lightly, sliding another finger into her heat. I rubbed my beard back and forth across her thighs and her back arched off the desk.

"*Yes*," she gasped. "That's what I thought about."

"What next?" I held her hips and swirled around her clit, fucking her slowly with my fingers.

"At the bar," she moaned. "I thought... I thought you were sexy. Hoped you would kiss me."

"I should have."

Her thighs tightened around my ears. "The first time on your bike. I pictured you pulling over on the side of the road and fucking me against the first building we found."

I thought of Luna's hair wrapped around my wrist, her palms flat on a brick wall, back bowed as I took her from behind.

"*I should have*," I grunted, then increased the pressure of my tongue. Firm, even strokes right against her clit as I stroked her from the inside.

"I wanted to suck your cock on that motorcycle, Beck, *Beck, Beck*." Her fingers yanked at my hair. I shoved her farther across my desk, sending even more meaningless office supplies tumbling to the ground. One leg hoisted over my shoulder as I licked her clit fast, hot.

No goddamn mercy.

"After you come on my tongue, you're going to drop to those knees and suck my cock, sweetheart."

She squealed at that, mouth wide, these breathy, sexy sounds tumbling from those lips. I did the fanciest tongue work of my life as she writhed and panted and yanked the hair from my head. I knew that everything about this moment was different, that everything with Luna would be *better*. The ugly voice in my subconscious was quieter now. Softer. Replaced by a feeling of trust.

My hand worked beneath those skirts and I palmed her

breasts with the other, let her nipples harden as I sucked her clit between my lips.

"Oh my god, like *that. Like that like that*—"

Luna climaxed with her entire body—screams, moans, limbs trembling, hands slapping down onto the desk as I held her to my face while she rode out the aftershocks. I would have happily kept going, licking her over and over until she tapped out. But that wasn't what she had in mind.

Not at all.

Luna da Rosa sat up on that desk. Put her foot on my chest and *shoved*. I fell back into my desk chair, surprised.

"What are you doing?" I asked, because I could have guessed and I wasn't sure I deserved it.

She leaned forward, palms on my thighs, and ghosted her lips along my ear. "I'm going to get on my knees and service you, *sir*. Like you told me. How does that sound?"

My fingers flexed on the chair. "You don't have to do that. Those were just words. A fantasy."

"You would deny me the pleasure of feeling your huge cock hit the back of my throat?"

My brain sparked, shorted. Went entirely black. My jaw felt seconds away from breaking. "Sweetheart."

"Mr. Mason." Her mouth teased mine, biting a little. "Why are you restraining yourself, Beck? You think I can't handle the beast?"

I growled at her, lip curled.

She gave me a hard, bruising kiss. "I'm going to have this cock, Beck. And you're going to come down my throat. And you're not going to hold back, you hear me?"

She sank to the ground, layers of her skirt fanning out all around her. Her fingers slid over my knees, tugged down my zipper. She reached in, freed my cock—already leaking, aching for her.

"Where do you want those hands?" she asked. She knew. Luna had figured out my little obsession with her hair.

"Your hair," I bit out.

"Then do it."

So I speared my fingers into all that brown-and-gold silk as she lowered her plump lips all the way down.

ower.
There you are.

That had been what was missing — or rather, taken from me—as the media and my fans had descended with their bloodthirsty insults.

It was my power, being slowly drained away as I tried to correct a mistake that would never, truly, be corrected.

It was my power, being drained away because I gave it away to *strangers*. My twelve million fans didn't really know the true me. Money drained it. Greed drained it.

But not now. That glow over my heart was back and in full force, demanding me to service this sexy, filthy hulk of a man sitting in front of me. A man who had spread my legs and eaten me out with a hungry abandon, growling and licking and groaning and shuddering. Seeing his shaggy, bearded face between my legs had ignited a thrill I'd never experienced before.

But now it was my turn. Beck the beast was *mine* to play with—to tease and taunt and to be overcome by.

The cock I released was miraculous. Thick, veined, perfect. Big. Really big. And I wanted it all.

He speared his fingers into my hair and I gave into it—gave into the pure sexual need that threatened to consume me. The second my lips caressed the tip of his cock we *both* groaned. His fingers gripped my hair, and I slid all the way down, enjoying the stretch, his taste, and my immediate arousal. Sex, for me, was always fun and hot. Being raised in Coconut Grove meant I had no shame when it came to bodies, pleasure, sexuality. I fucked around and hooked up and had fun with lots of men— in summary, I'd given a lot of blow jobs.

This was the blow job to end all blow jobs. Like our kiss on the bike had been for me, I wanted this experience for him to be everything. I wanted to reward his bravery, his heart, his giving nature. I wanted to reward his tongue's masterful work.

I wanted Beck as mindlessly out of control as I'd been. My lips hit the base of his cock and then I slowly, slowly dragged my mouth all the way up. Let go with a *pop*.

"For the love of *fuck*," he grunted. "Don't you dare stop."

I squirmed at that, bit my lip. Gave him my teasing eyes. "Maybe I will."

His fingers tightened in my hair. Twisted. Trapped my face an inch from his dick. I was so hungry for it my tongue flew out, desperate for another taste. "Do you want it or not, sweetheart?"

"Yes, more, *yes*," I begged, hands flying forward. I gripped him with two hands, lowered my mouth and sucked his cock with enthusiasm. The utterly gratified sound he made was the most erotic thing I'd ever heard. It rumbled from somewhere deep in his chest, and it was because of *me*. Beck gripped my hair as I sucked his cock, my legs shaking, body on fucking fire. His groans were perfect, the way he gasped my name, his begging, his pleading, the rough way he handled my head. I wanted it, wanted more, and when his palm slipped beneath my shirt to squeeze my breasts, I lost my mind. Was sucking him fast, bobbing my head, letting him work my nipples as I moaned around his hard flesh.

He yanked on my hair, stopping me.

I was panting, out of breath. "What... what's wrong?"

"Tell me you're close again."

In response, I tried to squeeze my legs together. Needy. Nodded.

Beck was moving in a flash, dropping from the chair and laying his big body on the floor. I was picked up and deposited neatly over his mouth. His tongue slid through my pussy and my head fell back at the divine contact. I put my hands on his broad chest and rolled my hips, fucking Beck's mouth, enjoying this luxurious exploration. In front of me, he was fisting his cock and I watched it like live porn—Beck's head beneath my skirts, tongue in my cunt while he fucked his own fist.

"So hot," I moaned. "Beck, is this... is this how you touch yourself?"

His voice was muffled by my skirts but clear enough for me to hear: "I touch myself and I think about you."

"I like it," I whispered. "Very much."

His fist was moving faster now—tongue working in unison.

But I needed my lips on him.

I batted his hand away and lowered my mouth to his cock, sucking him deep as he worked his tongue on my clit. When was the last time I'd done this—when was the last time sex had been this *fraught*? His groans against my sex only made what he was doing hotter, better. The deeper I sucked his cock, the hotter I got, and the hotter I got, the faster his tongue flew. His palms were gripping my asscheeks, spreading them apart as he devoured me. I was fisting him fast, taking as much as I could—seconds away from climax. I started to scream, started to wail, started to rock my hips over his face. I was going to climax with his cock in my mouth and there was nothing I needed more.

His thumb slid through my folds and slipped inside. Euphoria rushed over me, a blinding ecstasy, and I cried out around his cock, coming hard and fast.

Beck did too.

Oh, and it was glorious. One long, beautiful groan that seemed to contain a lifetime of pleasure—a hot rush of salt—our orgasms in blissful unison. When we finally, *finally*, stopped moving, I collapsed off of Beck, onto my back. Wiped my mouth. Tried to catch my breath.

Uh-oh uh-oh uh-oh.

There I went again. Falling. He rolled over and placed his head on my stomach, breathing heavily. And I stroked his hair, the sweat on the back of his neck. Listened to the sound of his breath start to slow.

"I'm kidnapping you tomorrow," I said, still panting. "You're calling in sick from work."

"Yes."

"You're not even going to fight it, are you?"

"Not a chance in hell."

I stroked his temple. "When was the last time you ever fake called in sick?"

"I've never even considered it. And I'm going to guess that Luna da Rosa doesn't take days off either."

"I never get sick," I explained.

"Bullshit." He chuckled.

"It's *true*." I laughed. "You don't spend your entire life mainlining kale smoothies and experimenting with vitamin C supplements without gaining the immune system of, well, *me*,

I guess." Another stroke, this time through his beard. "Not even when I was a waitress in high school and college, I never played hooky. Never skipped a day of class in school."

"Why now?" he asked. We both sounded dreamy, floaty; voices rough from our orgasms.

"Because you inspire me. And I've got decisions to process."

"Okay then."

"You don't want any more details?"

"Doesn't that ruin the kidnapping?"

I giggled and he kissed my fingers. "I want to ride your bike, so can you pick me up?"

"And *I'm* kidnapping *you*."

"Semantics, Beck. And I want to do what we just did. Like a hundred more times."

"That can be arranged, sweetheart."

My toes curled against the floor.

Uh-oh.

43

BECK

*L*una's text the next morning gave me the time to pick her up on the bike and nothing else.

I'll pack all of the essentials, the text said. What followed was a bunch of winking faces and videos of fireworks.

I guessed she liked what we'd done yesterday in my office.

I know I fucking liked it. I loved having Luna's soft mouth wrapped around my cock while I ate her out. When I came, I felt a brick tumbling from my walls.

She was breaking me. But not in a bad way.

I'd stared at her texts for a while last night, knowing that if I sent *Okay* back to her, she'd tease me about it tomorrow. Instead I sent, *I am prepared to be very sick tomorrow. But I know that after our date—*

I deleted "date." Retyped it. Thought about it. Kept it in.

Luna da Rosa was also turning me back into an awkward teenager again, apparently.

But I know that after our date I will feel incredible. You make me feel incredible.

I hit send. Wondered if that was weird, but it was the truth.

Her reply came instantly.

You make me feel incredible too, Beck.

By the time I roared up to her gigantic mansion on my motorcycle, I couldn't wipe the grin off my face even if I'd wanted to. And when Luna walked barefoot through the grass towards me, I understood just how gone I was for this girl.

I wasn't a religious man. But I sent something like a prayer to the sky—that my parents would leave us be. That the MC would fade into the background. That Wild Heart would be fine and Luna could be mine.

Please.

Before she could even open her mouth, I had her by the waist, pulling her in for a long, sweet kiss.

"Good morning," I said. "I'm very sick today. How about you?"

She gave a cute little cough. "It's the flu, I know it."

I smoothed tendrils of hair from her face. She wasn't wearing makeup, so I could see the freckles across her nose.

"Do you want to come see inside my house? And I'm only asking because my best friends are on the back patio and they're dying to meet you."

"I look okay?" I asked.

"You look hot," she said. "Come on. Brutus is in the back too. You'll love him. He's our free-range Saint Bernard."

"Brutus?"

She held my hand as we walked beneath the palm trees that lined her driveway. "He's a rescue pup, but he hates being confined. That's why we let him roam about the enclave."

"Huh," I said. We walked through her courtyard, which had a fountain and huge, flowering plants and wind-chimes hanging from the tree branches. It was very... Luna.

"Come on in," she said, looking shy. "This is my home."

I stepped into a house filled with color and light and green things. Every room was open, filled with rugs and throw pillows, candles and plants. The ceiling had lanterns and string lights. Large windows opened up onto a turquoise pool. It was massive, expensive-looking. There were photos everywhere—of Luna and her family, her travels, her friends, awards from her work and magazine covers she was on.

Very, *very* Luna.

"Is that Big Dick Beck?"

Luna's eyes widened, but she couldn't contain the laugh that bubbled up from her. "My friends are out there and that's Daisy, by the way."

Outside, lounging with their feet in the pool, were three powerful-looking women with smiles on their faces. All three wore giant sunglasses, bathing suits, and sarongs.

"When I told them about my sick day, they all agreed they needed one too. Although they're off doing other things today."

"And people." The red head smirked. "A lot of us will be fucking. Two of us to be exact."

"And one—me—will be dialing all of the European princes I know for a booty call," Daisy said. "Come on over, Beck. Luna was just giving us a detailed depiction of your penis."

I put my helmet down. "Nice to meet you. Happy my dick can be of service."

Daisy gave me a mock salute. I shook hands with the tall blonde woman—Emily—and the smirking auburn-haired beauty—Cameron. Daisy was wearing an orange wig and gave me a high five.

"I'm sorry the media's been tearing you apart, Beck," Emily said. "Been there. Literally. As in like months ago. It feels horrible."

I looked at Luna, who gave me a little nod. "It was more of

a surprise than anything else. I feel worse about what they're saying about Luna."

Luna gave a little shrug—but her expression was more serene than I'd ever seen it. "Eh. What are you gonna do?"

"That's my girl," Cameron said.

"Luna's told me how much all of you support each other," I ventured. "That's a nice thing to have."

Emily gave a knowing smile to Luna. "We protect each other, all right."

A shaggy dog jumped out from where he must have been hiding in the flowering bushes. Saw me and leapt toward my face.

"Oh my god, Brutus, *no*," Luna squealed. But I was already sinking to my knees and giving Brutus a hug.

"It's okay," I said. "I know him."

"You know *Brutus*?" Daisy asked. "How?"

"Your neighbors must have gotten him from Lucky Dog," I said. "I didn't realize it was *this* Brutus. They said they lived in a quiet neighborhood. This must be dog paradise."

"Where did he come from?" Luna asked.

"Um... let me think." I sat back on my heels and Brutus immediately rolled over for me. "He and his sister had been left in a box on our doorstep by someone. Both pretty malnourished and skittish. Took about nine, maybe ten weeks but they warmed up, as you can tell."

"Brutus, in particular, can't keep his nose out of human butts," Daisy said.

I chuckled. "That sounds like Brutus."

I ran my palm over his fur, really damn happy to see one of my dogs in his new environment. We did house visits often after the adoption went through, but Brutus had been adopted a few years ago. He looked healthy, happy, safe.

He looked loved.

"He was a real sweetheart when we worked with him," I said. And when I looked up I caught Luna's friends giving her matching looks. Luna was blushing.

"Any other animals I should know about?" I asked, glancing over my shoulder.

"Frank," Cameron said. "He's our free-range parrot, but you'd know if he was here because he'd be calling you a *fuckface*."

"And?" I asked, because it felt like there was more.

"We've got a pod of dolphins in the marina that are horny as fuck," Daisy said proudly. "My kind of people. Although, on Valentine's Day, they usually make me feel more alone."

Cameron and Emily snorted.

"And Steve," Luna said, toeing the ground. She smiled at me from beneath a veil of hair. "Our rescued alligator. Lives in the lagoon. He likes when I feed him rotisserie chicken."

"He's not a vegan then?" I asked.

"Not even a little," she said. "He's a softie. You just have to watch your arms and legs around him."

Brutus curled at my feet, seemingly content in this weird environment of rich people and infinity pools and parrots and alligators.

"Are you ready to kidnap me or what?" Luna asked. "These perverts will be here forever, so we should get going." She lifted up her backpack.

"I'm ready," I said. "It's a pleasure to meet all of you. You should come to Lucky Dog sometime."

"I have a feeling we'll be seeing a lot of you, Mr. Big Dick," Daisy said.

I grinned, gave Brutus one last pat, and placed my hand low on Luna's back as we walked back through her house.

"You really told them about my cock, sweetheart?" I asked, bending down to nip at her neck.

She shivered. "I did. I described it in glorious detail. Is that okay?"

"More than okay."

I gave Luna her helmet, swung my leg over the bike and helped her on. Felt an immediate calm as her body wrapped around mine.

"Where are we going on our sick day, Luna?"

"We are going to a very private beach that doesn't have a name," she said. "But my parents used to take me there as a kid. It's a little wild and overgrown. You up for it?"

I squeezed her hands where they wrapped around my chest. "Yes. And what are we going to do there?"

She made a humming sound. "Eat this lunch I made for us before we skinny-dip."

This woman.

"Were you sent to this earth to kill me?" I asked, tightening my hands on the throttle.

"Oh, Beck," she sighed, laying her cheek on my shoulder blade. "I think I was sent to this earth to make you feel more alive."

44

LUNA

*I*t took only thirty minutes for Beck and me to come upon the private beach. This was the beach we used to frequent when I was younger, when my world was nothing but communing with nature and animals and the tropical environment around me. And during this not-really-sick sick day, when I needed to process the abundance of new information and feelings I had about myself, I knew taking Beck here would be the cure.

We coasted down the road, leaving the highway for back-country roads crowded with overgrown trees and bushes. The air was thick with humidity as I directed him to a tiny, dusty pull-off. We parked and he took my pack from me, depositing it neatly on his back as he grabbed my hand.

"Lead the way," he said.

I slipped my flip-flops off and zippered them into the pack. Flexed my toes in the wet earth, feeling a deep connection root there.

"On my social media accounts, I talk a lot about discon-necting from technology and letting yourself *be* in nature," I said. "And I haven't done that in years."

"Being a billionaire keeps you busy," he said.

"Still," I said, with a shrug. "It's interesting, isn't it?"

"Where's your phone now?" he asked.

"At home," I promised. I held up my empty palms. "It's only me. No articles or Twitter comments or emails from Jasmine or financial crises. I mean, all of that is still happening and Wild Heart is *this close* to falling to pieces. But all of it can wait until tomorrow, right?"

"Right," he said. "Plus you're sick. You can't be on your phone when you have the flu."

I tapped my temple. "Smart."

He gave me a playful grin that doubled my heart rate. "Should we go?"

I gave his hand a tug, pulling us along a sandy trail you'd never know existed if you didn't already know it was there. We hiked in silence, listening to bird song and the crash of waves that heralded the nearness of the ocean. Vines swayed, leaves tangled in our hair, we laughed as we tripped over roots and slipped under low-hanging branches. Beck's height kept him knocking against trees—but he was a good sport about it. And when we reached a giant mud puddle, he simply scooped me up and deposited me on the other side.

"How long have you been coming here?" he asked.

"Since I was little. My parents thought it was really important for children to feel at home in the wild, at one with nature. Veganism is usually connected to animal rights— which is important to me, obviously. But the other part of that is that factory farming and the meat industry destroy all of this." I waved my hands, indicating the wilderness around us. "Wild Heart is about preserving animals, humans *and* the earth. And that came from days spent here."

We stepped through one last tangle of trees onto a white sand beach, surrounded by high rocks. It was only about twenty-five feet wide and fairly calm—with clear, bright blue water.

And there wasn't a soul in sight.

"Welcome to paradise," I said with a smile.

Beck ran his hand through his hair, gazing out at the water with a look of wonder. I let him stand there for a moment, understanding the need to take it all in. From the pack, I unfolded a long white cloth and six glass containers filled with food. I sank onto the cloth, tucking the edges of my sarong beneath my bare legs.

"Let me feed you," I said, patting the spot next to me.

He reached behind his head and tugged off his white shirt, revealing a broad expanse of truly hairy chest. Lumberjack shoulders and a firm belly. He sank down next to me and I couldn't stop myself from closing my teeth around his bicep.

"Easy, tiger," he said.

I popped open each container. "Fried tofu. Quinoa. Watermelon and blueberries. Avocado and corn salad. Carrots. Corn chips."

"Corn chips?"

"They're vegan," I said, biting my lip. "I probably ate my weight in Fritos during study sessions in college. Also, I have no excuse, I still do that to this day."

His eyes crinkled at the sides. "Speaking of interesting food choices, what's the response been to your cheeseburger post?"

"One-half love. One-half extreme hatred," I said. "The people I've pissed off are still pissed off. And they keep piling up on me. I guess admitting that I even felt the temptation to eat meat confirms their view that I've lied this whole time. And the people who were never really that mad seemed to like it. Liked the honesty in it. Some people even sent me messages about their cheat days. Or other ways that they're less-than-perfect in how they express their core values on a daily basis but are working towards being better. That was really wonderful to read actually."

"I'm sorry about the extreme hatred," he said.

"I won't lie and say it doesn't hurt," I said. "But it's hurting much, much less now."

"You won't ever make them happy," he said simply.

I grabbed a fork and handed him one of the containers. "I saw one of your mug shots the other day," I said, and immediately watched his spine stiffen. "I think it was your last one."

"How did you know it was the last one?" he asked softly.

"You had this look," I said. "Like you'd already decided this was going to be your last time. Is that true? Before even meeting Willow, did you have a sense that you wouldn't go back inside again?"

Beck chewed for a minute and I let him think. "I was seventeen, about to do eight months. If I fucked up after that, I wasn't going to juvie. I was going to prison. Which is a big difference. MC members were always in and out of jail, in between prison sentences or awaiting trial. It was part of life, something to get through. It was a way to serve the MC and my parents."

The waves were soothing behind us, the ocean breeze a cool balm to the sticky heat.

"I guess I realized..." Beck drummed his fingers on his knee. "I guess I realized that all of my criminal activity was just me, trying to get their attention. Get their love. And they weren't ever going to give it. Right before my last stint, a loyal club member was returning from a five-year sentence. Logan. He'd taken the fall for a crime my parents had committed. They had been laundering counterfeit bills. But he had taken the fall happily, wanting to prove his loyalty to the club, to our family. It was... awful." Beck cleared his throat. "I overheard members talking at night about the shit that went down in there. Other rival MCs beating him up on a regular basis. For years. My parents never visited him, never sent money. And when he got out they didn't even say thank you. There was no reward for him. There was no love. It didn't matter what I did, or anyone did. They weren't going to care."

I scooted forward on the blanket, cross-legged, until our knees touched. Then I placed my hands over his. "Who showed you love growing up, Beck?"

A careless shrug, like it didn't matter. "No one, I guess. Willow and the other dogs in that program, when I was older. And now Elián. And it'd be hard for me to say it to them, but I love Wes and Jem too."

"Your family," I said.

"A family I almost lost because I can't do my fucking job," he said, anger edging his voice. I stroked the palm of his hand.

"You're fixing it," I said. "It's getting better. You didn't lose them."

He tucked a strand of hair behind my ear. "I felt okay during that video."

"You spoke from the heart," I said. "It was the most authentic thing I've ever seen. I envy that in you. Behind the walls you've built lives a man who isn't ashamed to be who he is. We can all learn from that."

He indicated the lush nature surrounding us. "This is who you are, Luna."

"It is. But money has changed everything in my life. Every single thing. And it's only now that I feel like I can really let myself see the fact that I allowed myself to compromise a core value of mine."

Beck leaned back on his hands but kept our knees touching. "Did you grow up rich?"

I slipped a piece of watermelon into my mouth, enjoyed

its rich sweetness. "My parents always had enough money, but rarely more than enough. And when they had more, they gave it away. Donated it. When I was entering that VC competition, I knew I wanted to found a company that would change the cosmetics industry. But I also knew that when I got that money I'd eagerly give it away. Never hoard it or keep it for myself. Instead a decade has gone by and philanthropy hasn't factored into my existence at all. Not one tiny bit. Instead I have so much money it's *laughable*. And yet at night I have anxiety dreams about not having enough. And during my workday, I'm constantly strategizing about ways to get more. Because I do need more. I have more employees, more salaries, more costs, more products, more, more, more."

The waves behind us curled in, white and frothy, and beneath I knew the ocean floor was teeming with fish and other sea creatures.

"I no longer feel right about the role of money in my life. And the fact that, whether I like it or not, it contributed to the situation I currently find myself in. That... *greed*." The word felt like a sin. It certainly was to my parents. Greed was the worst of human weaknesses because it meant others around us would never have enough. "Money, image, branding. It's all interconnected and the way I'm living right now isn't right. It's not entirely *wrong* either..." I scratched my head, thinking.

"But before the fraud though," he said. "Your company was changing things. That's not bad at all."

I thought about what Wild Heart stood for, the policies we had in place. "No, you're right. That's true too."

I cut watermelon in half, passed him a slice.

"The Miami Devils are runners," he said. "Money, guns. People, sometimes. Cars. Anything of high value, you can pay a member of the MC to run it from one place to the next. They don't give a shit what it is. They don't have *values*. Their only need is money."

I tilted my head, listening.

"My parents have always wanted a criminal empire, hidden inside a club. They've always wanted money. Shitty thing is that most motorcycle clubs aren't gangs, aren't criminals. Just groups of people who love riding bikes and enjoy their freedom. In Miami, my parents have stolen that freedom. Turned it into violence. And they're too deep in it now. This is how they'll live until the end." He reached forward and tugged on a strand of my hair. I smiled at him. "Not you though. You're at the beginning."

I held his hand, put it to my lips. "As are you, Beck Mason."

Hope was taking root in my heart. I leaned forward and kissed him for a long, long time. It was a sweet, exploratory kiss. My fingers slid into his hair. His arms wrapped around my waist, pulling me into his lap.

"It's time for the next part of our hooky date," I said, untangling myself from his warm body.

"You're sure?" he asked, voice rough.

In response, I tugged on the strings of my sarong, which dropped to the sand. Slowly untied my bikini top. Let it drop. Watched the transformation on his face—from emotion to a lust that stole my breath. I very deliberately slid the bikini bottoms down my legs and stepped out of them.

"Are you coming?" I asked. I backed down the sand, staring at the mountain of a man who was standing up. All muscle and hair and commanding strength. When he slipped out of his trunks, his thighs were thick with power. And that now-famous cock jutted away from his body.

Beck was magnificent. And he was prowling toward me in the water.

The water was at mid-thigh—it was bathwater-warm,

gentle. Lapping at my skin like a lover, like *Beck*. The air was sticky, scented with flowers and there wasn't a soul in sight.

He reached me in seconds and dropped to his knees. Pressed his face between my breasts and inhaled the scent of my body. His head tilted up, the look on his face reverent. Worshipful.

"I'm not coming, sweetheart," he said, fingers gliding along my thighs. "You are."

45

BECK

*L*una stood naked in crystal-clear water—an image that would be burned into my brain. I was ready to be taken by her, to give her every piece of myself. If I couldn't share all of my past yet, I could share this. My body and its desires.

I landed on my knees in the soft sand. Kissed between her perfect breasts. Taking one, and then the other, fully into my mouth as she clutched at my shoulders. I scraped my teeth across her nipples as my hands did filthy things beneath the waves. Like slip between her legs to find her clit; like stroke my index finger across it as I licked patterns across her nipple.

"Beck, what are you doing?" she gasped. "I thought... thought we were going to swim naked."

I could see her expression of joy. Needed to ask her permission for what I wanted to do to her.

"I want to fuck you on the rocks," I said. My finger slid inside her and she shuddered everywhere.

"Do it," she sighed. I groaned against her skin, scraping my teeth along her ribcage, slowly fingering her as my mouth moved down her stomach. I was hungry for her, could barely contain my sexual pleasure when my tongue found her clit. Lapped at it like the water around us.

"Beck, oh *god*," she sighed.

I held her hard to my face, steadying her in the waves so I could enjoy her sweet pussy out in the open like this. My tongue dove deep inside of her body as I gripped her ass cheeks. I let my mouth move without purpose. Just tasting.

But she was already shaking. Already pulsing her hips forward.

"Are you close already?" I asked.

"You're just... it's too good," she moaned. "Your tongue, it's like... it's like..." I fluttered feather-light strokes diagonally across the bud, and Luna wailed. "It's like *magic*."

I sucked her clit between my lips and hummed, giving her a hard vibration. She yanked my hair and wailed louder. This woman was going to come on my face in the middle of the goddamn ocean and I was fucking *here for it*. I wouldn't stop now—not when the woman I was gone for needed something. So instead of tasting delicious Luna, I licked hard circles around her clit as fast as I could and she screamed. The climax hit and the strength left her body—allowing me to hold her up as I licked her down—the taste of her pussy mixing with the sweat on her body, the salt of the waves.

"You are so unbelievably beautiful," I rasped, looking at her from my place on my knees. Luna was wide-eyed and panting.

"Please fuck me, Beck," she said. And then I was standing all the way up, wrapping her legs around my waist, and walking toward the closest flat rock.

"I didn't bring condoms, sweetheart," I said, kissing her ear. "I'll just keep eating that gorgeous—"

"I want your cock bare," she said.

Flash went my brain.

"*Luna,*" I swore, laying her on that rock and fisting myself —enjoying her spread out in front of me. "Are you safe?"

She nodded, reached forward to glide her fingers with mine along the length of my shaft. "Protected. Clean. You?"

"Same," I said. I took her mouth in a kiss meant to be gentle—but she had me snarling in seconds.

"Don't you dare hold back on me, Beck," she said. "I want you to take it all."

I flipped her over and yanked her up onto her knees, letting the beast take over. I leaned in and *bit* her ass cheek. She squealed and pushed back.

So I bit her harder.

"That's how I like it." She sighed, cheek to the warm rock, dark hair fanned around her. My palm slid up the back of her thighs, dipping in between. I teased her clit and licked inside of her, licked as deep as I could, getting her close again.

Because I wasn't sure how long I would last.

"*Please, please, please,*" Luna chanted.

"Is that Luna, begging for my cock?" I teased gently.

Her fingers scrambled at the rock ledge, gripping. "I'd do anything and you know it," she replied.

I gave her a ringing slap on her ass and she arched back. Gave me a look over her shoulder so filled with lust I abandoned any other plans I had for her ass and lined up my cock right at her pussy.

Luna smiled. "Please, Beck."

I slid the first two inches inside, giving her time to adjust— to my size, the angle, the fact that we were having sex. Sex I believed that would change everything. She was tight and wet. I had the impulse to slam all the way in.

"More," she said, and there was an edge to her voice I hadn't heard directed at me before. But I'd heard it in her office.

A command.

I fully seated my cock inside of her.

I wasn't going to survive this.

"More, more, more," she cried. I wrapped the strands of her hair around my fist. Yanked. Slid all the way out and slammed all the way back in.

Luna turned her head around. "It's too intense," she whimpered. "Beck, it's too... too *much*."

"I've got you, sweetheart," I said, giving my hips a roll that sent her body pitching forward. She sobbed my name. "Tell me what you need."

"To come," she said.

Biology took over. I kept hold of her hair with one hand and began to fuck her thoroughly, as if nothing else in the world mattered except her pleasure. And nothing else *did* matter—I could admit that now, watching my cock slide in and out of her pussy, hearing the way she cried my name, like the sound of it got her hot.

This *scene* got me hot—fucking this woman on her hands and knees on a rock in the middle of a private beach. Even *if* someone was watching us, fucking *good*. Let them see it—let them see how obsessed I was with this woman.

I drove into her from behind with long, even strokes that made her scream and gasp and cry out as I pulled on her beautiful hair. But as she got close, I pulled out and flipped her back over. Slid inside her body with her legs around my waist. Angled my pelvis so I ground against her clit as I let her have it, fucking her fast, with no sense of control.

But our mouths spoke a different story. I fucked Luna like an animal—but kissed her with all the tenderness I had, both hands in her hair as I drank her in. Trying to show her how she made me feel.

Luna's orgasm rushed over her—and I was swept away too.

I cried out against her mouth as I emptied inside of her. The release was too good, too perfect, too real, like it was never going to stop.

She stroked my face, held my gaze as I rode out the pleasure.

She kissed my cheek. My jaw.

Forget one brick falling. Luna had officially sent my walls tumbling down. I pressed our foreheads together. She was still staring at me with dark eyes. Eyes that saw me for who I was, completely.

Who showed you love, Beck?

No one had shown me love, not then. Not at all.

But I knew who was showing me love now.

46

LUNA

*I*t was Friday night and I was staring bleary-eyed at my computer. I was sitting cross-legged in my living room on a meditation cushion, wearing yoga pants and a giant tee-shirt, hair in a messy ponytail.

I felt... ready.

I was going to start Wild Heart's Foundation.

And I'd never been happier.

The only distraction I'd had in the last seventy-two hours was the fact that Beck had fucked me into a literal *sex daze* on that rock. I found myself staring out the window more than usual, replaying everything we'd done on a dirty little loop inside my brain.

Beck's fingers, yanking on my hair.

Beck's mouth, tasting me everywhere.

Beck's miracle of a cock—which had done what I'd fantasized about. Stretched me perfectly, filled me just right. Stroked nerve endings into a deep, delirious fire of sensation that made me scream. Was it any wonder I couldn't stop thinking about that filthy fu—

The doorbell rang, storming through my hundredth

sexual daydream that day. It was after ten, which meant probably Daisy, looking to borrow body glitter before heading out
on some extravagant yacht adventure.

"You can take my glitter but you have to bring it back this
time, Daze," I called out, yawning into my hand as I walked
toward the front door. "I might need it this weekend—*oh*."

Not Daisy at the door.

Beck Mason. Holding his helmet under one arm and a
delicious-smelling plate in the other.

"Hi," he said, looking shy.

"Hi," I breathed. I knew I sounded obsessed but who
cared. "What are you doing here?"

"Um. I know you've been really busy the past few days and
we haven't seen each other since, you know, our date. I made
you vegan peanut butter cup cookies. Or tried to."

I lifted the cloth to find twelve irregularly shaped cookies
that looked half-burnt, half-undercooked and absolutely
delicious. "I usually only can make macaroni and cheese
from a box. And Jem wasn't there to help. They're probably
terrible."

"I think this might be the most adorable moment of my
life," I mused.

His lips lifted. "Well, I think you're adorable too,
sweetheart."

Swoonsville, population: Me.

"It's ten at night and you came over here to see if I was...
up?" I asked, tilting my head.

"Sure. Is that okay?"

"I believe the kids call that a *booty call*, Mr. Mason. Next
time text me an eggplant emoji."

"A what?" he asked, brow furrowed.

I laughed. "Never mind. Come in. I need a break anyway. A
billionaire's job is never done but a girl's gotta eat. I've also got

kombucha, your favorite. And also leftover noodles with lemon-pepper tofu—"

He dropped the plate on the island and pulled me in for a dramatically passionate kiss — bending me over backward and tangling his hands in my hair as our mouths moved together hungrily. After long, sensual minutes, we both came up for air.

"I've been thinking about kissing you all day," he said.

"Same," I panted.

He placed me back on my feet and kissed the top of my head. "I'll have some of that kombucha."

"Excuse me, what?"

Beck shrugged. "I'm trying new things. Vegan things."

"Interesting," I mused. I opened up my refrigerator and cocked my head inside. "Check out what I had in here in case you ever showed up unannounced."

It was a six-pack of ice-cold Heineken, backlit by the fridge light like a beer commercial.

"I'll have that, please."

I winked. "Excellent choice."

We smiled at each other with fucking hearts coming out of our eyes probably.

I watched Beck move through my house, touching the plants, examining the framed, funky art pieces. There was a huge wall of photos that he paused next to, stepping back to take it all in. The photos were mismatched: in between cute pictures of me with Cameron, Emily and Daisy were family shots with my parents and grandparents, trips to see extended family in Mexico and Italy. Volunteer work both here and in other countries. That magazine article I had hanging in my office, declaring Wild Heart's ability to *change the world*.

I was also currently standing in my mansion wearing a very simple outfit that still cost thousands.

"Does it make you hate me?" I asked Beck, completely out of the blue. "Seeing, you know, all of this?"

He gave me a rueful smile. "Still processing, I'm guessing?"

"Kind of," I said, pulling my right leg up into a tree pose. "I was working on research to start the foundation, that's why I'm asking. I've got money on my mind."

"I'm happy to hear it," Beck said. "And no. It doesn't make me hate you. I do still feel uncomfortable with it."

This was open Beck. Vulnerable Beck. I let that truth sit for a minute in the air between us. Gave it space to breathe.

"The difference between how much money you have and how much I have is like… it feels as huge as the ocean," he admitted. "You just… have it. I don't."

"I get it," I said. "I really do. But this is my home, my life, and I want you to feel okay here. Comfortable. We could work on it. I want… I really want to work on it for you. Maybe you won't feel entirely comfortable now, but… eventually?" There was a note of hope hanging at the end of *eventually*.

It was also the first time either one of us had verbalized anything beyond the current moment.

"I think I will feel comfortable eventually," he said. "I'd like to work on it."

I tucked my hair behind my ear, suddenly shy. "That makes me happy to hear."

He kept staring at the wall of photos. "Now that I know you better, this is who you are, Luna." He tapped an old picture of me. "You're the girl in these photos *and* the CEO standing in front of me. Didn't you tell me we all get to love what we want in this world?"

"Sounds like me," I said, laughing a little.

"You should love what you love."

Beck turned around, continued to stare at all the pictures while I ate cookies and admired the lines of his shoulders.

He tapped a photo of me. "Where's this?"

"At an elephant sanctuary in Thailand where my parents and I stayed for a bit."

He pointed to the next one. "And here?"

"A bike fundraiser for literacy programs in Miami schools," I said.

He tapped the famous one—me holding that million-dollar check.

"Businesses can do right by the world," I said, looking at the picture. "I'm starting to believe that again. Believe in our mission."

"I'm proud of you," he said. His big body took up so much space in this room; I was transfixed by it. I was glowing. He caught my look, responded with his own. In two large strides, he was right in front of me. I blinked then I was being lifted in the air and deposited on the island.

Beck stepped between my legs. Reached up and undid the tie in my hair.

I loved this little obsession he had.

"I didn't come over here for a... a *booty call*," he said. "I don't want you to think that."

"What if that's what I want though?" I said, wrapping my legs around his waist.

He inhaled my hair, roamed his teeth along my throat.

"I haven't seen your bedroom, Luna," he whispered, tone dark and delicious.

"Allow me to show you, sir," I said.

47

BECK

"I should Instagram this," Luna said, popping an entire cookie into her mouth. She was wearing my shirt and sitting next to me in her gigantic bed—white curtains, white bedding, green plants and a fountain in the corner. It was like laying in a cloud.

"Cookies that delicious, huh?" I asked, head leaned back on my arm.

"I meant *this*." She pointed at my cock, still half-hard.

I grinned, covering it up with my hand.

"Don't *hide it*," she squealed. She grabbed another cookie, handed it to me. "But in all seriousness, you did good, Mr. Mason." She had a bit of chocolate on her lip—I leaned in, licked it off, kissed her cheek.

She was flushing when I leaned back. "I didn't think you were such a romantic, to be honest. A romantic *and* a fuck machine."

"Fuck machine," I repeated dryly.

"Very much so." She bit her lip. "I like it."

I fisted my hand into her shirt. Tugged her all the way until our mouths met again. "Weren't you the woman who just held me down while you sat on my face?"

Another flush, a graceful lift of her brow. "Vegan goddesses can be fuck machines too."

I nipped at her jaw, reluctantly letting her go. After Luna had lowered herself over my face, I was lost in lust for hours, devouring her through orgasm after orgasm before flipping her over and taking her hard. But she wasn't wrong about the romance either—like our ocean sex, everything intense was followed with sweetness.

I stroked her bare ankle with my thumb. "You haven't posted that picture of us from our date on your page."

"Spying on me?" she asked.

"The staff at Lucky Dog is obsessed with you," I hedged. "And maybe."

"Which date though?"

"Our first one."

"Beers at Dean's?"

I shook my head. "Burgers."

She tapped her chin. "We've had a lot of dates. One might even say we're *dating*."

"One might."

She picked up her phone, found the photo in question. "You mean this one, right?" There it was: Luna laughing as I kissed her cheek. "One might even say," I said, gathering my courage, "that you're my girlfriend."

She couldn't contain her excitement. "Does that make you my boyfriend?"

"If a forty-year-old man can be someone's boyfriend," I said, attempting a shrug.

"Oh, he can," she replied. She typed away on her phone. Chewed on her lip. Bounced her knees a little. Flipped her phone around to show what she'd just created.

There we were, available to be judged, loved and hated by Luna's twelve million followers. Her caption read, "Boyfriend and girlfriend."

I cleared my throat. "I like it," I said, voice rough. "Jasmine might not."

"I am publicly declaring my relationship with the executive director of the nonprofit I'm helping—" she started.

"—a man from Miami's most hated crime family—"

"—and a woman the city of Miami currently believes clubs seals in her spare time to make lipstick," she finished.

My lips twitched. "What a pair we make."

"I think Jasmine might call this *a public relations nightmare*."

"And what do you call it?" I asked. This felt like trust to me. This felt like... like...

"The real me," she said.

Real.

I swallowed my sigh of relief.

She lay down, placing her head on my chest. My fingers immediately went to her scalp, scratching as she purred.

"I like this you," I said.

"I like this me too."

Long minutes went by before she spoke again. "Can I ask you an intimate question? And please know you absolutely do not need to answer it."

I stiffened. She felt it, sitting up. She waited, as patiently as she waited for Penelope to eat from her hand.

"Yes, you can," I said. I still felt at odds with her extreme wealth, the casual money so fucking obvious everywhere I looked when I'd walked through her doors. I was honest when I told her I was *trying* to feel comfortable.

Because I wasn't there yet.

Naked in her bed though? That was a different story.

"Did your parents ever... lay their hands on you?" she asked, voice soft and gentle. Face open and non-judgmental.

I weighed out the consequences of telling the truth. But couldn't I be honest with a woman that was now my *girlfriend*?

"Do you mean was I ever hit?" I asked. "Yes."

Her nostrils flared. But she didn't speak yet.

"Getting smacked around was part of the culture there," I admitted. The member hitting me for knocking his beer over wasn't the only time. "Georgie, not so much. But I took back-hands from Rip."

She placed her hand over my heart, cupping it—like she was keeping it safe. "No one deserves that. I'm so, so sorry."

"They're not worth your apologies," I said. "My parents are worth less than dog shit on the bottom of a shoe. The only reason they're even present in my life right now is because—"

Her mouth pinched with concern. "Wait. Have they contacted you?"

I lifted a shoulder. Looked away. "I... think I've seen them a couple times. Riding past Lucky Dog. It's their usual intim-idation."

"But I thought you said you hadn't spoken or interacted with them in twenty years."

"I haven't."

"Until I put Lucky Dog all over the internet," Luna said, fingers clenching in the sheets. I covered them with my own. I felt comfortable telling her about the times Rip slapped me around. I *didn't* feel comfortable telling her that the few ride-bys I'd glimpsed had me afraid for the first time in two decades.

"I gave you permission," I said. "All of this is because of *them*. Not you. It's their fault. And the fault of the media. Of gossip."

Her eyes searched mine. "I feel responsible. Dragging you into a spotlight you said you didn't want."

"Except now my nonprofit is actually raising funds for the first time ever and more dogs are going to get rescued," I countered. "And now I have you."

Her breath hitched. Her fingers traced my jaw, swept along my lower lip. "I'm opposed to violence. But I would commit real atrocities against your parents, Beck."

"Stay peaceful," I said, half-chuckling. "Not worth it, remember?"

"You're worth it though," she said, leaning in for a lingering kiss.

And then she lay back down on my chest, falling asleep shortly after. And I held Luna like that all night long, breathing in her sunshine scent, wondering how the hell *I'd* gotten so lucky.

Terrified that it couldn't last.

48

LUNA

One week later

"*W*hat would be the foundation's focus areas?" Sylvia asked me. We were sitting in the Wild Heart conference room with Rebecca, my CFO, and Jasmine. The real work of the foundation would start next week—there was lots of structure and strategy to work out before we could begin—but I was too excited to wait. I thought Sylvia and I could put our heads together about the vision. And most importantly: the impact.

"Three focus areas," I said, reading from notes I'd scribbled late last night. Beck had fallen asleep with his shaggy head on my lap on the couch. I'd stroked his hair and dreamed my way through ideas. "People. Animals. The environment. Divided like that. Grantees who fit in those categories would apply specifically and maybe... maybe each category would have its own team of people. A program officer... a separate budget. Different priorities to fit those category needs."

"You could site visit," Sylvia suggested. "It'll be hard with your schedule but—"

"I'd love to," I said, letting my heart feel that glow.

"It'll make *great* press," Jasmine cut in. "Luna da Rosa, back to changing the world."

"I'm not having my company start a foundation to garner good press," I corrected Jasmine.

"It doesn't mean we can't garner good press *from* it," she shot back. "The fate of Wild Heart ultimately lies with your ability to ensure the public trusts you again. A process that can be sped up with a story like this. You get to donate your money. The nonprofits get to receive money. The extra *bump* to your reputation is an added bonus."

But the tone of her voice was *starving* at the phrase *bump to your reputation.*

I looked to Sylvia, who was regarding me closely. "What makes you feel uncomfortable about this, Luna?" she asked.

I pulled my hair over one shoulder and mindlessly braided it.

"Being manipulative," I said. "Using the foundation as a way to make people like me. I'd never want to be that person. It's... slimy."

"You don't get where you are in the world without a bit of slime, trust me," Jasmine argued.

"She's not wrong," Sylvia said carefully, "we're all a little slimy. But what I hear you saying, Luna, is that you'd like to be... different."

I knew what people had said about me in this industry when I won the VC award. They'd mocked what I'd declared on that stage, labeled it childish, naïve. *People say it's too hard to make real change in the world anymore,* I'd said, keeping my eyes on my parents in the front row. They were my anchor. *All the damage has been done. Well, I never, ever thought it would be easy. How could it be? We're talking about dismantling a system that has been in place for hundreds of years. But suddenly we live in a world where we can't all try and do better?*

"I know it's naïvely optimistic of me to try and do this and *not* use it for my own personal gain," I said softly, "but I'd like to..." I glanced at the photo on my desk of me and my fundraising stand. "I *will* do better. The media will focus on the nonprofits receiving the funds. Not the foundation."

"You're the one giving away the *money*," Jasmine said.

"They're the ones actually doing *the work,*" I said, leaving no room for her to argue.

She sat back in her chair, arms crossed.

Sylvia glanced at her watch. "I have to go to my next meeting. Luna, let's schedule for next week with the accountant. There's a whole hell of a lot of paperwork for us to start processing before we can start accepting applications."

"I'd like the first gift to be for Lucky Dog though," I said. "They can fill out an application like everyone else, but I've spent weeks working with them and can speak to their value. Feels silly not to end my time working with them by granting them much-needed funding."

"I like it," Sylvia said. She swept out of the room, about to close the door when she turned and said, "For what it's worth, you can be philanthropic without coming off as manipulative. The foundation should be announced, and people should know about it. It doesn't mean you have to present yourself as the rescuer. You could present it from the heart. An expression of why philanthropy matters."

I thought about Beck, sharing such an intimate conversation with Jimmy for the camera. The way they weren't trying to *guilt* people into money, but giving a piece of themselves. *Here's my heart and soul... What are you going to do with it?*

"The media and Luna da Rosa will have a complicated relationship for a long time," she said. "They can't control you. And you shouldn't let them control you now."

She closed the door behind her, leaving Jasmine and me to regard each other like sparring partners.

"Your time with Lucky Dog has done wonders for your damaged reputation. Giving money through your foundation to your new boyfriend with the criminal past will only make things worse," she said.

"It's not to *Beck,* it's to Lucky Dog," I said. "I don't think anyone can debate the fact that they're amazing."

"The media and the public won't see it that way," she said.

"The media and the public don't control my decision-making," I said, biting off the word *anymore.* Thinking about what Sylvia had said. *Trying* not to use the media to manipulate was as exhausting as pandering to them, seeking their approval.

Maybe I should just *be.* Let the chips fall where they may.

Like Beck would do.

"Listen," she said, uncrossing her arms and leaning across the table towards me. "I've been working with Derek's team like you asked. Their research indicates that your reputation after Ferris Mark has improved, of course. But barely. And I don't believe the upward trend will sustain into the future. The next mistake you make—and you will make one because you're in charge of a billion-dollar company—and they'll descend on you like vultures."

I braided faster—then let go. Inhaled. Exhaled. Thought of Beck speaking into the camera—*Luna has more integrity in her little finger than most people have in their entire bodies.*

I didn't have to direct this company from a place of fear.

"Let them descend," I said. "The force of what Wild Heart's foundation could do is bigger than tabloids and Instagram trolls."

Jasmine was silent for a minute, drumming her nails on the table. *Tap tap tap.*

"Moving on to other agenda items. You got invited to be a last-minute keynote speaker. Tonight," she said.

"Seriously?" I asked. "Why?"

"It's the Miami Business Woman of the Year award. Prestigious."

"I know it," I said. "I've been nominated before. So have Cameron, Emily and Daisy. That's super last-minute though for an event that huge."

Tap tap tap went her nails.

"The keynote speaker came down with the flu this morning. This year's organizer is Alissa Hendrix."

I perked up. "Oh, I love Alissa." She owned a storefront called Ruby's Closet that sold trendy, bohemian clothing and vintage furniture. It was like Anthropologie, but on a smaller scale, and she'd recently expanded from her Florida stores up into the Carolinas. I hadn't seen her in years.

"She loves you too," she said.

"What on earth am I speaking on in... six hours?"

"*The Changing Landscape of Business in Miami*," she said. "I'll work on a speech for you. Staff can have it ready in an hour."

"Sure," I said, brightening. "This is good news, then?"

"Great news," she said. "Tonight you're being accepted back into the world of business in Miami. It's still a long road but this is the first step we need. Means they don't all hate you anymore."

"Or some of them do, but they'll play nice for tonight," I added.

"True." *Tap tap tap.* "Actually... I have an idea for your speech tonight, now that we're chatting about it."

I grabbed a pen and my legal pad. "What is it?"

Jasmine leaned in, with a gleam in her eye I didn't quite like. "If you're going to insist on giving funds to Lucky Dog—"

"I insist."

"—what if we used it?"

I put my pen down. "What do you mean?"

"I think you need a real *push*. It's not like these awards are well known anywhere else but here, but if I got media and camera crews there, it could be shown on the news. Shared on social sites. Go viral a little. It would be one of those short videos everyone sends around that makes you cry."

"Why would my speech about business go viral though?" I asked. "It'll be inspiring but boring. It's not a cat with one eye who can only get around with help from his best friend, a duck."

I would know. I was the person who watched all of those videos.

"Would you bring Beck as your date?"

"Of course. If he's around." I had to glance at my paper to hide the silly smile I couldn't hold back. *Beck Mason. Your boyfriend.*

"Surprise him."

I tilted my head. Kept braiding. "How...?"

"If he's there, you could announce the launch of the foundation—"

I opened my mouth to protest but she talked over me.

"—and then tell the audience that the executive director of Lucky Dog is here in the audience this evening and he doesn't know he'll be receiving... what? How much of a grant were you going to give them?"

"A million dollars," I said, and even Jasmine looked

momentarily startled. "Spread out over four years probably. Four installments. It would really be the investment they needed to grow and expand without having to constantly worry about closing their doors."

"See?" she said. "You're already talking as if you know."

"I do know. I've been giving this a lot of thought," I said.

"Cameras would zoom in on Beck, looking surprised. Grateful. Maybe even crying a little. Emotional."

I was already shaking my head. "Beck would *hate* this."

"Beck would play along. For the cameras. Would be great for his image too." Jasmine tilted her head, as if two puzzle pieces were slotting together. "He would come off as the executive director with the heart of gold."

Which was who he was, through and through. Even the random tabloids that kept recycling his mug shots and bringing up his past weren't doing too much damage to Lucky Dog's reputation. Those who screamed the loudest were dimming; those who saw the true value of Lucky Dog's mission were donating. Beck had made two more videos with adoptive families since the one we did with Jimmy. Both had been successful. In each one, he was a little bit more comfortable, owning his voice and his story with more confidence.

"Surprise Beck and play the whole thing off like a cheesy, inspiring video with me as the hero, swooping in to save the poor nonprofit?"

"*Yes*," she said, snapping her fingers.

"No," I replied. "And Beck asked me to never make him feel that way. Ever. I'm not going to do that, Jasmine."

I'd spent the past week sifting through the background noise and deciphering the *real* lessons the universe was trying to teach me. I'd already shifted my messaging—pulled back from Lucky Dog and let Jem lead the spotlight online. Re-dedicated myself to the work of Wild Heart and our core values—Wild Heart represented more than this one mistake. We were an example, an innovator.

On social media, I only posted when I truly wanted to. And when I did, it wasn't filtered or airbrushed; it wasn't *on-brand* or strategic. It was purely me, purely fun.

Beck featured prominently now in all of my pictures—with his permission of course. And for every cute comment we received, there was a negative one: about me, Beck, Beck's family, Lucky Dog, motorcycle clubs in general, women, and on and on. I was noticing that the trolls were coming back in full force and I still didn't care. Fans or trolls, friends or strangers, none of it was real.

Just like Sylvia had said.

"Sometimes it's about the bigger picture, Luna," Jasmine cut in. "Sometimes it's about being the leader who thinks long-term and does anything to save the company that she loves."

I opened my mouth to argue back. The devil on my shoulder shook awake. Peered around. It wasn't because I was actually thinking about using Beck. But because I was suddenly consumed with the worry that my cheerful optimism was going to sink Wild Heart. I could see our offices behind the wide-open windows—the people who relied on me, the employees whose paychecks covered their mortgages, the impact I truly believed we could make in the industry once we'd gotten past this horrible rough patch.

Was my vision clouded by my feelings for Beck?

And yet I knew it wasn't. I knew it deep, deep down, in that part of your soul where only the truth shines through, scary as it might be.

I was back on the right path.

And I was going to stay that way.

"No surprises," I said firmly. "And actually..." I looked at my schedule—there was one clean half-hour without anything tagged to it. "Actually, I changed my mind. I'm going to write the speech."

"That's a bad idea."

"I'm not taking opinions on it," I said cheerfully.

"I'll still have cameras there," Jasmine said, chin lifted.

"Which is great," I clarified. "Cameras are great. *Not* on Beck. Are we clear?"

"Sure," she said.

I passed my thumb over the picture of me in front of my stand. It was time to go make that girl proud.

49

BECK

*L*una was going to be here in a few hours. I was fighting off the urge to scowl around the office until she got there. Elián was out interviewing a potential family. Wes was coordinating new volunteers. Jem was working happily with Penelope.

I was supposed to be responding to these community event invitations.

Instead I googled Luna's name.

I shouldn't have. In the past week, we'd spent every single night together at her house. I'd never been happier, lighter. More content. I'd never been as *obsessed* as I was with Luna. Every night our lust for each other only increased. It left me low on sleep and dazed at work. *Sex drunk* Wes had called it, giving me a standing ovation yesterday in the office.

Sex drunk was right. My thirst for Luna never seemed to end.

I shouldn't have googled her. I knew the internet had nasty shit to say about her, me, our relationship. But I felt like I needed to see her face, hear her voice for a minute. Luna's

TED Talk was the first thing that came up. She'd mentioned it many times but I'd never seen it.

I clicked on it.

When she walked across the stage in the video, I felt proud of her. I'd never seen her so dressed up and professional. Beneath her name on the screen, it read: *Founder and CEO. Self-made Billionaire.*

That ugly voice in my head—the one I'd been able to shut out this week—took notice of it all. Luna's charts and numbers and arguments about why businesses could be profitable without mistreating people, animals, and the environment. She was charming and funny. Smart.

"*The cosmetics industry thinks it can hide behind claims that animal testing is a necessary evil,*" she was saying. "*That working with factories that pay people pennies per hour is efficient. Just business. These industries believe they can use women's bodies to sell us products and yet their boards and upper management are staffed entirely by men.*"

My heart was crashing against my rib cage. It was hard for the high school dropout in me to watch while sitting on shitty, donated office furniture. Luna was a slick, brilliant businesswoman who spoke before hundreds of people. She'd become just a woman to me—a woman I was falling for—but a woman without labels.

Her labels were real though. MBA. Self-Made. CEO.

And she's been using you all along.

I sat back in my chair. Funny how those insecurities came back as soon as I let my guard down. As soon as I... trusted.

I scrolled through the page, Luna still speaking about industry standards in her video. I felt so damn attracted to her in that moment *and* so damn aware of our differences.

Differences that would never change.

My mouse hovered over an article someone had left at the

bottom. *Just a reminder of who Luna da Rosa's new boyfriend is,* the comment said. My left fingers curled into a fist.

I clicked on it.

It was an old article from the *Miami Dispatch*. It was a time-line of the Miami Devils' criminal activity in the city—when they'd started, when they'd first become a problem. There were a few old pictures, old videos. My stomach clenched as I scrolled, unable to stop. In the middle of the screen was a faded-looking picture of my parents, me standing off to the side. It had to have been taken by a member that had defected, like me. It was the inside of the clubhouse—just the sight of it brought back the smell of smoke and tension. My parents were deep in conversation; I was leaning against a wall with my arms crossed. Surly. About fifteen years old. Gangly, all limbs, already too tall.

I looked mean as hell.

I *looked* like I belonged there.

"Yo, Beck?" It was Wes, kicking in my office door in his usual manner. "Luna's here, working with Penelope. Wanna see her?"

I nodded, clicking out of the website. I turned to see Luna smiling happily down at a dog that had changed beneath her care. Luna was all light, all hope.

Too successful.

Too different.

My heart begged me to keep trusting her—because we'd spent the last seven days fucking each other and sleeping together and talking till dawn and you couldn't fake that kind of connection.

My head, however, begged me to be realistic.

*P*enelope stared at the treat in my hand like it was the only thing that mattered in all of existence.

Which, to a dog, was objectively true.

Still—I got a kick out of her golden eyes, trained on mine. Trusting. No more skittishness.

"Paw," I said.

She presented it, pressed it into my open hand. *Click* went the clicker.

Penelope got her treat.

"Good girl," I praised. I looked at Jem, who was nodding encouragingly. She'd dyed her lime-green hair hot magenta and had doubled-up on black eyeliner. She looked like a punk rock princess. And the covert glances she kept shooting toward Wes every time he walked past us had me wondering if he'd finally asked her out on a date.

"Down," I commanded Penelope. She lay flat on her belly. "Roll over."

She did, giving a wiggle that made me laugh. I gave her two treats and lots of praise. I sank to my knees and smoothed a hand over her head as her tail wagged. It was hard to believe her progress since Beck had rescued her the first day I'd shown up.

"Have you considered submitting an application to adopt Penelope?" Jem asked.

I fought a gigantic smile. "I hadn't... I mean, I hadn't thought about it much. In my mind, I pictured us doing this forever."

"Well, you could do it forever. If you were her dog mom."

I teared up at that.

Jem laughed. "Don't *cry*, I'm just *saying*."

"Do you think it would be a terrible idea? What if I don't know how to be a dog mom?"

"It's not a terrible idea," she said. "I think it's the best idea I've ever heard. You'd be a strong candidate." Her wink was sly.

Glow went my heart.

Beck was walking toward us from across the campus. He and Elián had been busy this week. I'd recommended a few board members to Elián—people I knew with brains for long-term planning and investing for nonprofits. Beck was practicing his elevator pitch, had even spoken to a couple of church groups. A slow and steady progress.

"He's really leaning into it more now," Jem said, helping me up from the ground. I stayed next to Penelope, one hand on her head. "You were the jump start we needed."

"You would have figured it out eventually," I said, which I believed to be one-hundred-percent true. "I'm only happy I could help. Your social media game has been on point, by the way. You'll have this place on the map in no time."

"Learned from the best." She winked. "I like everything you're posting now. You always seemed real and like, approachable. But I did also think you were perfect. I kinda like seeing you not perfect."

I watched Beck cross the yard.

"I kinda like everything that's happening right now in my life," I admitted. For the past week, Beck and I had been drunk on each other. At night, he picked me up from Wild Heart on his motorcycle, drove me to my mansion and we fucked each other until dawn. Our appetites were insatiable—*Beck* was insatiable. He didn't just fuck me, it was an endless, erotic exploration with his hands, his palms, his fingers, his tongue. He sent me to space and brought me back down to earth. In between, we'd eat snacks and tell stories and swim naked in my warm pool beneath a canopy of starlight.

And I woke every morning with a hard, naked Beck melded to my back, kissing my neck and stroking my hair.

I'd been late to work every day this week. But I wasn't able to conceal my silly, light-hearted smile. It was constant now, and Beck was the source.

"I told you," Jem said.

I gave Penelope another treat for being cute. "Told me what?"

"Second chances. You got one and you didn't fuck it up."

I reached over. Squeezed her shoulder. "It was touch and go there for a while. Wild Heart's going to be in financial trouble for a long time until I can re-right the ship."

Jem was silent, watching me.

"But, yes," I finally said, "I didn't fuck it up. You were right. Plus, I got Beck out of it."

I flashed her a goofy smile. She surprised me with a hug, wrapping her arms around my waist. Penelope barked happily as I squeezed Jem around her narrow shoulders.

My throat tightened.

It was more than Beck that I'd gotten.

"Hey, can I ask you something random?"

"Sure," she said, stepping back from me. "What is it?"

"The day we filmed Jimmy's adoption video, what did Beck whisper in your ear? To you and Wes?"

"Oh," she said. "He said..." She tapped her lip, thinking. "I've always seen your value."

My chest constricted. "I do too."

"I know," she said. "You see everyone's value. That's who you are as a person."

I looked at my fingers, now absent of my ever-present and very on-brand, gold rings. I had sold them yesterday, was sending the money directly to the elephant sanctuary where my parents were volunteering. I never wanted to be ashamed of earning my billionaire status. But I was pretty sure I didn't need to be adorned with jewelry that cost such a hefty price.

"Did Wes ask you on a date?" I whispered, changing the subject. Jem shook her head.

"No, but I asked him. We're going tonight."

I gave her another squeeze before letting go. "Your eyeliner is flawless."

Jem touched her cheeks. "Thank you. And, uh, I'll go put in a good word with the boss about your application to adopt Penelope."

My heart lurched forward. I looked down at the dog I loved.

"Thank you," I said. Watched her walk away and give Wes a *very* romantic-looking high five.

"Luna."

I turned around to find Beck, by himself, grinning at me.

"Mr. Mason," I said. No one was around, so I wrapped my arms around his waist and let him give me a giant, Beck-sized bear hug. His fingers found my ponytail, tilted my head back.

Claimed my mouth with a kiss that was a bit too filthy for the workplace.

"I missed you," he said.

"It's only been eight hours since I saw you this morning," I teased.

"Feels like longer." He ghosted his lips over my temple.

"Remember when I told you we could start going to events together and you could be my date?"

"Where are you taking me?" he asked.

"I've been asked to fill in last minute as a keynote speaker at an event tonight honoring women business leaders in Miami."

His eyebrows shot up in surprise.

"My thoughts exactly," I mused. "Want to come and watch me give a speech?"

"Of course," he said, although an odd pause preceded the words. A hesitation. "I won't embarrass you?"

"What? Of course not," I said, tilting my head. He hadn't asked me a question like that in a week. I was hoping we were both working past the frequent *impasses* we'd had when we first met. "I happen to think you'll be the hottest guy there in a suit."

"Those places have people that aren't always that welcoming to a guy like me."

"I guarantee you'll be a better person than most of the people on that beach," I said.

"Wait, where is it?" he asked.

"Middle of Ocean Drive, on the beach."

His expression darkened.

"What?"

He looked past me for a minute. "Should be fine. It's a Friday night and that tends to be Devils territory this time of year." His jaw looked tighter than normal.

"Okay," I said, concerned. "If you don't feel safe, you don't have to—"

"You're speaking?" he interrupted.

"I think I'm going to announce the foundation," I said. "I'm writing my speech in a bit."

He relaxed. "I'd like to be there, Luna."

"I'd like you to be there too," I admitted.

Then he bent down in front of Penelope and cupped her face in his hands. They were sharing some kind of communication I couldn't read, but the sight of it tugged my heart forward.

I swallowed the words I wanted to say. Really, they were begging to be liberated. *Hey, this might be totally weird but I love you?*

I'd already semi-practiced it in the mirror a couple of times. I'd almost said it half a dozen times this past week, and *not only* when Beck was giving me an endless array of exquisite orgasms. It was watching the tender way Beck worked with the dogs here, the same tenderness reflected in his interactions with Wes and Jem. His comfort with Elián. The many small ways he was trying to be the leader everyone believed him to be.

Beck Mason, truly vulnerable, was the most beautiful thing I'd ever seen.

But it was probably too soon, right? He'd only been my boyfriend for *seven days*. Yet here I was, standing in the middle of a field filled with rescue dogs, being held by a meat-eating, leather-wearing giant I was in love with.

Standing here, watching Beck, the man I *loved* with the dog I loved, I knew now where this new path was taking me. This journey I would get to walk.

And not alone.

Tonight, I promised myself. I would tell him tonight.

And I sent a plea to the universe that Beck Mason felt the same way.

51

BECK

"*I* look normal, right? I'm worried I look like the Hulk pretending to be a rich person."

Elián, Wes and I were in the administrative offices at Lucky Dog. They'd both gone emergency suit shopping with me immediately after Luna had invited me as her date to this event. I'd been desperate for their company, a distraction from the anxiety I felt after seeing her video. That old picture of me.

The truth was I wanted to see Luna give that speech. And I was scared shitless to be around people who probably thought of me as garbage.

"I believe the word girls would use to describe you is *total babe*," Wes said, with exaggerated air quotes and absolute sincerity.

Elián hid a smile.

"A babe?" I asked dryly.

"Oh, yeah," Wes said, drumming on his knees. "Luna's gonna be fucking psyched you're her date, boss."

I tugged at the tight tie, wondering how people wore these to work every damn day. It made me feel like I was choking.

"Luna said there might be potential donors there tonight?" Elián asked, right to business. I nodded.

"You gonna schmooze 'em?" he asked.

"Yes," I said firmly. "With Luna there, I feel like I can do anything."

The words tumbled out freely—I was helpless to stop them.

"You got it *bad*, bro." Wes grinned. "But we all saw it coming from a mile away. Right, Elián?"

Elián chuckled. "There was water cooler talk."

"Yeah, yeah," I said, trying to shrug it off. "More donations came in today, right?" I asked Wes.

"Yeah, they did. But, uh, I don't know. They're kind of trickling off. Still more than we ever got. But I think we're hitting the end of it, maybe."

I exchanged a look with Elián, who lifted a shoulder. "I agree with Wes. There's only so much attention people are willing to give through Luna. I think it's time the donors become our donors. Our relationships."

"Which means talking to them," I finished.

"Which you can do now," Elián said. "We dodged the gap. It's been 30 days and we're doing really well actually. It's time to move on, think of the future, you know?"

I blew out a breath. "Okay. Anything come in the mail I can use for stories?" I found that if I focused on an exchange like I'd seen between Jimmy and Wes that day, being vulnerable felt easier somehow. It was a truth I was revealing, not a half-lie to manipulate someone into giving me money I'd owe them for.

"I'm glad you asked, boss," Wes exclaimed. "Check out this shit."

He walked over, bobbing his head as usual, and handed

me a card from New York City. The return address label said "Quinn-Cavendish III."

"We have any adoptive families this far away?" I asked.

Elián shook his head. "Not that I remember."

I opened the card—it said "thank you" on the front. Inside was a picture of a dog I remembered well.

Matilda.

She'd been a huge pitbull; craggy face, giant body. We'd found her abandoned here but were completely out of space. I couldn't just let her go and I refused to send her to a shelter where I knew she'd be a candidate for euthanasia. We'd been in extreme luck—a friend of Jem's, Sasha, had been in town and mentioned she worked at the Manhattan Island Animal Rescue shelter. She escorted Matilda back to New York City, but that was two years ago. Last I'd heard, she was still in the shelter, waiting to be adopted.

A picture fell out. A wealthy-looking white man in a suit stood with his arms wrapped around Matilda. Behind them, with a matching smile, was a white woman who looked like the lead singer in a punk band. Partially shaved head, tattoos everywhere. The couple didn't fit, at least at first glance.

But the love they had for each other would have been obvious to anyone.

And they were holding Matilda—our Matilda—like she was their most prized possession.

Dear Lucky Dog, the note began. *My extremely brilliant— and incredibly convincing—girlfriend Roxy forced me to adopt Matilda one night early on in our courtship. To say this dog has changed my life irrevocably would be an understatement. She has brought me an unconditional love I have never experienced before. We heard recently from Sasha that Matilda came from your fine establishment, so on this first anniversary of her joining our family, please let us extend our sincerest gratitude. You have made our lives wonderful.*

The bottom was signed: *Best regards, Edward Christopher Cavendish III.*

Elián grabbed the picture. "Matilda. I thought she'd be in that shelter forever."

"Me too," I said, throat tightening. I knew the story I could share now if someone asked me.

"Oh, and that fancy dude sent this too." Wes dug in his pockets and pulled out a check.

Edward Christopher Cavendish the whatever had sent us five grand. A sticky note was stuck to it that read: *My rich boyfriend is extremely rich. Don't worry. I'll make sure he sends even more next time.—Roxy Quinn.*

"What a mismatched couple," I muttered. But the check felt right. The check was ours, not from Luna.

Elián pinned the card next to a picture that Buzz had sent us a few days ago—Jack Sparrow looked right at home on Buzz's boat. He was not dressed in a full sailor costume. But he proudly wore a bandana covered in tiny fish.

"Think I've got a few stories," I said, clearing my throat.

As Wes left to respond to emails, I turned to Elián, crossed my arms. Fidgeted a little in my jacket. "I guess it is time for you and me to start making a five-year plan or whatever. Do... investments."

He cracked a smile. "Yeah, we gotta do those investments."

"You know what I mean. You're right. Luna's not going to be helping us forever."

"I don't know about that," he said slyly. "She fucking loves it here. She even seems to like the grumpy douche who stomps around grumbling all day."

I pinned him with a serious look. "You, uh... you think she actually does, though? Like me?"

"*Luna?*" Elián said. "She's been walking around with hearts for eyes ever since she met you. She's almost as obsessed as you are. Look, and now she's taking you to be her fancy date. You mean a lot to her."

"Think she understands I've never, ever been invited to be in a room full of people like this tonight?"

He lifted a shoulder. "Who cares? You're going now."

I knew why I was feeling this way—I was entering Luna's world tonight. And not the world I usually saw her in—kneeling in the dirt so she could pet Penelope or working on mock-ups with her staff at her office. This was *billionaire* shit. The next level.

"I'm not sure I measure up," I admitted.

"You measure way the hell up," Elián said, clapping me on the shoulder. "Don't ever forget it."

I hoped I did. Really fucking hoped.

Because I was pretty damn sure I was head over heals in love with Luna.

52

BECK

I parked about a mile from Luna's event, needing the air. Needing a walk to clear the crop of worries that had invaded my thoughts. Worries that I loved Luna and she couldn't possibly love me back.

Worried that we'd always be too different to ever be anything more. Worried that her pet project—Lucky Dog— was merely a means to an end and she'd drop me like a hot potato.

I hated giving these thoughts power. But they were loud. Louder than normal. Which was why as I walked along the sidewalk I didn't notice the group of motorcycles and riders beneath a palm tree.

Or my mother.

"Evenin', son," she said, in a voice like steel.

I stopped, mid-stride—turning slowly.

Time had not been kind to my mother—although she still gave off a dangerous air I was sure terrified the younger recruits. People assumed it was Rip, my father, who handled the Miami Devils with an iron fist.

They couldn't have been more wrong.

Georgie wore her leather vest. Seven other MC members stood behind her with a coolness that didn't hide their intent. They were here to intimidate.

I was standing there in a three-piece suit on my way to see my billionaire girlfriend. From the smirk on Georgie's face, she caught the irony.

I debated walking past—ignoring the problem—but something told me they wouldn't let me off that easy. And the last thing I wanted was them showing up at Luna's event.

My old instincts rose immediately. But I wasn't a scared, desperate kid anymore. I was a forty-year-old man who'd spent two decades building the life I wanted. I didn't look down. Didn't cower or hunch my shoulders.

I strode up to my mother with a quiet fury. One I'm sure she recognized.

"What the fuck are you doing here, Georgie?" I asked as soon as I reached them.

My mother actually winced at her given name. But I hadn't called my parents "Mom" or "Dad" since I was fifteen. I wouldn't start now.

"We ride on Friday nights down here, you know that," she said with a sniff. "Certainly didn't think I'd see my son heading towards those lights over there in a monkey suit. Must be that new rich girl of yours."

Fire burned up my spine. I knew it. Knew they were keeping tabs on me and Luna. How could they not? She was one of the wealthiest women in the city, for fuck's sake. A mark.

"How have the past two decades been?" She tried a motherly smile I didn't buy.

"You need to leave us alone," I said, voice low.

"And you don't belong here," she spat out, dropping the act.

"You don't know shit, Georgie," I snapped.

She looked impressed with my temper. "There's a lot of work for you in the MC, Beck. We can forgive your twenty-year dalliance. Especially if you bring all that money the rich girl's been giving you."

"That money's nonprofit," I said.

The guys standing around her all smirked. As did she. "Right," she said, as if we were all in on the joke.

I took a step closer—registered the other members fully taking in my size for the first time. I'd always been tall, but I was carrying fifty pounds more muscle than I had at eighteen.

"If you come near me or Luna ever again, I'll call the cops and have you all fucking arrested," I said softly. Dangerously. "Do not threaten my new life, Georgie. You'll lose."

Her face looked exactly like it had the day I'd asked her about applying for community college. *You really think they'll let you in?*

I was turning on my heel, fists clenched at my sides, when she said one last thing. "You honestly think you fit in this new life?"

I stopped. Hated myself for it.

"You're a *Mason*. Which means you're goddamn motorcycle trash. These new rich people in your life, your new girlfriend included, will never, *ever* think of you as anything more."

What had I said to Wes and Jem the other day? *Never forget your value*. I'd said it because of this moment right here, because holding tight to your value was hard when people who were supposed to love you called you *trash*.

"And if you think that woman doesn't secretly feel the same way, you have another thing coming, son."

I walked the hell away. Because Georgie Mason didn't deserve a response.

Because this situation didn't deserve my time.

Because I didn't want the Miami Devils to see how much my mother's words affected me.

53

LUNA

*T*he event was Miami's Business Woman of the Year award and it was a glitzy, glamorous affair held at the country club right on Miami Beach. Tables draped with white tablecloths sat on the beach and local elite business folk mingled with piña coladas in their hands. News stations and camera crews were out, covering the event since it boasted some of the wealthiest members of our community. The organizer was a woman named Alissa Hendrix and she was currently walking toward me in a white suit. She was a tall Black woman, about ten years older than me, and she radiated competence.

"You've had the worst month," she said, lips curved into a graceful smile. She kissed my cheek and squeezed my hands.

"It'll be okay," I promised. "I can't tell you what it means that you invited me to do this. The attendees aren't going to storm the podium with pitchforks, are they?"

"Nope," she said. "When our speaker got sick late last night, I thought of you immediately. I understand the complications of your situation, believe me. And I think you're a model for how leaders move forward after scandal. By reorienting their values and placing them at the center of their decision-making. Admitting wrongdoing, taking responsibility. It's not easy. You could have taken several much easier ways out. Many leaders do."

"I... I guess I never even considered that," I said.

"Exactly," Alissa said. "That's why you're here, Luna. Also, there's an incredibly handsome man in a suit staring at you right now."

When I turned around and saw Beck Mason in a tailored, dark-blue suit, my body went up in flames. "Oh, that's... well, you know who that is, right?"

"The man who runs Lucky Dog." She didn't say, *the ex-con with a criminal family*. And I was pretty sure it was on purpose.

"Beck's my date tonight."

"Lucky you," she mused. "Come find me in a few minutes and we'll get you up on that stage."

Beck moved through a crowd that naturally parted for him. Lucky *me* indeed. Beck Mason in a suit was a sight that could have stopped rush-hour traffic. He looked even taller, the blue suit made his eyes stand out even more. Hair combed, beard neat and trimmed, hands in his pockets like he wasn't sure what to do with them.

I knew what I wanted him to do with them.

"You look so handsome," I said as he approached. Unable to stop myself.

"You look... perfect," he said softly.

I fingered my dress. My gown was orange, floor-length, completely open in the back with a high neck. I'd pinned my hair all the way up.

I'd dressed for Beck, one hundred percent.

"Can I kiss you here?" he asked.

"I'd expect nothing less."

He stepped forward. Smoothed a palm down my spine,

tugging me into his chest. Caressed his lips over mine. A tease.

I gripped his beard and kissed him hard.

When he pulled back, there were shadows in his eyes I hadn't seen before—it felt like he was memorizing my face—like he'd never see me again.

"Are you okay?" I asked, hand on his chest.

"Yeah," he said. "I'm fine."

But it had a note of falsehood I didn't like.

"Are you nervous?" he asked.

"Less now that you're here," I said. Which was a lie—Beck watching me speak gave me gigantic butterflies; telling him later tonight that I loved him had me so nervous I worried I might float away.

Strangely—that false note in his voice had me nervous too.

"You're going to dazzle them," he said.

I gave him a kiss on the cheek and smoothed down his tie. "Thank you. And you look like the respected executive director of an up-and-coming nonprofit. Go get those donations."

Beck nodded at me. Squeezed my fingers with that same shadowed look again. "I'll see you up there, sweetheart."

He moved through the crowd, stopping to chat with a small group of people at the bar. Beck was stepping into his leadership and I couldn't have been happier or prouder. From the stage, Alissa waved me over and Jasmine gave me a wry look from behind one of the tables. I lifted my chin, walked right past her. A few news vans had shown up, cameras blinking. The coverage would be positive regardless—a hopeful sign that Wild Heart was regaining its footing.

I was going to give this damn speech from my heart. *Not* take the easy way out.

And then take the hottie in the suit home and tell him I was in love with him.

54

BECK

I held a beer and watched the woman of my dreams climb the steps to a small stage in the middle of the beach. Luna da Rosa looked extraordinary—strong, confident, brilliant.

I couldn't help but feel like an outsider. A fake, pretending to fit in this society I'd never once belonged to. The group of businesspeople I'd just spoken to had been polite but prissy. Almost dismissive. They dripped with Rolexes and diamonds and designer labels—and when I told them I was Beck Mason, executive director of Lucky Dog, I'd caught a shared look between them all. So I'd stumbled through the elevator pitch Elián had been helping me with, fucking it up halfway through, and I wasn't surprised when they made their excuses to leave.

You're a Mason. Which means you're goddamn motorcycle trash.

I swallowed a growl of frustration. Knew Elián and Wes and Jem and all the dogs were counting on me. And the last thing I needed was Georgie Mason's bullshit making me feel bad for no reason.

As if sensing I needed her, Luna caught my eye from the stage. Like she'd done for me when I'd made the video, I placed my palm over my heart. She caught the gesture. Beamed at me like she'd done the first day we'd met.

"Good evening, Beck," Jasmine said. She wore her usual sour expression.

"Hey," I said, taking a sip of beer. Luna was talking on-stage with a tall woman, both gesturing excitedly.

"I'd still like to set up that meeting with you. To discuss your image."

I looked at her. "Luna said it wasn't a problem weeks ago. It still isn't."

Just a reminder who Luna da Rosa's boyfriend is.

"Will you continue seeing her?" she asked.

"Yes," I said firmly, before nerves could get the best of me. "*Of course.*"

"Then this is always going to be a problem." Jasmine held out her phone to show me a random tabloid article. I should have ignored it.

But I looked anyway.

One of my mug shots—I looked young and hungry and snarly—had been paired next to a still of Luna the night of her TED Talk. I looked like a feral animal. Luna looked like a glowing corporate princess.

The comparison wasn't lost on me. I was a goddamn human, after all.

I shrugged, training my eyes back on Luna. My anchor.

"Luna sees otherwise," I said shortly.

Jasmine huffed a little, as if my very existence was a frustration.

"Listen, Beck," she started. I turned at the sincerity in her tone. "If you... if you're serious about Luna, you need to take a hard look at how you affect her. Her reputation as a spokeswoman, as the personal brand for Wild Heart, is what makes them so successful. She won't stay down forever."

"I agree," I said. "Look at her up there." On stage, with the sun setting behind us and the light in shades of pink, Luna glowed. Chin lifted, shoulders back—she was a woman comfortable in her own skin, a warrior leading her company through the next stage of battles. A true leader. I looked at the crowd's faces, their awe. Luna's charm was cranked all the way up. It sparked off her like a storm of lightning.

"If you agree, then you'll do what's best for her," Jasmine said, indicating the people around us. "You won't hold her back."

"I would never—" I started to say—harshly—but Jasmine was already gone, moving back through the crowd.

You won't hold her back.

Her words lodged themselves in the darkest, weakest corners of my thoughts.

I usually knew a match when I saw one, but it was hard when our worlds were so fucking different.

There was a loud roar from the street behind me. Twenty motorcycles drove past, slow enough for me to see the screaming skull on the back of their jackets. There was no way they'd be able to get into this beach—too much security—but they were sending me one final message.

Goddamn motorcycle trash.

That would only hold back that beautiful woman on the stage.

55

LUNA

*T*he words of my speech swam before my eyes. My fingers wouldn't stop trembling. Which was unusual for me—I didn't fear public speaking. But I did fear the anxiety that was storming its way in. Facing a crowd of people who'd had nasty things to say about me just the other week.

I thought about Beck that day with Jimmy. Courage. Value. The bravery of speaking your truth and not caring about what others might say.

I put my phone down. Flipped it over so I couldn't see the speech I'd written. It was a good speech, but I was going to have to flay myself open without any prompts tonight.

I was going full-on Beck Mason.

"Good evening, everyone," I said. "I'm incredibly honored to be here this evening with all of you, the women I respect most in this community." I swallowed hard, caught Beck in the crowd. I couldn't read the strange look on his face. "Ten years ago, I had two goals in mind. To create a successful cosmetics company that could change the beauty industry and its horrible animal testing practices." I swallowed. "The other was to make enough money I could give it all away. The first one I've done—or I did, until I made a huge mistake and decided to partner with a company that didn't match my values. And for that I've apologized, but allow me to repeat myself—I am truly sorry. Please know Wild Heart has been following through on all of the promises we made to ensure this never happens again. It was absolutely my fault, and it was absolutely a decision based entirely on greed and not justice."

I looked down at my notes, seeking comfort, then remembered I was winging it.

"The second part isn't true," I continued. "I'm speaking now to everyone on this beach who is extraordinarily wealthy, like me. Who is extraordinarily successful, like me. Isn't it interesting how the more you make, the more terrified you become of losing it? I'm sitting on more money than I could realistically spend in a lifetime and yet I hoard it for myself."

I paused—the audience was shifting in the sand. I could hear throats being cleared.

"I take my role as a young, female entrepreneur seriously. It's a level of success that has been denied to women in our society. I am proud to be here, proud of my best friends, who have also worked incredibly hard to be here while maintaining their ethics and integrity. That's no easy feat," I said, catching Alissa's eye. "I am proud to have founded a company that I poured my blood, sweat and tears into. But money can be directed towards good or evil, nonprofits, or in my case, more yoga pants than a woman could ever wear."

A smattering of laughter—but it was very, very true.

"We all get to direct our money in the way that matters the most to us. That could be our families, our children, our pets. Our homes, our art. Books, travel, adventure. To pay our bills so we don't lose our home. To pay for gas so we can visit a loved one in the hospital every day. Because I have so very much of it, I believe it should be given away. That is *my* choice. The one I'm rededicating myself to, having lost my way."

My voice wavered a bit at the end. I paused. Took a breath.

"I want to live in a world where humans and animals and the natural world have value. I never want that taken away." I looked right at Beck. "From anyone. Tonight I'd like to formally announce the Wild Heart Foundation, which will act as the funding arm of the Wild Heart company. Philanthropy will be at the heart of our company moving forward. Giving back. Paving the way for even more corporations to give even more of their profits to community organizations that are changing things for the better." I swallowed, thought about that girl in the picture, sandy hair and a happy heart. "Philanthropy will be at the heart of my life, moving forward. Because it's time. And I believe all of us can agree that we have the power to chart our businesses on a better course. That is what I believe *real* business is about. And that is how I believe the women in this audience can stand out, do better, be better. A rising tide lifts all boats, as they say. Let's lift them all."

I looked at Alissa, who nodded in approval. "Thank you," I said into the microphone. The audience clapped—really clapped—but I felt shaky, light, dizzy, weird. Side effects of being honest, I guessed. The audience was still clapping. I smiled. Waved a little. Made my way off the stage to find Beck.

But I was crushed—Jasmine, gripping my elbow and pulling me towards a trio of cameras.

"I need to find Beck first," I said to her.

"Interviews first, Beck second," she said. A mic was shoved into my face and ten years of public relations training kicked in. As the event continued around us, I gave a handful of interviews about the foundation—all while scanning the crowd. Where was my boyfriend?

And by the time I finally extricated myself from Jasmine and camera crews, I spotted his broad back. Walking down Ocean Drive.

Away from me.

56

BECK

I knew two things as I watched Luna declare her values and her dreams for the world up on that stage.

I *was* in love with her.

And I had to end it.

I stayed long enough to watch her finish her speech and give interviews—watched the crowd surge toward her. Cameras and reporters were trying to get to her. The applause after her speech was enthusiastic. If Luna had been looking forward to starting fresh, tonight was that night.

You won't hold her back, will you?

"Beck, wait."

Luna's voice, floating toward me in the crowd. I was making my way to the street, which was filled with the usual tourists. People were out, having a blast along South Beach, while I was having my heart broken.

"Beck, wait, where are you going?" There was a blur of orange and then an arm, yanking me behind a building.

"Hey," Luna said. "Where are you running off to? Was my

speech okay? Do you want to go out for celebratory tacos later tonight?"

She was babbling, bright-eyed. Flushed.

My fists clenched at my side, desperate to kiss her. Hold her one last time.

I took a step back, putting distance between us. "Your speech was incredible. You're incredible—" I broke off, voice thick.

"Why, thank you," she said. "You were my inspiration."

I looked down at my feet but no extra courage was there.

"I bumped into my mother and her crew on the walk over here tonight," I said. "She wanted to drop by to remind me that I'm motorcycle trash that will never belong."

Fury slashed across Luna's face, twisting her mouth. "That's categorically untrue, Beck Mason."

"Is it?" I asked.

Now it was Luna's turn to step back. "Of course it is. You know that. You're so much more than your family or your past. You're... you're *everything*."

Her words stunned me for a second.

"Jasmine doesn't think so," I managed, coughing out the words.

She looked confused. "Jasmine? Wait, what did Jasmine say to you?"

"She told me I was always going to be a problem for you. My past. My family. I was holding you back."

Luna grabbed my hand like she knew I was trying to back away.

"I don't know why she would say that," she said. "And I'm truly sorry she did."

"I'm not," I said sadly. "We've talked so much about authenticity, Luna. Honesty. The truth. Doesn't part of you believe that to be the truth?"

"Not at all." She gripped me tighter. "Besides, I don't care. You *know* I don't care about that, Beck. I only care about you."

"I'm not so sure," I said, feeling like a bastard. Feeling more like a bastard when I realized it was the truth. I *wasn't* sure Luna still didn't feel the allure of Instagram comments and branding opportunities. It had been her life for ten years, after all.

Luna let me go. Our line in the sand was forming and I wasn't going to budge.

It was better, really, if I didn't.

"If I cared that much about my reputation, how come I never stopped working with you?" she said, swallowing over and over. Like she was trying to fend off tears. "Your past and your family have been an issue since literally the beginning. You told me. Jasmine told me. I could have cut contact with you a hundred different times and didn't. Because I... I..." She stopped.

"Maybe you should have," I said. "If my mom is showing back up in my life again, we have a problem. It will always *be* a problem, Luna."

"You never changed your last name," she said quietly.

"What?"

"You never changed your last name," she said, louder this time. "I just realized. Your last name is recognizable and hated and you could have legally changed it twenty years ago. But you didn't."

My jaw worked, teeth grinding. "Your point?"

"It's the same as why you started the nonprofit even though you knew you'd struggle being the leader. You, Beck Mason, are no longer held hostage by the demands of your family. You don't care. If you did, you'd be Beck Smith right now. But you kept it like a badge of honor. I think you kept it to remind yourself they don't matter to you. What did you say about them the other night? *They're worth less than the dog shit on the bottom of a shoe.*"

Having my words thrown back at me like that didn't feel so great.

Neither did admitting she was right about my last name.

"That doesn't mean we're still going to work out, Luna."

"Is *that* what we're discussing right now?" Her dark eyes flashed. "Whether or not our relationship will be successful?"

"Luna," I said. Gentler this time. Her face lit up with hope and I died a little bit inside. "Tell me you actually see a future between the two of us. I have four hundred dollars to my name and zero formal education. I'll never be a vegan or a shaman or a yoga instructor or some charming, witty guy you can take to functions filled with rich assholes. We don't *look* right."

"Who cares what we *look* like?" she shot back.

"You do," I said.

She took a step back, a deep hurt in her eyes. It felt like I was being carved out, gutted. Georgie's words wouldn't stop, I was helpless to resist them. *You think your girlfriend will ever see you as more than just motorcycle trash?*

This was a fantasy and I'd known it all along.

"Beck," Luna begged—and she was crying now. "Please don't do this. Whatever it is you're about to do."

"I don't think we should see each other anymore," I said, every word dragging from my throat like a heavy stone. "We've had a lot of... fun. But you and I both know it's time."

Silence hung between us—punctured by people laughing, shouting, the ocean waves. Luna looked completely shocked.

"Well, that sucks," she said finally. "Because I'm like totally and completely, in love with you, Beck Mason."

Who showed you love, Beck?

Luna. Luna does. Or did. It was too tempting to cast off my doubts. Run off into the sunset with the rainbow billionaire.

But we'd only be having this argument a month from now. I knew it.

"Okay," I said. Like a coward.

Which pissed her the hell off. Which was fine by me—I preferred her anger to her tears.

"Walls back up, huh?" she said. She lifted her chin, wiped her cheeks. I didn't reply. "I know it's scary. I know we have to trust each other. But guess what? I trust you, Beck. I trust you and I'm in love with you."

"I don't trust you," I said, the truth of that startling me. There'd always been a grain of it left in there—the differences in our power, our status, our wealth were so shockingly high, how could I not?

She went still as a stone. Fury gone. Tears gone. Energy zapped back in. She looked silently devastated.

"That's that, then," she said. "If you don't trust me, we can't be together."

"Right," I said.

Her lip trembled. "Right," she repeated. "I guess we're over."

"I guess."

Without another word, Luna da Rosa walked away from me, head held high. And I watched her, watched her until she blended into Miami's nightlife crowd. Watched the love of my life take my heart with her.

I wasn't ever going to get it back.

But it was for the best.

57

LUNA

*N*ights like these were the reason why the enclave had been built. Why Emily, Cameron, Daisy and I insisted on building mansions next door to each other. Because I couldn't, wouldn't, was *physically unable* to crawl through the front door of my house.

Instead, as I waited for my driver, I sent a single text to our group chat: *Beck broke up with me.*

Immediately, Cameron texted: *We'll be here when you're dropped off.*

I'd stashed my phone in my purse and pasted a fake smile on for Alissa. After I'd left Beck Mason, the love of my life, I'd calmly walked back to the event and proceeded to network like the CEO that I was. There were a number of business-women committed to making future, substantial gifts to the Wild Heart Foundation.

I would have been over the moon—finally feeling like *me* again—if my heart hadn't been ripped out.

That truth sat like a heavy stone in my stomach, weighing me down all night. A night I barely got through. I'd just told a man that I loved him and he'd responded with *I don't trust you.*

I couldn't blame him.

The billionaire devil on my shoulder had claimed another victim. Wasn't I probably to blame? From the moment we'd met, Beck had suspected I was using Lucky Dog for my own reputation. *And I was.* Or I had been. That wasn't exactly the right way to start off a relationship with someone.

As I waited for my driver, feet aching, head aching, heart numb, Alissa waited with me. She leveled a cool gaze my way —like she could see all of my secrets.

"I believe in what you said tonight. The way money affects us, changes us. I'm awake most nights, terrified I'll lose everything. When the truth is, I don't need any more cash, that's for sure."

My jaw clenched. "Yeah. That's me all the time now."

I raised my arm when I saw my driver, hailing him over.

"Is it true Wild Heart lost its contract with Fischer Home Goods?"

"It is," I said, preparing to say goodbye. Alissa handed me her business card with a smile.

"We're not a mega-corporation like Fischer. But we're women-run, independent. A lot of things we sell are eco-conscious. Vegan. Wild Heart might be the right fit for our stores. We've been looking for a cosmetics line to feature."

"In Ruby's Closet?" I asked, incredulous. They were *way* smaller than Fischer but I admired them *so much more.* "I've, I mean, I've always been a huge fan of your store."

"Maybe Wild Heart should contract with a business that matches your values better," Alissa said. Then she gave me a wave before walking away.

Through the fog of sadness shone a small ray of light. A direction. Sylvia would love it.

I loved it.

I went to step into the car when suddenly Jasmine

appeared, looking dour as ever and strapped to her phone. But she did perk up a bit when she saw me.

"People loved you," she said. And she wasn't wrong. "Can you do a couple more interviews with the news before you leave?"

"No, I'm going home," I said. I felt slimy enough already. "Jasmine, I need to ask you a question," I said. She was still staring at her screen. Ignoring me. "*Jasmine.*"

My tone was sharp enough that she looked up. "What?"

"Did you tell Beck that he was only ever going to hold me back?"

She swallowed. "I mean... yes. It's true though."

"So... Beck just dumped me."

There it was—a gleam of victory in her eyes.

"Which I'm guessing might have been your plan for this evening all along."

"Like *you two* were going to last?" She laughed, but *with* me, like I was going to join her. Like we were going to cackle the night away, laughing at poor Beck. "You can be real with me, Luna. You don't have to pretend anymore."

I tapped my fingers on the door. Tilted my head like a hawk. "Okay. I won't pretend anymore. You're fired, Jasmine."

Her face registered total shock. "Excuse me?"

"We're on different journeys," I said with mock sympathy. "I don't want you on mine. Love and light." I flashed her a peace sign and slipped into the car. She was outraged, yelling at me as we drove away.

"Can you take me to my house, please?" I asked my driver. But my voice broke on *house.*

I sat back. Let the tears fall freely.

You'll be here soon, Emily had texted. *We've got you.*

Which I needed, desperately. Because the only man I'd ever loved didn't love me back.

And when we finally pulled up, they were standing there, like they had that night three weeks ago. The Charlie's Angels of Friendship. They scooped me up and took me inside, listening to my tale of woe. Our breakup. Beck's face in the crowd. The audience applause. His mother. Jasmine.

They ran me a hot bath and plopped me right into it. Poured me a glass of wine. Held my hands as I cried.

"I'm already prepping the yacht with corn chips and spin instructors with vegetable names," Daisy said. I half-giggled, half-sobbed. "Just say the word. You ever been to a private island owned by a European prince? I'll take you and your spin instructors there."

"Corn chips sound nice," I hiccupped.

"Shhhh," Cameron said, handing me an open bag. "We'll go spend way too much money on lingerie tomorrow, okay?"

I nodded. Ate a corn chip. Felt worse.

"I know you abhor violence, Moon. But the three of us will junk-punch anyone you tell us to." Emily stroked my hair in a gesture so maternal it caused another wave of tears. "You want to make a list? We'll clear our morning schedules."

"I love you guys," I said.

"We love you forever," Cameron promised.

58

LUNA

Two weeks later

The Wilson Family Center was a cheerful-looking building with a white picket fence outside and a wildflower garden spilling over with blossoms. A row of palm trees in the front gave it a sense of privacy from the busy street out front.

Christian, the program manager, waited with Sylvia and me while my driver came to grab us.

"We're really happy you both could make it," he said. "The kids here love Wild Heart. They're big followers of yours on social media. It'd be extra special if the funding we need for our new kitchen came from the Wild Heart Foundation."

"I agree," I said. "Submit your application by next month and I'll have the board take an extra special look at it. Also, the makeup skills displayed in this tiny house put me to *shame*."

The Wilson Family Center was a twelve-bed shelter for homeless youth in Miami and their kitchen was in dire need of repair. The kids couldn't cook or take cooking classes without it. The visit today was merely to verify what I'd already learned—they were doing incredible work that deserved long-term support.

I'd also donated almost all of my kitchen supplies to them (minus the blender Cam had rigged that could have been a military-grade weapon) and a handful of other furniture pieces for their lounge. I'd been slowly stripping my mansion of items over the past two weeks—I had *more* than enough, and there were plenty of nonprofits nearby who told me they could use new tables or better chairs or artwork to brighten up play areas for children.

I was happy to oblige.

I'd been dazzled by all the kids at the Wilson Family Center showing off their different makeup styles to me, their hair colors, their vibrantly-painted nails and clothing. It was a place of joyful, warm spaces that helped youth transform from isolated to embraced. Art as healing was at the center of their programming, and that artistry extended out into the way they dressed and accessorized their bodies.

Christian also might have mentioned last week how much the kids loved makeup. And I might have sent like a one-year supply of products their way ahead of time.

"Well, we appreciate it. We've also been looking into starting a therapy animal program, to help the kids when they're first with us, before they start to feel safe. I know you worked with that nonprofit Lucky Dog. Do you think the director over there might have any contacts?"

All the air left my lungs.

"Beck Mason, you mean?" I didn't need to clarify with his name. But I was suddenly desperate to say it out loud. To hear it spoken.

"Yeah. I know his nonprofit works with rescue dogs, but I

thought he might know who in Miami is running therapy dog programs. The kids would love it." I could see it in my mind's eye clearly, how perfectly therapy animals would augment this program. The unconditional love, the sense of caring for a living thing. It was like the program Beck had done when he was in the detention center.

"You should definitely call him," I said. "He's great. Like really great. A truly beautiful soul, you know?"

Sylvia was giving me an odd look—sympathetic but also confused.

"Oh. Cool," Christian said. "I'll give him a call, tell him you sent me his way."

"Sure." I faked a big smile, feeling itchy. "Well, our ride is here." I took Christian's hand, shook it. "Please send in the application. I look forward to reading it."

Christian waved at us as we drove off.

"I'm really, really happy we did that," I said, noting the total happiness I was feeling in the moment, even with the mention of Beck. "I know we've both been busy with Wild Heart stuff but—"

"It's important," Sylvia replied. "It's the mission moments that keep you going. And you got to see the benefit of your foundation *and* makeup. A twofer."

"I did," I said, looking out the window. "The only hard part is wanting to give all the money to all the nonprofits everywhere."

Sylvia smiled, but she looked tired. We both were. Tired but weirdly energized—working with a purpose. The last two weeks we'd been hard at work crafting the structure of the foundation, hiring staff, working with the accountant. We still needed to hire a director and program managers. It was daunting. Thrilling.

Funding wouldn't be available for months, but I was doing some early site visits for qualified candidates, learning what they needed and the best way our program could truly help. It was the perfect distraction from the other work I was doing—rebuilding Wild Heart's reputation from the ground up, basically. There was a flurry of positive press after my speech and announcement, but now I mostly ignored, well, any form of media that came my way.

The only way out was through—the only way out was dedication to why Wild Heart had been founded in the first place. We re-signed with our original supplier and took tours of their facilities to confirm their promise. Started new production. Wild Heart formally signed an in-store contract with Ruby's Closet, and as soon as we had enough product, it'd be rolling out in Alissa's stores. Our footprint would be smaller for a while, but I was okay with that.

At least we were back to doing the right thing. I'd never been more at peace. Professionally-speaking.

By day I buried myself in hard work.

By night I was completely and utterly miserable. Heartbroken in every sense of the word. I couldn't meditate. Couldn't focus long enough to do yoga. Feeding Steve brought me no joy and our continually horny dolphins only brought out a strange jealousy in me. *At least they get to have love.*

Daisy, Cameron and Emily kept me busy and affirmed. We ate vegan ice cream and watched bad movies. They brought me donuts and let me cry for no reason. Daisy even took me out on her yacht one night, where we drank a bottle of champagne *each* while bemoaning our single life. And maybe she convinced me to jump naked into the ocean with her too.

It all helped—in that I needed soothing and comfort and platonic love to keep me going.

But my heart stayed broken and missing Beck so much it felt like I couldn't breathe. I thought breaking up meant that the love you felt for that person abated slowly over time, as you accepted that you weren't to be. You *weren't* soul mates or forever companions or life partners. You were done, broken up.

That wasn't happening for me. I loved Beck, fully, the same as I did the night we ended. Every second, every minute, every hour. My heart beat *Beck* and my pulse beat *Beck* and my body ached and yearned and craved Beck.

And my Instagram posts were capital "s" Sad. I didn't say we'd broken up, but I did take a lot of pictures of sad, empty ice cream containers or shared lonely lines of poetry. If people wanted the real Luna da Rosa—well, she was heartbroken.

"Can we talk about the email you sent late last night?" Sylvia asked.

"Of course," I said, expecting it. "Does that sound like it will work? I have a meeting with my accountant tomorrow to work out the logistics."

She gave me a long look. "It does work. I think it's the right thing to do. You think the person you were the night I met you is gone. But that's not true at all, Luna. That twenty-two-year-old visionary is sitting right in front of me."

I looked out the window at Miami Beach, shimmering blue. "That means more to me than I can say," I said, tears in my throat. "It wasn't a hard choice in the end. Just had to listen to the right voice."

She was talking about the email I'd sent letting her know that ninety percent of my CEO salary would now be directed to the Wild Heart Foundation as a private gift. I didn't want it to be received with the perception of strings or make the staff give me more power. But it was the right place for it to go. It's where it belonged.

"You'll be okay? Financially?" she asked.

"I'm a billionaire," I said. "Ten percent of my salary is still more than enough. The rest of that money is sitting there, being spent on worthless things. This community deserves that money."

"If Jasmine still worked here," she said slowly, "she would tell you to issue a press release, announcing your charitable gift. This would garner you an immense amount of good media."

"No thanks," I said, voice clear. "Sometimes we need to do good things just to do them."

"Spoken like an extraordinary woman," Sylvia said.

I squeezed her hand, tears in her eyes.

"You know, I never asked you," I finally said, throat tight, "why did you give me Lucky Dog to work for? Was there any reason beyond you thought they looked like the right fit for me?"

Her smile was mysterious. "Charlotte and I adopted our dog from them four years ago, when they'd recently opened. I met Beck then, was incredibly impressed with his heart and his spirit. I could see how little money they had and always wanted to do more for them." She shrugged. "Our dog, Betsy, is the best thing that's ever happened to us, besides getting married, of course."

"I didn't know Betsy came from Lucky Dog," I said, happy to hear it. "That place really is special." I was surprised I'd gotten the words out. My eyes were already filling with tears at the memory of standing on that campus. Seeing Beck with Penelope for the first time.

Sylvia was still staring at me. "It is. And I know you, Luna. I knew you'd love it."

We were pulling up to Wild Heart, slowing down to the curb. She opened the car door and said, "And for what it's worth, Charlotte and I are total opposites in every sense of the word. So different that a lot of people around us laughed when we got together. Swore we'd never make it." She lifted a shoulder gracefully. "Of course we've been together for twenty-five years now, so what do they know?"

She slipped out of the car and I stared back at her, open-mouthed. She had been playing nonprofit-fairy-godmother *and* matchmaker.

It would have made me laugh with delight if I didn't want to curl up in the fetal position and cry.

My phone buzzed.

Jem. She'd texted me a picture.

Biting my lip, I opened it. Heart racing. We hadn't talked since the night Beck and I had broken up. Missing my little Lucky Dog family was like the shitty icing on the shitty cake. But I didn't want to impose—wasn't sure what Beck had told them.

Thought you'd want to see this, Jem said. It was a picture of her and Wes, smiling at the beach, holding rainbow sno-cones.

GIRL WHAT I texted.

Dating for two weeks now! She wrote back. *We miss you!*

Me too. I miss you so much, I sent before I could stop myself. My phone had about a thousand draft text messages to Beck that I didn't send. *I love you. I'm sorry. I miss you. Please take me back.*

I don't know if this is still on the table, but Penelope is officially available for adoption starting today, she wrote. *Do you still want to submit an application for her?*

I did. Desperately. I wanted a dog and I wanted Penelope specifically.

But fear held me back. Fear that I'd never be able to stop

thinking about Beck when I looked at Penelope, since Beck was the man who'd rescued her.

I need to think about it. I'll let you know, promise. I said.

Jem didn't respond.

59

BECK

*E*lián and I had been looking at designs for the expansion we were now planning on our campus— adding another fifteen kennels and a second training space. At the rate new funds were coming in, I was going to be able to hire at least four new trainers and another two administrative staff to help Wes. We were already scouting out our second location near the Redlands.

It had been the most financially successful two weeks of my entire life.

It had also been the worst two weeks of my entire life.

I hadn't truly smiled since the night of Luna's speech, and had spent so much time grunting in response to things, Jem had thrown up her hands and said, "You have to speak with words, not sounds, Beck." Then she'd stomped off to see Wes, which I didn't blame her for.

The pair had been dating since Luna and I had broken up. Maybe their new love was one of the reasons why I couldn't seem to do anything but grumble, growl and throw things around my office.

But it was Friday—exactly fourteen days after I'd broken

up with Luna—and I was exhausted. I wanted a beer and my bike and the high-speed of a solitary ride to drown out my thoughts.

Instead, I was being surprised by the Carlisle Foundation again.

"Albert's not here," the older Black woman from before said, coming through my office door. "It's just me this time. I'm Justine. I'm sorry Albert's a giant asshole."

I barked out a surprised laugh and she chuckled. "It's true. I thought you'd been made aware of our arrival or I wouldn't have hassled you with those questions. And I know I'm dropping in on you now. But it's purely to apologize. Our visit didn't sit right with me.

I reached forward, shook her hand. "Apologies not necessary. I was looking at our expansion plans. Elián and I were going to walk the grounds in a minute. Want to come along?"

"Please," she said. "Lead the way."

Although I'd been glowering about like a bastard, this was actually my fifth tour this week—and I'd spoken at a church, a synagogue and a Girl Scout troop. Each time it was hard; each time it also got a little bit easier.

"We *are* investing now," I said, walking her past Penelope's kennel. My throat tightened and I had to look away before I lost it. "We've had three new board members come on who have been lending their experience to set up our... stock portfolios." That wasn't entirely the right word but I threw out a phrase I hoped sounded smart. Justine seemed impressed and I was grateful I didn't have to explain the nitty-gritty details. Which I didn't really get yet, but I was happy we had experts helping me learn. "Our first strategic plan will begin in November."

"Wonderful. You're really not that far behind for being a

grassroots nonprofit," she said. "You're right on target. The Wild Heart exposure certainly helped, I'm sure."

We reached the end of the field and I stuck my hands in my pockets. "Luna da Rosa is a very generous person."

"That she is," Justine said. "I've always admired her."

I'm still in love with her.

"I admired her too," I said quickly. The only reason I'd been able to stick to my decision to break us up was that it seemed like everything was getting better for Luna and Wild Heart. Her foundation was getting attention and I'd seen her on the news, making a call for nonprofits to start sending in proposals.

Without me in her life, she was rising. I'd been the one holding her back.

That is categorically untrue and you know it, Beck Mason.

Well—except that Luna's voice was in my head constantly. Begging me to change my mind.

"The kennels will be built in a semi-circle here. I'd like to put in a state-of-the-art training facility right there, where the edge of those trees are," I said, pointing things out to Justine. "Building offices will need to go in so we're not in trailers anymore, but I might save that cost after we expand. We're also looking at a second site near the Redlands, since it's a stray dog dumping ground. We could have an emergency triage area for those new dogs and then funnel them to our program, others, an emergency vet."

"And five years out?" Justine asked.

"Five more staff. Salaries increased fifty percent across the board. Better benefits. I'd love for our board to be stable at fifteen members, we only have six right now."

We were strolling back through the cages—Beatrix, looking mournful. Penelope, looking like she missed Luna. Sunshine was panting happily as Elián led her through a few last exercises—she'd made big strides and would be ready for her forever home any day now.

"Things are peaceful. Hopeful, here at Lucky Dog," I said to Justine. "Different from two months ago when we believed we would have to close for good."

"You're a great ambassador for your cause, Mr. Mason," Justine said. "I don't see why you shouldn't come down to our offices, give this speech in person."

"Oh," I said. "Um, thanks. I've been feeling more comfortable lately."

"Being the executive director isn't easy, but I can tell you've got the passion for it. Being a Mason isn't easy too."

My head whipped her way. "Excuse me?"

She nodded. "I'm born and raised in Miami, Beck. I know who you are. And I saw that video you made, the one where you spoke about your value. Leaving your family. That's an inspiration too. Courageous, like you said. Not shameful."

I blew out a breath, kicking a rock with the toe of my boot. "Thank you for saying that."

She patted my shoulder. "Now can I go take a look at that dog over there?" She was pointing to Sunshine.

"Sure," I said, amused. Wondered if there was a match brewing. I let Elián take her over and set up a possible interview. Neither my mother nor my father had reached out in the last two weeks, which was fine by me. Seeing her once had been enough to send me spinning back to all of those dark places.

I didn't want to do it again.

But it left me unsettled. Because I'd told Luna they'd be persistent, that they'd be an issue for us forever and ever.

And they were silent—as usual. No ride-bys. No bumping into MC members on the beach or seeing them on Ocean Drive. But this had always been their way—a little bit of emotional manipulation here or there to keep me on my toes.

Except... was that significant enough to end my relationship with Luna?

In the office, Wes flagged me down. "Groovy bundle of mail today, boss." He was permanently smiling now because of Jem, and even my cold heart couldn't be angry about it.

"First, these three checks." Wes handed them over and I recognized the names immediately: *Cameron Whitbury, Daisy Carter-Kincaid, Emily Stanton.* Each check was in the amount of $250,000. On the back of Daisy's check was a post-it note that read: *The three of us love Lucky Dog. But we are of the opinion that you're an asshat for dumping Luna.*

Cheeks hot, I jammed the post-it note into my back-pocket, heart hammering.

"This is next level," Wes said.

"Holy shit. You're right," I replied, still amazed that the people in Luna's world had access to money like this. "We'll be..." I swallowed hard. "We'll be set for a couple years with these. If we're careful."

"Right? Also *this*." Wes slapped a large white envelope down. It was a packet from the Wild Heart Foundation. Inside was a short letter.

From Luna.

The sight of her happy handwriting felt like a sucker punch. I sniffed. It was probably my imagination, but I thought I smelled oranges.

To the staff of Lucky Dog, thank you for allowing me to spend time with you. Your organization is truly a place of magic and miracles and I feel incredibly fortunate to have known all of you.

"Have known" felt like two sucker punches.

When we first met I also guaranteed a large financial gift to Lucky Dog on top of volunteering my time. I've attached a *funding agreement—the first from the Wild Heart Foundation. It would be a privilege to award Lucky Dog with our first grant early next year. The award would be $1 million over four years. I know how strategically you've been focusing on securing your financial future. I hope this gift allows you the flexibility to pay your bills while achieving your wildest dreams. All the best, Luna da Rosa.*

"This is like a fuck-ton of money, boss." Wes whooped, clapped his hands. "Can you *believe it*?"

"No," I said, voice rough. "I almost can't believe it." I thought of Willow—the way she'd stared at me the first day we met, like she knew I'd rescued her. The first night she'd spent with me in the jail cell, she had been terrified of the clanging doors. A sharp sound that made her shake. I had stayed awake all night, petting her, making her feel safe. I know it sounded cheesy as hell but that night literally *was* the first day of the rest of my life.

And now? We wouldn't have to turn away dogs just like her. We'd continue to rehabilitate. Save. The matches between dog and person that had the power to change lives.

Luna had done it. It was more than I ever could have hoped for. Almost two million dollars had landed on my desk today because of the woman I still felt devoted to. She was following through on her promises—her actions matched her words.

"Jem! Elián!" Wes was yelling for them from the door. My heart was hammering—thumb stroking across Luna's handwriting. Jem and Elián burst through the door, faces surprised.

"Did someone die?" Elián asked. "Why are we all yelling?"

"Because we just received almost two million in the fucking mail," I said, smile breaking across my face. A real one.

Elián came over while Jem squealed and leapt into Wes's

arms. He kissed her cheek as she giggled, spinning her around.

Elián gave me a half-hug, laughing and holding up the checks like he couldn't believe they were real. "Told ya working with Luna was a smart move."

"You were right," I admitted.

Luna was trusting me to spend this money well. Even with our breakup, she was showing me that she cared. That she trusted me.

Daisy was right. I was an asshat.

60

BECK

*B*eatrix was finally going home.

Wes, Jem, Elián and I all came out for this adoption interview because, according to Wes, "the lady who wants Beatrix is fucking *dope*."

I needed a happy story right now. It was a few days after Justine's visit and the big donations from Luna's foundation and her best friends.

I literally ached with missing her.

The only thing I could focus on—really, the smart thing to focus on—was Lucky Dog.

Jem had Beatrix on the leash. Beatrix's big head came up to her waist. She wasn't the snarling, terrified beast she'd been when we'd brought her in more than two months ago. But I was still wary. If Beatrix didn't like you, she didn't like you.

And I doubted she'd like the woman standing in front of us.

"Victoria Whitney," she said, holding out her hand like the Queen. I didn't know if she wanted me to kiss it or shake it or what. We all just stared at it until she placed it back on her expensive-looking handbag. Victoria was a white woman in her sixties, white hair, giant diamonds in her ears. She held a black umbrella to shield her from the sun, and her nose was tilted high.

"Beck Mason," I said. "This is my staff. I'm sorry, but did you say you're here for *Beatrix*?"

A curl of her lips. "Yes, well, I've flown all the way from Philadelphia because my arch-nemesis, Bitzi Peterson, told me I *had* to get my dog from your nonprofit. I was going to go *pure-bred,* as you can imagine."

She said this in a whisper, as if the tattooed ex-convicts standing around her were the kind of people who cared about a dog's pedigree.

"But Bitzi won't wear anything other than the makeup from that Instagram model. What's her name? *Luna da Rosa.*"

My back stiffened. "Luna?" I croaked it out like a teenager.

"Bitzi told me that if *Luna da Rosa* says this place is all the rage"—she sniffed around again, like she didn't quite believe it —"then it's all the rage. And I am nothing if not *all the rage,* darlings."

Who the hell was this woman?

"Uh, okay," I said, hands in my pockets. "What kind of dog companion are you looking for? Beatrix requires a lot of work. And love."

She lifted a shoulder. "I have love." She said this with a slight sadness, which piqued my interest. "And a sinful amount of money. Beatrix would live a life of luxury, I'll tell you that."

"Beatrix used to have to fight dogs. She was chained up every hour of the day," I said. "Luxury is fine. Love is more important."

Victoria turned around, eyeing Beatrix with a new appreciation. "A fighter, you say? Just like me."

Elián smirked at me from behind Victoria. But I was

watching dog and human carefully.

"Would she protect me?"

"Bullmastiffs, as a breed, are very loyal," I said. "She'll love you forever."

She touched the string of pearls around her neck. "I've had some things stolen from me quite recently. I had hired a team of men to keep them secure." Victoria fixed her gaze on Jem. "I think I've learned my lesson about hiring *men* for things, right, darling?"

"Dogs are better," Jem agreed. "No offense to my boyfriend over there."

"None taken." Wes beamed.

I hid a smile, watched Beatrix sniffing her way toward Victoria's high heels.

"Is she trained?"

"She is now," I said. "But she'll need firm direction. Jem, can you let her off the leash?"

Jem did, and Beatrix began wandering off, following her nose on some scent.

Victoria snapped her fingers and said, "Halt."

Beatrix stopped. Turned.

Victoria pointed at her feet. Beatrix went.

"Sit," Victoria said, like an empress giving orders.

Beatrix sat. All four of us watched wide-eyed as Beatrix laid her giant head against Victoria's leg, and stared up at her.

Victoria smiled. Placed a hand on top of Beatrix's head. "She's quite a good girl. Very pretty."

Beatrix wasn't pretty, but I wasn't going to disagree.

"Would you like a collar made of diamonds?" Victoria cooed down at her. "I'll have one made for you as soon as we return."

"How about I take Victoria and Beatrix around for a bit?" Jem asked. "See how they do?"

I mouthed *They're a match* and Jem flashed me a thumbs-up. I watched them make their way through the field, Beatrix staring at Victoria like she was the center of her universe.

"Wouldn't have guessed that one," I admitted.

"It's not always obvious," Elián said. "You know that."

I clapped him on the back. "All right then. Back to those new grant applications."

"Hey, so, since we're all standing around, Wes and I were wondering when you were going to admit to Luna that you were wrong and get back together so we can have a little goddamn peace around here?"

"Bull's-eye, bro," Wes said beneath his breath.

I turned with my meanest scowl—but Elián wasn't having it. "Beck, I'm your best and oldest friend. You think Scary Beck even has an effect on me anymore?"

"I'm not trying to be scary," I growled. They both snorted.

After a minute, I cracked a small smile.

"There he is," Elián said. "Mr. Sunshine."

"Fuck off," I said, but it lacked heat. "And you know it was for the best. I might have broken us up early, but we were going to break up eventually."

"I don't know, boss," Wes said, rocking back on his heels. "*I* think you're terrified to be in love with her. Because you never had it. It takes courage to embrace love. To not let the shame win. You taught me that."

I shifted on my feet, totally uncomfortable.

"Do you really think... like *really* think a woman like that would love a man like me?"

"Yes," they said in unison.

"You're a lovable dude," Wes said. "Luna owned up to her shit. Apologized. Made changes. Is moving on."

"You're the *leader* of this place," Elián continued. "You need to own that. Because if we don't have Big Lovable Beck to do the work that needs to be done, then everything Luna did for us is going to go to waste. You're already stepping into it. Doing the things Luna would want you to do. What's keeping you from being with her, really?"

Wes didn't have to say it. It was another bull's-eye.

"Money. Our differences. My family. Her reputation," I said. I'd been repeating this list to myself for weeks now—a reminder.

"Except," Elián said, "when you were with Luna, you'd never been so happy and comfortable. We all recognized it. Luna's the *one*."

The one.

I mean, I fucking *knew that*. Knew it deep, deep down.

"But going all in," I managed, "being with... with Luna would mean..." I blew out a breath, stalling. "Trust."

"All of the trust," Elián agreed.

"It's scary shit," Wes said. "You can do it though. Look at Beatrix over there." I did, watched her trotting around the campus with her eyes on Victoria. It was a leap—a risk—but it was going to pay off for her. She was going to be loved. Forever.

"If Lucky Dog had a heart, it would be you," Wes said.

"That true?" I asked, coughing through a knot of emotion lodged in my throat.

"*Yes*," they both said again.

"Okay, *Jesus*, I get the point." I was trying not to smile, but their faces were so serious I couldn't help it.

"In case it's not, you know obvious or whatever, I love you guys."

"Ah man, I love you too," Wes said, hugging me hard.

Over his shoulder, I arched a brow at Elián, who was grinning.

"I love you too, Beck. And you should go get Luna back."

61

LUNA

*H*eartbreak was going to be my reality forever and ever and ever.

I knew that because I was at our monthly Drag Queen Brunch at Mordecai's Bistro—my *absolutely favorite day*—and I was a hot mess of misery.

Daisy, Cameron, Emily and I sat in our usual horseshoe-shaped black booth in the very back of the restaurant. They had looks of *extreme* concern on their beautiful faces. Lady Raquel, our favorite server, diplomatically placed a mug of steaming liquid in front of me. It was frothy, with a design of a flower in the middle. "Chamomile, cinnamon and almond milk," she said. "Healing for a broken heart."

"I don't have a broken heart," I said with faux cheeriness. "Everything is great. Wild Heart's doing *super well*—"

"Shhh. Drink your drink, honey. You're so sad you're making everyone else in here cry into their food." Lady Raquel said.

"I'm really fine," I said, voice cracking at the end. "You guys can stop looking at me like you all just re-read *Where the Red Fern Grows* and sobbed at the ending."

"Grown women don't read children's books where dogs die in them," Daisy said. "That's only you, Moon. And you need to go talk to Beck and force that big biker to realize he's your *soulmate*."

"I know," I said. And that was even *sadder*. "But he doesn't think we belong together. He believes he'll hold me back or whatever else nonsense words he spouted at me that night. But they were... they were just *words*. And Beck's a man of action—"

I stopped because the romance authors were streaming into Mordecai's and taking the booth right next to ours. Cameron's eyes widened and Emily craned her neck to see if they had paperbacks with them. Usually they came bearing notebooks and sticky notes and highlighters, with messy hair and wearing old sweatpants. *On deadline*, they'd all complain, and then we'd all listen in as they untangled messy plot holes and brainstormed conflict ideas. The four of us had been low-key stalking these authors for the six years we'd been coming here. I personally had improved my oral sex technique from listening to the author with giant blue glasses scream about blow jobs at a volume completely inappropriate for a restaurant.

And now she was complaining about the book she was writing. As we quietly drained our mimosas while *super obviously* listening, blue-glasses-author dropped her head on the table while another author, wearing a shirt with a giant taco on it, patted her back sympathetically.

"My book is basically all telling and not showing," she was saying.

"You'll fix it. You always do," taco-lady murmured.

"*I'll never fix it and it's garbage*," blue-glasses-author wailed.

"You need ways in which the hero can show the heroine

how he feels," taco-lady said. "You know he needs to do some—"

"*Actions.*" I blurted the word out just as taco-lady said it. I caught her eye and I flushed.

"Unrelated to what you're talking about," I said, waving my hands.

"Also can you *please* tell me what happens to Salvio in book five?" Daisy whined. "I've been waiting *forever.*" One of the authors had an extremely popular and long-running series about a bunch of brothers who owned a winery and Daisy was obsessed.

"Oh my god, ignore her," Cameron said to the romance authors. She gathered us in, like a football huddle. "Luna, what's going on in that pretty brain of yours? I can see you scheming."

I blew out a breath. "If Beck has a certain view of who he is, especially in comparison to me, then I need a way to show him. Show him what I see when I look at him. Not... not what he believes to be true. What his mother said or Jasmine or the media or anything else."

"Show him why you love him," Emily said with a sweet smile. "What would do that? Is there anything Beck wants? Has done? Maybe from his past?"

I sipped my broken-heart-latte, courtesy of Lady Raquel. It smelled like baking cookies with my mom and tasted like nostalgia and comfort. *Alchemy.* If this was an elixir for a broken heart, it was working.

What did Beck want? He wanted me, at some point. And maybe, hopefully, still did. He wanted Lucky Dog to flourish.

Willow.

"Emily, do you think Derek's team of super savvy tech people could help me out with something?"

"Of course," she said. "What is it?"

I flashed a real smile for the first time in days. "I need them to help me find a dog."

62

BECK

I'd been at my tiny kitchen table for hours. I had tossed copy after copy of the application, scribbling through sentences. It was harder than I thought, forcing my words into a kind of sense. Making them match, even slightly, the feelings that I had. I'd never been good at this, and as I sweated and erased and crumpled up paper, I hoped that it would be clear.

It was all I had.

So when there was a knock at my door, I was completely startled. Other than Elián, not many people had been to my run-down apartment.

Imagine my surprise when it was Luna da Rosa in a white dress and a crown of flowers.

And she was clutching a stack of papers to her chest.

"Luna," I said, like she was a dream.

"May I come in?" she asked. Her smile was shy.

I blew out a breath. My heart was trying to climb out of my chest. "Uh, what are you doing here?" I was trying to figure out how clean my apartment was. I never had visitors.

"I brought you a gift," Luna said. And I wanted to kiss her so badly I forgot how to breathe.

"I, uh... I have a gift for you too," I said, stepping back to let her into the small space. I was barefoot, in old sweatpants and an undershirt. She slid past me and I inhaled her sunshine scent like an addict. Watched her look at my kitchen, my tiny living area, peek her head around the corner toward the bedroom. My furniture was thread-bare and not a single picture hung on my walls. But she had no judgment, just curiosity.

Then she sat in one of the chairs, kicked off her sandals. I had spied on her Instagram feed for the first time in two weeks last night. She was sad. Really sad. It was painful to see.

"I was thinking about ways that I could show you how much I love you," she said, voice clear. "To dissuade you from having any doubts about me or my intentions or my feelings. And so, with the help of my friends, I did a little digging. Talked to some people. And uncovered a mystery for you."

"A mystery?" I asked, hung up on the fact that Luna had said the words *how much I love you*.

I assumed she'd abandoned our love. Yet here she was— surprising me, as usual.

"With some keen internet sleuthing, I tracked down the program coordinator from your class at Positive Results twenty years ago. He's still there, and he's still amazing. In fact, I think the foundation might be considering them for a gift soon." She gave me a fun wink and I couldn't help but smile.

"Wait... you mean Eric?" I asked.

Luna nodded. "He remembered you."

"But he's worked with thousands of inmates at this point," I said.

"He remembered *you*," she said, "because of how gigantic your heart is. And he remembered Willow and looked up the family that had adopted her. I know you said they'd never written you back, that you never knew how her life had turned out."

My heart was thudding loudly in my chest.

"Eric called them, asked if they'd be willing to send any pictures. Of course, they were. There was some mix-up with their address way back when you'd been trying to contact them. They'd moved, never got your letters. It was never because they didn't want you to be involved."

"I thought..." I started, but couldn't continue. *I thought they didn't want me.*

"I know," Luna said kindly.

She placed the pages down and slid them across the table toward me with a delicate reverence. "Willow passed away in her sleep when she was thirteen years old, about nine years after she was adopted by the Harrison family. Who, according to Eric, loved her to pieces."

They had. Even the scanned, older pictures I held in my hand showed Willow sitting by a Christmas tree wearing a Santa hat. On a hiking trail on a leash. Running at the beach, sleeping by a fireplace. Humans, her family, were in every shot —petting her, holding her, running with her. They were photos of love and devotion between human and animal.

"Eric spoke with their son, who was a kid when they got Willow. He told Eric to thank you, profusely, for bringing such a loving dog into their lives."

I wiped at my eyes, which were suspiciously wet. "She was happy."

"She was very happy, Beck. Very loved. Very cherished. You gave that to her."

I couldn't speak for a minute, was too fucking overwhelmed with everything. When I could finally clear my throat, I said, "Why did you do this for me?"

"This is who you are, Beck," she said, tapping the pictures. She placed her hand over mine, threaded our fingers together. Her touch, after missing it for so long, felt euphoric. "This is what I see when I look at you. This is why I love you. I'm sorry, so very, very sorry, if I ever made you feel used. Or like a charity case. I'm sorry if you ever felt like my time with you was just to rebuild my reputation. Nothing could be further from the truth. All this time, I thought Lucky Dog was my happy place, a shelter from the storm. A refuge." She leaned over, brushed our lips together. "You're my happy place, Beck Mason."

I didn't even think—just acted, as usual. I wrapped an arm around her waist and pulled her into my lap. Our faces were still close as I brushed the hair from her forehead.

"Thank you," I said. "Thank you for... I never knew, you know, and I thought maybe they were ashamed of where Willow came from."

"They weren't," Luna said, stroking my hair. "They couldn't have been prouder of where she'd come from. Couldn't have been prouder of the work *you* had done for her."

I pressed my forehead against hers, palm between her shoulder blades. "We got the money, Luna. From the foundation."

"I'm so happy to give it to you." She smiled. "It's for you. And Lucky Dog. It's for more dogs like Willow."

Trust. No more walls. No more fear. My heart was wide open.

"I wrote this for you," I said, handing her the piece of paper. My fingers were shaking slightly.

"For me?"

"For you." I locked my arms tight around her. Now that she was in my lap, I wasn't ever going to let go of her.

"Lucky Dog assessment for Penelope's adoption," she read.

Stopped, eyes flying up to mine. "Jem told me she was ready but I... I never said. I figured, you know, you would have given her to someone else."

"Keep reading," I nudged.

"*As a staff member at Lucky Dog, please give your assessment of why you think Luna da Rosa is the right home and family for the dog in question.*"

I hadn't written much—wasn't my style, and it was too hard. But what I'd put was all feeling.

She cleared her throat. Read the truest words I'd ever written: "*Before I met Luna, I lived a life based in fear. Fear that I would never be more than my past. Fear that I would never be the leader I knew I could be. Fear that I would never know love. I know better now. Luna da Rosa sees the value in all and she sees the value in me. Which means, as an adoptive dog parent, she would give Penelope a life of love, and organic dog food and kombucha. Most of all, Luna would love her with an open heart. Anyone would be lucky to have that kind of love in their life. I only hope she still loves me back.*"

Beneath that was a box—I checked *approved for adoption.*

"I'm sorry for what I said, Luna," I said. "I'm sorry for letting all of those old habits get in my way. I'm sorry—"

She put a finger on my lips. "No more apologies. I love you, Beck. So much."

"I love you, Luna," I said, "so very, very much."

And then she was kissing me, and laughing, and my hands were in her hair, and holding her tight, and I didn't realize that love could fill a room but it could. It was everywhere. Luna was my magic, my transformation. If any woman was my alchemy, it was the rainbow billionaire, shining on my lap like the rays of the sun.

"If you look in that fridge," I said, nuzzling her neck, "you'll find six bottles of ginger-peach kombucha."

She laughed, kissing my cheek ten times in rapid succession. "I *knew* you loved it. Also, I've been drinking Heineken all week."

I kissed her—hard. Threaded my fingers through all of that hair. Scooped her up and carried her into my bed. It was too easy, too perfect, to shift all of those layers away so I could kiss every inch of her legs. Lick and tease her sex until she was arching off the bed, fingers in my hair. Let her guide me inside her body so I could take her, fuck her, show her how much I missed her. We were nothing but gasping mouths and hands and a pleasure so strong my body trembled. Hours passed and we didn't stop—didn't stop kissing. Didn't stop touching. Exploring. I gave her every single thing that I had, every vulnerability. Every feeling. And when she came for the final time, tears rolled down her cheeks.

As the sun set, we lay curled around each other. Sweating, out of breath. Happy. She cupped her hand over my heart again. I held it there.

"Thank you for showing me love," I said.

Luna entwined our fingers. Kissed me sweetly. "This wild heart will always be yours, Beck. Now can we go get our dog?"

EPILOGUE

LUNA

Six months later

*B*eck and I were preparing to be on camera.

We were sitting in our living room, squished onto a couch by the fireplace. Penelope was sitting on Beck's lap, tongue lolling, looking happy and adorable and clearly obsessed with her dog dad.

I was obsessed with him too.

"You two cuties just hang for a second while Wes and I get set up," Jem said, hair dyed electric blue to match the blue engagement ring on her finger. Wes had popped the question on the campus at Lucky Dog, placing the ring on the collar of a puppy Elián had rescued a week ago.

A puppy that Wes and Jem were now planning on adopting.

"Boss, this video is going to be *tight*," Wes said, bobbing his head and scoping out the visual logistics of the room. Ever since Wes and Jem had taken over Lucky Dog's social media presence, their beautiful videos of dog adoptions had become viral hits.

Penelope laid her head against Beck's chest. He smoothed a palm over her fur, watching me with playful eyes.

"Whatcha thinking about, Mr. Mason?" I asked.

He reached over, curled a strand of my hair around his thick finger.

"I think you know," he said, the words a quiet growl. I felt myself flush. Six months into our relationship and my big, bearded, meat-eating, beer-drinking boyfriend continued to fuck me with a passion I was addicted to. I'd woken this morning with his head between my legs—not an unusual occurrence—and after two blinding orgasms the man had flipped me over and fucked me literally *senseless*.

"I might need reminding later," I said, tapping my lip with a fake quizzical look. "Perhaps in the hot tub?"

Beck's grin was wolfish. "That can be arranged, sweetheart."

I leaned in for a kiss but Penelope got there first, licking us both on the cheek. I laughed, wiping her slobber off, before giving her a huge hug. Penelope had moved in with me immediately and brought me so much joy it was impossible to categorize. She came to Wild Heart with me every day, hanging out in different offices, running on the beach and getting fed way too many baby carrots by Sylvia. She was calm, gentle, curious and I worried my heart would burst from loving her.

The only thing I loved more was Beck.

Beck had moved in right after Penelope. I'd been worried, since my mansion and the ostentatious wealth of Bluewater had always made him wary. But Emily, Cameron and Daisy—not to mention their husbands and boyfriends—had become our family, showing Beck every day that he was valued and loved and welcome. Beck had even taken over feeding Steve, who adored him—as much as a three-legged alligator can show his adoration. And Brutus spent more time at my mansion than any other—I often came home to find Beck napping on the couch with Penelope, Brutus sprawled out on the loveseat.

His motorcycle was parked in my garage and our fridge was stocked with beer and various meats. Although I made him eat vegan dinners with me half of the week.

I filled our walls with pictures of Beck and Elián, Jem and Wes, Willow and her family. And now, our walls were slowly filling with pictures of Beck, Penelope and me—our little family on our many, many adventures.

"Thanks for making time for this," Jem said, sitting down about ten feet away with a video camera and some note cards. Wes stood next to her, hand on her shoulder. "I know you two have been super busy."

"All in a day's work," I said with a shrug. "*This* is what's important."

Jem smiled. "I can't get over how cute you three fucking look."

I bit my lip as I grinned over at Beck.

"Yeah, yeah," he said, faux-grouchy. "We can get on with it."

"He's a *four* on the grumpiness scale today," I stage-whispered to Jem.

He responded by leaning over and kissing me on the cheek.

"What does Penelope mean to you?" Jem asked.

Beck nudged me to go first.

"Okay," I said, scratching behind her ears. "I first saw Penelope more than a year ago. She was a stray dog living behind my offices at Wild Heart. She was, um, pretty skinny." My throat tightened. "Scared. Didn't trust me or anyone else. I think she was really, really afraid."

Beck shifted next to me, entwining our fingers together.

"She needed love," Jem said, nodding.

"She needed a lot of love," I said. "I started feeding her. Gaining her trust. Showing her that I was..." I glanced over at Beck—"that I was the person that I said I was. This was during a time when I'd... lost my way. Penelope was the first step in finding myself again."

Jem beamed at me from behind the camera. I'd been donating ninety percent of my salary to the Wild Heart Foundation for six months now and I'd never felt more purpose in my entire life. The foundation was thriving—the first round of grants would go out soon—and every time I visited a nonprofit, my heart glowed and glowed and glowed.

Wild Heart was rebuilding—slowly. But our products were back to being cruelty-free and Ruby's Closet had ended up being the perfect partner for us.

I was matching my values, my business, my money, my time—having them reflect the world we all wanted to see.

A better one.

My life was less focused on image and always focused on integrity. And if I ever got anxious, or concerned, Beck was there to remind me of who I really was.

"And, Beck, you were working with Penelope too, right? Without Luna's knowledge?" Jem asked.

He nodded. "The first day I met Luna was the first day I brought Penelope to the rescue. We hadn't known that we'd both been feeding her."

"I remember that day," Jem said.

"So do I," he said, smile secretive. "We, uh... well, Luna and I had been at an *impasse*. Penelope helped us get past it."

Lucky Dog was thriving too. Beck was building more

kennels, hiring more staff, expanding to their second location. I'd gone to see him speak at an event the other night and had been blown away at his quiet confidence, the way he captured the audience's attention and demanded they consider Lucky Dog. He *was* a leader—he just hadn't seen it.

"Why rescue?" Jem asked.

"Because even a skinny beach mutt that is terrified to trust people has value," I said. "We all do. Sometimes it takes a while to earn that trust. To show them your love."

Beck was silent but squeezing my fingers hard. He'd let his chin rest on top of Penelope's head—and when he turned to look at me, his eyes were shining.

"How'd you know Penelope was your match?" Jem asked. "And I should mention that Beck has a unique talent for matching dogs to humans."

"Penelope..." I paused, looked at the man next to me. My opposite in every way. "Penelope made me work to earn her trust. It didn't happen overnight. I think that makes our connection stronger."

Beck kissed my shoulder, chuckling softly.

"What has Penelope done for you as a family? Is she settling in well?" Jem asked brightly.

"Penelope is everything to us," Beck answered. "We're very happy to give this dog the home she deserves."

"And I think she's settling in well," I mused, laying my head on his shoulder. "Beck thinks I don't notice that he feeds her food from the dinner table."

"I would *never*," he said.

"He's a softie, just like you told me," I said to Jem.

He pulled me in close, lips on my hair.

Click went the sound of a camera—it was Wes, looking especially excited.

"Can I post this picture of you three?" he asked. He flipped the phone around so I could see it: I was laughing, Penelope looked calm and content, and Beck was looking at me with a gaze of astonishment.

"Of course," I said, remembering how hard that had been even six months ago. But when you were this happy, the opinions of strangers really couldn't touch you at all.

"Here, can I see that?" Beck asked. Wes handed him the phone. Beck's smile was mysterious as his fingers moved over the keyboard. I petted Penelope and snuggled in closer to my gentle giant. My happy place.

"What do you think about this caption?" he asked, lips at my ear.

Beneath our photo, he had written:

It wasn't obvious, at first.

People wouldn't believe it.

But I knew a match when I found one.

EXTENDED EPILOGUE

Two years later

BECK

The knock on the door that led to the groom's suite was suspiciously *Daisy*-like. I was fiddling with my cufflinks and trying not to mess up Derek's expert handiwork with my tie.

I was nervous. As hell.

"Who is it?" I asked, ear at the door.

"*Code word: 696969*," came the response. Yep. Daisy.

"Didn't ask for a code word," I said, lips tipping up.

"Doesn't matter, Big Dick Beck. We brought you a present," she stage-whispered.

Curious, I opened the door. Emily, Cameron and Daisy stood in teal bridesmaids dresses holding bouquets of colorful wildflowers.

And they had matching mischievous grins.

"What do you want?" I asked, crossing my arms over my chest.

But I was already smiling.

"Listen. You have exactly twenty minutes before the wedding planner marches down this hallway to grab you before your ceremony begins," Emily said. "And we have exactly twenty minutes worth of distractions."

"Jude's staging a mini-coup as we speak," Cameron smirked. "And if that doesn't work, we're going to unleash our children. See how long it takes your planner to wrangle them up."

"Which will be freaking *ages* because our children are monsters," Daisy said dramatically.

"Or," Cameron said, thinking, "we could unleash Penelope. And your two new puppies. That's a dangerous combination."

A few months ago, Luna and I had adopted a pair of bonded puppies that had been dropped off at Lucky Dog's doorstep in a plastic container. Penelope had taken to nurturing them immediately and the mansion was now filled with three times the canine chaos.

We couldn't have been happier. In fact, all three dogs would be standing with us during the ceremony—squished between Emily, Cameron and Daisy to Luna's left, Elián, Wes and Jem to my right.

"What does that have to do with a present?" I asked.

"We kidnapped your bride," they said in unison.

"*What?*" I asked.

Beaming, Emily nodded her head down the hallway. "Why don't you close your eyes and let us deposit her safely in this room. For a private first look, just the two of you."

"Luna's... wait, Luna's nearby?" We'd spent only last night apart but I was an emotional wreck because of it. I hadn't slept in a Luna-less bed in two years—and I planned to never do it again. But West, Jude and Derek had dragged me out for a night of fine scotch and poker with Elián and Wes.

Luna had been dragged out for a night of dick-themed drinks and endless dancing by the three women standing in front of me plus Jem. I know because I'd gotten a dozen drunk voicemails from all *five* of them.

They had sounded wasted but extremely happy.

"She's right down there. In her dress. Waiting for her almost-husband," Daisy said.

My heart tried to climb out of my chest.

"Twenty minutes, right?" I asked, already sitting back on the bed. I covered my eyes.

"You got it, BD," Daisy said.

"Thank you," I said, voice rough. "For everything. Always."

Discovering my Lucky Dog family had been my greatest privilege—until I'd found myself welcome in Bluewater's community. Luna's closest friends had become my own, and we were surrounded every day by love.

"We love you, Beck," Emily said. I heard rustling. Recognized Luna's footsteps. A closed door.

Silence.

"Mr. Mason, I presume?" Luna's voice, laughter in her words.

I opened my fucking eyes.

Luna da Rosa stood in front of me like a wildflower bride. Long white dress, simple. Arms and shoulders bare, tan skin shimmering. A crown of lavender on top of her beautiful hair.

"Luna," I rasped. "Luna, you're..."

She smiled. Took a step closer. I wrapped an arm around her slender waist and had her on my lap in a second. Her legs came around to straddle me, hands cupping my face.

"You're the most beautiful thing I've ever seen," I managed. "And I'm the luckiest man in the world."

"Seems like we're at an impasse again," she said, eyes bright. "Because I think *I'm* the lucky one. You've always been a hunk. But in a suit?" As if to demonstrate, my almost-wife rolled her hips—right across my lap. "I won't make it through the ceremony, *sir*."

"Is this why you snuck in here?" I said, chuckling darkly. I ran my nose along her throat, nipped her jaw with my teeth. Another roll of her hips.

"Maybe," she sighed. And then she kissed me—it was a kiss of promises, of longing, of everything we'd been through to get to this point. Although now I was wondering why we'd waited so damn long. If I'd known what being loved by this woman would feel like, I would have proposed at that damn burger joint.

"What do you need, sweetheart?" I asked, already stroking my fingers up her thighs, through her slick center. She gasped. "Tell your husband."

"You're not my husband *yet*," she said. Her hands were working at my fly, tugging it down, freeing my cock. I groaned —louder than I intended to. Her eyes widened, hand coming to cover my mouth.

"*Shhhh*," she said, half-laughing. Her other hand gripped my cock. I wrapped my fingers around hers. We stroked my cock together, in unison, my groans quieted by her palm. Her eyelids fluttered. "You don't... you don't want us to get caught, do you?"

I ducked away from the hand covering my mouth. "I *want* my wife to ride me."

I'd barely gotten the words out before she was hovering herself over my cock and then lowering inch by sweet inch. We didn't have time for slow or sweet or sensual—but even still, there was so much beauty in this moment. Her gorgeous smile, the flowers in her hair, our beach wedding—happening in fifteen minutes—our friends, our loved ones, our dogs.

All of our dreams, coming true.

"Yes, *Beck*," she sighed, mouth coming to mine. I gripped her hips beneath her white wedding dress and moved her up and down in a quick, steady rhythm I knew would get her off. We kissed, gasped, sighed—stared into each other's eyes as the pleasure grew. And grew. With a palm on my chest, she shoved me back on the bed, rode me fast, head thrown back. I watched my wildflower bride steal this moment of ecstasy— looking as happy and joyful as she'd always been. It was never hard being with this woman—this ray of fucking sunshine whose big heart only seemed to grow bigger every day.

"Come for me, sweetheart," I whispered, tilting my hips up, brushing my thumb against her clit. I watched her face change, felt her orgasm, felt my own climax rush through me.

A transformation.

True alchemy.

"Wedding sex is the *best* sex." Luna sighed, starting to laugh. She was a panting, grinning mess on my lap and I couldn't stop myself from wrapping her in a giant hug. "I think this is a first look for the record books."

"Just wanted to make sure you had enough fireworks," I said, kissing her temple.

"Mission fucking *accomplished*." She touched my face, my hair, as if her fingers were memorizing me. "Are you ready to go get married, Beck Mason?"

I was going to show this woman love for the rest of our lives. Every damn day—and in every way I knew how.

"I've never been more ready," I said—and meant it. And then we strolled hand-in-hand onto that beach filled with our family and friends and dogs. And I finally married the rainbow billionaire with the wild, open heart.

A NOTE FROM THE AUTHOR

Dear reader,

Thank you for reading Luna and Beck's sweet, funny, sexy and emotional love story. To say I was obsessed with these two would be an understatement. In fact, the hardest editing challenge for me was stopping them from leaping into each other's arms from their very first meeting. But I will say—making these two opposites truly work for their happily ever after was pure joy.

Of course, working with Lucy Score, Claire Kingsley and Pippa Grant to bring you the Bluewater Billionaires series was an absolute delight (more on that in the acknowledgments).

This story was very personal to me. I was a fundraiser for more than eight years; six of those spent at a grassroots nonprofit that helped homeless women re-enter the workforce. Many of them—like the staff at Lucky Dog—had been in and out of the criminal justice system. Many of them, on the first day of class, expressed a deep sense of worthlessness.

Of lacking value to our community because they were homeless, poor, female, lacked a certain amount of education, were single mothers, etc. They had been labeled and deemed *trash* —quite literally. Although by the time they graduated our program, the words they would use to describe themselves were dramatically different: strong, courageous, beautiful, hard-working, intelligent, brave. Seen. Valuable. Important. It was my greatest privilege to bear witness to their transformations over the years—and I will never, ever forget their stories.

My husband and I also recently adopted a rescue dog named Walter. I've always been a dog-lover—so I understood the connection and love that could exist between human and pet. But I'll never forget the memory of a scared, shaking Walter being placed in our arms on his adoption day. And I'll never forget what Walter had looked like in the kennel the day he was scheduled to be euthanized—a stray from the street, nothing more. As anyone who even casually follows me online knows... Walter is the light of my life.

It's no surprise, then, that I'm equally drawn to programs like the one I envisioned for Beck, Jem and Wes. And luckily there are many out there if you experience that same passion. But the one I drew from the most for details and inspiration is called the *Marley's Mutts Pawsitive Change Prison Program.* Marley's Mutts is a dog-rescue nonprofit, and Pawsitive Change is run in state prisons in California. Inmates and at-risk shelter dogs are paired together for 14 weeks—both working on a process of rehabilitation and transforming together. The program is also run at California's juvenile facilities for girls.

If you're interested in supporting them, you can find out more (and donate) at :

https://www.marleysmutts.org/pawsitivechange/

Love,

    Kathryn

ACKNOWLEDGMENTS

For Lucy, Claire and Pippa: thank you for making this entire process a freaking blast. Your intelligence, humor and kindness are a source of light in our indie world. Keep it shinin'. (If you've never met these women in person, they are as brilliant as they appear online). Creating the Bluewater world—and getting to write Emily, Cameron, Luna and Daisy—was amazing from beginning to end. Who knows what those Wealthy Widows will get up to at the next HOA meeting? I'll bring the flasks.

For Faith: who is not only my best friend, but the world's best developmental and content editor. Thank you for all of the brainstorming and pep talks and supremely brilliant edits, as always.

For Bronwyn, Jodi and Julia—beta readers extraordinaire. The three of you caught *everything*—and made me work hard for that HEA. Thank you for your eagle eyes and perfect feedback.

For the Hippie Chicks: thank you for being the most beautiful and hopeful group ever. I think Luna would *totally* be at home in our little bohemian circle of good vibes.

Always always for Rob (and Walter)—my beloved little family of nomads. Thank you for the road trips, the camping, the endless cups of coffee and the daily reminders that I don't suck at writing. I made Rob *promise* to take me on a vacation to Miami if I finished this book so... you know... I've got a suitcase packed with a bikini and a dozen flower crowns. Meet me in South Beach?

ABOUT KATHRYN

I'm an adventurous hippie chick that loves to write steamy romance. My specialty is slow-burn sexual tension with plenty of witty dialogue and tons of heart.

I started my writing career in elementary school, writing about *Star Wars* and *Harry Potter* and inventing love stories in my journals. And I blame my obsession with slow-burn on my similar obsession for The *X-Files*.

I'm a born-and-raised Philly girl, but left for Northern California right after college, where I met my adorably-bearded husband. After living there for eight years, we decided to embark on an epic, six-month road trip, traveling across the country with our little van, Van Morrison. Eighteen states and 17,000 miles later, we're back in my hometown of Philadelphia for a bit... but I know the next adventure is just around the corner.

When I'm not spending the (early) mornings writing steamy love scenes with a strong cup of coffee, you can find me outdoors -- hiking, camping, traveling, yoga-ing.

HANG OUT WITH KATHRYN!

Sign up for my newsletter and receive exclusive content, bonus scenes and more!
I've got a reader group on Facebook called **Kathryn Nolan's Hippie Chicks**. We're all about motivation, girl power, sexy short stories and empowerment! Come join us.

Let's be friends on
Website: authorkathrynnolan.com
Instagram at: kathrynnolanromance
Facebook at: KatNolanRomance
Follow me on BookBub
Follow me on Amazon